KNIGHT OF THE GODDESS
BRIAR BOLEYN

Cover Design by Artscandare Book Cover Design

Proofreading & Editing by Rachel Bunner, Rachel's Top Edits

Interior art by Bryanna, Bree Reads 85 (Instagram)

Map by Angeline Trevena, Step By Step Worldbuilding

Flourish Art by Polina K, Emmie Norfolk, Gordon Johnson (GDJ)

CONNECT WITH BRIAR

Grab the FREE & STEAMY bonus scene I wrote for Queen of Roses, find out about my latest new releases, giveaways, and other bookish treats:

http://briarboleyn.com

If you love this series, find me on or apply to !

I love hearing from readers:

author@briarboleyn.com

Acknowledgements

For two little boys who love to dress up as dinosaurs and dragons and would love to ride an exmoor or meet a girl who can shoot flames from her fingers.

CONTENT WARNINGS

Blood of a Fae is a dark fantasy romance series that deals with topics which some readers may understandably find triggering.

A trigger and content warnings list may be found at the end of the book. Use the hyperlink in the Table of Contents.

Please keep in mind that reading the content warnings list will spoil certain plot elements. Avoid reading the trigger warnings list if you do not have any triggers and do not wish to know specific details about the plot in advance.

CONTENTS

THE CHARACTERS

From the Court of Umbral Flames
KAIROS DRAVEN VENATOR, Prince of Myntra
LYRASTRA VENATOR, Regent of Myntra
ODESSA DI RHONDAN
CRESCENT DI RHONDAN
GAWAIN
TAINA
HAWL, an Ursidaur
ULPHEAS, a Royal stitcher

In the Rose Court of Camelot
MORGAN LE FAY, Empress of Myntra
MEDRA PENDRAGON, Daughter of Orcades le Fay and Arthur Pendragon
KAYE PENDRAGON
SIR ECTOR PRENNELL, Master-at-Arms
GALAHAD PRENNELL, his son
DAME HALYNA, a Knight Commander of the Royal Guard
LANCELET DE TROYES, Knight of Camelot
GUINEVERE OF LYONESSE, High Priestess of the Temple of the Three
DANIELO CASTELLANO, a chef of the Rose Court

In the Court of Brightwind
MARK, King of Tintagel
CAMILLE, Queen of Tintagel
From Rheged

MADOC, a leader of refugees
AMARA, a healer

The Creatures
NIGHTCLAW, an exmoor
SUNSTRIKE, his mate
TUVA, eyes of the High Priestess

The Deities
ZORYA, goddess of the dawn
MARZANNA, goddess of death
DEVINA, goddess of the hunt
PERUN, their brother
NEDOLA, goddess of fate
VELA, high goddess of the fae
KHOR, her mate

At the High Fae Court
GORLOIS LE FAY
RYCHEL, a lost girl
SARRASINE
TEMPEST
LORION
DAEGEN

PRONUNCIATION GUIDE

Aercanum: AIR-kay-num

Agravaine Emrys: Ag-ra-VAYN EM-ris

Amara: ah-MAH-ruh

Ambrilith: AM-bri-lith

Atropa: uh-TROH-puh

Avriel: AV-ree-el

Bearkin: BEAR-kin

Belisent: buh-LI-sent

Brasad: BRAH-sad

Breena: BREE-nuh

Cavan: KAV-uhn

Cerunnos: Ser-UHN-os

Daegen: DAY-gen

Devina: DEH-vee-nuh

Ector Prennell: EK-tor Pren-ELL

Eleusia: EL-oo-see-uh

Enid: EE-nid

Erion: EH-ree-on

Eskira: es-KEER-ah

Ettarde: eh-TAHRD

Exmoor: EX-moor

Fenrir: FEN-reer

Fenyx: FEH-niks

Florian Emrys: FLOH-ree-an EM-ris

Galahad Prennell: GAL-uh-had Pren-ELL

Gawain: GA-wayn

Gelert: GEL-ert

Glatisants: GLAH-tis-ants

Gorlois: GOR-lwah

Halyna: Ha-LEE-nuh

Hawl: HALL

Haya: HI-uh

Idrisane: ID-ri-zayn

Javer: JAH-ver

Kairos Draven Venator: KAI-ros DRA-ven Veh-NAH-tohr

Kastra: KAS-truh

Kaye: KAY

Khor'a'val: KOR-a-VAL

Khor: KOR

Khorva: KOR-vuh

Lancelet de Troyes: LAN-suh-let deh TROYZ

Laverna: la-VER-na

Leodegrance: lee-oh-de-GRANS

Lorion: LOHR-ee-on

Lucius Venator: LOO-shus Veh-NAH-tohr

Lyonesse: LEE-oh-ness

Lyrastra: LIE-rah-struh

Madoc: MAH-dok

Malkah: MAL-kah

Marjolijn: mar-jo-LYN

Marzanna: mar-ZAH-nuh

Medra: MEH-dra

Meridium: MEH-ri-dee-um

Myntra: MIN-truh

Nedola: NED-o-la

Nerov: NEH-rov

Noctasia: nok-TAY-zhuh

Nodori: no-DOH-ree

Numenos: NOO-meh-nos

Odelna: o-DEL-nuh

Orcades: OR-kay-deez

Orin's Horn: OR-inz HORN

Pelleas: Pel-LEE-us

Pendrath: PEN-drath

Perun: PER-uhn

Rhea: RAY-uh

Rheged: RAY-ghed

Rychel: RYE-chel

Sarrasine: sa-ruh-ZEEN

Selwyn: SEL-win

Sephone Venator: se-FOHN-ee

Siabra: SHAY-bruh

Sorega: soh-RAY-guh

Tabar: TAY-bar

Taina: TIE-nuh

Taryn: TAIR-in

Tempest: TEM-pest

Tuva: TOO-vah

Tyre: TY-ruh

Ulpheas: UHL-fee-us

Ursidaur: UR-si-dor

Uther: OO-thur

Valtain: val-TAYN

Varis: VAR-is

Vela: VAY-luh

Verdantail: ver-DAN-tail

Vesper: VES-per

Vespera: ves-PAIR-uh

Ygraine: Ee-GRAYN

Zephrae: ZEF-ray

Zorya: ZOHR-ee-uh

BOOK 1

In the heart of spring, a child shall rise,
From royal blood, a king's demise.
Born of sister, born that day,
Kings shall fall, in disarray.

When springtime blooms, the babe is blessed,
Born of kin, from the king's own nest,
A sister's child, the kingdom shakes,
The death of kings, the birth awaits.

Born of power, in endless night,
To cast down realms, a dark birthright.
Both fae and mortals, their thrones shall swirl,
In the child's hands, lies the end of the world.

The Child Prophecy

Beware the dread curse of Three,
The sword, the spear, the grail's mystery.
Blood calls to blood, the dark shall rise,
Forged by the gods under sacred skies.

The words written on the stone which held the sword Excalibur.

PROLOGUE

I pushed open the door to the room, my heart brimming with anticipation.

He was awake. Kaye was awake.

Despite everything the healers had said, despite Guinevere's proclamation, he was awake.

Things could only get better from here. I would help him. Slowly but surely, he'd come back to his full strength.

I'd introduce him to Draven, my husband. Together, we'd help my brother to heal.

I'd have to tell Kaye about Medra. Orcades's daughter. How happy he would be to have a niece. I knew he would quickly grow to love the little girl. I imagined Kaye chasing little Medra through the halls of the castle and smiled to myself. How good it would be to have a child's laughter here after so long.

My pulse quickened as the door swung open. Daylight spilled from the windows where the curtains had been left open.

As I entered, a shadow passed over the room as if clouds had suddenly darkened the sun.

The room seemed to shift, dimming to an ominous shade.

I looked to the bed, and a harsh cry escaped my lips.

Kaye sat rigidly upright. His once-vibrant eyes were pools of emptiness. The pallor of death clung to his frail form.

Horror gripped my heart. I had seen this before. I felt my limbs beginning to tremble and clutched the skirt of my gown, desperate to hold on to disbelief.

Yet there was no denying this nightmare.

A groan. Kaye was struggling to get out of the bed. His movements were sluggish and uncoordinated.

Moments before, I had been longing to see him sit up. But not like this. Not like this.

My body felt anchored to the spot as a weight of despair settled upon me.

Across the room, Kaye slid out of the bed and began to walk laboriously towards me.

I let out a whimper.

His approach held none of the warmth I had yearned for. No embrace awaited me in those lifeless arms. Only a sinister threat in the clacking of his jaw and the sight of his pale white teeth.

The room had become a chilling stage. Elongated shadows of moonlight stretched across the floor where moments before there had been sunlight.

We were cursed. The Pendragons were cursed. The gods frowned upon us.

No. I knew better. There were no gods.

I could not move.

My brother drew closer. Limbs bent with unnatural stiffness as they slowly lifted.

Disbelief clung to me like a suffocating shroud.

And then I understood.

He needed me.

Heartbreak surged within as I stared at those empty arms.

This was not the joyous reunion I had envisioned mere moments before.

But perhaps it was all I deserved. All I could hope for.

I stepped forward into the waiting embrace of my brother's arms.

Death. Death was where I belonged.

In the end, I let love consume me.

CHAPTER 1 - MORGAN

I woke with a jolt, covered in a sheen of sweat.

The baby was crying.

"Just turn over and go back to sleep, my love," a deep voice murmured in my ear. "I'll go to her."

A moment later, I heard the pad of heavy footsteps. Then the creak of a cradle and a familiar crooning lullaby. Within seconds, the crying had ceased. Even I felt easier in my heart, listening as Draven sang.

I turned over with a sigh, knowing the return of sleep would not be forthcoming. The sickly gray light of dawn peeked through the long curtains and reminded me of my dream. I shivered.

I snuck a peek across the room to where Draven was rocking Medra in his arms. He had eyes only for her when he held her. I smiled to myself. Should I have been jealous?

She wasn't even our baby.

And yet somehow, she was now.

She was family. Our family.

"She'll want milk, Draven," I reminded him. I knew he knew this. I also knew he hated to give her up to anyone else.

He glanced at the little bottle of expressed milk that sat on the windowsill. It was empty now. Medra had finished it off earlier in the night.

She could have spent all night with her wet nurses. She had two of them, after all, the hungry little thing.

But Draven preferred to keep her close to us as much as possible.

Truth be told, I think he believed she was only safe when she was near us. And after all we had been through, all we had seen, I couldn't blame him for his fear.

Though it did mean less alone time for the two of us. More waking at night to the plaintive cries of an infant.

But Medra was motherless. Parentless. I would not resent her for her demands. Nor be anything but grateful that my mate had accepted a child not of his blood so easily or wanted to keep her close and protected.

"We won't always be able to keep her this close," I said out loud.

He glanced at me and frowned.

"I'm sorry. I know..." I shook my head. "No. I don't know. I'm just... sorry."

I was. Sorry. Sorry Draven had lost his own daughter. Sorry we couldn't keep Medra this close to us always.

But with what we had to do still lying ahead, I knew it was impossible. There was no way I was bringing a child into Rheged. And I knew Draven wouldn't want that either, no matter how much he already adored Medra.

Loved Medra. He loved her. I knew this.

And as for me? If I were being honest with myself, the truth was that I had kept my distance from Medra to an extent, afraid to get attached as quickly as I might have in the past.

Orcades's death was fresh in my mind. My sister. Medra's mother. If she had lived, what else might have been?

No matter what mistakes she had made, in the end, I had found myself loving her.

And I had vowed to care for her daughter.

"You are the most beautiful thing I have ever seen in this or any world."

They had been Orcades's last words as she looked upon Medra. Just after the cryptic riddle she had cited.

"Who meets their death devoid of love shall surely face their end. But one who gives their soul away, eternity extends."

"She's grown overnight," Draven remarked, bouncing the baby who seemed in no hurry to be delivered to her wet nurse for her next round of feeding.

"Isn't that the sort of thing everyone always says about babies?" I smirked but eyed my niece nonetheless.

In fact, Draven might have been right. Medra *did* look bigger. Her legs seemed longer than they had the night before and her chubby little arms were pushing at the seams of the white nightdress she wore.

"You may be right," I conceded. "Is this a fae trait? Rapid growth in infants?"

"Not usually." He rubbed his nose against the baby's. "We're longer-lived, so we often tend to mature more slowly than mortals. But then, you're special, aren't you, Medra? Aren't you, darling?"

He used a special tone of voice which might have made another person slightly nauseous. But hearing that dark, deep voice take on such a sweet tone just for my niece sent waves of warmth spreading through my body.

This man, this colossal figure with the presence of a mountain whose voice could take on the intensity of crushed rocks and whose gaze could instantly cause those around him to tremble with instinctive, primal fear... Well, it was an incredible thing watching him transform the moment he cradled our niece in his massive arms.

The colossus became a kitten.

I watched as the gray shadows played upon Draven's features, emphasizing the rugged contours of his face. His beautiful green eyes melted as he looked down at the baby with an expression of pure affection.

Then he looked at me, and his expression shifted.

"What's wrong?" His voice had taken on a tinge of concern.

I shook my head. "It's nothing."

"It's not nothing." He reached forward and touched my skin, just below my breastbone. "You're clammy. You've had night chills. What was it? A dream?"

I nodded slowly.

"Tell me," he said softly. "You know you can tell me anything."

I did know that.

I took a breath. "A dream, yes. A very disturbing one."

I told him briefly, careful to leave out the dream's conclusion. Where I had decided to simply... give myself up to Kaye. To surrender.

What did it mean? Was I losing myself to despair? I hadn't thought so before now, but the dream... it had shaken me.

"He's been on your mind a great deal. It's natural. I've been wrapped up in this little one"—he bounced Medra gently—"but you're filled with concern for Kaye."

"And there's nothing we can do," I said hollowly. I sat by his bed for hours each day, speaking to him, reading to him. But it was pointless. No matter what I did, he didn't even seem to know I was there. "That's what Guinevere said."

The young high priestess had seemed to become an expert on such things almost overnight. Even such strange supernatural events like Kaye's cursed sleep.

Kaye slept and he did not wake. He did not eat or drink. He seemed frozen in time. Neither dead nor alive.

Too similar to the horrible undead children from Meridium than I cared to admit. At least, in my waking hours. But in my dreaming mind, a part of me must have feared that was exactly what Kaye would eventually become.

"He *will* wake, Morgan," Draven said. "You know that. Once we've destroyed the grail..."

"He's bound to the chalice. That's what Guinevere said. She said it *holds him*. But what does that mean?" I asked sharply. "Will destroying it help him? Set him free? Or will it destroy them both?"

I hadn't been brave enough to ask Guinevere the question directly. Perhaps she knew but hadn't dared to offer the answer.

Draven watched me silently for a moment. "Let's go and ask her today. After all, it's better to know, isn't it?"

"Knowledge doesn't always equal happiness, Draven. You know that," I said, bitterness filling my voice.

"No, but at least then you'll be equipped. Prepared for whatever you have to do. Whatever you decide to do." He hesitated. "If she says destroying the grail will somehow hurt Kaye..."

"Would I still destroy it?" I sat up in bed and wrapped my arms around my knees. "I have no choice, do I? They must be destroyed. All of them. The grail, the sword. The spear, wherever the hell it is."

"They're not all necessarily evil. The sword..."

"Yes, it helped me. When it wanted to. And only me. Think of all of the countless others that it's killed simply because... what? They didn't possess my exact blood type?" I felt almost guilty saying the words out loud, as if I were betraying Excalibur somehow, failing to appreciate what the sword had done for me, how it had saved me. "It might not be fully evil. But Arthur planned to use me, bound to the sword, to execute his plans. While the sword exists and I exist, that's still a possibility."

I let the words hang in the air, unspoken. Arthur was no longer alive. But another, much more malicious king was.

A king I had seen—or thought I had seen—once in a dream. A king who preferred to work from the shadows, pulling my brother's strings.

Gorlois le Fay had never reached out to me. Never directly.

Did he even know I existed? Did he know where I was? What did he want from me, anyhow?

Whatever it was, I doubted it was a simple family reunion. Not after what Orcades had said.

Gorlois had somehow gotten the grail into Camelot and into Tyre's disgustingly, deceptive hands. Or Cavan, as he was truly called. Cavan, the High Priest of Perun.

Had Gorlois ever truly wished to help Arthur magnify his own power? Or had it all just been a ploy of some sort? To sow chaos in Pendrath? To weaken Pendrath still further?

Or to get at me in a way I couldn't even see yet. Was that what Kaye really was? A way to strike right across Eskira and into my very heart?

If so, I couldn't critique the plan. It was working. My true father's downfall and destroying the three objects were all I could think about most of the time.

No matter how hard Draven tried to distract me with other, healthier occupations.

Now, his hand brushed my chin, lifting my head. "Hey. Look at me, silver. I'm still here. Where did you go?"

"I'm sorry. Distracted, I guess." I tried to smile.

Medra let out a sharp, complaining sound that made it clear she was just about done waiting for this dull conversation to be over and for milk to arrive.

"We'd better go," Draven said, his attention turning back to her immediately.

I smiled. A real one this time.

"Wait. I'm coming with you. We'll find her wet nurse. And then breakfast?" I scrambled out of bed and started pulling out clothes from the wardrobe.

Draven and I had taken up residence in a suite of rooms across the castle overlooking the city. It was strange not to be in my old little tower room with its view of the gardens below.

But overall, it was a refreshing change. There were no old memories in this suite. It had been used for visiting noble guests. The room was richly decorated and well appointed like any suite in the castle, but it was also completely generic.

The new memories Draven and Medra and I had made in the suite were all good.

So far. Except my little nightmare.

I pushed that thought away. Because a nightmare was all it had been. Not a true dreaming. Just a simple nightmare. My own mind was trying to frighten me. Trying to sow doubt.

I wouldn't let myself become my own undoing. Not when I had real enemies to contend with.

Draven had placed Medra back in the cradle for a moment where she was fussing as he strapped something to his chest. He let out a frustrated oath.

"What is that?" I glanced over, curious, as I finished buttoning a leather vest and tucking a muted, rose-colored blouse into my trousers.

Draven's expression was distracted. He was tightening some sort of a sash and criss-crossing leather straps over his chest and shoulders.

When he was finished, he reached for Medra.

I gaped as he began trying to stuff the squirming, cranky infant into the pocket he had created against his torso.

"Here, let me," I said quickly, stepping forward and taking Medra from him.

"It's a carrier," he answered, a little grumpily. "For an infant."

"Ah, I see." I tried to quell the twitching in my lip and carefully did not make eye contact as I lifted Medra over the pouch and tried to dangle her legs so that they would drop into the holes just so.

"She's so squirmy," I complained.

In answer, Medra let out a shriek of protest and kicked her legs as I tried to lower her in.

"If she'd just hold still a moment," I complained.

Now it was Draven's turn to hide a smile. Not very successfully.

I tried again, waiting until Medra had finished getting her kicks out.

"There." I looked with satisfaction as the baby's legs finally slid into the waiting holes, her bottom settling into the pouch as her tiny fists raised and rested against Draven's chest. "She looks quite comfortable," I observed.

Medra leaned her soft pink cheek against Draven's tunic. She seemed to be settling in for the ride.

"Well, she does like me best, you know," he teased.

"It's no joke. She really does. Everyone can see it. You're wonderful with her. And... well, I'm not... used to babies," I admitted.

He raised his eyebrows and grinned. "And you think I am?"

"Well, you certainly have a knack for it. An instinct."

He tapped a finger to his chin, still grinning. "I believe they call it a maternal instinct, do they not?"

"Shut up," I growled playfully. "I suppose I must be lacking mine."

"It has nothing to do with male or female. You have it. She's bonding with you, too. In time..."

"Yes, in time." I looked at him and the baby, suddenly imagining Medra running through the castle on her own two legs. I could teach her to read. Show her my favorite books in the castle library. Or teach her sword fighting down in the practice yard. Of course, with Draven and Sir Ector and Dame Halyna all nearby, she'd have a lot of help with the latter.

The baby carrier Draven wore was crafted from a study linen and embroidered with flowers. It had clearly been used before.

"Where did you get it?" I asked.

"Hawl and I were discussing how Bearkin cubs simply hold on to their parent's fur and are carried about on their backs, or even their undersides. Lancelet overheard us and mentioned that her mother had used a carrier with all of her children—and that sometimes her father had worn it, too." He shrugged. "Well, it piqued my interest..."

"Of course it did." I smiled.

"And so she offered to try to find it."

"I'm so glad she's been visiting her family," I murmured.

He nodded. "She brought it back from her family's home in the city yesterday. Her mother said I could keep it as long as I wanted. You're welcome to try it, too, of course." He flexed his shoulders. "It's quite enjoyable." Then he eyed me. "You look quite enjoyable, too."

His tone had changed, taken on another meaning entirely. His eyes moved over my body, pausing over the tight bodice of my leather vest, the curve of my waist, then passing to my hips snug in their trousers.

He made a pained sound, half-growl, half-groan. "I suppose I could pass her off to the wet nurse. We could have breakfast in bed."

"Don't you dare. You've promised baby Medra a ride," I chided. "Besides, I just got her into that contraption."

"Fine," he assented. "But later..."

"Yes. Later." I bit my lip, feeling a familiar heat instantly kindle between my thighs at the sound of the word and its connotation. An entire afternoon in bed, perhaps. To banish the nightmares.

Draven leaned forward, one hand cupping Medra's head, covering her tiny ears.

"In the meantime," he whispered, his voice husky and low. "I'll be imagining doing so many things to you, Morgan. Many, many things. *Later.*"

He stepped forward and kissed me, a kiss slow and simmering, his lips warm and firm against mine, and a quiver went down my spine as my own imagination began to dance.

We stepped out into the corridor and began making our way down to the great hall.

Usually one of the wet nurses slept in the little servant's room outside of the main bedroom so we could call on her during the night. But Draven liked the freedom of having bottles prepared so that we could keep to ourselves. This worked out fairly well... except when the newborn had a sudden appetite surge.

I glanced at Medra. It was actually miraculous she was being this patient. Usually, the infant would have been a squalling ball of rage by now. But Draven's proximity seemed to calm her. It always did.

"Hawl keeps some bottles of expressed milk in the kitchens in a cool place. They're replenished every day or two. Chances are we can find one to give her. If not, we'll have to summon a nurse," Draven said, explaining his plan.

I nodded. He had concerned himself with the details of tending to Medra much more than I had. Feeding her, cleaning her, changing her. Oh, I helped, of course. And we were very fortunate to have servants. But I knew Draven believed she was our responsibility, that we should be doing as much as possible by ourselves.

I bit my lip. Except... we couldn't. Not for much longer.

Soon, Medra would be left alone again. Her life would dramatically change once more. The people who were supposed to care for her, gone in an instant.

And would we return?

It was cruel. So cruel for a child to have to go through.

I knew, for I had gone through it myself.

Was that why I was already pulling away from her?

"Have you given more thought as to who we'll ask to care for her?" I asked carefully.

We'd entered the Great Hall. The seat of my brother's power.

Draven paused, his hand running over Medra's small back as he looked around the room.

The king's throne—the monarch's throne, I corrected myself—stood alone on the dais. Orcades's had been cleared away.

"Whosoever pulls the sword from this stone shall be the rightful ruler of all Aercanum."

They were Orcades's words. My heart ached as I remembered my sister's blood-rimmed lips as she had spoken them. I didn't like to think about what she had truly meant. The throne should remain empty. It wasn't waiting for me. It was waiting for Kaye, I told myself. It always had been.

I caught Draven looking at a pile of dried out rose petals that had somehow still not been cleared away.

"Roses." He shook his head disgustedly. "What sort of a man can ruin something as beautiful as a rose." He looked over at me. "You'll always be the queen of roses in my mind. And that throne over there—it will always be rightfully yours. Just as your sister said."

"Don't say such things," I said quietly. "Isn't one throne enough for me? It's already one throne I didn't want."

"No one who wants power—"

"Should ever get it," I finished. I wrinkled my nose at him playfully. "Yes, yes, I've heard your kernel of wisdom before. But perhaps it's simply that those who don't want power are too timid and incompetent in the first place to desire it. Perhaps they know they're unsuited to it."

Draven looked amused. "Timid? Incompetent? Is that what you think you are?"

"No," I admitted. "Well, not timid."

He lifted his chin and laughed. "Certainly not since I've known you. If you ever were." He eyed me curiously. "Were you? Ever?"

"I had to keep my head down when I was a child," I replied. "So I tried my best to seem so." I thought back to my childhood in the castle after my mother died. "I spent years avoiding my father. And then years mostly avoiding Arthur." I met his eyes. "Then I found you."

He held my gaze, rock-steady. "And now you never have to pretend to be timid again. Be everything you truly are. That's all I'll ever ask of you, my silver one."

I stepped forward, careful of Medra, and lifted my lips to his.

If the kiss upstairs had been a simmer, this one was a burning spark that threatened to become a blaze. When I pulled away, I was panting.

Draven's wavy, tousled, black hair fell over his broad shoulders, longer than ever. Clad in black trousers with a leather jerkin open at the throat, he showcased pure, raw strength. His green eyes stared back at me, hungry and haunting.

Mine.

I felt suddenly bewildered. Overwhelmed. What man was this who had shadows and darkness at his very fingertips?

But something in his darkness called to my own. He was my perfect complement in every way.

"I am the luckiest woman, mortal or fae, in all of Aercanum to have a mate such as you," I said slowly. "Did you know that, Kairos Draven Venator? Have I told you?"

He grinned like the rogue he was. "No, but you should. Daily."

I rolled my eyes.

"But that throne..."

"No, no, no," I interrupted. "Nice try. I asked you first. Have you given any thought to..."

But Medra trumped us both, letting out a high-pitched wail that filled the hall and showed no signs of stopping.

"We'd better go straight to the kitchens," Draven shouted over the crying.

I nodded and followed him out of the Great Hall and away from the lingering scent of dead roses.

CHAPTER 2 - MORGAN

For thousands of years, the world I lived in had been shaped by the fae. But for most of my life I had counted myself as half-mortal. And like the mortals around me, I had been too blind or too stupid to understand the unseen strings that pulled at us.

Alternative option: Somewhere in twilight's embrace, a war that most mortals had managed to live in blissful ignorance of had raged on in the background. We had lived in ignorance, too, of the way fae had once treated us. We had not been their equals, but in many cases, their slaves.

But history books were written by the victors. And those who won wars usually did not wish to dwell upon previous losses or tales of how their grandparents had been not kings and queens but slaves.

Or at least, that was the Pendragon way of it. We had always been rather blinded with our own sense of pride.

Outside of Pendrath, however, Rheged had always been something of a mystery. Even as a child, I had heard tales of their reputation as a brutal, aggressive nation known for secrecy.

Now I wondered how many of the stories were true.

Their king, Nerov, had certainly played my brother false, offering aid and then withdrawing it only to attack. But perhaps he'd had no other choice. What was really going on within that dark kingdom?

In the past weeks, parties that seemed to come from Rheged had been attacking Tintagel and spreading as far as the northwestern borders of Lyonesse.

That night in the tavern, after my brother's death, had been the first announcement of many.

The raids had passed Pendrath by, at least for now.

In the meantime, I had scoured the maps of Eskira and Myntra, searching for the seat of my father's power. The court of Gorlois le Fay.

I had known it would not be clearly labeled on any map. Still, when I looked at the northern mountains of Rheged—mountains said to be so deadly and unscalable, so rough and rocky with their peaks far above the clouds—I felt... a pull. Nothing more. But a pull.

We would start in Rheged, I had decided. And along the way, we would find out why the attacks had begun and find a way to make them stop.

In the meantime, troops from Pendrath and Myntra had been bolstering Tintagel—when they could. Understandably, a foreign monarch who had only so recently seen Pendrath as a threat to his people and dominion did not wish to let in too many of our forces.

Lyonesse had rejected almost all of our help, preferring to stubbornly fight alone.

I thought again of Rheged. Fenyx had been fostered there. He had been a brutal, cruel man. Was his cruelty fostered in Rheged, too?

When Draven had first come to Camelot, Sir Ector had told me a story of how the new Guard Captain had supposedly helped to murder almost an entire royal family. It was a bone-chilling tale. One which Draven had told me the truth of—a long story, and one for another day.

But suffice to say, murdering infants was, thankfully, not a part of his long and adventurous past.

A loud wail broke my concentration. Medra was still crying. Now at an increasing volume.

Beside me, Draven was focused on shushing and bouncing her as we walked quickly through the grandeur of the Rose Court's long, stone corridors.

Picking up our pace to a jog, we navigated past brightly-colored tapestries and candles flickering in iron-wrought sconces. The air carried the faint scent of beeswax mingled with the perfume of centuries-old wood and dusty stone.

As we reached the entrance to the kitchens, the atmosphere changed.

I felt my own stomach rumbling as the air became thick with the savory scent of roasting meats, the tantalizing fragrance of freshly baked bread, and the underlying notes of herbs and spices.

The sound of clattering pots and the sizzle of something delicious being cooked on an open flame provided a cozy backdrop of noise. Wooden beams crisscrossed overhead, holding the essentials of any good kitchen—rows of hanging herbs and dried ingredients. Long, sturdy tables lined the center, holding pots and pans and other culinary tools.

Kitchen scullions bustled hurriedly through the room with purpose, some tending to the roaring hearths, ensuring the flames beneath the pots were just right. Apprentices stood at stations, slicing fruit or kneading dough for pastries.

It was a wonder to me that so little had changed with Arthur's death. Life in the castle went on much as before, even without its king.

As Draven and I entered, a hush fell over the room and the banging of pots and chopping of vegetables came to a standstill.

One by one, the kitchen staff turned towards us. I saw a few kitchen maids and apprentices, hands dusted with flour from making the morning bread, exchanging glances of excitement.

Apparently, not everything had remained the same. My role had changed. Much as I would wish to forget that.

Trying not to blush awkwardly, I was relieved when I spotted Hawl. The Ursidaur was towering over one of the cooking stations, stirring something in a huge, copper pot.

A tall, white, cook's hat was balanced precariously on their brown, furry head.

As we approached, Hawl whipped the hat off and threw it on the floor with a short-tempered growl that sent the scullions nearby scurrying away.

Next to Hawl stood a short man with sun-kissed skin and a balding head who I recognized as the head cook. Now the man looked up from his cutting board with a patient smile.

"A tradition, nothing more, my friend," the cook said soothingly in the warm accent of Lyonesse.

"A ridiculous accoutrement," Hawl snapped. "That hat was more likely to fall into a pan and start a fire than serve any real purpose."

"You need not wear it," the cook said appeasingly. "Your reputation as a culinary maestro precedes you. It was a silly thought, the hat, nothing more. A gesture of honor. I deeply apologize."

Hawl grumbled, sounding slightly embarrassed. "It is... nothing. You wished to share a piece of your culture." The Bearkin cleared their throat. "It was a kind thought."

The small chef beamed. Then he seemed to finally notice Medra, Draven, and me standing nearby.

His eyes lit up as they fell on Medra.

"Ah, a visit from the little one and her family! We're whipping up something special this morning, Your Radiance," the cook promised me. I opened my mouth to tell him there was no need for such formalities, but the man was already rushing on. "Your friend, Hawl, here is a virtuoso of the culinary arts…"

"Danielo helped," Hawl interjected, deadpan.

"A little, a little. I helped a little," the cook said, waving an arm but looking pleased. "We are making the most divine stew, My Serene Sovereign. A stew like none will have tasted before." He touched a finger to his lips, then looked at Medra who had momentarily stopped crying, and his eyes widened. "But little one, you have no wish for stew, do you? You seek only the milk. Never fear, I will fetch it for you."

He turned on his heels and moved towards one one of the staircases leading down to the cooling cellars below the kitchens.

"Serene Sovereign?" Draven murmured.

I glared at him. "Hush. Hush immediately."

"Whatever you say, My Radiance," he whispered.

I kicked his shin before I remembered he was holding a baby. He yelped, and I saw one of the passing apprentice's eyes widen in shock.

Yes, I longed to say. The Empress of Myntra is terrifying indeed.

Since entering the kitchen, Medra's bawling had stopped. Instead, she stared wide-eyed at Hawl in total silence, watching their every move.

The Bearkin tended to have that effect on her. She was completely mesmerized.

Draven let out a sigh of relief at the reprieve from crying. "So you've made friends here already, I see," he observed to Hawl.

"Danielo Castellano is a great improvement on the company I was forced to keep in your fleet," Hawl growled. "He is a talented cook, a man of taste and refinement."

I hid a smile. Draven had told me all about the very inhospitable Vemak Bear-Killer who Hawl had encountered on a Myntra ship.

"He certainly seems to admire you," Draven said.

"We get along well," Hawl acknowledged. "Our interactions have been collegial."

"So everyone has welcomed you? There haven't been any… issues?" We did *not* want a repeat of Vemak in the castle kitchens.

Hawl's gaze softened as they looked at me. "I have been mostly accepted. Of course, some fear me. They always will. Others are overly curious and stare with their bulging, beady human eyes. I'm used to it."

"But you're comfortable?" I pressed, deciding not to dispute Hawl's assessment of mortal eyeballs this morning. The Bearkin tended to have a rather dismissive view of humans and fae at the best of times. But then, with the state of the world, who could blame them?

"As comfortable as any of us can be as we while away these tedious days," Hawl complained, dropping a large knife onto the cutting board beside them with a thud that made me jump. "Waiting, waiting, and more waiting."

Draven glanced down at Medra, then ran a hand gently over the baby's head. I wondered if he felt guilty for not minding the wait.

"Sunstrike's wing couldn't be helped," I reminded Hawl. "But yes, I share your impatience to get on the road." Though I felt a little guilty for admitting it in front of Draven.

"Her wing is healing nicely," Hawl conceded. "I looked at it again last night."

"The exmoor?" Danielo had reappeared. "Have you shown them what you've made for the exmoor, my dear friend?" The chef bounced up to us, holding a bottle of milk in each hand.

I looked towards where Hawl stood over the copper pot and raised a brow. "What's in the pot, Hawl?"

Was it my imagination, or could Bearkins actually blush?

"Hawl?" Draven prompted.

But it was Danielo who eagerly answered. "The most tender cuts of venison, slow-cooked to sweet perfection and infused with yarrow, comfrey, and chamomile." He waved his hands towards his nostrils and drew a long, luxurious sniff. "Ah, heavenly. And of course, it shall be served with the pâté, already plated and prepared."

"Pâté?" I inquired.

"Elk liver pâté. Seasoned with the finest healing herbs, fresh burdock and dandelion, and blended with brandy, garlic, onions..." Danielo waved a hand. "Well, I'm sure you do not wish for a full list of ingredients, Divine Elegance."

I cringed. "There is truly no need for such formalities, Danielo. Please, call me Morgan. After all, I'm not even your sovereign."

"Ah, it is true I hail from fair Lyonesse," Danielo agreed. "But if only—"

Here, Danielo was elbowed by Hawl and quickly smothered whatever he had been about to say. As it was likely something borderline treasonous about how he wished I ruled all of Eskira, I was infinitely grateful. I had heard similar things mentioned a few times already by some of the staff and had been quick to quell them.

"Seems rather rich for breakfast," Draven observed. He glanced at me. "I'm not sure that Her Divine Radiance and I..."

"Oh, it is not for you!" Danielo cackled jovially and clapped his hands together, while I glared at my mate. "Though any creature would be fortunate indeed to sample them. But no, no. These creations are for the beasts. The cats. You know, the exmoors."

"Venison stew and elk pâté for the exmoors," Draven drawled. "Huh. Really, Hawl?" There was a smirk on his handsome face.

"She needs her strength," the Bearkin growled, as if anticipating a challenge. "What you may see as delicacies, I see as nutrient-rich, healing grub."

"She does, of course she does. I'm just..." Draven coughed. "Just impressed that you're putting so much care into her recuperation."

"Oh, the female exmoor is all they talk about, all they think about. Dare I say—" Danielo began.

"No, you may not," Hawl growled. "Ridiculous for you to imply I might be so invested. Like a Bearkin with a cub. Absolutely ridiculous." The Ursidaur slammed their paws down on their cooking station, then stalked off towards the nearest doorway.

Danielo watched the Bearkin go, bewildered. "What did I say?"

"I think Hawl believed we might be teasing them," I explained.

"Pâté," Draven murmured, shaking his head, the hint of a smirk remaining. "Pâté."

"Hush up," I hissed. "Or Hawl will soon be doing more than growling at you."

Draven grinned. "I'd like to see them try. But very well, I'll stop teasing." He looked down at Medra who had been slurping happily on the bottle he was holding for her for the last few minutes. "I suppose Hawl is worried that... what? Their reputation as a bold warrior might be compromised if word got out they were bringing fancy feasts to a cat?"

"And as you're in no position whatsoever to point fingers..." I noted.

Draven grinned. "Precisely." He tapped a finger to his lips. "In fact, remind me to have a talk with them about balancing the responsibilities of parenthood with those of a seasoned warrior."

"I'll be sure to get right on that. Can we carry some of that stew out to Sunstrike?" I asked Danielo diplomatically, trying to change the subject and finally get out of the kitchen and out of everyone's way. "Or the pâté if it's ready?"

"Certainly, certainly. I'll prepare a platter while you eat your own breakfast upstairs," he assured me. "One of the scullions must surely accompany you and carry it, however. It may be quite heavy."

I smiled. "I'm sure I can manage. I'm stronger than I look."

After a hearty but pâté-free breakfast in a mostly empty dining hall, I found myself carrying the exmoor's tray from the kitchen with Draven and Medra marching behind me as we made our way out of the castle. Danielo had been correct. The tray was rather heavy, but nothing I couldn't manage on my own.

"I wonder if there's insect powder in that pâté," Draven muttered.

I wrinkled my nose. "What?"

"Just something Hawl suggested back on the ship when we were at sea. Specifically, dried cockroaches were what they had in mind."

"The exmoors do seem to have a broad palate when it comes to food," I said, thinking of how I was fairly certain I had caught Nightclaw eating a frog the other day. "But I'm not sure they'd stoop to cockroaches. Blech."

Draven laughed. "Be warned. Hawl thinks they're very nutritious. Bears are known to eat grubs and other insects, you know. They might be sneaking them into our food even now."

"Surely Danielo would stop them," I said, a little horrified.

Draven chuckled. "Danielo has far too big a case of hero-worship to stop Hawl. Perhaps our Bearkin friend will have a sweetheart before long."

I snorted. "I highly doubt that. I don't think Hawl is interested in, well, romance and that sort of thing." I thought for a moment. "Not that we know much about the romantic life of Bearkins. Or what Hawl's preferences are. Do they usually stick to their own kind?"

Draven shrugged. "There aren't many of them left. Perhaps they can't be so choosy."

"Well, whatever you do, don't you dare ask them, or worse, tease them about Danielo," I threatened. "Let's just be happy Hawl's made a new friend and mind our own business."

"Yes, my Serene Sovereign," Draven said with false meekness. "Whatever you say, Your Royal Radiance."

I shot him a deathly stare which swiftly changed to a grin as I realized where we were.

We had almost reached the roost.

CHAPTER 3 - MORGAN

D espite Draven's teasing, I knew he was worried about Sunstrike, too. And while the elegant cuisine Hawl had crafted for the exmoors might be a little excessive, if the food really did improve Sunstrike's recuperation, I knew Draven would be thankful.

He was simply in a difficult position. Torn between eagerness for his battlecat to recover and a desire to remain as close to Medra for as long as he could.

The sun was shining warmly overhead as we entered the perimeter of what Sir Ector had labeled the "Winged Roost."

The Master-at-Arms had really outdone himself, especially considering how little time he'd had to prepare suitable accommodations for two massive creatures—ones which the people of Camelot found both utterly terrifying and fascinating, so rare and strange were they.

An ancient stone tower had been repurposed into something suitable for the large cats. Part of the wooden roof had been cut away, providing a huge, circular opening, allowing the battlecats to take off and land freely. The remains of the roof had been left as large awnings, which provided shade and shelter for the exmoors, while a large secluded alcove had been set up on the ground floor with soft straw bedding to offer a padded nest.

But most ingenious of all was what Sir Ector had done to the walls. Elevated perches and platforms had been strategically positioned on the exterior of the tower to allow the battlecats to climb and survey the castle and grounds from various levels and positions. Nightclaw in particular seemed to love creeping up to these vantage points, just as any feline might.

Dotted around the roost were large, sandstone blocks with textured surfaces. As we approached, Nightclaw was standing on his hind legs beside one of them, scratching and sharpening his long claws while an audience watched, oohing and aahing.

The fact that the two battlecats frequently had an audience was both a source of amusement and annoyance to Draven and me.

Word of the rare creatures staying at the castle had spread quickly throughout Camelot thanks to their dramatic arrival on the night of the king's death. Once the funerals and days of mourning had passed, many citizens seemed eager to find something to be, well, excited about. Something that had nothing to do with tragedy or war.

Nightclaw and Sunstrike had provided the perfect distraction.

So many residents from the city and visitors from the villages surrounding Camelot had started to gather at the Winged Roost that it had gotten to the point where Sir Ector had to set up benches and built a fence around the roost. A few guards were regularly stationed nearby to keep out trespassers, though there had only been a few.

The fences were more for the viewers than the exmoors. After all, it was not as if the exmoors could not easily defend themselves from the overly curious and bold or simply fly away.

So far, however, the tourists had managed not to become exmoor food.

There had been one incident in which a young man attempted to sneak into the exmoor's roost and fetch a handful of fur for his lady love to make into a pillow. To Nightclaw's credit, he had only ripped off the poor young man's trousers. Though, considering how the young man had shrieked and wailed, one might have thought he had lost a chunk of his buttocks as well as his pants.

The craze for exmoors had extended all over the city. In the markets, artisan stalls offered battlecat-themed trinkets, drawings, and other souvenirs. A new inn, The Sunstrike, had been erected to serve the tide of travelers, while a tavern had renamed itself The Empress's Exmoor. A blatant attempt to win royal favor, but secretly, I rather liked the name.

Thankfully, the crowd outside the roost was small today.

It had been raining earlier, and I assumed this had caused many to disperse. Those who remained were pressed eagerly against the fence. I caught sight of one small girl standing on a fence rail, waving a little stuffed version of Sunstrike. The exmoor's yellow eyes were made from bright yellow buttons.

My gaze quickly moved to the tall, slender figure of a young woman standing all alone further along the rail. She had short, cropped, blonde hair, and even now, the sight of her profile and the brutal scars on her cheek made my heart tighten.

As if feeling my eyes on her, Lancelet turned her head.

"Ah, look who it is," she drawled as I approached. "Our Regal Eminence, Our Divine Grace—the Rose of Myntra." She glanced down at the tray I carried. "Oh, Your Imperial Majesty, who dared to load down your noble arms with such a vulgar burden?"

I flushed with heat, but then spotted the mischievous look in her eyes. She was mocking me, yes, but not trying to be cruel. I nearly sighed in relief. We had moved past the cruelty. Slowly but surely, my friend was letting me back in.

"I rather like that. The Rose of Myntra." Draven let the words roll over his tongue. "Who came up with that one? Was it you?"

Lancelet snorted. "I'm offended you even had to ask that, Draven. No. I suppose it was someone in the faction."

Ah, yes. Even more awkward than the entire castle kitchen coming to a standstill was the fact that a new faction had quickly arisen following Arthur's death. This small group—and I prayed to the Three that it *was* small—believed I should not only be empress of Myntra but queen of Pendrath, and perhaps even all of Eskira.

The last thing I needed right now, as we tried to make amends to our northern and southern neighbors, was a group of overly fervent supporters starting rumors I had plans to take over the continent, starting a new war between kingdoms as a result.

I groaned and said as much.

"But you could, you know," Draven declared, bouncing Medra in the baby carrier. "If you wanted to."

There was an impish glint in his eyes. Fortunately, Lancelet saw it, too.

"I'm not even going to dignify that with a response," I said. "And keep your voice down. There's a crowd."

He looked around. "They're nowhere near us. You worry too much. And it's true. If you wanted to rule Eskira, you certainly have the power to do so."

"Eskira is divided into peaceful, independent kingdoms already. And I have no wish to rule. I haven't even begun to properly rule Myntra, now have I? It's not as if I'm exactly bursting with experience."

Before Draven had left the Court of Umbral Flames, he had left Lyrastra as regent with Odessa as the power behind the throne. I had done nothing to even deserve the title of "empress" yet. Perhaps that was why, beneath the embarrassment, it also stung. I was a fraud. A prince's consort, yes.

But a savior? A ruler? No.

"You'd have her colonize Eskira?" Lancelet's eyes had narrowed in on Draven. "Seize power? Destroy our independence?"

Draven shrugged. I knew that he was mostly saying what he was to annoy her—but in small part because he happened to believe it. A fact that made me vastly uncomfortable. "If that was what the people wanted. Majority rules, doesn't it?"

"That's mob rule," Lancelet said seethingly. "What we have always needed is government by the people, for the people. A truly organized and equitable system where everyone may have a say, from the lowest commoner to the highest noble. Not a monarchy based on blood lineages. It's beyond primeval." She glanced at me. "No offense."

I shrugged. I wasn't offended by the idea that monarchy was an ancient, incredibly unfair system of ruling a kingdom. Perhaps when Kaye was king, we could even begin to discuss the possibility of eliminating it.

"It so happens I agree with you, generally speaking. It's not as if the people in any of these kingdoms had a say in selecting their rulers. Hereditary succession is a joke. That's why I broke the mold." Draven winked.

"Yes, it was ever so bold of you to put the royal daughter of one kingdom on the throne of another," Lancelet said sarcastically. "Nobles, commoners. The entire system is a travesty."

"I suppose I might have chosen a peasant girl," Draven said, stroking his chin thoughtfully. He looked at me and grinned. "But then, I didn't fall in love with a peasant girl, did I? I fell for you, silver one."

He blew me a kiss, then grinned wickedly as Lancelet made a sound of disgust while I went red to my roots. Now I *knew* he was only doing this to drive her mad.

"I was hoping to speak with Guinevere today," I said quickly, desperate to change the subject. My misbehaving mind had gone straight to the bedroom at the sight of Draven's grin, and I needed to get it out again.

Lancelet furrowed her brow. "She's not here. Obviously."

"Right. Of course not." I took a breath. "But perhaps you could take me to her. She's at the temple, I suppose? I thought you might like to accompany me. It..." I fumbled. "It would be nice to spend some time with you." I looked at Draven meaningfully. "Alone."

Draven chuckled.

Lancelet nodded. "I could walk you down if you want the company."

There was a collective gasp from around us and not a few shrieks.

The sound of beating wings filled the air.

"Nightclaw," I said, without having to look. He was so close, I could sense him. He had been hunting.

"Out hunting?" Draven guessed. "Was he successful?"

I closed my eyes and mentally reached for Nightclaw, feeling his emotions. Triumph, hunger. "Yes." I opened them again. "He's bringing meat to Sunstrike. She'll be happy about that."

"Well, you'd better get that tray to her before he does or Hawl will be offended if she doesn't touch it," Draven suggested. "They can have a feast together."

"That tray is for the exmoors?" Lancelet peered at the large plate of minced and jellied meats. "Is that... pâté?"

"It is. Hawl is very eager for Sunstrike's recovery."

"Clearly." Lancelet met my eyes. "Well, they're not the only ones."

"I'll take this to Sunstrike and then you'll come with me to the temple?"

"You know, I just got here," she pointed out. "I was delivering a message to one of the healers from Kasie. But yes, I'll go back with you."

"About Kaye?" I asked sharply.

Camelot had many healers and the foremost of them had been brought to the castle over the last few weeks. But the only two I truly trusted to care for my brother were Guinevere and Kasie. The others seemed completely bewildered by Kaye's state and determined to only offer physical remedies and answers. One had even claimed Kaye was fully conscious and choosing to remain prone—even though that was obviously not true, for my brother did not eat or drink yet remained exactly the same day after day.

That healer had been sent swiftly packing.

Lancelet nodded. "There's a fine apothecary among them. Kasie sent for some herbs."

I felt my shoulders sag. "Oh. I see."

"Nothing has changed," Lancelet said gently. "You would be the first to know if anything had happened, Morgan."

I nodded, then eyed the roost where the sounds of roars and tearing flesh had started to emanate. The crowd around us looked simultaneously disgusted and delighted.

"Why don't we skip walking to the temple? As you said, you've just come from there."

Lancelet frowned. "You don't wish to speak with Guinevere after all?"

"No, I do. But why don't we fly? You've never ridden on Nightclaw, have you?"

"No, but I..." Lancelet began.

"Excellent. You're not frightened, are you?"

She frowned. "Of course not!"

"Good. Then I'll deliver this, ask his permission, and we'll go."

"Ask his permission?"

But I'd already started to walk away. I caught Draven's eye for a moment. He seemed to understand.

"I'll be here, waiting for you to get back." He flashed me a grin. "Without Medra."

The wooden doors of the roost swung open as I stepped through, but I quickly pulled them shut again behind me. I could hear a few sounds of disappointment from the people waiting and hoping to catch a glimpse of the exmoors.

But as far as I was concerned, they had already had the privilege of seeing Nightclaw fly overhead and land with his catch.

The battlecats weren't pets or performing animals in some sort of a circus or play. They deserved their privacy.

They had already been remarkably patient with all of the fuss they'd been receiving. If I were one of them, I realized, I wasn't sure I'd have been able to show the same restraint in not eating the crowd already.

With that in mind, I made a mental note to instruct Sir Ector to have visitors' access restricted to just a few hours at midday. The circus had gone on long enough, and our exmoors had been more than patient.

Blinking in the sunspecked light, my eyes quickly adjusted to the shadows of the overhang above.

Across from me, in the center of the tower, the two exmoors were engrossed in devouring the deer Nightclaw had brought back. I knew they'd sensed me entering, so for a moment, I simply watched.

Nightclaw's dark ebony fur, thick with golden stripes, gleamed in the broad rays of sunlight from the opening above. I smiled to myself. How beautiful my exmoor was. How far he'd come from that first day I'd met him in the royal menagerie, when his sleek and lustrous fur had been so matted and unkempt, his gold stripes dulled by neglect and malnourishment.

Sunstrike's coloring was more subdued, but she was no less lovely. Her gold-brown fur blended with the courtyard's hues as she matched her mate's fervor in feasting upon the fresh, raw meat. Both cats' wings were furled by their sides, quivering in anticipation as they ate.

I hesitated, glancing down at my tray, uncertain as to whether the cats would have an appetite for more.

But as I waited, Nightclaw let out a deep rumble and stepped away from the deer, gave a languid stretch, licked his lips, and then padded over to me.

Our eyes met in unspoken recognition, and I felt a thread of happiness weave through me. Tucking the tray under one arm, I reached out a hand and gently stroked his head, right between his tufted, lion-like ears.

"I've missed you," I said softly, feeling his happiness at seeing me, sensing his contentment. "You did well hunting today. That deer is huge."

I felt him begin to purr under my hand.

"How is your mate's wing?" I asked. I gestured to the tray. "Hawl prepared all of this for her. To help speed her recovery."

Nightclaw didn't answer, just eyed the tray, then serenely turned and padded back over to the deer. Approaching Sunstrike, he licked her neck, then bit it playfully, drawing her attention to me.

As the female exmoor watched curiously, I crouched and carefully placed my tray down beside the dead deer.

The two bowls Hawl and Danielo had put there had seemed enormous down in the kitchens. But now, compared to the deer, they seemed rather small.

"I suppose this could be your dessert," I suggested, standing back up. "Or a snack for later?"

Nightclaw nudged his mate, clearly trying to convey that it was meant just for her. Sunstrike made a sound of annoyance, but backed up and began to unfurl her wings.

From what we had eventually been able to gather, the younger exmoor had gone off hunting by herself on one of the windier days we'd had. When the wind had picked up and became a strong spring storm, Sunstrike had already been tracking her prey—a large tusked boar—and, understandably, hadn't wanted to give it up.

But when the boar ran into a dense patch of woodland, Sunstrike had recklessly followed. And that's when her injury had occurred. Snagging herself painfully in the trees, the delicate membrane of her left wing had ripped.

When she hadn't returned, a distraught Nightclaw and I had flown after her. When we found her, the wing was a wretched sight, torn and tattered and dripping with blood.

But now, as Sunstrike carefully opened her wing to its full length, I could see how significantly she had already healed. The golden threads that veined the membranous surface seemed to glow with renewed vibrancy. Her fur had regained its lustrous sheen. Though the mending process was not quite complete, her wing showed huge improvement, and I felt filled with relief.

I also knew I'd have to tell Draven we'd be able to leave within the next few days, which might not be exactly what he wanted to hear.

But in the meantime...

"I don't suppose you'd fancy another flight?" I said to Nightclaw, touching a hand to his fur again to sense his response. "Just a quick one? With another rider?" I hesitated. "I wouldn't normally ask, but this one is very special to me."

I'd only requested this of him once before, and that had been my mate. It also hadn't really been a question. We'd been under attack then and desperate to get into the fight.

But this wasn't going to be a battle. Just a short flight over Camelot.

Perhaps I wanted to show off a little. Or perhaps I simply wanted to share a little of the joy the exmoor had given me with my friend.

After all, few could say they had ridden on the back of a battlecat.

I felt Nightclaw's acceptance. There was no reluctance or hesitation. He'd already eaten his fill and was prepared to go.

I saddled him while Sunstrike nibbled on the delicacies I'd brought her, making little sounds of appreciation. Nightclaw watched her the way I sometimes sensed Draven watching me—as if he couldn't take his eyes off her. As if she were the most beautiful thing in the world to him.

"We'll be back soon," I murmured. "You won't have to leave your mate for long. Just a quick jaunt to the temple. Maybe a few circles over the city. You can leave me there and I'll walk back."

The exmoor said nothing, not that I'd expected him to. But I knew he understood every word.

When we emerged from the roost, the crowd let out a roar of excitement. Amusement mixed with annoyance again, and I knew Nightclaw felt much the same.

Then I saw the little girl was still there, waving her tiny stuffed Sunstrike eagerly.

Before I could help myself, I met Nightclaw's eyes and inclined my head in a question. The older battlecat let out a long-suffering sigh. Then he padded over to the fence, right up to the little girl.

The crowd went silent. I watched the little girl's eyes become wide as saucers.

Then, slowly, she reached out a hand through the slats in the fence and touched Nightclaw's fur.

She squealed with glee. "Mommy! Mommy! I touched him! I touched an exmoor!"

I could see envious looks in the faces of adults in the crowd around her. Well, too bad. This wasn't about to become a regular thing.

Lancelet was still waiting in the same spot on the other side of the enclosure. Draven had disappeared, probably to tend to Medra, and Sir Ector had replaced him.

The older knight was smiling from ear to ear as Nightclaw and I came towards them.

"You do that every time you see one of them, you know," I observed.

Sir Ector continued beaming. "I'll never get over the sight. They're incredible animals. Absolutely incredible. It's a privilege to simply have seen them. The honor of a lifetime to have been able to care for one."

Nightclaw made a deep rumbling sound as if acknowledging the truth of what Sir Ector had just said.

"You have a lot in common with Hawl, you know, Nightclaw. Don't let it all go to your head," I chided, running my hand along his sleek side. "All of this attention. I suppose you'll want me to buy you a stuffed Sunstrike at the market to bring back to her next."

The exmoor chuffed forbearing as if to say I was being ridiculous.

Sir Ector laughed. "He understands every word we say, doesn't he?"

"They both do," I confirmed.

"Marvelous," Sir Ector said with no less wonderment. "The intelligence of these creatures. Why, we have no idea what they're really capable of."

I cleared my throat. "Did Lancelet tell you she's about to ride one?" I felt a little bad, as I realized Sir Ector would have loved the experience just as much if not more as my irascible friend. But it was too late. Perhaps Nightclaw would be very, very patient with me and concede to take my dear mentor for a ride another time.

"What an honor," Sir Ector breathed, looking at Lancelet with delight. "Are you nervous?"

Lancelet did indeed look a little nervous. Her fair skin had paled a little as Nightclaw had approached. Now her lips thinned decisively. "No. Not at all. Why should I be?"

"Of course, you aren't," Sir Ector said encouragingly. "Why, you've…"

I knew exactly how he'd meant to finish that sentence. Fortunately, he caught himself. "You've done much braver things." He cleared his throat. "It's a small task for one such as you. I won't deny, I'm envious."

"Well," I said quickly, "we'd better go." I flashed Sir Ector a smile. "But it'll be your turn soon. I promise."

"I'll hold you to that," he said cheerfully, watching as I climbed onto Nightclaw's back, then helped Lancelet clamber up behind me.

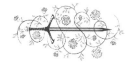

If we had gone straight to the temple, we would have been in the air only a few moments.

So instead, I gave Nightclaw free rein, instructing him only not to stray too far.

We circled over Camelot, flying over familiar sights. The castle, the markets, the temple.

I caught sight of the arena Arthur and Fenyx had used to test Excalibur. I had sat in the royal stands while Lancelet had been down on the sand. From where she was perched behind me, I felt her tense up. She'd seen it, too.

We flew out further, passing over the Greenbriar River where the harsh stone lines of the Temple of Perun held my gaze. Perched defiantly on a small island in the middle of the river, the temple's aura of conquest and cruelty clashed with its serene surroundings.

I remembered what Guinevere had said as we stood outside the temple that night. The temple should never have been built in such a place. For the isle was named Avalon, and even Guinevere, an outsider from Lyonesse, had known the legends—that the place was said to be one of the seats of the goddesses' power.

At that moment, as the armies of Tintagel and Lyonesse had stood on the riverbank opposite us, I had wondered what she had meant precisely. I still wondered now.

She had said they could not touch us there.

But would the island itself have stopped them? Or had Guinevere meant herself? Or me?

We passed over the island and flew across the countryside. Below us, a patchwork quilt of green fields unfolded. Emerald-hued farmland, tidy hedgerows, and quaint villages.

Small cottages with thatched roofs and smoke curling from chimneys nestled amidst the lush and peaceful hills and valleys. Nightclaw's wings beat with powerful grace as we traveled over meadows filled with bright spring flowers, streams glinting like silver snaking through the landscape, and woodlands with their canopies a mass of vibrant greens.

"It looks so peaceful down below," Lancelet said from behind me, echoing my thoughts. "As if nothing has changed."

But it wasn't the truth. The villages might look untouched, but they had faced losses of their own. They had given their sons and daughters to Arthur's war. Who knew how deep their sorrows ran.

In the city, the people had lost not only soldiers, but their youngest, most precious children. The babies my brother had slaughtered, blinded as he had been by a cryptic prophecy.

The prophecy Orcades had turned into her reason for being. For Medra's being.

Now we flew through the sunshine. But darkness was coming. I could feel it. I wondered if Lancelet sensed it, too.

"I'm with you, you know," she said, surprising me. "I'm with you through it all, no matter what." She cleared her throat. "No matter what came before. I hope you know that."

Had I? Had I known that?

"I know," I said softly. "I never doubted you. But if ever I gave you cause to doubt me, I'm truly sorry. You are my most dear and trusted friend."

"Friends to the end," Lancelet said. I heard the grimness in her voice.

"It won't come to that, Lanc," I said, using an old nickname, one I hadn't used since we were children, and trying to sound as if I meant it. "Besides, you're supposed to be appointed as regent soon..."

"For fuck's sake," she swore. "I won't be your regent, Morgan. Did you really think I'd go through with that? That I'd stay behind and keep a throne warm for you?"

"For Kaye," I said automatically.

"Or for Kaye," she concurred. "It doesn't matter who it's for. You're going to have to pick someone else."

I knew there was no point in arguing.

"Perhaps Guinevere..." I started to say, then stopped. The new high priestess would have much work of her own to do.

"Guinevere could take on anything she put her mind to," Lancelet said. "But you'll have to speak to her about that."

I nodded but said nothing as I looked down over the rolling hills.

I touched a hand to Nightclaw's warm fur. It was time to return to the temple.

CHAPTER 4 - MORGAN

I didn't hear the goddesses' voices when I entered their temple like some of the most devoted did. But then, I never had.

I only heard Merlin's.

When I stepped between the white marble pillars into that familiar courtyard, Merlin's was the face that danced before my eyes. Her lips turned into a half smile, her expression full of kindness, serenity, and wisdom.

The temple was full of echoes, memories, and death. It felt haunted to me now and always would be.

All around, worshippers milled to and fro, kneeling in prayer before the colossal statues of Devina, Zorya, and Marzanna before rising and leaving their humble offerings of flowers, grain, and scrolls.

But when I looked at the people who had come to worship, I saw shadows behind them. The forms of Arthur's soldiers, the fallen bodies of priestesses, and beyond it all, the look on Merlin's face as Fenyx's blade cut through her.

"It will never feel the same, will it?" Lancelet had been leading the way. Now she walked back over to me as I stood, hesitating beneath the shadow of the temple pediment. "Not without Merlin."

I looked past her, trying to form a response. On the edges of the courtyard lay the shrines of Perun and Nedola, the two siblings of the pantheon. Lingering on the fringes, they had always received less attention in Pendrath than the Three.

Now I saw that Perun's altar had been recently neglected altogether. Where once soldiers had visited and laid their weapons to be blessed, now the shrine sat barren. While a few women and a man sat in contemplation by Nedola the goddess of fate's shrine, Perun's seemed to have been intentionally abandoned.

I supposed it made sense, considering Perun had been my brother's favorite of the gods—and the god had done nothing to help him in the end. Now that Arthur and his cronies were dead and gone, Perun's temple would also be neglected and unvisited.

"Did you know," I said slowly, "that in Myntra, the Siabra have their own temples where the Three are depicted? But instead of showing the three sisters as mortal, some have fae traits."

"I suppose that makes sense. After all, we craft the gods in our own images, don't we?" Lancelet said with a shrug. "We always have, since the very start."

I gave a choked laugh, then dropped my voice. "I'm fairly sure that's sacrilege. What if... you know... *she* heard you."

"Who? Zorya? She's made of stone."

I choked. "Not her, you idiot. Your... you know. The woman who holds a special place in your heart. Guinevere!"

"The woman who holds a special place in my heart?" Lancelet snickered. "Is that what you're really calling her?"

I reddened. "Well, what am I supposed to think of her as?"

"She's the High Priestess, for one. You could call her that."

"I know that. Of course, I know that. But to you..."

"She's everything to me," Lancelet said simply, and the words went through me, right to my heart, reminding me of my own devotion to Draven. "But she belongs to the temple now."

I studied my friend. "So... that's it then?"

"I never expected to have a happy ending, Morgan." She said the words with such resignation. "Is that what you're so worried about?"

I threw up my hands. "I have no idea. I just thought that... Well, you know. You aren't usually the type to give up easily."

"I haven't. Given up, I mean. I'll still be with her. That won't change."

"Here? In the temple, you mean? But you also said..."

Lancelet brushed me off. "Speak with Guinevere."

I wanted to ask more. Wanted to ask exactly what Lancelet's feelings for Guinevere were. Wanted to ask how this could work when one person was supposed to be eternally celibate as High Priestess and one person was decidedly... not. Or at least, hadn't been as long as I'd known them.

But I also knew it wasn't my right to ask those things. This was between them.

So I just nodded. "So you really don't believe in any of this?"

"Now?" Lancelet shrugged. "Guinevere believes. I believe there are things we can't understand. But do I believe the Three really exist? That I should, what? Pray to them and hope they heal my scars?" She shrugged. "No. I don't. Does that shock you? I didn't take you for much of a believer yourself."

I thought for a moment. "I never have been. I suppose I'm a hypocrite. But I respect the traditions. I respected Merlin."

Lancelet watched me. "And now?"

I knew she meant now that Guinevere was the high priestess.

"I'll respect her successor, too. Merlin chose her after all." I looked over at the towering sculpture of Zorya with her arms outstretched to summon the first rays of the dawn. Beside her, Devina posed mid-stride with a spear in her hand, her eyes dancing with laughter.

I thought of how the hunters had prayed to the goddess of the hunt in the forest that night so long ago.

The third sculpture was cast in dark obsidian. Marzanna looked neither young or old, but simply foreboding, with her necklace of bones and her sharp sickle. But she received more than her share of worshippers. The small scrolls and papers littered around her feet attested to that.

Mortals would always be desperate to reach into the world of the dead somehow, and Marzanna represented a chance for that. She was said to be merciful to the mothers of lost children, kind-hearted to widows and orphans. But in the end, all had to meet her and none could escape the path she waited on.

As for me, I might have spent the rest of my life in this temple, or close to it. I was free of that fate now. I glanced over at Nedola's shrine. Should I be thanking the goddess of fate for that?

"Lancelet, Morgan. Welcome." Guinevere's voice echoed through the courtyard in a melodic cadence that had all heads instantly turning towards her. Like Merlin, I had to admit, she had quickly developed a commanding presence all her own.

She walked towards us slowly, one of the temple healer's, Kasie, following closely behind her. Clad in a flowing white gown edged in threads of silver, Guinevere's curvaceous form reminded me of a bell's graceful silhouette. Soft, brown curls framed her face. She moved with poise, an embodiment of serenity in a space meant for the divine, but a discerning gaze could unveil the subtle shadows etched in her doe-brown eyes, forged on her journey to the sacred seat of the high priestess.

"Guinevere," I said, forcing a smile. "It's good to see you." It was still strange to see her in the gown of the high priestess. Strangest of all was seeing the peoples' heads turn towards her as if she truly were the new Merlin.

Not the new *Merlin*, I reminded myself sharply. The new high priestess. No one could ever replace Merlin, and Guinevere would never try.

It was right that the people of Pendrath respected the new high priestess—and if Guinevere could offer them hope and comfort during this tumultuous time, then so much the better.

It certainly wasn't as if the royal family were doing such a wonderful job of it.

"You wished to speak with me privately," Guinevere said, her expression serene as always. "Come, this way."

I didn't bother asking how she knew. Perhaps it was simple intuition. Perhaps it was just a logical guess. Perhaps the bird on her shoulder had told her.

Tuva, the owl, swiveled her head and looked back at me from luminous, lantern-like gold eyes. I quickly looked away.

When I lived in Camelot, I had never seen the owl with Merlin. And yet when I returned from the Court of Umbral Flames, the owl had appeared. In her last days, Merlin and the bird had seemed inseparable.

Now the bird clung just as closely to Guinevere's shoulder. Following her everywhere, the bird's eyes watching everything and everyone around.

Guinevere led the way back through the temple, into the corridors reserved for those who served in the complex, and then to a private chamber.

Stepping in, I was relieved to find it wasn't the set of rooms Merlin had used.

This room was already Guinevere's own, pretty and peaceful. The walls were covered in pale, ancient murals that showed scenes of nature from across Pendrath. The floor boasted a delicate mosaic pattern in blues, greens, and purples. Brocade-covered chaises were positioned along the walls, inviting those who met with the priestess to sit and share their worries. The scent of a familiar herb wafted through the air from a bronze censer hanging high in the center of the room.

Lavender. That was the smell. A calming herb.

Very appropriate. As if Guinevere knew exactly the topic I planned to bring up.

Somewhere along the way, Kasie and Lancelet had vanished. Now Guinevere sat down on the edge of a chaise and gestured for me to do the same.

Now that I was here, I felt a little awkward. But the more I had been through, the less I felt the need to mince my words.

I looked directly at Guinevere. "You know I wish to destroy the grail. I need to know, Guinevere. Will doing so kill my brother?"

The brown-haired girl—for she was still so very young, hardly older than I was, that I couldn't help but think of her that way—gazed back at me, unspeaking. She had been through so much already in her young life—as had I. Now she stood ready to take on the burden of becoming the new spiritual leader of Pendrath.

Reaching up a hand to the owl on her shoulder, she gently stroked her feathers with a practiced motion. The bird hooted, almost tenderly, then with a flutter of wings, took flight and alighted on a perch across the room.

I felt impatient. "You said we hadn't lost everyone who could tell us about the objects of power. What did you mean by that? It's been weeks since then. Do you know anything that can help me before I leave or don't you?"

A look appeared in Guinevere's eyes that was almost disappointed. I felt chagrined. My tone had been too harsh.

I opened my mouth to apologize, but she was already speaking.

"It's all right, Morgan. You're right."

"I am?"

She nodded. "Perhaps I should not have said what I did that night."

Now it was my turn to feel sinking disappointment.

"Because the truth is," she continued, "I don't know. I don't know everything. And what I do know is..." She made a gesture of frustration, unlike anything I had ever seen her do before. "Shrouded. Confused. Not useful. At least, not to you right now. You need hard facts, and right now, I'm trying to make sense of it all." She took a deep breath. "All I can promise you is that I'm doing my best."

"I know you are," I said, finding myself wanting to give her the comfort it was evident she couldn't give me.

"Yes," she said directly, looking at me. "It may kill Kaye as you fear. No. It may not kill him. That is the true answer. I don't know. Knowing that, what will you do now?"

I felt shocked into silence.

Then the answer was on my lips. It required no deep thought because I had no choice.

"I'll still destroy them. I have to."

"I understand," Guinevere said quietly. "There is an expression. 'The calm before the storm.' They say it in Lyonesse."

Her brown eyes held mine, and I felt goosebumps spread over my skin.

"We have the same saying in Pendrath," I said. "Probably all over Eskira."

The high priestess nodded. "The calm—it's almost over."

This had been calm? I opened my mouth to say as much but Guinevere was already rising to her feet.

Clearly, our meeting was at an end.

Holding the door open, she seemed almost eager for me to leave. But as I moved through into the corridor, she touched my arm.

"I'm sorry," she said. I looked at her, but her eyes were downcast. "I'm sorry for what you must endure, Morgan. I'm sorry for what is to come. I'm sorry I can't be of more help."

At the time, I thought she meant Kaye.

Or the quest. Destroying the grail, the sword, finding the spear. All of it.

"Thank you," I said awkwardly, and stepped out. "It's all right, Guinevere. I understand."

I'll never be sure I really did.

CHAPTER 5 - DRAVEN

I had the training hall all to myself.

Or, as Gawain might have said more truthfully, I had frightened everyone else away.

The burly, red-haired man sat on the sidelines now, mopping his brow with a cloth. He was winded, I knew, and strained and aching.

I had done that to him. I might have felt guilty. But the truth was, I felt only a little frustrated. I had pushed my partner too far, and now there was no one worthy to spar with.

No one but my own shadow.

And so I danced with that. Parrying and thrusting. My feet moving swiftly over the stones, worn smooth by countless drills.

I was breathing hard but nowhere near reaching my limit. And my limit was what I wanted to find. What I had to find.

I gave another thrust, my blade cutting through imaginary resistance with a metallic hiss of air. I pivoted, spinning and striking, engaging my unseen adversary. The phantom opponent I could only see in my mind's eye.

How much time passed? Who could say. I was relentless.

Until finally, I felt the sweat glistening on my brow.

Still, I pushed on. Shadows formed around me.

On the walls, the torches flickered and sputtered as a living cloak born of my darkness rose around me.

I intensified my assault, imagining the thing I feared the most. Not for my sake, but for hers.

I imagined a moment I couldn't help her, couldn't save her. I imagined us apart.

I threw myself forward, tendrils of darkness spiraling from the tip of my sword. I forgot about Gawain. I forgot about the room around me. There was only myself and my imagined foe. I blurred. Merged with the shadows. Moving between patches of darkness at will.

Nightmarish visions flitted through my dark. Forcing themselves into my mind. I saw her taken again. Tormented. I saw her scream, saw her call for me.

Teeth clenching, I spun, furious at a future that wasn't even real. Terrified it somehow would be.

And then flames flared through the shadows. Burning so bright, I was forced to shield my eyes.

And she stepped through. The source of it all. My guiding light. My burning star.

CHAPTER 6 - MORGAN

"How long has he been at this?"

I watched, fascinated as Draven sparred with his own shadow. Moving almost too fast for me to follow as he relentlessly drove himself on.

I'd come from visiting Kaye. Unsurprisingly, nothing had changed with my brother. I'd sat beside his bedside for an hour, speaking to him, reminding him of memories we'd shared, telling him the latest news—about Medra, about the exmoors; even about my visit to the temple, though I'd left out what it had been about. When I ran out of things to say, I'd picked up the book I'd been reading to him and continued to the next chapter. When I'd run out of breath, I'd finally left. I would return the next day. And the next.

Until it wasn't an option any longer.

On the bench along the wall, Gawain looked up at me. "Hours."

"Since you and he began? Or since he started... this?"

"Since he started fighting himself instead of me," Gawain replied matter-of-factly. He crossed his arms over his chest. "I think he's doing a better job testing his own mettle than I ever could."

I stared. "Have you seen him do this before?"

Gawain laughed. "Have I seen my friend fight his own demons of darkness for hours on end? Literally rather than metaphorically speaking, you mean?"

I clenched my jaw but said nothing as Gawain glanced up at me and tried to look reassuring.

"Not since we were more than children. After a particularly horrible fight with his father." He studied Draven. "Perhaps not even then. Not like this."

"What *is* he doing exactly?" Though part of me already knew.

"Well, you know Draven," Gawain said, raising a hand to run it through his sweat-soaked hair. "He isn't a man who fears for himself. He fears for others. The ones he loves."

My throat felt choked up.

The room around us had dimmed from my mate's shadows. Now the torches finally gave up their last breaths, sputtering and dying.

I sensed rather than saw Gawain rise to his feet.

"Perhaps I'll see you at dinner," he said, touching his hand gently to my arm. "Hopefully both of you."

I opened my mouth to ask how he could leave his friend. Then as he left the room, I understood.

He hadn't left Draven alone.

He had left him with me.

I stepped onto the sparring floor, my palms already open.

Across the room, Draven was enmeshed in darkness, a shadowy form, his features shapeless.

I ran towards him, hands raised.

Flame upon flame shot forward, piercing through the darkness, hitting the walls, coming closer and closer to Draven's shape.

The shadows shifted as if in surprise. Then they began to dissolve.

I caught the look on Draven's face as he turned towards me, face illuminated by the flames. Weary numbness, a driven intensity, quickly replaced by sheer shock.

I felt a little surge of triumph.

"You singed me," he said accusingly.

I laughed. "I could have done worse if I'd been trying."

He looked behind him at the black markings on the wall. "Those will be tough to get off."

I shrugged. "Flame wielders need a sparring room, too." The castle of Camelot was not just for swordplay now. Not when fae of flame and shadows dwelled within it these days.

"Gawain said you've been at this for hours," I said softly. "Will you come with me now?"

He nodded.

I slipped my hand into his as we walked down the hall, studying his profile and waiting for the ceaseless intensity to drop away.

But it didn't show any signs of disappearing.

"What's on your mind?"

He glanced down at me, then pushed his dark hair off his forehead. "Not sure what you mean."

"Going to play it like that, are we?" I sighed. "Why don't I help you tell me then? Kaye is in some sort of nightmarish endless sleep and I've been preoccupied with him. But in the meantime, there's been Medra to care for. You've taken the lead on that. She's been... Well, you've become closer to her than anyone. I know you love her. Deeply." Draven said nothing, but I knew he was listening. I took a breath. "And soon I'll be taking you away from her. But that's not the worst of it."

"Oh, no?"

"No." I shook my head. "Your sister. Rychel. We hardly talk about her. But she's a constant pain in your heart." For all we knew, she was already dead, a small voice in my head said. But I wouldn't accept that. And I knew he wouldn't either. "We don't know what's happened to her. And I've been so wrapped up in this idea that's consumed me. Destroying the grail, the sword. Finding the spear. We don't even know where to start. We don't even know where Rychel *is*. But we need to find her. I haven't forgotten about her. Though I know it might seem like I have. I swear I haven't, Draven. I hardly had a chance to know her, but I care about her, too." I swallowed hard. "At the very least, for your sake. Because your heart is aching for her loss. Aching not knowing what's happened to her. Please don't think I don't know that."

Now it was his turn to sigh. I felt his hand squeeze mine back. "I know. I know, Morgan." I watched his broad shoulders stiffen. "As for where we start. Rychel will be at the heart of it all. I know her well enough for that. She'll be exactly where we need to go. She'll be where the spear is."

"How? How do you know that?"

"She gave your father the grail," he said simply. "She wanted to get to the heart of his power. She'll be where the objects were kept or where they were made. We'll find her where *he* is."

"Is that why you were training so hard? Because you're afraid we'll have to fight him to get to her?"

"Afraid?" He said the word sharply. "I'm not afraid. Not for myself. I would gladly lay down my life if it meant getting Rychel out of there."

My heart clenched.

"Or if it meant shielding you from danger, Morgan. Or Medra." He set his lips in a hard line. "But we're going right into danger. Into the worst of it. And I don't know if we'll be coming out again."

My eyes widened. "Is that really what you think? You?"

Draven of all people was the source of my hope. My optimism. It felt wrong to hear him sound so bleak.

"We're coming out again," I promised him, with more surety than I felt. "We'll succeed. We'll be together."

Draven wouldn't look at me. His eyes studied the stone floor ahead of us. "I can't..." He took a deep breath. "I can't watch you go through something like that again, Morgan. Like with Fenyx. I'll do anything to stop it."

His hand slipped out of mine, and I watched him curl it into a fist and slam it against the other. "And I wasn't even there for the worst of it."

He prowled ahead without waiting for me, moving into the Great Hall.

The vast room was empty. Most of the castle was in the dining hall for supper. Even from this distance, we could catch the loud roar of voices. I had been trying to lead Draven in that direction. He needed hot food in him and then some rest.

He paused to stand before the throne of Camelot, his back rock-hard and tense.

I'd never seen him quite like this before. Simmering with something too similar to fear. It was unsettling. Strange.

I was too used to Draven being the one to comfort me. To have him always be the strongest one, the one I could lean on.

But now his strength was proving to be his weakness. If he kept pushing himself like this, he was going to snap.

How long had he been approaching this point? Hiding his true fears from me? How long had I been letting him?

Was it since that terrible night he'd found me with Fenyx? How much had I been hiding of myself since then?

I looked past Draven at the Rose Court Throne.

Fashioned from a rich, dark wood, its surface displayed an intricate design of carved thorns and blossoming roses.

Looking at it, I suddenly thought of a way to knock Draven out of this dark stupor. It wasn't a solution. Just a temporary distraction.

Still, it might be good for him. Good for us both.

I moved past him until I was facing the throne.

In my lifetime, I had seen two men sit on the imperial seat. My father and my brother.

I couldn't remember the last time I had touched the thing. Even as a child, I had never dared to sit upon it, even for a moment as a child might do in play.

Now I turned my back and slowly sat down.

The throne was massive and the seat was hard. How had Arthur managed to sit there so stoically for hours on end?

I placed my arms along the sides and leaned back.

"What are you doing?" Draven sounded idly curious, nothing more.

"You wanted me on the throne, didn't you? Here I am." I smiled coyly. "But it's a big chair. There might be room for two."

"Now I know you're fucking with me." Draven's voice had turned slightly hoarse. "Come, let's go to dinner."

"Not until you come and share this throne with me. I insist. You're my mate after all." I parted my thighs slowly, then ran my hands down over my leather trousers.

Draven let out a low growl. "What are you doing, Morgan?"

I honestly wasn't quite sure. In fact, part of me was afraid to find out. Especially since there was a crowd of people a few corridors away, all happily enjoying their dinner.

But for now, the Great Hall was completely abandoned. And all of the servants would either be serving in the hall or eating their own meal in the kitchen below.

In other words, this throne was ours for the taking.

"I should think it was perfectly clear." I let my hands wander over the planes of my stomach, over the white tunic I'd pulled on that day.

Then slowly, slowly up and over my breasts, cupping them a little, feeling the hardness of my nipples.

But then, I'd already known my nipples were hard. They'd been hard ever since I'd come up with this unhinged, probably catastrophic idea.

"I want," I said slowly, "to feel you inside me. Now. Here. On this throne."

I watched Draven swallow slowly, then touch a finger to the ring he wore in his left ear as if he were considering my proposition.

"Don't pretend you're actually stopping to think about—" I started to say with exasperation.

And then he was above me.

Lowering his face to kiss me as his massive body hovered over me, his hands resting on the back of the throne, his legs spread out on either side of mine.

He practically covered me and the entire throne, and he hadn't even sat down on the thing.

"Maybe," I said breathlessly, between kisses, between tongues darting desperately in and out of one another's mouths as if we hadn't touched or tasted one another in years instead of just the night before. "Maybe I overestimated the size of this throne. You're rather large in comparison. On second thought…"

I felt Draven give a low, throaty chuckle. "Too late for second thoughts. But thank you. That's high praise from my mate."

"That's not what I meant. I mean, it's true. You are… gifted. Endowed." I felt my cheeks heating. "Both things are true."

I tried to compose myself, but there was no point in bothering. Draven's hand was sliding down my blouse, over my pebbled nipples, then down over my stomach, and slipping into my pants, to the place between my legs where I was already slick and wet. As his fingers touched me there, I whimpered.

My eyes darted about. No one had entered the hall. No one had heard me.

"But if we continue this," Draven said as if reading my mind, his breath hot against my cheek, "someone *could* hear you, Morgan. Anyone could. Anyone might walk in. Anyone might see."

I knew he was trying to call what he saw as my bluff. To give me a last way out.

But he didn't know me very well if he thought I'd actually back down. My backbone was steel. Smart or not, I was doing this.

And then one of his fingers slipped inside of me and I moaned.

We were doing this because I couldn't fucking wait long enough for him to carry me back up to our bedroom or take me against a wall in some cramped broom closet.

"I think," Draven said with surprising casualness considering he had a finger inside my pussy, "we'll need to do this the other way around."

"What?" I mumbled, already a mess of hot desire.

He withdrew his hand, and I had just enough time to moan a protest before he had flipped our positions, picking me up and raising me over him as he sat back down on the throne.

"Is this what you had in mind when you invited me here, Morgan?" he asked as I pressed against him, feeling his cock pressing hard against his trousers. I writhed against it a little in anticipation, then moved my hands down to help free it from the confines of his pants.

"What? No foreplay?" Draven pouted. "I want to *taste* you."

"Oh, by the Three," I breathed. "Now? Here?"

There was a gleam in his eye. "Now. Here on this throne. I want to leave traces of your juices all over this fucking chair. Let's call it a belated present for Arthur."

"That's... slightly disturbing. But very well." The thought of Draven's mouth pressed against my clit was too much to resist.

I shimmied out of my trousers, then let Draven pull my tunic over my head for good measure. Then my underthings.

Now I was bare.

Naked and bare and in a very, very public place.

Still, even fear wasn't enough to trump the wave of lust I was riding.

"Uh, uh, uh," Draven warned, waving a finger as I tried to cover my breasts. "Don't you dare. This was your idea, after all."

I groaned. First one way, then another as Draven caught me by the hips and lifted me back onto him, raising me to the perfect level for his mouth to access.

His tongue slid over my wetness, caressing my softest places. He pushed my thighs further apart and then buried his face between them.

"Oh, fuck," I whispered as he dragged his tongue over me. "Oh, goddess."

"I'll make you a true believer, Morgan," he swore, circling my clit with his tongue and sliding a finger inside of me. "But it's my name you'll be calling, not any goddess's."

I tangled my fingers through his hair and moaned, "Draven, please." I wanted this. But I wanted him more. Much more. "I need you. All of you. Inside me. Now."

"And I need you," he said against my flesh. "Do you know what the sight of your body does to me, Morgan? Do you know what the taste of you does? You make me wild. You turn me into a mindless, depraved creature." He gripped my hips so hard, it hurt. "But it's time to stop this game. If we keep going, I won't be responsible for how far it goes. Not tonight." He drew a deep ragged breath. "Not in the mood I'm in."

I looked down my body, my bare hips inches from his lips. I looked down at my mate's tense face.

"I don't care," I whispered, stroking the edge of his jaw. "Take me here. Take me how you want me. Fuck me on this throne."

He started to open his mouth.

"Don't." I put a finger to his lips. "Don't tell me you haven't thought about it. If not here, then the Umbral Throne. Don't tell me you haven't fantasized about tearing my clothes off and mounting me on your cock..."

He groaned, a sound low and full of need. It echoed loudly off the stone walls around us, and I flinched but went on.

"That you haven't thought about mounting me on your cock," I repeated, "and ravaging me senseless."

"Sounds like you've been thinking about it, too," he growled. "More than once."

"Maybe I have. Maybe now's your chance."

"Maybe you'd better come then, so I can fuck you the way you clearly want me to," he snarled.

He moved his mouth back against me, and I gasped so loudly, the sound echoed from the walls. His tongue was hard and relentless—like his swordplay in the training hall. He licked and stroked and then thrust his tongue inside me and fucked me with it while his fingers rolled over my clit.

I'd never come so fast or so hard.

Stars crashed into my vision, blinding me for a moment. Hot warmth spread over me as I clenched, gasping, my hips tilting backwards.

He caught me, holding me steady before pulling me forward towards him.

"Remember," he said, his voice a husky whisper. "You asked for this."

And then he was driving into me, his cock pressing against my entrance as I cried out—forgetting we weren't truly alone.

Draven's mouth was hot against my breasts. His hands ran up and down my sides, then cupped my ass, holding me more firmly against him.

That was when I heard the voices.

A low chattering. Unmistakable. The sound of nobles.

From the sounds of it, they were on a tour. A fucking guided tour.

One voice was louder than the rest. A man. He was chattering cheerfully and seemed to be describing the castle's stonework. A castle connoisseur.

Draven slowed but didn't stop thrusting completely. He kept his cock pushed into me, forcing small sounds of pleasure from my lips, even as my ears cocked, listening, praying the group would take a detour, pass by the throne room. Why the hell weren't they back in the dining hall at this time of night anyhow?

I moved my hips automatically as Draven made a deep thrust, and a moan escaped my lips as the voices drew nearer.

"Oh, fuck. Oh, fuck," I whispered. "We have to…"

"We have to what?" Draven's teeth nibbled on my neck. "Fuck more?"

"We can't let them see us," I said desperately. "I've changed my mind, I…"

"No."

"No?"

"You can't change your mind."

"I can bloody well change my mind whenever I want to," I said hotly.

"About this, yes," Draven said, teeth sinking deeper until I gasped. "Do you really want me to stop?"

"N-no…" I breathed. "But…"

"So. We're here. Let them see us."

He sounded so pragmatic. So blasé.

"I'm naked," I hissed. "You're not."

He grinned. "Ah, so that's what it's about." He shrugged. "I can be naked next time."

I groaned. I wasn't sure there would be a next time.

I could hear the tour guide's voice crystal clear now.

"And now, if you follow me into the next part of the castle, there is some excellent masonwork dating back two centuries. It's particularly well preserved along the columns of the Great Hall, also known as the throne room…"

I recognized the nobleman's voice. Baron Bertram Cadogan. An eager, excitable little lord who had recently been invited to join the Privy Council and help advise our new monarch—or regent, in the meantime—on important decisions.

He had also enthusiastically taken it upon himself to welcome visiting nobles from rural provinces.

Apparently his welcome extended to tour-giving. They must have finished up dinner early.

"This isn't a joke," I moaned. "We have to go. Of course I want this. But I didn't truly expect to be seen… Can you imagine what they'll make of me if they see… us…? This?" I could barely form words.

"Tsk, tsk," Draven said, running his hands over my bare arms. "You're shaking, love. Just look at your breasts. I didn't think your nipples could get any larger." He shook his head in admiration. "Have I ever told you that you have the most beautiful breasts of any woman I've ever known?"

I knew exactly what he was trying to do. Stir my ire by making me think of other women he'd been with.

"Don't you dare even try to change the subject," I hissed.

Just as the footsteps entered the Great Hall.

"Ah, yes, if you step this way, you can see the roses engraved right into the stonework along each arched window," Sir Bertram was saying enthusiastically.

They were in the room now. Right there with us.

Fortunately, they were still near the entranceway, moving slowly along the pillared edge of the Great Hall, apparently inspecting the windows. But if they turned the corner to their left just slightly, they'd have a full view of the dais, the throne, and... all of me. Sitting fully on my mate's lap. Where Draven was sunk to the hilt, as it were. A poorly chosen phrase I had read in a romance novel I'd found in the castle library once.

Draven was grinning cheekily up at me. "I'd better just do what I do best then." And he lifted his hips to fill me.

I gasped, moaned, groaned all at once.

Instantly, Sir Bertram's voice stopped.

Draven's hand was over my mouth. I felt my eyes bulging.

"I say," Sir Bertram started. "Did anyone else hear that? A strange sound..."

"It sounded... familiar," one lady in his audience said. She giggled. "Almost as if..."

"No, that's quite impossible," Sir Bertram said, sounding completely shocked. I could almost picture the little nobleman straightening his back. "No one would dare to use the throne room for such a thing. It would be a violation. An utter desecration."

Draven's cock buried inside me as he thrust again. Despite the distraction, I felt myself squeeze hard around him. I bit down on his hand as he moved again and again, opening my body for his invasion little by little.

"Keep your eyes on me. Only on me. Do you hear me?" Draven growled. "Don't think of anyone else. Don't look at anyone else. Eyes on me, only me, always."

A scream was building in me. Try as I might to keep it down, it was bubbling up, welling up inside with every thrust of Draven's great, glorious fucking cock.

My mate's hands pinned my hips, holding me in place. "You were fucking made for me, my silver. So why not let them see you take me like you were meant to? After all, we were made for this. Let them stare, let them watch, let them envy."

It was tempting. Part of me wanted to do just that. And in another moment, I wouldn't exactly have a choice. I couldn't hold it in much longer. I could feel the scream rising in my throat as Draven stroked in and out of me, increasing his speed.

I saw him start to lower his hand to stroke my clit, and my eyes widened in panic, my lips starting to part.

"By the Three, if anyone is around that corner…" I heard Sir Bertram declare stoically. "You'd best stop this nonsense this instant, or I swear, I'll send for the empress herself and…"

And then poor Sir Bertram and his coterie must have stepped around the corner.

There were gasps. Some shocked. Some admiring. Some both.

But they were all short-lived.

Shadows swept around us, concealing us from view.

"There," Draven whispered. "Is this what you wanted?"

"Took you long enough." I gasped as he shifted his fingers against my swollen clit, stroking it until I whimpered loudly.

A heat was building inside me as the shadows swirled and shifted around us.

"I believe it's time this tour took a slight detour," Sir Bertram announced hurriedly to the group. "Perhaps the gardens. Or perhaps we'll continue this tomorrow. Yes, or better yet, next week. Once I've conferred with the castle staff on the best route we should take on future tours."

I pictured the poor man wiping a handkerchief across his brow.

"By the Three, I had no idea this room was considered closed to the public at dinnertime," he moaned, his voice becoming more distant as the group moved across the room.

"Why, I do believe you'll be invited to a very special private meeting with the empress soon, Sir Bertram," suggested the same woman who had giggled earlier. "I only pray it won't end in your banishment."

She snickered to show she was only teasing, but I still heard poor Sir Bertram let out a pained groan of fear. I hoped she had gotten a good eyeful. The cheeky lady.

Then their footsteps were moving out the door and I was alone in the spun web of shadows with my mate.

A fever was simmering in me. My scream had been suppressed, but now the tension in my body was searching for another way out.

"Look down, Morgan," Draven said, his tone odd. "Look down and see yourself."

I did as he said and gasped.

Liquid fire was moving under my skin, beneath the markings that were usually silver.

"You're boiling over inside, aren't you?" he observed, sounding amused at my predicament. "Let yourself erupt for me. Come for me, Morgan. Come for me, my queen, my empress."

He pushed deep into me, and I cried out, my orgasm exploding in a wave of white heat and burning stars. Scorching flames danced over my flesh and pushed into the shadows around us, mixing fire and darkness together.

I screamed without caring who heard us, my voice echoing off the stones. I felt my mate groan and burst at the same time, his release filling me with a second source of pleasure.

When it was over, Draven's mouth danced over my breastbones.

I shivered. His mouth hovered right over my scars. The ones Florian had carved into me. It seemed so wrong to be marked even now with another man's name when there was only one I would ever willingly belong to.

Draven traced the scars with his fingertips. "Someday these marks will fade. These scars you wear like shields against the world. Marks of your resilience, testaments to your strength." He met my eyes. "They don't bother me, Morgan. Just like nothing that came before this, before us, could ever bother you. The lovers we had, whoever they were... They're meaningless now, aren't they?"

It was true. I felt no jealousy. No pain. Not even when I thought of Vesper. And as for the lovers Draven must have had? And I had no doubt there had been many. I felt only pity for them. He had left all of them behind.

He was mine now. Here, now, and forever.

"When I see these scars, do you know what I really see?" my mate asked.

I shook my head.

"I see forever with you by my side. Because long after these scars have faded away to nothing, I'll still be standing beside you. You and I? We're eternal."

There was a lump in my throat that I tried to swallow. I had no words, so a kiss had to do. I pressed myself against him and kissed him with everything I had and tried to convey eternity.

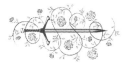

Later, we lay in bed. Breathless from another wild coupling.

My body felt wonderfully heavy. I rolled over and rested my head against Draven's shoulder, one arm stretched languidly over his chest.

"What are you thinking of?" I asked, looking at his profile in the dark. "Missing Medra? I can send for someone to fetch her if you want."

I caught the edge of his smile. "No. It's good to have a night just you and me. There will..." He cleared his throat. "I know there will be many of those ahead."

In other words, he had to get used to it now.

"I know you'll miss her," I said softly. "It's all right to acknowledge it. She'll miss you, too. It's terribly unfair. To her and to you."

He nodded. "Do you know... she reminds me of Rychel."

"Does she? How?"

"Even for such a small thing, she's precocious. So quick to learn and grow. She's only six-weeks-old, but she can already bring the bottle to her mouth. Did you know that? That's something only six-*month*-old infants can usually do, Morgan. The nurse told me."

"I didn't realize that," I said, realizing I knew even less about babies than I'd thought. "How... incredible." I tried my best to sound impressed.

"Isn't it? And she recognizes faces already. I think she has for weeks now. She's so intelligent. She knows you and me, and her wet nurses, of course. Today was the most remarkable thing. I placed her on the floor on her stomach, and when I turned around to fetch her toy and then looked back at her, she was sitting up by herself."

I was startled. That did seem more advanced than usual for one so young. "Truly? She sat up? What did her nurse say?"

"I don't think she believed me when I told her, actually," Draven said. "Medra had already toppled over again by then, of course. Her nurse seemed to think it was an impossibility."

"She's part fae though," I said slowly. "That must be why she's so precocious, as you say. Mustn't it?"

I wondered if I had been anything like Medra. Had my mother cooed over my every new achievement and discovery just like Draven was doing?

"I don't think so." Draven sounded doubtful. "Even for a fae, this is... something else."

"Arthur was only mortal. What *something else* could there be?"

Draven shrugged. "Who can say. But she'll do great things, that one. My little Medra." He gave a sad laugh. "If she's anything like Rychel, we'd better hope she doesn't blow up half the castle."

I propped myself up on my elbow, a little alarmed. "What? What's that supposed to mean?"

I started to imagine a flammable infant. What if Medra had powers like my own... only could access them much, much sooner?

He chuckled. "My little sister, in her pursuit of understanding wind patterns, once built a self-propelled sailboat. She convinced one of the stable boys to help her, and they set sail on one of the artificial ponds in the gardens. The 'self-propulsion' turned out to be a bag of explosive powder that she'd invented. I've never seen two people swim faster back to shore in my life."

He rubbed his chin. "Another time, she tried to help our father with a fireworks celebration in Noctasia. Oh, without telling him, of course. He would never have asked any of his children for help. This was before she realized it was going to be utterly impossible to ever earn his love or his favor."

"Poor Rychel," I murmured. What a waste of a father they'd had. Not that mine had been any better.

"She mixed in the wrong ingredients to whatever she'd been planning. The entire fireworks display wound up being a rainbow of chaos. Women's dresses on fire, panicked screaming. That sort of thing." He laughed. "My father was humiliated. Which would have been wonderful, as far as I was concerned. Except he found out who did it, of course. I had to hide Rychel for a week until he'd forgotten about it. Moved on to the next person to be furious at."

"Of course, not all of her inventions went wrong," he continued. "She once promised me she could make bubbles larger than I was. And you know, she really could. She poured her formula into one of the grand fountains in the palace." He snorted. "The next thing I knew, bubbles the size of horses and sheep were floating around the halls, and the fountain had turned into a frothy mess."

"That sounds charming." I leaned back against the pillows. "Like something out of a children's tale."

Then I remembered. There had been few children in the Court of Umbral Flames to enjoy such spectacles. Only the very rare half-fae, half-mortal ones like Rychel. And like Beks.

"She doesn't have magic, you know." There was a weariness to Draven's voice. "Not like you or me. Or if she does, she has no idea how to access it. She's incredibly smart, but she can't... She can't protect herself."

"Even with magic, we can't always protect ourselves," I reminded him softly. "But I know what you mean. You must be very frightened for her." I hesitated, then added, "We'll be on the road soon. I saw Sunstrike's wing today. It's almost healed."

I wasn't sure if this would comfort him or not, but it seemed to be enough. He lay back and stroked my hair. Soon we had drifted off to sleep.

CHAPTER 7 - MORGAN

The cottage was on fire. I stood, transfixed, watching it burn.

The air was thick with the acrid scent of smoke. As I watched, sparks from the burning timbers of the cottage flew into the meadow of wildflowers that surrounded it and began to ignite.

The entire place quivered with an unsettling energy. Flickering flames danced wildly against the backdrop of the starlit sky.

I lifted my hands, then dropped them again uselessly by my side. One could not fight flame with flame.

And Draven was not here.

I had thought this was a true dreaming. Now I questioned that assumption. If Draven was missing and the cottage was burning, perhaps this was simply a nightmare after all. Like the one I'd had of Kaye.

A very vivid nightmare. One I very much wanted to wake up from.

With that thought, my uncertainty was put to rest.

In the doorway of the burning cottage, a figure of a man was emerging.

He came slowly towards me, as if he had no care for the flames. As if they could not harm him.

Wild tendrils of gray hair aglow from the flying embers framed a face etched with the fortitude of tempest. Gray eyes, fierce and forbidding, burned at me with an intensity that pierced through my stupor.

He wore a suit of gold and silver armor, the finest I had ever seen. Behind him flowed a cape of brilliant scarlet.

Slowly, he came towards me. As if he had all the time in the world.

"What have you done?" I snarled, furious at the look I saw in his eyes. "What right have you to come here?"

Before he answered, I feared what he would say, and as the words left his lips, I wished I had never spoken them.

"The right of a father," the man said unnervingly. "The right of a loving father who wishes only to see his daughter."

"Loving? Is that what you call this? Destroying my home?" I was fighting back tears but refused to let him see that.

"You call this shack a home?" The man shook his head and laughed. "You have been away from your *true* home too long, Daughter, if you believe this was a fitting place for you."

"I will decide what is or is not a fitting place for me to reside," I said angrily.

It was a dream, I told myself. I could rebuild it.

But what was the point? He had found me here twice now. He would only come again.

"I don't want you here. Can't you see that? I have no wish to see you."

A scowl came over his face. "You hardly know what you are saying. Your mother's treachery took you from me. Poisoned you against me. Do you know how long I have been looking for you? Seeking you?"

I watched, fascinated, as I saw him try to force the scowl from his face and replace it with something else. He seemed to be seeking to show emotion. Perhaps, yes, even something akin to the love he claimed.

But he was ancient. Timeless. He was hard and cold, and bitterness seeped too strongly through his veins.

He could not show it no matter how he struggled. Eventually he gave up, his face returning to its glacial state.

"You're wrong about my mother."

He stopped on the path.

"I saw what she believed about you," I continued. "She believed you truly did love me."

I had been wrong about his ability to convey emotion. A look of shock crossed his face.

Then it cleared into an arrogant serenity I hated. "In that case, you must return to me. Surely you cannot doubt me if that is what she believed."

I curled my lip. "She believed you loved me. That does not mean I believe it. She also believed you would fail to protect me. And so she took me away."

"She stole you away," my father thundered. I flinched as the trees around us shook and the blades of grass in the meadow shivered. "She took what did not belong to her."

"I belong to no one," I shouted back. "Not to you. Not to anyone. You do not possess me, Father."

And as I screamed the words, a sense of familiarity came over me. As if it were not the first time I had said this thing to him.

I struggled for calm. "I know what you did. To the children of Valtain. Your own peoples' children."

"You know nothing," he replied with disdain. "You do not even know your own true name or why you were created. You are ignorant. Empty. Without me."

"Oh, and you would educate me, I suppose? Turn me into, what? Someone like you?"

"Your mother was wrong," he said, ignoring me. "I would have protected you."

The words struck me to the bone. Perhaps because they were, of course, what any child would long to hear their father say.

Part of me even wondered if I should believe him.

Then I remembered Lancelet.

"Perhaps. Perhaps you would have saved me. After all, I was your own flesh and blood. But the other children? You cared nothing for them."

"Because they were nothing like you," he said coldly. "Nothing like us. The others are beneath us and always have been. Most know and accept their place. You have no idea, Daughter, of how far above them you belong. Above all of this." He swept out his hands.

"I don't want to belong there. Towering over, what? Humanity? The fae? Is that what you think I aspire to? Is that what you think would bring me happiness?"

"Happiness?" The gray-haired king tossed his head back and laughed. "Happiness is a word invented by mortals to bring hope to their bleak and pathetic existences. A passing feeling, nothing more. You may feel it countless times, Daughter. True pleasure. I have felt it more times than you could fathom."

"I can only imagine what brings you pleasure," I said, wrinkling my nose. "Watching your peoples' children become mindless, slavering, undead creatures—did that bring you pleasure? Or perhaps when you took from them what you wanted—their souls—that brought you greater pleasure?"

I had hoped to catch him off guard, take him by surprise. But I was disappointed.

He merely smiled. "The thing that gives me the greatest and most lasting pleasure? Power. The ways I might acquire it. The pleasures of accruing it. Let me show you what great pleasure power might bring to you as well."

I was tempted to tell him then that I was an empress but that it brought me very little pleasure and not a little lost sleep. But then I realized with a start that I had no idea if he knew that fact about me already or not. And if I told him, I would be telling him things he did not need to know.

"Why find me here?" I asked carefully. "Why in dreams? Why not come to me yourself? If you're so powerful, why haven't you found me before this?"

I already knew why—or could guess. My mother's markings had shielded me.

But when Draven had saved my life and bonded to me, I had gained a new power. The power of true dreaming.

And only then had my father finally been able to catch up with me, here, in this place that should have been my refuge.

"I have thought I sensed you from time to time," my father murmured. "Sensed your power growing." He examined me closely as if looking for clues, and I cringed.

"Where did your mother take you?" he demanded finally, apparently unable to see all that he wished.

"You truly don't know?" I was incredulous. "You, the all-powerful High King of the fae? You still don't know?"

"I am much more than a mere king, and you shall tell me." His face grew impatient. "What harm can it do? I found you here, didn't I? I will never stop, Daughter. I will keep coming. Keep hammering against the walls of your mind until I have seen everything I need to see. And then... I *will* come for you."

The threat made my throat constrict. "Love," I whispered. "You speak of love. But how is this love, Father?"

His face hardened. "Love and fear and need are wrapped together. They are much the same. You have not learned this lesson yet. You are still a mere child. Your mother ensured that you would never grow up properly. That you would never take your place by my side as you should have."

I thought of Excalibur and the grail, which had been sent to Arthur from Gorlois's court. A poisoned gift. Did my father realize I had two of the objects now in my grasp? Why had he ever let either of them go in the first place?

"You need me," I said softly. "But why? Why do you need me so badly? You have other children. Orcades... You had Orcades..." Too late, I stopped.

My father's eyes flashed. "Orcades? You know of your sister?" His eyes narrowed. "You saw her? Where did the two of you meet?"

He didn't know. Didn't know his daughter was dead. Or that she had died trying to undo everything he stood for. Right down to giving birth to a child she hoped would be his undoing.

But I would never let this man know Medra even existed. I would keep her far away from her grandfather, no matter what it took.

My father took a step towards me. "Where are you? Tell me, Daughter. Enough games. *Tell me where you are.*" The voice was ancient and primeval. I sensed the compulsion there. My father was powerful, far more powerful than Fenyx. And yet the compulsion was a cloud of smoke, and in my mind, I pushed it away and saw it evaporate.

His face clouded with impatient fury, and he took another step, then another.

I backed away, matching him step for step, but he paced on.

"I love you, Daughter. As I love all my children."

Yet I knew it for a lie.

I shook my head. "Your love is a disease."

He frowned. "That stings, Daughter. Let me teach you true love. The way your mother never did. Let me teach you the ways of your people, the ways of the fae. You have grown up soft and weak and mortal." He said the words with such derision. "For surely she hid you in some mortal lands. With a farmer perhaps? Or a shepherd? Did you grow up smelling the scent of manure on your straw-filled pillow at night? Come with me, and you will never face hardship again. Come with me to a place where perfumes and silks will delight you and where all around you will worship at your feet."

He paused. "Your brothers and sisters will welcome you, Daughter."

I caught my breath and he pounced as if knowing how his words had caught my attention. The knowledge that I had other, living siblings. And the awareness that this man standing before me represented what might be my only chance to ever know them.

"How they would welcome you, Daughter," he murmured intoxicatingly. "With feasts and with songs. With banquets and celebrations. The long-lost sister they hardly knew. You were a mere babe when your mother stole you away from us. Return to your family, Daughter. Return to us."

He snatched a hand out towards me.

I was caught by the arm.

A loud clash erupted around us as if lightning had struck the spot where we stood.

I screamed, and as if from a distance, heard my father shouting.

Then he was in my mind. Not merely inside my dream. But my inner mind.

But so, too, was I in his.

I saw a corrupt Valtain court. The air was heavy and sweet with spilled ambrosial wine. Indulgent feasts stretched out on tables, filled with decadent offerings, some so terrible, my mind could not fathom them. My brothers and sisters entwined in lascivious dances, draped in exquisite garments adorned with gemstones that sparkled like corrupted stars. Their laughter was a discordant symphony that echoed through the twisted corridors of my memory. I saw two men, my brothers, struggling over a beautiful mortal woman. And when they could not agree on who would possess her, one slid a sword from his belt and sliced her in half. They laughed. How they laughed then, drunkenly sliding in the pool of her blood.

Nearby, my father sat on his throne and looked on, bored and indulgent.

I looked further.

I saw my father, drained of his power and weakened in a great battle centuries before. His court had fallen. His children were dead or scattered. His vast empire was destroyed.

I saw him striving to regain what he had lost in any way he could. Forced to face off with Myntra one hundred and fifty years ago, he avoided another battle like the one he had lost, tricking them into their self-imposed curse of barrenness and taking the power he gained from sacrificing Valtain's children. He wrapped their souls like a precious newborn, carrying his newfound power to a mountain stronghold, so near to the clouds, it might have been the heavens. A palace so near the stars that they seemed touchable.

I saw darkness stretching like tendrils over Aercanum. The darkness of my father's designs. First Eskira, then Myntra, and then all of Aercanum, until all fae and mortals were under his dominion and all lesser creatures were slaughtered or enslaved.

I saw a future of my father's making. The one he dreamed about. A world awash in blood. I saw my friends slaughtered and dying. I saw my mate's face drenched in gore.

I saw and I saw and I saw until I wished to see no more. I pushed and I shoved, then I screamed and stabbed and cut and tore until my hands were claws and knives, scrabbling at my own mind to get the things I had seen out, to get him out, for he was scanning and searching, and I knew once he had found me, he would take and take and never stop taking.

But no matter how I slashed and scratched, the thunderous, baleful presence that was my father would not withdraw from that place he had no right to be.

I was weary and hard-pressed and close to losing hope.

And then I remembered the cottage. Blazing with flames.

I lit up like a bonfire in the night and burned my way out of my father's hell.

CHAPTER 8 - MORGAN

In what was becoming too much of a habit, I woke drenched in sweat and sat bolt upright.

Next to me, Draven was groggily waking. Fumbling with blankets, he reached out a hand to touch my hip.

"Morgan, what is it? Another nightmare?"

I didn't answer. My eyes had already flown towards the pool of moonlight by the window where a man stood silently with his hands wrapped around his throat.

Draven's gaze followed mine.

"Ulpheas!" He sounded angry. A man had intruded on our bed chamber. And for Ulpheas, this was not the first time. "What's the meaning of this? What the hell are you doing here?"

The stitcher's blue eyes were wide and panicked. Catching my breath, I spotted the tear tracks on his cheeks.

I knew this wasn't what Draven thought. "Ulpheas," I said, trying to keep the panic from my own voice. "What is it? What's wrong?"

The courtier's hands had not moved from around his throat.

As my eyes became more accustomed to the darkness, I saw why.

From Ulpheas's hands clutched around his neck, blood dripped down onto the collar of the fine silk suit he wore.

"Oh, gods. Ulpheas..."

Draven was already leaping out of bed and moving across the room, pulling the shirt he had been wearing the previous day from a chair.

"Don't," Draven shouted to the courtier. "Don't move..."

But it was too late.

Ulpheas fell to the floor, his protective hands falling away from the gash at his throat.

Cursing, Draven tried to catch him as he fell.

I was already scrambling out of the bed to help, but as I stepped onto the floor, my feet slid in a pool of slippery blood and I nearly lost my footing. Clutching the bedpost, I stood, looking on helplessly as Draven crouched beside the courtier.

"Tell us who did this to you," my mate demanded. "We will avenge you, Ulpheas. Tell us."

Only a gurgling sound came from the dying courtier's throat.

Powerless, we watched as the honey-haired young man's eyes turned vacant and expressionless.

Draven touched the wound at Ulpheas's throat. "An arrow wound. The gash was severe. He couldn't have spoken even if he'd wanted to. His vocal cords were severed."

The shirt Draven had been holding, hoping to stem the flow of blood from Ulpheas's wound, lay discarded beside him.

We looked at one another over the body.

Was this my father's doing? Had the fae high king seen so far into my mind that he had gotten to one of our stitchers already?

I opened my mouth to begin to tell Draven what had happened in my dream, but a banging at the door cut me off.

"Who the fuck is it?" Draven bellowed. His face was dark with frustration. Unable to act, unable to help.

"Now isn't the best time," I called, trying to temper his words and guessing it was probably some poor servant with a breakfast tray. Though it was far too early for breakfast.

"Open this door right now." It was Lancelet. She hadn't stopped pounding, merely shouted above the sound of her own thudding fist. "Or I swear to the Three, I'll break it."

Her voice was pitched high with desperation.

There was only one thing I knew that could bring her to such a state.

One person.

Guinevere.

I scrambled across the floor, feet still sticky with blood, and opened the door.

"What is it? Has something happened to Guinevere?"

Lancelet nodded, her fist still half-raised. "She began convulsing. Kasie and I... We brought her here. They're down in the Great Hall." Her eyes widened as she looked past me to where Draven was lifting Ulpheas's body into his arms. "Ulpheas! But how...? I thought he was in Tintagel."

"He was," Draven said grimly, coming towards us carrying the courtier's limp body.

Lancelet looked at me. "Did he come to, you know... harm you?"

I shook my head. Somehow, I already knew that wasn't a possibility. Except for one slipup, long ago, Ulpheas had been loyal to Draven. "No. He came to warn us."

Draven's head swiveled. "How do you know that?"

"Let's get downstairs," was all I said. "I'll tell you more there."

When we got to the hall, Guinevere was already back on her feet, one hand resting on Kasie's shoulder. She looked as if she were recovering from great pain.

Tuva perched on her shoulder, chirping softly, as if the bird were concerned for her priestess.

Others had joined them. Galahad, Sir Ector, Dame Halyna, and Gawain stood about in a cluster, looking anxious.

As soon as I entered, Guinevere's eyes met mine. I caught a look of sympathy.

Then the room erupted into chaos as everyone noticed Draven behind me, carrying Ulpheas's body.

"How is this possible?" Sir Ector demanded. "He was in Tintagel."

"He's a stitcher," Lancelet said, rolling her eyes characteristically. "But that's what I said too."

Sir Ector furrowed his brow. "Was it an attempt on their lives?" He glanced at Draven and me. "Did you do this?" I knew he was asking if we had slaughtered Ulpheas in self-defense.

I shook my head. "No. He was like this when he arrived. I believe he came to try to warn us."

"Warn us of what?" Galahad asked, coming up beside me. He grimaced as he looked at the blond-haired man's body. "Poor Ulpheas."

"Yes," I agreed. "It was the last thing he did. He must have pushed himself incredibly hard to manage to stitch such a distance after he was already so gravely wounded."

"Can we get a message to King Mark? Find out what's happening over there?" Dame Halyna said, her voice cool and reasonable. "Perhaps this was all some sort of accident."

I shook my head. "It's impossible. Crescent isn't set to return until at least tomorrow."

Crescent, an experienced stitcher as well as Gawain's husband, had gone on a double mission. First, he was to journey to Lyonesse and pay yet another visit to Lady Marjolijn, plying her with his customary charm into accepting one of our stitchers as King Mark had done.

With a stitcher in every court, we would have a connected network and be able to alert one another in the event of an attack. Just as I believed Ulpheas had been trying to do tonight.

Next Crescent was to return to Myntra and check in on the progress of one of the new arches being built to link the Court of Umbral Flames to the Rose Court.

I had destroyed the one connecting the two temples, but a new one had been built on the rooftop of the Camelot castle. Its companion arch in Noctasia was not yet complete.

There were quite a few stitchers amongst the Siabra. But few were as trustworthy as Crescent. We had some lined up to potentially take up the court position in Lyonesse, but as Lady Marjolijn had rejected all of our offers before this, we hadn't thought to have any stationed in the castle.

"There should be at least one stitcher working on the arch being built along the road to Tintagel," Galahad noted. "We could send troops to fetch them immediately, couldn't we?"

On my other side, Draven nodded. "Mariah. She's overseeing the work. An excellent stitcher. Reliable."

"Good," Lancelet said with relief. "Let's send for her."

"We can send for her, yes," I said. "But we already know what's happened. Ulpheas took an arrow to the throat. This wasn't some mere hunting accident."

The hall became quiet.

I looked around the room. "Tintagel has been attacked. King Mark is besieged. Ulpheas came to warn us, yes, but to also seek our aid."

Sir Ector was already nodding. "That would make sense."

Dame Halyna met my eyes. "Things must be in a very bad state already if Ulpheas arrived as he did. The battle must be in full swing."

I rested my hands on my hips. "Which is why we can't wait."

"Leave now?" Lancelet shifted on her feet eagerly. "I'm ready. We take an hour or two to prepare, leave as soon as the sun is up. Gather all the troops we can..."

But I hardly heard her as she continued chattering. I was looking past her to the High Priestess in the pale blue and white robes with the owl on her shoulder.

"Guinevere, what did you see?" I interrupted.

Lancelet stopped talking.

"She was convulsing on the floor when I found her," Kasie said softly. "A vision, I think."

Guinevere's eyes were serene and steady as she gazed back at me. "I saw Brightwind."

My heart sped up. "So I'm right? They're under attack."

She raised a hand to stroke the owl on her shoulder. "Yes. Brightwind will burn unless we come to their aid."

"Who is attacking them? More raiding parties?" But I thought I already knew the answer. The raiding parties had been a mere preview for what was happening now. My dream—it couldn't be a mere coincidence. My father had found me. In more ways than one.

Guinevere didn't reply. She simply looked at me disconcertingly until finally, I looked away first.

"I'm leaving now," I announced to the rest of the group. "Not in the morning. But now, as soon as I can be ready." Draven touched my shoulder, and I immediately grasped his hand. "With you, of course, my love, if you'll go with me."

If he had been shocked to hear me say I was leaving at once, he showed no sign of it. He simply nodded. "By your side, always."

"What do you mean 'now?'" Sir Ector demanded with a frown. "How can you leave? Surely you're not going to ride down the road to Tintagel alone, Morgan. You need support. It will take time to gather our soldiers. And as we've already determined, there is no stitcher nearby."

"Draven and I don't need to stitch," I reminded him. "Not when we can fly."

There was a murmur amongst our friends.

Sir Ector's dark face flushed. "That's asinine. If something should happen to your brother, why, Morgan, you're our only..."

"Your what?" I shot back.

The noble knight shook his head mutely.

"He's right, Morgan, and you know it," Dame Halyna said reasonably. "Everyone knows you don't want the position, but Kaye can't accept it and Medra is... well, she's not a possibility."

Not after Tintagel and Lyonesse had bluntly stated they would never accept Arthur's daughter as queen.

Which suited me fine, as Kaye would one day be a fine king, with his niece cared for and protected by his side.

"It's our job to keep you safe, whether you like it or not. Sir Ector is only pointing that out," she finished.

I knew she was right.

"I accept that you all believe I'm the only choice." I steeled myself. "And I accept that some of you may even believe that Kaye will never wake up. Even so, there are only two people here who can ride those exmoors. Two people the exmoors will accept. And you're looking at them."

I met Draven's eyes. "If we leave now, how long will it take us to get there?"

"I admire your tenacity," Hawl's voice boomed out. "But the female's wing is hardly healed."

I turned to see the Bearkin striding in, flour dust covering their furry arms.

"I know you care for her, Hawl," I answered. "For both of them. As do I. More deeply than you can know. But this is our ally we're talking about. We cannot let King Mark stand alone. Sunstrike and Nightclaw will understand that. We have no choice." I looked at my mate. "Besides, I've thought of an idea. Sunstrike's wing is newly healed. If she'll permit it, I'll ride her, and Nightclaw will take Draven. That should lighten Sunstrike's load a little at the very least."

Hawl shook their head but said nothing. But Draven nodded.

"Now, how long?" I asked Draven again.

"It's hard to say. But they fly at incredible speeds. It was unbelievable how swiftly they passed over those mountains on our way to you."

"Brightwind is farther than the Ellyria Mountains from Camelot," Galahad pointed out. I wished he hadn't.

"Hours are better than days," I said firmly. "They could be under siege as we speak. But for all we know, the real battle may be yet to begin."

Sir Ector cleared his throat. "If the court stitcher arrived like this, it suggests King Mark was directly attacked. We must prepare ourselves. The king himself may be dead. Tintagel may already be lost."

If that were the case, then Pendrath would have lost its best ally. The one most likely to trust us. The kingdom that had allowed our stitcher into his court, a move that was supposed to provide them with added protection.

I could only imagine how Lyonesse would react. If Brightwind fell, unfairly or not, Pendrath would be at least partially blamed.

"I know that," I answered. "We still need to go. Now. Ulpheas spent his last breaths getting here to beg us for help. For all we know, King Mark sent him. If the king is dead, well, then at the very least, perhaps we can help the king's family." King Mark had a wife and children. Among them was his heir. They would be sheltering in the city's royal palace.

Unless their enemies had penetrated that far already.

I refused to believe it.

"King Mark wouldn't have sent Ulpheas if there was no hope. Surely most of us standing here have some knowledge of military history. Sieges can go on for days, weeks, even months. Just because Ulpheas is dead doesn't mean the city has already fallen. There's still hope," I insisted.

Though, conveniently, I avoided acknowledging that the Three only knew how Ulpheas had taken that arrow to the throat unless he'd somehow been in the very heart of a battle.

"For all we know, he didn't send Ulpheas at all. We really have no idea what happened," Dame Halyna pointed out. "We're making a great number of assumptions right now."

I clenched my jaw stubbornly. "Then Draven and I will fly over to Tintagel, check things out, and fly back again if all is well. Sound good?"

Dame Halyna's lips quirked. "Oh, Morgan."

"You couldn't hold me back if you tried," Hawl growled. "I'll be marching come dawn, with or without you, humans."

"Oh, I'll be right there with you," Lancelet declared. "And my horse can outrun you, Bearkin."

"Sir Ector has found me a steed that will hold my weight, so don't hold your breath," Hawl retorted.

Lancelet snorted and seemed ready to continue the verbal jousting, but I interjected impatiently.

"Enough. You'll all follow Draven and me. As quickly as you can. With as many of our troops as you can gather, Sir Ector and Dame Halyna."

"At least some of those are already in Brightwind, thank the Three," Dame Halyna murmured.

With the repeated attacks on his borders, King Mark had permitted us to station a few regiments in Tintagel to provide a small measure of support for his own soldiers.

"But only a few," Galahad reminded her. He turned to me. "Morgan, I hate to say it, but we don't even know for certain that Ulpheas *came* from Brightwind."

I gritted my teeth. "Brightwind is where we know he was last, and so Brightwind is where I will go now. If he'd left Brightwind, he'd have told us, wouldn't he?" I looked at Draven, and he nodded. "Good. Then he was almost certainly still in the capital."

But suddenly, there in the back of my mind was something I didn't even want to think about or dream of mentioning.

I didn't know if the last thing Ulpheas had done was stitch to us... or if I had somehow stitched him here myself.

Once, in my moment of greatest need, Draven had come to me—disappearing off the back of an exmoor and arriving in the dungeons of Arthur's castle as I was being tortured by Arthur's Lord General, Fenyx.

In the midst of my nightmarish battle of minds with my father, had I somehow sensed Ulpheas's similar distress and instinctively stitched him to Camelot?

But no. There was no reason to think that was a real possibility. Especially when we still had no idea who was responsible for Draven's instantaneous arrival in the dungeons in the first place. It might have been me who did it—or it might have been him. Some quirk of his own fae magic. Who could say how these things worked? It had only happened once. Once was not a basis from which to draw conclusions.

Draven's hand gripped my arm gently, pulling me away from the group as the others engaged in a new discussion as to how quickly they could leave and whether those who could be ready faster should depart immediately, followed by Sir Ector and Dame Halyna with the larger contingent of troops.

"There's another possibility, Morgan," Draven murmured.

"Oh?" I said lightly, wondering if we'd been thinking along the same lines.

"You know I came to you once. Perhaps if we tried it together now..."

"No." Some warning prickled at the back of my mind. "No." I shook my head. "It wouldn't work."

Draven gave me an assessing look but didn't press me, for which I was grateful.

"I'll get your armor," he said. "And everything else we need. You finish up here. I'll meet you at the roost."

I gripped his hand before he could stride away. "Thank you. For... everything. For not doubting me just now."

His eyes shone very green. "It will be my great honor to fight at your side once more." He leaned down and kissed me, quickly but fiercely. "All or nothing, my silver one."

"In dreams as in life," I whispered back, tears threatening the corners of my eyes as I remembered our cottage.

I couldn't tell him. Not yet.

Not until this was over.

CHAPTER 9 - MORGAN

In my heart, I knew I had been right about Brightwind.

And yet when we finally saw the fires burning from a distance, I was still shocked.

Below us, the sprawling city of Brightwind lay ensnared in the grip of an insidious siege. Spreading out for miles around the city were dark foot soldiers moving with sinister purpose.

I had seen fighters like these once before. Draven and I had battled them by air in Myntra. They had come for Rychel and the grail then. Some had stayed to lay waste to the Court of Umbral Flames. We had stopped them.

But today? They may not have come with their dark, sinewy flying mounts, but right now, there seemed to be so many more of them.

Thousands upon thousands, like ants crawling up endlessly from the ground, they spread over the earth, moving tirelessly towards their target.

Like the forces that had attacked Myntra and those who had ambushed Draven's troops as they came ashore off the western coast of Eskira, all of the foot soldiers were masked. Their helmets were crafted in the image of death itself, forged from the same foreboding black metal as their spiked armor. The helms bore skeletal features with hollow, glowing eye sockets. It was impossible to say what lurked within. Were they all fae as I assumed? Mortal? Or something worse?

Shrouded in their obsidian armor, the enemy infantry bore an array of menacing weaponry. Some brandished curving blades. Others wielded long, jagged halberds, their tips adorned with runes that pulsed with unnatural energy.

For now, the city of Brightwind was untouched.

Fires burned on the battlefield where they must have been lit by King Mark's soldiers as they fought through the night.

Now dawn had come, but as a gray, sickly thing. A hazy fog hung over the air, mixing with the smoke and terrible stench of death.

As Draven and I soared on the exmoors overhead, the magnitude of the destruction that had already been wrought unfolded beneath us.

Brightwind, surrounded by a ring of Tintagel forces, had somehow stood resilient. Yet the air crackled with the tension of an imminent breach. The infantry seemed an unending tide, relentlessly clashing with our beleaguered allies. The ring was a slender thing, and the brunt of the battle drew ever closer.

My heart quickened as I glimpsed King Mark. Catching Draven's eye where he flew beside me on Nightclaw, I pointed.

The king was a figure of regal defiance, heavily armored and riding a sturdy white steed through the fray, surrounded by a group of elite knights who followed as close to their liege as possible, their faces protective and watchful.

King Mark's very presence among his troops was a rallying cry, I knew, and yet the act was dangerous in the extreme, for if he were to fall, his troops would surely lose hope.

We flew past the inner ring guarding the city, over the king and his knights, past the second ring of troops engaged in battle, to the outer edges of the fray where new, fresh groups of foot soldiers were joining the dark fae forces every minute.

Flying high overhead in the cloud cover, we had not been spotted yet. We had the element of surprise as we decided where to strike first.

My pulse quickened as I caught sight of a twisted, horned helmet that rose above the others.

The man—for I knew not what else to call these creatures for now—rose above his fellows. He was a colossus, shrouded in an aura of terror that seemed to radiate from the ground upwards. A tableau of carnage surrounded him—fallen bodies of Tintagel soldiers strewn like discarded pawns at the feet of a malevolent giant.

As I watched in horror, one not-quite dead soldier crawled valiantly through the mud towards her sword.

Just as her hand touched the hilt, the general's form towered over her. His halberd came down. She screamed, and even from our great height above, I heard the woman's cry. Then, the sound was abruptly cut off as the dark creature's weapon sliced through the back of her skull.

"Don't," Draven cried sharply from beside me, and I realized belatedly that my hands were raised to strike.

But it was too late.

Something had alerted the general below. As I looked back down to the earth, my eyes met his.

My heart leaped as the master of the troops began to bark instructions to the forces around him. Foot soldiers maneuvered into swift formations. Archers notched arrows. Soldiers began to crank an arbalest loaded with bolts.

A volley of missiles flew through the air.

I could hear Draven shouting to fly low and turn.

I could sense Nightclaw was already doing so, moving Draven out of harm's way.

But Sunstrike and I were in tune in a different way. The younger battlecat was swift and light, yes, but also inexperienced. She had carried me stoically this far, but now I sensed her weariness.

As I fed her my thoughts, a hand to her fur, I felt her struggle to respond with the speed Nightclaw had. She turned, ever so slowly as it seemed to me. And then she began to climb, flying higher rather than lower, heading for the clouds. I sensed her newfound fear as the arrows began to hiss around us.

But there was nothing for it. I hunched on the great cat's back, my head against her coat, urging her on and praying Draven would cover our retreat.

Quick-witted as always, he had already done so. When I looked back over my shoulder, I saw him sculpting a path of safety for us, shadows cloaking our withdrawal as he and Nightclaw sped towards the projectiles and ensnared them, shadows coiling around arrows and missiles, hurling them back down towards the earth.

A few moments later, Nightclaw soared beside us.

We flew above the clouds, letting Sunstrike get her composure back. I could feel the young battlecat's heart racing and struggled to remind myself she had never been in this sort of fray before.

I shouted the thought to Draven over the whistling wind. "She's never done this before. She's frightened."

He urged Nightclaw closer until we were flying neck in neck. "I know. We should send her back. Join me on Nightclaw."

It was not a terrible idea.

And yet as Sunstrike heard his words, I sensed her immediate reaction. Her utter refusal to return without her mate, to leave us behind.

Not my first battle, I felt her say, in emotions if not in words. Not my first. Back on the beach. I helped.

"She did," Draven said begrudgingly as he understood her message. "But this..." He shook his head. "This is very different."

I looked at Nightclaw, but the cat's eyes were focused ahead of him. I got the impression he would not tell his mate what to do but would leave it to her.

"She wants to help," I said carefully. "She's fast. I can guide her. We'll just be more careful."

"They'll be watching for us now," Draven said grimly. "That large one down below, the general..."

"That large what?" I prompted. "What the fuck *are* those things, Draven? Men? Fae?"

Draven shook his head. "Fae, I'd assume. Well-trained, impassive. Very well-controlled."

I snorted. "Impassive? Is that what you'd call it? They're brutal. Nothing like any human soldiers I've seen."

Draven gave me a searching look. "Think of who they work for."

We had never spoken of it outright. But I knew we'd shared the same idea for a long time.

"Right," I said darkly.

"It's probably easy to be impassive when something worse awaits them back home if they fail," he pointed out.

"Why send out those raiding parties if this was what my father had all along?" I demanded. "What was the point?"

"To rattle us, to frighten us," Draven answered. "To test Tintagel's strength. To see where he should first attack. Tintagel is the closest kingdom after all."

And Pendrath was next. Followed by Lyonesse.

And then what? Cerunnos? Until all of Eskira was under Valtain control?

"Total dominion," I said miserably. My father must have had this attack already planned out, if not under way, by the time he found me in the dream.

"If I had to guess," Draven said, "I'd say this battle has been a long, long time coming." He looked over at me. "What's the plan?"

"Get down there and fuck shit up?" I suggested.

My father may have been a military mastermind. But I had my own style. Blunt and to the point.

He grinned. "How elegantly put."

I shrugged. "I'll use fire. You use... whatever the hell we're calling what you can do. And we'll see if we can help King Mark."

"Shadow wielding. It's rare among fae, but not unheard of." He sighed. "Fine. But Nightclaw and I will stay close and shield you. If things get too hot, you and Sunstrike head back up into the clouds."

I touched Sunstrike, making sure she understood. She was eager and excited to go back down. But she was a little afraid, too. I knew she'd be more careful.

"We're ready. Let's go."

We flew to war.

The blood-soaked earth stretched out below us like a canvas.

Sunstrike flew swiftly. She was young and nimble, if lacking experience.

Small flames danced in my hands, ready to unleash on the forces below us.

Beside us soared Nightclaw. If Hawl was right, the older exmoor was the veteran of countless battles. He moved with a sure and primal grace.

Astride him sat my mate, commanding shadows as easily as one might wield a blade.

Below us, the dark fae foot soldiers now found themselves confronting forces beyond their darkest imagining.

I ignited my flames. Trails of searing fire cascaded down from my fingertips, raining over the masked hordes like divine retribution.

The obsidian armor that made my father's infantry look so fearsome and unassailable now began to sizzle and melt under the assault of my flames.

But I had seen my own abilities in action before. It was Draven beside me who I found truly impressive. Unleashing himself on our enemies below and invoking the very essence of true darkness.

As Nightclaw surged forward, the two of them became a shadowy blur amidst the chaos of battle. Darkness clung to the exmoor's form as Draven lashed out with coils of shadows, manipulating an inky abyss to devastating effect.

Ethereal black blades slashed through the ranks of our enemies, cutting them down in great swathes.

Animated by Draven's will, shadows ensnared groups of foot soldiers with an otherworldly grip. Dark tendrils writhed and clung to our foes, sapping the life from their bodies as they hacked and cut fruitlessly at the intangible coils embracing them.

I watched as huge lines of my father's foot soldiers convulsed and then collapsed, lifeless husks in armored forms.

As the lines of foot soldiers fell, Draven extended his powers, weaving a veil of shadows to provide cover for our weary allies, concealing their movements as they moved to new and stronger positions and disorienting the dark fae forces, obscuring their vision and muddling their attempts to pursue.

I watched gleefully as the general stomped and screamed at the soldiers around him.

More arrows and missiles launched into the air towards us, but this time, Sunstrike and I were prepared. We didn't have the same bond as the one Nightclaw and I shared, forged of trust and time. But she was his mate. And I was her rider's. And that meant a great deal to us both.

So trust blossomed and grew swiftly as we flew through arrows streaking and projectiles soaring over our heads.

After a few minutes, I realized that Sunstrike was enjoying herself. The smaller battlecat veered and swerved midair with impressively deft motions, becoming more and more confident in her maneuvers as she took me precisely where I needed to go.

As we flew low over the battlefield, bursts of heat emanated from my palms as I unleashed my torrents on the foes below us. Flames erupted in brilliant hues, consuming the enemy ranks as an inferno swept over the battalions, leaving behind charred remnants.

My flames danced in harmony with my mate's shadows. The light to Draven's darkness. Together we created a symphony of devastation. The battlefield became a tapestry of fire and shadows as we fought on relentlessly, holding nothing back.

Gradually, exhaustion tugged at the edges of my senses. But beneath me, Sunstrike soared on with fierce determination. Pushing tendrils of damp hair out of my face, I met her resolve, and together, we burned brighter than the flames I conjured.

When a wave of raucous cheering finally erupted from the Tintagel soldiers spread on the field below us, I knew the battle would soon conclude.

The dark fae foot soldiers were scattering, their forces decimated by the combined might of the Tintagel troops and my mate and me. Even from my lofty vantage point, I could see their disarray. The dark general's authority could not reverse the tide of their defeat. I wondered what awaited him if he made it home to my father's court. I hoped his fate would be all that he deserved.

I could sense Sunstrike's elation. She purred with accomplishment, her fatigue forgotten in the face of our victory.

Across the expanse, Draven and Nightclaw hovered, both watching the retreat of the dark forces.

My mate's eyes never left the general as he struggled for control of his fleeing infantry, and immediately, I understood. We could not leave the leader of our enemy's forces standing to fight another day.

Before I could move Sunstrike into position, Draven had beat me to it. Guiding Nightclaw into a swift descent, he dove upon the general like a shadowy tempest.

The dark fae lord must have heard the beating of battlecat wings. He turned to face his unexpected adversary, hoisting a halberd in one hand.

But it was useless. In a blur of motion, Draven extended a hand, almost lazily, and from his shadows emerged a dark, slender blade. The shadow knife sliced through the air with a preternatural precision. As the dark general, caught off guard, struggled to parry, Draven's onslaught danced around his defenses, and in a final, sweeping motion, cleaved his blade through the general, slicing through armor and flesh and rending both in two.

I shuddered, suddenly reminded of the scene I had witnessed in my dream. The memory of my brothers struggling over an innocent mortal woman, and when they had not been able to come to an accord...

But this. This was different. When Draven moved in violence, he was a punishing force of justice. I had no qualms over this type of bloodshed. Watching my mate execute our enemies did not leave me feeling pity or nausea. It left me filled with a strange and wild joy and pride that could easily have turned to desire.

Draven swooped upwards, flying Nightclaw towards where Sunstrike and I hovered. Though weariness clung to him, our eyes met in the shared satisfaction of a hard-fought victory.

Below us, the city was free from its siege. A handful of soldiers continued their struggle, pushing back the last of the enemy who had not retreated. But they were mere skirmishes, echoes of the once-thunderous clash of thousands.

I scanned the sea of soldiers for King Mark and, with relief, found him. He had been unhorsed and was limping. Only a few knights remained by his side. But he was alive and looked as if he would remain that way.

I lifted my eyes back to meet Draven's but found my mate's gaze had shifted. He was staring at something off on the horizon.

I followed his train of vision, and a chill touched my heart.

A new legion of foes flew towards us, filling the sky with their foreboding silhouettes.

Down below, the cheering of our allies had ceased. An ominous silence grew as, one by one, the Tintagel troops turned towards the sound of beating wings.

As the new forces approached, the drone of wings became an incessant roar.

Horror gripped me as I saw our adversaries more clearly and the truth spread out across the skies.

Dark riders drew nearer on flying beasts with sinewy frames covered in leathery skin. In every way, they were like the ones we had seen when we battled in the air above Noctasia, except these had one significant advantage: knifelike beaks protruded from beneath beady black eyes matching the sharp, slender talons which extended from their wingtips. The beasts looked nothing so much as strange and horrific featherless birds. Dark and terrible, I was not surprised by the silence of our allied soldiers down below.

But it was not these raptor-like creatures that made my heart race faster now.

No, it was the flying beasts at the vanguard, full of raw power and moving with unnerving speed that held my attention.

Their chests were covered with plates of armor like knights' horses, and they advanced with a precision that bespoke years of training.

They were battlecats.

CHAPTER 10 - MORGAN

Beneath me, I felt Sunstrike shudder in shock. How quickly our elation had turned to horror.

I looked over at Draven. His face was hardset and grim.

I understood how he must be feeling. In an instant, my belief that our battlecats were somehow singular in their existence had crumbled, replaced by the stark reality of an entire legion of exmoors approaching.

If my mindset had been shaken, I could only imagine how much more Sunstrike's had.

She'd been born in the wild. Her mother and siblings were slaughtered by my brother's henchman when she was no more than a newborn. She'd fended for herself until finally joining our group. Nightclaw was the only other exmoor she had ever known.

Now I glanced at Nightclaw and knew the same could not be true of him.

A subtle vibration was coursing through Sunstrike. A mix of awe, trepidation, and a curious recognition.

I felt trepidation of my own. What we were about to ask Sunstrike and Nightclaw to do seemed antithetical to their existence. To war against their own kind... It was an unsettling paradox. But one which fae and mortals faced with all too great a frequency.

I stroked Sunstrike gently, feeding my concern to her. Did she wish to go back? I could fight from the ground. There was no need for her to continue to fly.

No, she responded, quickly and firmly. She would fly and she would fight. She would not be left behind.

I glanced at Draven and saw his own apprehension. He flew Nightclaw closer to us.

"She says she'll fight," I called. "She wants to fly."

Draven nodded reluctantly, his eyes focused entirely on his battlecat. I could sense his worry—and Nightclaw's as well. This would be a very different kind of battle. Was Sunstrike ready for it?

I gently stroked the exmoor's fur, trying to calm her disquiet.

When I cast my eyes at the field below, I saw to my relief that King Mark and his knights were quickly rallying the Tintagel forces back into position. More than that, they had formed a new strategy swiftly. Archers, crossbowmen, and other ranged units were moving into place, quickly finding elevated locations on small hills. Behind the forces out on the fields, all along the city ramparts, more archers were running out to take up positions.

I spotted ballistae and catapults being rolled forward, ready to launch projectiles. Large nets were being dragged up beside them. If these could be launched by ballistae, they might be able to ensnare a battlecat midair.

"Can we do this?" I said to Draven, trying to keep my voice casual.

His jaw was tight as he answered, "We'll have to."

Nightclaw simply roared. A mighty, deafening sound that echoed across the sky and caused heads below us to turn upwards.

Good. He had reminded our allies that we had our own flying beasts. Only two, admittedly, but Draven and I had shown what we could do with them already.

Still, I had to admit we were at a severe disadvantage. Not only in numbers but in terms of energy. Believing the horde of foot soldiers to be the only wave we would face, I had spared nothing. Now I flexed my hands and prayed I would have enough left to finish what we had started.

Draven's constant glances of unease, both at me and at Sunstrike, were not helping matters.

I scowled at him. "Stop looking at me like that, Draven."

He forced a grin and opened his mouth. Presumably to say something reassuring.

But whatever he was about to say was cut short by the cacophony of shrill cawing that filled the air. The battlecats in the vanguard had peeled away to allow the raptors to take the forefront in the attack. Now the birdlike beasts propelled through the air, knifelike beaks pointed downwards.

With deadly accuracy, they dove into the troops of Tintagel's infantry, skewering soldiers on their elongated beaks, lifting them high into the air before letting them fall again.

I watched in horror as soldiers fell like discarded ragdolls, their bodies splitting open on the hard ground below.

Faced with this new macabre onslaught, King Mark's once-steadfast soldiers struggled to hold their ground. Terror painted their faces as they confronted the new and horrifying foe.

And the attack hadn't truly even begun. Not yet.

I looked at Draven, horrorstruck. If Tintagel could not hold the line, what hope did we have?

Again and again, the raptors struck, diving in and out, plucking men and women into their gaping maws. A trio of raptors turned it into a sick game, tossing three soldiers back and forth between themselves, yanking on limbs and tearing flesh, until, one by one, they let the foot soldiers plummet to their deaths.

The frontlines were wavering. I saw knights riding back and forth and shouting commands and encouragement, only to be plucked off their own horses and swept up into the air screaming. I'd lost sight of the king and could only hope he'd gone back behind the city battlements.

Our allies on the ground were doing their best to counter the airborne threat. Archers loosened arrows and ballistae crews launched their projectiles skywards. But many of the shots went astray, missing their targets in the chaotic sky. The raptors were simply too swift.

A cheer from a contingent of soldiers went up as a projectile finally struck true and a raptor tumbled down from the sky. The ground trembled as the creature and rider hit the earth.

But for the one raptor and rider that had fallen, two dozen or more Tintagel soldiers had been picked off in the meantime.

"What are we waiting for?" I screamed at Draven.

I knew why he hesitated. He was afraid for me. Going in amongst the raptors would be much different from simply enveloping the fae foot soldiers in flames from above. We'd be fighting one-on-one, dueling in the air as we had above Noctasia.

But unlike the battle over Noctasia, Draven and I were separated. We'd be fighting alone, without one another to draw from.

Still, there was no help for it. Surely two riders on two battlecats were better than one. We could cover more ground.

I watched a raptor toss a screaming young soldier up in the air then snap him in half with its merciless beak. I'd had enough.

Without waiting for Draven to respond, I urged Sunstrike forward. We surged into the fray.

Flames flew from my fingers as we sped towards a pair of dark riders on raptors. The air crackled with heat as I directed a torrent of fire, first at the riders, sending them screaming and spinning off the backs of their mounts, and then at the raptors themselves.

One of the creatures tried to fly towards us, snapping and cawing, its sharp beak coming perilously close to Sunstrike's head. But before it could close its beak, I sent a searing cascade engulfing its nearest wing, melting the leathery flesh and leaving the bird screeching in pain as it plummeted downwards.

I watched as soldiers on the ground immediately ran towards it and finished the raptor off, then I turned my attention back to the skies.

Across from Sunstrike and me, Draven and Nightclaw were also engaged. They were speeding across the skies towards a grouping of raptors. Shadows thick as midnight erupted from Draven's outstretched hands, wrapping around three of the raptors' taloned wings like heavy chains.

Shadows spread outwards, clinging to the raptors and their riders, engulfing them in darkness. Blind and disoriented, with their wings pulled down by heavy chains, the creatures faltered in their flight and began to fall, their riders plunging from their backs as their mounts followed.

The sky radiated with the panicked cries of our fae foes and their winged beasts.

I grinned until my face hurt.

Perhaps we could do this.

And then I saw him. The commander of this incoming battalion. Mounted on an ashen silver battlecat, a fae rider clad in armor of darkest embers. Spiked pauldrons rose from his shoulders like twisted spires. A helm, adorned with cruel, angular motifs, concealed his visage.

Beneath him, the battlecat he rode moved with a predatory grace towards my mate.

We were too far for me to shout, too far for me to have any hope of catching Draven's eye.

I touched a hand to Sunstrike, knowing it would be enough, and she sped forward, her wings beating hard against the air.

Even as we moved, I knew we would be too late.

Draven's back was turned. He was focused, battling another raptor-mounted rider.

The ambush unfolded, and there was nothing I could do.

The fae attacker raised his hands.

A thick coil of darkness snaked through the air, and I gasped at its familiarity.

The coil lashed out, looping around Draven's neck and pulling tight. I could almost feel the suffocating pressure, the darkness that threatened to unseat my mate and send him hurtling downwards.

With a surge of adrenaline, Sunstrike and I swooped forward to intervene.

The air sizzled with the heat of flames as I threw ball after ball of fire towards the fae who was attacking my mate, desperately trying to draw his attention to me.

What happened next, I had not expected.

I succeeded.

Caught off guard by the unexpected assault, the fae relinquished his hold. The coil around Draven's neck dissipated, and I watched in relief as he regained control of Nightclaw.

The fae attacker turned towards me, steering his battlecat towards us.

My flames had seared a piece of his armor, but he seemed otherwise unharmed.

Now the attacker raised his hands. Pulling off his helm, he held it beneath one arm as he looked across the skies at me.

I understood I was facing the true leader of this army—of both the foot soldiers below and this second winged wave.

Beneath the intricately crafted helm, the fae man revealed a striking visage. Long hair, so fair it was essentially white, framed a face characterized by sharp cheekbones and a pointed chin. A pair of piercing, sapphire-blue eyes gleamed against skin so ageless and alabaster that it seemed impossible this man had ever been touched by the harshness of battle.

There was a look in the fae's eyes that sent a jolt of recognition through me I could not place. Perhaps it was the unveiled cruelty, I told myself. I had certainly seen that before in more than one pair of fae eyes.

Then he spoke, his voice pitched to carry above the wind, the fray, and the sound of beating battlecat wings.

"I've come to fetch you, Sister."

I flinched. "Who are you to call me 'sister?'"

But memory was streaming through my veins. Try as I might to deny it.

The man smiled thinly. "Come now. Don't tell me you've forgotten your older brother, Daegen. Why, I bounced you on my shoulders when you were a small child."

The memory coalesced. Bounced? No. He had not bounced me. He had dangled me, screaming, from a balcony until my mother had torn me from his grasp and sank to the ground with me clutched in her arms, sobbing.

"You tortured me," I said coldly.

Daegen clapped his hands together. "Ah, she does remember." He leaned forward in his saddle. "Your mother's not here to protect you now." He gestured to the markings on my arms that peeked out from beneath the Flamebloom armor I wore. "And those won't save you. Not now that you've left your pretty nest, little bird."

"I don't know what you mean," I said, feeling a cold chill come over me.

"You could only hide behind those marks for so long, Morgan. And behind the island. You've left it far behind now."

"The island?" My heart sped up a little. "What island?"

"Avalon, of course," my brother said disdainfully. "Why else would your mother have chosen a mortal to warm her bed? Disgusting woman to sink so low after the honor our father bestowed upon her, choosing her to be his queen."

My mind was racing too fast to pay much note to his insults.

"You know, you did well for such an ignorant girl," Daegen commented derisively. "To hide from our father as long as you did. But I suppose you had no idea how you were even doing it. The markings, the island. And then you were too stupid to stay where you were shielded." He leaned forward again, his smile turning secretive and seductive. "Tell me, Sister, what blade is that you carry?"

I touched a hand to the sword strapped to my back. Excalibur. I had brought it with me, not truly expecting to need it. But like it or not, it was the best weapon I'd ever had.

"Tsk tsk," Daegen said, wagging a long, slender finger. "You should have left it where you found it. It wasn't yours to take."

In horror, I realized I had opened myself. Alerted my father to my presence here somehow. By drawing on my magic—fueled by the markings. By leaving the safety of Camelot and its proximity to Avalon. And lastly, by carrying Excalibur with me into battle. Was the blade truly still so attuned to him that he had sensed its presence with me?

Or had he merely known the lure of Tintagel at war would be enough to draw me here?

I felt open and exposed, naked and vulnerable.

"Taking things that don't belong to you seems to be a habit, Sister," Daegen observed. "Like that mount." But instead of gesturing to Sunstrike, he pointed to where Draven hovered on Nightclaw a little ways away, listening and staying close.

"Our father's," I said, with a dawning realization.

"Yes, of course. Who do you think trained him in such tactics? When he escaped, it was a loss. An insult."

"Nightclaw didn't want to be our father's mount any longer," I said angrily. "And it sounds as if our father should really be used to such losses by now."

His battlecat. His wife. His daughter.

"As if a dumb animal really had a choice in such a matter," Daegen sneered.

Nightclaw roared, and for the first time, I realized what Daegen was holding in his hand. A whip. To control his own battlecat.

I curled my lip in disgust. "They're intelligent creatures. And yet you whip them? Is that my father's way?"

"Our father's way is one of might and power. And conquest. You would do well to remember that. When I return you to him, he will reward me, and you will see the true magnanimity of a fae high king—all that and more." He smiled a secretive smile.

"Good luck with that. I have no plans to return with you, Brother. You would do well to leave here now, while you still have the chance," I said as boldly as I could.

Daegen tipped his head back and laughed. It was a cruel and familiar sound. A prickle crossed my skin as I wondered if I sounded anything like that when I laughed. He was family, after all.

"You and the object you carry can come with me now," my brother said. "Come easily, and I'll spare these mortals down below. There's no reason they must be drawn into our family squabbles."

I knew he was lying. After all, my father's forces had attacked Tintagel first.

"And if I don't?"

He shrugged. "Then all below you will die in agony." He glanced over at Draven for the first time with a glimmer of interest. "And this man. The Siabra. He is your mate, I take it? Coupling with your enemy. How very much like your mother."

"Shut the fuck up," Draven growled. "If you think you're taking my wife anywhere, you're as mindless as you look."

"So the pleasantries are over then?" Daegen said with a smile. "I'll take my sister and I'll take the beast you ride. You and the other one are swill."

And then, before I could even blink, he had thrown out both his hands, dark blades extending in each direction.

One swept towards Draven, and from the corner of my eye, I saw Nightclaw veer and heard Draven shout.

The other sped towards me. I lifted my hands to ward off the expected blow that never came, and as I did, I heard Sunstrike cry out in pain and fear.

I caught sight of a wing, ripped to shreds.

And then my exmoor began to topple.

For a moment, I dangled in the saddle, struggling against the pull of gravity.

But as Sunstrike spun and spun in midair, plummeting faster and faster, my feet slipped from the stirrups.

And I fell.

CHAPTER II - MORGAN

I plunged downwards, feeling the raw rush of wind around me. For a few moments, it whipped past me like a tumultuous symphony that I could do nothing but listen to. My mind was blank, devoid of fear or panic.

Then I felt the sword strapped to my back begin to slip from its sheath. I reached my hand back, struggling to grasp the hilt, but it was too late.

Excalibur was gone.

Reality sank in. I turned my body and glimpsed brown earth rising up below me in a dizzying blur.

Panic filled me like a flood. This was it. This was how it ended. Killed by my own brother.

The sickening sensation of free fall engulfed me. The air roared past, screaming over my ears as it tore at my clothes and streamed through my hair like a wild beast.

I tried to think of Draven. Of all of those I loved. I closed my eyes and I tried to prepare for my end.

There was nothing else I could do. Nothing.

Something slammed into me, knocking the breath from my lungs. For a moment, I actually struggled against it, but the force was too strong.

Firm arms wrapped around me, enveloping me like a shield.

My eyes popped open. Draven.

The wind was too loud for us to speak, but I saw his eyes. Green and... terrified. He feared we truly might die. Yet he had caught me.

He had slowed my fall, I realized. We were still hurtling downwards but at a slower speed than before.

The ground was very close now.

It rose up towards us.

Soon. Very soon.

I shut my eyes, gritted my teeth, and wrapped my arms around my mate.

We hit the earth.

It was not a pleasant feeling. If the breath had been knocked out of me when Draven had collided with me in midair, this was a thousand times worse. I could only lie there, gasping airlessly, and wait for my diaphragm to eventually return to normal. As the air began to fill my lungs again, I looked upwards and saw a sight I had not dared to hope to see.

Nightclaw would never have discarded his rider or allowed Draven to do what he did unless the cat himself had good reason. In any other situation, the exmoor could have easily caught me himself and carried Draven and me both to safety.

But his mate had been in danger. Her wing ripped to shreds.

And so he and Draven had acted the only way the two males could.

They had split up, each to save the ones they loved.

Now above us, Nightclaw circled slowly with Sunstrike supported over him. The female exmoor was still stubbornly beating one wing. She could never have landed on her own, but with Nightclaw's help, her deadly descent speed had been reduced.

I watched as Nightclaw guided his mate away from the battlefield and began to bring them both down some distance from us, towards the forest treeline that stretched to the south.

As they disappeared from sight, there was a coughing sound. Belatedly, I realized I was lying on top of Draven.

Scooting off quickly, I watched as he got his bearings and caught his breath.

We were in a small grove. Or what had been one until recently. All of the trees were blackened and charred. I must have destroyed it while flying with Sunstrike because some of the trees were still smoking even now.

We had landed in a good spot, sheltered from the battle and relatively hidden.

Overhead, in the distance, raptors and battlecats dove and struck. Arrows flew and missiles soared. The battle was clearly not over.

My brother, Daegen, was nowhere in sight. I hoped he would assume I had died in the fall.

I looked down at where Draven still lay on his back and grinned. "Now that was a nice surprise."

"You—" He coughed again, a hacking, wheezing sound. "You didn't expect me to be... so acrobatic..." He coughed again, pounding on his chest. "Did you?"

"I expected to be dead right now," I said matter-of-factly. "But I should have known you'd once again be full of surprises."

"That's... me," he said, with another gasping cough. "Can't have you getting bored with me."

"Bored?" I leaned over him, brushing his dark hair off his forehead. "Never."

I pressed my lips against his, kissing him softly.

And as I did, I tasted something metallic and familiar.

Blood.

I sat back, my heart beginning to speed up. "Now why don't we pull you to your feet?"

"I find I much prefer..." He paused to cough, turning his head away from me. "I much prefer to recline."

"Get to your feet, you stubborn bastard. I want to take a look at you." Heart hammering, I stood up and reached my hands down for him to take.

He groaned, then very slowly pushed himself up onto his elbows. "What's there to see? I'm not very impressive."

"I'll be the judge of that, you insufferable man," I said. "Besides, you're just hunting for a compliment."

He tried to grin up at me, and I glimpsed a hint of the pain he was concealing. "Standing is overrated."

"Up," I said, clenching my jaw. "Now. Not a request."

He took my hands, surprising me, and heaved himself to his feet.

The scent of blood mixed with the rich scent of earth was stronger as I stepped behind him. Crimson ran down his back over the metal plates of his cuirass. There was a split in the plates where something had penetrated. A tree branch. Sharp and short, it had slipped between the plates. The force with which he had hit it must have been immense as we landed.

"We rolled. I felt something. Just a scratch," Draven said breezily.

Of course, his easygoing tone was contradicted by him having to stop and catch his breath twice as he spoke.

"There's a fucking tree branch sticking out of you, you can hardly breathe, but it's just a scratch?" I glowered at his back, then gingerly reached out a hand and touched the branch. It was sticky with blood, and I could see the irregular edges of torn flesh all around it. "We need to get this off you."

"That's what they all say," Draven joked.

I had no witty reply. Feeling suddenly frenzied with worry, I moved to help him, hands trembling as I pulled off the encumbering layers of metal. The clang of armor hitting the ground echoed through the grove.

I moved to stand in front of Draven, and my heart sank. The other end of the tree branch had penetrated the thick, padded layers of the gambeson beneath. I could see the uneven, blood-coated ridges of the wood poking through from the other side.

Draven caught my hand. "Morgan, it's nothing. Truly, I'll be fine."

He could have been right. I knew fae healed unusually quickly, Draven in particular. I had seen that for myself before. A mortal man would probably have died instantaneously.

Still, I shook my head. "We need to get you to a healer. You're not invincible, Draven, no matter what you might think."

He smiled, and a trickle of blood ran from his lip, sending my heart crashing.

"Besides," I said softly, touching his lip with a finger, "no matter how much you might think you're fine, I can't stand to see you in pain. Any sort of pain. Just as you can't stand to see me in any. Surely you can understand that."

He caught my hand and, raising it to his mouth, kissed it. "Fine. For you."

He dropped my hand and shrugged his shoulders with care as he winced. "And perhaps because this damned tree branch hurts a little more than a mere sliver."

He groaned and moved to lean up against a nearby tree.

"I'm not surprised," I started to say but the sound of beating battlecat wings cut me off.

I turned, expecting to see Nightclaw landing behind me.

But instead, Daegen's sapphire eyes pierced through me. My older brother smiled triumphantly as he slid off his silver battlecat. "Caught you."

"Can't you tell when you're not wanted?" I said sweetly.

"Pardon me, Sister. Am I interrupting a tender moment?" He peered at Draven with interest. "Or perhaps your mate is conveniently on the brink of death? That would simplify things nicely."

"He's fine," I snapped. "Strong as an ox. Healthy as a horse."

From behind me, I heard Draven mutter, "Fucking bastard."

Daegen put a hand to his ear. "What was that? Not a very polite fellow, is he, Sister?"

His arms struck out, and coils of shadow shot past me. I let out a cry and turned to see them wrapping around Draven, binding him to the tree.

"What's this?" Daegen said exuberantly. "Not even going to try to stop me, Siabra?"

"I don't need to," Draven said through a clenched jaw. "She can do it easily."

"Letting a woman fight your battles? Is that how your people do it?" Daegen's expression was disdainful. "You'd never survive in my father's court. Such weakness would never be tolerated."

"We'll never be in your father's court," I said.

"Well, he won't. You certainly will. Father knows best, Morgan. And he says you're coming back to us."

"Fuck off, Daegen. Just fuck right off."

"I can't, sadly. Besides, this is too much fun. And too easy."

The worst part was I knew he was right. Draven was struggling against his bonds, but the fact that he hadn't broken them already meant his wound must have been worse than he'd let on.

Furthermore, we'd exhausted ourselves fighting in the skies.

As I looked around the grove, I realized just how much time had passed.

We'd arrived at dawn. Now a gray twilight blanketed us. We had fought through the day and into the night.

I knew my power would return to me. Even now, I could feel it replenishing. But if my power was a sea, then I had dried it down to a mere pond. I could access it, but there was no guarantee it would be enough to beat my brother who had arrived far more recently and was fighting fresh.

Still, I knew how to do one thing. I could bluff.

"How does it feel to know you'll never be our father's favorite, Daegen?" I demanded. "You must be pretty low down in the ranks if he sent you here to fight a mortal battle, after all. Fetching me like some glorified courier—is that all you're used for?"

Daegen flushed red. "You know nothing of the honors that have been bestowed upon me, Sister. Why, next to Lorion, I am the greatest weapon our father has."

"Lorion?" I grabbed onto the name. I had heard it once before, in the true dreaming I'd had of my mother. "So you're next to Lorion, not above him? He surpasses you? How fascinating."

"We are both commanders in our father's army," Daegen insisted, glaring at me from behind his brilliant blue eyes.

"How does it feel to be a second-best weapon?" I shot back. "No, not just second-best. More like third or even fourth or fifth best. Because I'm willing to bet our father loves his precious grail above you or Lorion. And what about the spear? I've heard it's his favorite weapon."

"The spear..." Daegen began. Then his eyes narrowed. He laughed.

I cringed, knowing what was coming.

"The grail and the spear and the sword," he said slowly. "And just where is the sword, Sister? Have you lost it?"

"I put it somewhere safe," I lied. "Very close by."

"You lie badly," Daegen said. "You've lost it. Do you even have the grail? If not, our father will be very displeased."

"Why do I care if he's displeased? I care nothing for his pleasure."

Daegen hissed. "Ignorant girl. If you care nothing for his pleasure, you should at least fear his wrath."

"And perhaps you should fear *me*. Have you ever thought of that?" I demanded, standing up straighter and lifting my chin. "You have no idea what I'm truly capable of."

"That might have been true at one time. But now?" Daegen laughed. "You have no idea who you even are. I doubt your powers are anything to brag about. And without the sword? You're nothing."

I swallowed my pride, realizing he might be right. Daegen wasn't Fenyx. He wasn't a man pretending to be fae. He was truly fae, and I had no idea how much latent power he had left.

Could Draven and I make a run for it?

I pushed my senses out, seeking Nightclaw and Sunstrike. But I could not touch them. Perhaps they were too far off. Or perhaps they were simply exhausted and resting. I could not expect help from that quarter. They had already done enough.

From behind me, I heard Draven murmur, "You'll have to draw from me. Take what you can. Take everything."

I nodded ever so slightly, but had no plans to do as he said unless I had absolutely no other choice. Every moment we lingered, stuck here with my brother, Draven was losing blood. What would happen if I drained him dry before we could get him to a healer?

"You hesitate, Sister. You make no move to strike me. Shall I tell you why?" Daegen taunted. "It is because you are weak. Because you are a liar. Because you are not worthy of our father's praise."

My eyes flashed. "So why do I have it then? Why does he want me back? Why does he love me? Why does he care for me above all of his other children? Above you?"

Daegen's gleeful look dissipated. "I shall never truly know the answer to that."

"Now that is a lie," I said victoriously. "You do know."

"You've forgotten so much. It's truly entertaining," he said with a forced smile.

Daringly, I took a step towards him. "So enlighten me. Who knows, perhaps you won't even have to force me to go home. Perhaps I'll come willingly."

My brother opened his mouth, and I took another step forward, this time almost eagerly. There were secrets here. Right on the tip of Daegen's awful tongue. Perhaps today I'd finally get to hear them.

The haunting cry of an owl pierced the air, drawing my attention skyward.

Tuva. The gold and brown bird had something clutched in her talons.

A sword.

The moon was rising as the owl released the blade.

It fell, not as I had moments before with a painful thump, but with grace and purpose, spiraling through the air until it landed with a resolute thud on the blackened earth in front of my feet, dust and ash rising around it.

In a heartbeat, I had snatched it up and gripped it in both hands.

As I lifted the blade up in front of my face, the moon broke into full view above us.

Excalibur hummed with energy. The gleaming blade pulsated under the moon's gentle glow.

Overhead, Tuva hooted softly and flew off. I kept my eyes on my brother.

"Well, at least you haven't lost it as I'd feared," Daegen said, curling his lips.

But I knew he was unnerved by what had just happened.

"A small complication?" I suggested. "I won't be going willingly. No matter what family secrets you tell me."

"Fine," he snapped. "Let's deal with one problem at a time then."

He raised his hand, but this time I was ready. As a blade of shadow flew from his palm towards Draven, I moved Excalibur to block it. The shadow blade bounced harmlessly off the sword and vanished like mist.

"If you were a true Valtain and one of us," my brother snarled, "you would put him down yourself, even if he is your mate. He's weak. He's a burden to you. Free him from his misery."

I held Excalibur sideways with my right hand and lifted my left.

"Then it's a good thing I'm no Valtain," I snarled back, letting flames dance across the blade, turning it a hot, glowing red. "Because the only one I have any interest in putting out of his misery is you, Brother dear."

And then we danced.

Beneath a full moon, we danced, while beyond the grove, the clash of steel echoed through the night as the battle for Brightwind raged on.

I knew Daegen had been given instructions not to harm me. I also knew those instructions did not apply to Draven and that Daegen would defend his own life no matter what it took.

So to me, it was a dance of death.

I was an average swordswoman at best. When practicing in Sir Ector's training arena, I had been proficient. An apt pupil, not a brilliant one.

But with Excalibur in my hand again, there was nothing I could not do. My swordplay knew no bounds.

The air buzzed with tension as Daegen and I circled each other, eyes locked in unspoken challenge.

I lunged forward, Excalibur cutting through the night with a sharp hiss.

I missed but caught the look in my brother's eyes as he saw the flames dancing along the blade.

"Not afraid of a little heat, are you, Daegen?" I goaded him. "Don't tell me that pretty Valtain armor has a boiling point." I stepped away quickly as he slashed out with a black shadowy blade. "But then, it did the trick with your foot soldiers. Their armor melted and so did their flesh."

"I've been wounded before," Daegen said, a little breathlessly. "I have lived for countless millennia. I was here long before you were born."

But it wasn't true. I could see in his eyes that it wasn't true and wondered why he'd said it. Why lie about such a thing as being my older brother?

"Do you really think you can kill me, Sister? I, who have stood at our father's side for so long?"

"No," I said calmly. "But Excalibur can. Have you ever been touched by such a blade as this?" I let him get a good look at the flames that still moved like living fire over the blade, casting an eerie glow and illuminating the dust kicked up by our footwork like countless, tiny fireflies. "Tell me, has our father ever turned his fantastical weapons of power upon you?"

As I spoke, I realized I truly wanted to know the answer to that question.

"Why did he forge such weapons, anyway?" I continued, figuring at worst I'd distract him a little, at best I'd get some answers.

Daegen's shadowy blade responded with fluidity. I parried, then moved forward again, executing a series of quick slashes, Excalibur weaving seamlessly through the air.

One slash hit home.

Daegen let out a curse and clutched his shoulder.

"Fascinating," I said softly. "So that answers that about the weapon cutting through Valtain armor."

"I'll have new armor crafted," Daegen snarled. "Once I strip that sword from your body and drag your lifeless carcass back to our father."

"Tsk, tsk," I cautioned. "Killing me might get you into a heap of trouble. But I, on the other hand..."

I spun, the flames on my blade twirling in harmony with my motions. Excalibur clashed against Daegen's black sword. My brother moved as swiftly as I did, matching my every move, his shadow-infused weapon proving frustratingly elusive.

"I doubt Father would care if I killed you," I panted ruthlessly. "Maybe he won't even notice you're gone."

With a roar, Daegen came at me, his shadowy blade slashing towards me.

Instinctively, I blocked the attack, the clash resonating through the night.

Shadows and flames intertwined as we pressed our blades against one another.

"I hear those savages have made you their empress," Daegen spat. "What an honor."

"Better to serve the Siabra or mortals than the Valtain as you do," I said softly. "I am honored to have been chosen. I live to serve my people. Can you say the same?"

Immediately, I saw the truth in his eyes. If he could read me like a book, the reverse was also true. Daegen hadn't really cared about anyone but himself in a very long time. Perhaps ever.

"How sad, Brother," I said quietly, and I meant it. "To have no one to care for."

"I don't want your pity," he shouted, crashing up against me. "I don't require it. You speak only in words of weakness. Pathetic girl. Fallen sister. Shall I tell you what my honor will be?"

His blade cut through the air. I raised Excalibur to where I thought it would fall, but at the last moment, Daegen swerved. I felt a searing pain as the blade bit into my side.

"My honor will be to kill you, Sister. To end our father's pathetic search. For you are his only weakness," he snarled. "It will be an honor to end his torment and wield the sword you hold as I stand by his side."

As if in answer, Excalibur countered. I moved in a furious onslaught. I had already seen Excalibur become an extension of my will. Now I moved at the sword's behest, each of my strikes carrying the weight of years of betrayal and secrets kept in the dark.

The moon bore witness to our rivalry as Daegen and I exchanged blows in the grove.

And then, with a final, decisive strike, Excalibur pierced through my brother's defenses. I felt the moment the blade slid through his black cuirass. The look on his face was one of true shock. Perhaps he had been wounded before, yes, but not like this.

He crumpled to the ground, his eyes only on the blood seeping from his chest.

"You touched me. You touched flesh." His voice was full of incredulity. "Blood. You've bled me."

"Yes, there's quite a bit of blood, isn't there? But then, you've fought in countless wars, so..."

"With mortals. With... different fae. Not like this. So much blood." He lifted his eyes to mine with the expression of a sullen, hurt child. "How dare you?"

Suddenly, I felt tired, looking at my brother sprawled in the dirt.

"You came to me, remember? I didn't want any of this." I was so tired. What if this could all just stop?

"Let me go, and I'll withdraw our armies," my brother pleaded, telling me exactly what I wanted to hear. "This can end now. No more deaths. Isn't that what you want? You said you served your people. I offer you a chance."

"No, you offer yourself a chance to save your own life," I said, standing over him, Excalibur still raised. "How do I know you'll do as you say?"

"I swear it," he said, and the look in his eyes was truly pathetic. "By the sword you carry. By anything you choose."

I looked into his eyes, wondering if he was simply lying again. It was hard to tell. He certainly wished to live.

"Fine," I said. "Get up and go. Take every creature you brought with you. And never show your face to me again, Brother. I have no wish to repeat this with you."

"Agreed." Relief filled his voice. "I will not overstep your domain again. My father will simply have to send someone else next time he wishes to... communicate with you."

That should have been what warned me. The idea that my brother would so easily dismiss his father's favor and do anything to invoke his displeasure.

But I was so eager to see this battle end.

I turned to Draven. He had been watching us the entire time in silence. Though he had long escaped the coils Daegen had wrapped around him, now I saw his dark face had become paler than usual and he had one arm wrapped around the tree for support.

"Come, let's get out of here," I began to say just as Draven's eyes widened.

That look was the only warning I had.

I whirled, and there he was. My brother had risen from the dirt with shadows clinging to him like loyal servants. Shadowy knives emerged from his palms as he darted straight towards me.

Without a conscious thought, Excalibur surged forward, propelled by a force beyond my own.

The gleaming blade cleaved through the moonlight night, piercing Daegen's chest in a lethal strike.

My brother's shadows evaporated like smoke. I watched the brilliant sapphire of his eyes dim and fade as the spark of life left him.

Silence fell, heavy and oppressive, as I stood over his fallen form.

The taste of victory was bitter in my mouth as I turned away, Excalibur still in hand, towards the wounded figure of my mate where he stood against the gnarled shape of the burned tree.

Draven's eyes were warm and watchful, but he seemed hesitant to speak.

That was all right. I knew what I needed to say.

"I've been going about this all wrong," I said, hardly recognizing the sound of my own voice. It sounded hollow and far away. But I pushed on. "We don't need a healer."

I took a step towards him, strangely hesitant.

I had just killed my own brother. I had committed what some might call the greatest crime before the Three. Even now, in some small villages in Pendrath, one who killed a parent or sibling even by accident would be banished and shunned.

But then, Draven knew a little about murderous family members himself.

Still, I found it impossible to meet his eyes. What would I find there if I dared to look?

Then I had no choice.

"Healing can come later," Draven said as I stepped closer. "Look at me, Morgan." He gently tilted my chin up so I was forced to meet his steadfast green gaze. "You will find no judgment here. Not ever. Nothing you do will ever be wrong in my eyes. Everything about you and who you are is right to me."

I shook my head, hearing and not hearing. "But it's not right. Not really. It never can be. All of this... It needs to end. But first."

I took another step towards him. Could I not show there truly was some good yet in me?

I could do this thing. I had done it before. When we had not even been bonded yet.

Yet even then, there had been something linking us. Some thread of fate.

As Draven leaned against the tree, wounded and weary, I touched a hand lightly to his chest, opening myself to the familiar sense of our bond.

Closing my eyes, I focused on the energy pulsating within me, seeking the wounded recesses of my mate's body. The air seemed changed, fraught with the unspoken language of our joining.

A current passed through me, an invisible bridge spanning the gap between souls. Within my mind, I felt the raw edges of Draven's injuries as I traced the path of the branch that had pierced through him.

His pain echoed through my senses and fueled the urgency of my efforts.

I could kill, yes, but I could also heal.

The grove became a cocoon, shielding us from the outside world as the palliative power within me coalesced.

The moment hung suspended. An aura of light enveloped us. The grove crackled with unseen energy.

And then, like the echo of a fading song, it was done.

Draven stepped towards me, a hand pressed to his chest. The rips in his gambeson were still there. But the flesh beneath was whole once more.

"Faster than a healer," I remarked.

"Or to wait for me to heal," he agreed. "But you'll have spent yourself. You had hardly anything left to give, Morgan. You should have saved it. Not expended it all on me. I would have been fine."

I shook my head stubbornly. "Not good enough. I couldn't risk it."

Not when he was the one I needed most by my side, now and always.

I was shivering. He pulled me to his chest, and I felt my body relaxing. "Besides, surely the battle's almost over."

Seeing Tuva had changed everything.

Not only had the owl brought me Excalibur, with her very presence, she had brought us word of our friends.

There was hope. If the bird was here, Guinevere and the others would not be far behind.

But looking beyond the grove, I had only enough time to scan the battlefield and confirm that Pendrathian and Myntran troops had indeed joined our allies before the next storm swept in.

CHAPTER 12 - MORGAN

I t was no natural gale.

The promise of victory that had hung in the air unraveled with the storm's arrival, birthed from the unforgiving sea to the north of coastal Brightwind as sheets of rain began to fall.

The silver strands of water were illuminated by flashes of malevolent lightning. Overhead, the silent moon had vanished, replaced by clouds and the heavy rumbling of thunder.

Then the wind began. A killing draft surged forth over the coastal cliffs, slicing like an invisible scythe through ranks of foe and ally alike.

Soldiers were lifted into the air like leaves then tossed to the ground.

Up in the sky, even the riders on their raptors and battlecats were not spared. The wind struck them, carving through bodies like knives and sending riders and mounts tumbling down.

Frozen, I stood with Draven, my gaze fixed upon the approaching wind.

Small flames flared in my palms. But what was fire against a storm such as this, even if I could conjure enough to somehow make it meaningful?

The first gust had died down. Now we saw a second wave of wind sweeping across the plains again. Those who had somehow survived the first time were now being swept away.

"Run," Draven commanded. "We have to run, Morgan."

Yet something held me. Cold fury was welling up inside. This was my father's doing. He had lured me here to our ally's side. Sent my own brother after me. And then, even when I had killed my own kin in self-defense, he would not stop.

He would not relent.

This storm was his. It should not have been possible, even for a fae. But somehow, I knew it with every fiber of my being.

Draven grasped my arm, trying to tug me across the grove, but I wrenched away.

The wind was close now. The sounds of battle had been drowned out completely by the ominous roar of the approaching gale.

In another moment, it would be too late. Would we survive, or would we be lashed to pieces?

Rain hit my face, a thousand tiny, stinging arrows.

I ran then. Not out of the grove but into its very center. Lifting my arms overhead, I screamed. It was a primal cry, erupting from the depths of my being, born of desperation and from fierce defiance.

With arms raised high, something extraordinary unfolded.

My scream became an invocation, a plea that was somehow answered.

A shimmering veil materialized overhead. A shield.

The shield spread out with a brilliance like the first light of day, encapsulating Draven, me, and the small grove in its barrier of energy.

The killing wind, denied its prey, howled against the barrier fruitlessly.

Then the gust subsided and the air stilled.

I lowered my arms.

"It will come again," I said wearily, turning to my mate.

Draven's eyes were wide. "You can shield."

"I don't know what that was. I didn't know I could do it until... I did."

He was looking past me, out at the battlefield. "Do you think you could do it again? If we could extend it..."

"No." It killed me to say it. "I have nothing left. You were right. I don't know where that came from. But whatever it was, I can't. I just can't. I want to." I curled my fingers into my palms, stabbing my nails into them until the skin broke. "This is my father, Draven. He's doing this. Killing them. Killing us." My voice broke.

"Call Nightclaw."

"What?"

"Call him, Morgan. Call him now. Can you do it?"

"I... I already tried."

"Try again. Try now. For me."

I could hear the urgency in his voice. From a distance, I could hear the wind picking up again.

I closed my eyes. Was the battlecat near? Was he awake? Was he alive?

I reached out, pushing harder than I had before, struggling to sense the exmoor and his mate.

There. I touched him.

Nightclaw!

A feeling of acknowledgement. He was with Sunstrike. They were safe.

Guilt passed through me. How could I ask this of him when he had already done so much?

The battlecat sensed my hesitation. Tell me, he demanded, as obstinate as Draven.

I need you, I confessed. Here. Now. Can you come?

The response was immediate. A feeling of understanding and unwavering loyalty coursed through our connection.

A moment later, the grove shimmered with a burst of energy.

Nightclaw stood before me, proud and regal, his eyes reflecting the wisdom of ages I had long forgotten.

I felt relief but not a little trepidation.

"Now what?" I turned to Draven, shouting to be heard over the mounting wind and the sound of distant, unsettling screaming.

"Now you draw," he shouted back. "From both of us."

And then he grabbed my hand and pulled me hard against him while, with his other, he reached out and set his palm against Nightclaw's side.

"Do it, Morgan. Do it now," he urged.

Draven's touch was warm and grounding, anchoring me back to the present moment. His hand wrapped around my waist, holding me firmly against him.

I shut my eyes, allowing my connection to Nightclaw to reform, to deepen, then stretched out the bond encompassing Draven within it.

Draven. Where we touched, a current of power surged through my veins. The sensation was visceral... almost erotic. Euphoria danced over my skin, and I longed to revel in it, losing myself in the intoxicating merging of our energies.

What was the wind to this? Connected like this to my mate, what was a storm?

A low growl from Nightclaw brought me to my senses. We were a triad of power. Beside Draven, the exmoor was a pillar of earthy, steadfast strength, grounding me and stabilizing me.

As the battlecat's presence intertwined with my own and Draven's, a newfound clarity settled over me.

The wind. It was very near now.

I raised my hands and felt the air, sizzling and crackling upwards like sparks. But this was no fire. To face a storm, I needed a wall.

I visualized the shield I needed. I pictured it extending high over the battlefield, a dome that would guard my allies from the impending storm.

Focusing my intent, I began to shape it with my hands, tracing it in the air.

Raw power surged through my fingertips. The magic took shape, the shield coalescing around and above.

As it gained form, I kept my arms lifted high as the shield became a colossal canopy, stretching across the expanse of the sky, rippling with intertwined energies.

The killing wind reached the barrier.

There was a crashing sound like a wave breaking on rocks.

I felt the presence of the one behind the wind, and I screamed again, this time, words forming.

"Get out. You shall not have them."

I strained, struggling to maintain the shield as again and again the wind crashed upon it. The trinity of energies was a bounty of strength, but even such a formidable alliance had its limits.

Sweat formed on my brow. Every muscle in my body tensed as I drew deeper and deeper from my mate and the battlecat, sensing their energies ebb and drain as they flowed into me and were pushed out into the shield.

Time flowed and passed. Still I held the shield. Draven's face was a mask of tension. Nightclaw did not move. Still I held, still I drew, directing the flow of power.

Still the wind bashed against what we had formed. Still the wind blew.

We could not outlast it. My father was an unrelenting force that defied conquest or containment.

The shield, powerful as it was, could not endure indefinitely.

There was only one thing left to do.

I opened myself and embraced the wind.

The clash of energies was palpable. The shield's hunger was voracious.

I let it feed. Absorbing everything the wind had to give.

Godlike power flowed through me, carrying the weight of eons and the wrath of a deity scorned.

The fabric of the shield resonated with the clash. I felt my father's presence looming like a maelstrom bearing down.

Yet there was nothing he could do. I simply drew and drew, harnessing and encompassing rather than resisting.

I felt his fury as he faltered. And then withdraw.

The wind abated. A profound stillness settled over the battlefield.

We had won.

I looked down at my side and, with shock, saw Excalibur still glowing. The sword had been in my hand the entire time.

Not a trinity. A quartet.

"*Ferrum deae*," Draven murmured.

My head jerked up. "What did you say?"

"The sword. Another name for Excalibur. It means 'iron of the goddess,'" Draven said, meeting my eyes. There was something very solemn in his expression that made me uncomfortable.

"You're not fae, Morgan. Not after what you've done here today. You're a goddess." He gave a low chuckle, and I flinched.

"Don't say that," I replied uneasily. "What a ridiculous thing to say."

But it was too late.

The Three-cursed man was already kneeling in the dirt at my feet, his hands tracing the curves of my hips.

"You're my goddess, and I'm your knight," he said as he brought his face up to kiss my stomach and laughed again.

CHAPTER 13 - MORGAN

I knew he had been joking.

As we sat in King Mark's palace in his crowded council room at a long rectangular table, I told myself Draven had simply been joking.

I was fae. That was bad enough. I was no goddess.

Even though in the back of my mind, part of me knew what my father had just done out there had gone beyond the powers of any fae king.

The room around me was filled with the noise of advisors and nobles from Brightwind and other regions of Tintagel, all struggling to be heard over one another.

The battle may have been over, but this was a council of war.

I tried to focus on what was being said. Plans to invade Rheged. When and how to do so.

Lyonesse was being informed. They had sent no troops to the Battle of Brightwind as it had already been named. Without the help of one of our stitchers from Myntra, they had not even known the battle was taking place until it had been far too late for them to do.

The troops that had arrived to support Brightwind had been from Pendrath, bolstered by the extra troops from Myntra that Draven and I had kept stationed in Camelot as a precaution.

Pendrath, Sorega, Tintagel. Each kingdom's troops had sustained heavy losses. Tintagel's were by far the worst.

Though our friends had arrived late, Pendrath had held its own.

Now Gawain sat on the other side of the room nursing a broken arm on a chair along the wall, while beside him, Dame Halyna's left eye was covered with a patch that she likely would wear the rest of her days.

"We must attack immediately, sire," a tall, hawk-nosed noblewoman boomed, pounding her hands on the table to get King Mark's attention.

The king of Tintagel was a wary man, I saw. Unwilling to rush headfirst into anything, even after suffering such a brutal and unexpected attack on his people.

"That would be madness," Draven said, rising to his feet and towering over the table to glower at the woman. "You don't even know who to attack in the first place, let alone *where* to attack them."

"Rheged," a different advisor shouted from further along the table. "Obviously this was Rheged's doing. How can there be any question?"

"They came from the west," others agreed. "Rheged. Yes, it must have been Rheged."

"We hardly have contact with Rheged," King Mark said quietly. "What reason could they have to attack us? And with fae armies, besides."

"The fae came from Rheged," the first noblewoman insisted. "They marched in from there. That is all the reason we need to counterattack."

Draven shook his head derisively. "You've just sustained heavy losses. Do you really think you have the forces to attack Rheged without even knowing what awaits you there? Furthermore, where exactly in Rheged would you hit? The western border? That's a vast swathe of territory for an army to cover, let alone one that's just been weakened substantially."

"Our weaknesses are none of your concern," the noblewoman snapped. "You have no place here in the first place, *fae-blood*." She spat on the floor beside her. A murmur went through the room.

"Sir Joaquin, kindly escort Lady Izana from the council chambers," King Mark commanded. A dark-haired man nodded grimly and marched towards the offending lady.

King Mark looked around the table filled with his mortal nobles and advisors.

And then there was us. My friends and me. The fae empress with her strange markings, her fae husband with his horns, a Bearkin, a scarred knight, a High Priestess too young to be one. We were rather a strange ensemble of misfits by any estimation.

"Morgan Pendragon is fae, as is her husband," the king said slowly. "You all know this. You are also aware that both are our allies. And after today, we should count ourselves extremely fortunate to have them."

"Unless they were a part of this," Lady Izana shouted as she was prodded from the room by Sir Joaquin. "They might have conspired with the attackers."

"What utter rubbish," said a dark-skinned, elegantly-attired woman seated near King Mark.

Queen Camille had remained mostly silent, but now, she rose to her feet. "We do not dishonor our allies, Izana. That is not the Tintagel way. Was I the only one watching from the battlements as the fae empress"—the queen pointed across the table to me and every head in the room swiveled in my direction—"summoned some sort of shield to protect not only the battlefield but this entire city?"

I cringed. Apparently, the shield had been larger than I could ever have hoped for.

"She saved you and your children, Izana," the queen called after the noblewoman. "As she did mine. The Empress Morgan and her husband had nothing to do with this attack." She looked around the table. "Nothing. And anyone who thinks they did or who harbors such ignorant phobias of the fae will kindly leave this room now. We have no time to waste on such idiocy. Not when we need every ally we can get."

For a long moment, the queen looked at me, and I was terrified she would sink to the floor in a gesture of obeisance. But instead, Queen Camille simply nodded her head gracefully—a gesture between equals. Gratefully, I quickly nodded back, then watched as the queen sat back down beside her husband who was looking at her appreciatively.

The debate as to what Tintagel should do next and how to do it quickly resumed, though more politely this time.

A hand touched my arm. "You look exhausted."

I glanced over at Guinevere. "I slept badly."

In fact, I hadn't slept yet at all. We had been welcomed into the palace after the battle. Draven and I had been given a suite, and we had bathed then retired.

I had listened to the rhythm of Draven's breathing as he slept. But I had not dared to close my eyes.

Instead, I'd clutched the sheets, trying to stay awake. Afraid of what might happen if I let myself fall into a dreamworld again.

I knew I couldn't keep it up. I might last longer than a mortal, but eventually, I would have to surrender to sleep.

But in the meantime, I planned to hold out as long as I could. The thought of what—no, who—awaited me in my dream world... Well, it terrified me.

"You don't need to be here for this," Guinevere said softly. "Come. Walk with me."

I was surprised that she had no wish to remain at the council of war, but didn't need to be asked twice. Any opportunity to speak to the increasingly enigmatic high priestess was one not to be lost.

As I pushed back my chair from the table, I caught Draven's eye and he nodded slightly. Gently, Guinevere took my arm and led me from the room.

We walked in silence for a while, passing carved wooden doorways leading to chambers that held the suites of lords and ladies.

It took me a moment before I realized we were not alone. Lancelet had also left the council room. Now, she followed a discreet distance behind, ever vigilant.

We reached the end of the corridor where a large row of arched windows framed panoramic views of the azure ocean below.

The Brightwind palace bordered the sea to the north. A briny freshness filled the air as I pushed open one of the glass frames and let a cool breeze blow in.

Guinevere was very quiet beside me. The owl on her shoulder looked beyond me, staring out the window at the open sea.

"I'm surprised you left Camelot," I said finally, breaking the silence. "I never knew Merlin to do that. Leave the temple, I mean."

"Things were different in Merlin's time," Guinevere said simply.

I knew she wasn't deliberately trying to be provoking, but still, I stiffened.

"Merlin did all that was proper," I said.

"Oh, of course," Guinevere agreed, looking slightly surprised. "She was a fine high priestess. She conducted herself according to the will of the Three. She did all that was asked of her, and in the end, she made the ultimate sacrifice."

And had left Guinevere in her place without even telling me that she had chosen a successor.

"How do you even know what the will of the Three is?" I asked. It was a question I had always wanted to pose to Merlin. "It's not as if they speak to you, is it?"

Guinevere smiled ruefully. "We don't. We simply have to try our best and hope we're doing what the goddesses would wish us to."

I stared. "How on Aercanum can you ever possibly know what they wish?"

"We know they wish for peace. And for balance," she answered. "We would not serve them otherwise."

"Balance?" I shook my head. "At one point, my father had the three greatest objects of power in all the world. That doesn't seem particularly balanced."

"Yet now two are yours," Guinevere said, gesturing to the sword I still wore at my belt.

"Not mine to keep," I said sharply. "Mine to destroy."

As if in answer, Excalibur's hilt glowed briefly, then darkened.

"How did one man, fae or not, get so much power?" I said softly to the high priestess. "Can you tell me that?"

"There must be a long story behind it indeed." She looked at me until I glanced away.

"There is another name for Excalibur. My sister used it once. *Ferrum deae.* Have you heard it?"

Guinevere nodded slowly. "Iron of the goddess."

"Draven called me one. Only teasingly, of course." Why was I even telling her this, I wondered? "I suppose I surprised him when I formed that shield. I know I surprised myself."

"Did you?" Guinevere's expression was as calm as ever, but there was an assessing look in her eyes. "I should think it would be comforting."

"What? Being called a goddess?" I tried to laugh. "I assure you, it wasn't." *Empress* was overwhelming enough, but I felt certain she knew that already.

"No, not that. The other name Excalibur bears."

"Iron of the goddess? Why?"

"Well, it tells you the blade was never meant to belong to a man. Certainly not to your father, no matter how powerful he believes himself to be."

"Just how powerful do you think he is, Guinevere?" I said, sharper than I had intended. "As powerful as a fae high king? As powerful as, what? A god?"

"Why don't you tell me, Morgan?" she said softly. "He brought the storm, did he not? Do you know any fae who could do such a thing?"

I had seen fae do a great many things. Some strange, some breathtaking, some simply terrifying.

I had seen a winged fae who could not fly, and I had seen a small mortal boy with fae abilities he should never have had holding a shield over a city.

"I serve the goddesses wherever they take me," Guinevere said quietly. She was looking at the sword. "And something tells me the sword is trying to get back home."

"It *wants* to be destroyed?" I was less surprised by the fact that Guinevere believed a metal object could have wants of its own.

"Perhaps."

"Home. Wherever the hell that is," I said sourly. I somehow doubted anywhere my father resided could possibly be "homelike."

"Perhaps the goddesses are working through you more than you understand, Morgan," Guinevere said. "Have you ever thought of that? You wield their blade after all."

"I'm not a true believer. I'm not sure why they would."

"You don't have to believe. Not if they do."

I wasn't sure about her reasoning. But I wasn't about to argue either.

"You're saying they're granting me their powers? To balance things out between my father and me?"

"They might be," she answered judiciously. "That's one possibility."

I resisted the urge to throw up my hands in irritation. "I suppose you'll be returning to the temple soon. I understand you've left Kasie temporarily in charge."

"Who better to heal a kingdom than a healer?"

I wrinkled my brow. "Yes, but you must miss the temple." I knew most acolytes and priestesses could only dream of having received the honor Guinevere had been granted after only a few short months of living under the temple's roof.

She had not even been an acolyte. Merlin had simply selected her without any consultation or explanation.

I had no doubt Merlin had chosen wisely, but still, Guinevere sometimes seemed to lack a proper appreciation for the very great honor she had received. One that many women would kill for.

Well, if they weren't pacifist priestesses.

"Is there anything else you wish to speak with me about, Morgan?" Guinevere asked.

I got the sense that she was prodding, searching for an answer she already had. Just waiting for me to say it aloud.

I thought of my dreams. The burning cottage. I had still not told Draven about it. Last night, I had thought it best if he simply slept.

I could tell Guinevere. She was a reassuring presence at the very least. I might not understand her fully. But that didn't mean I didn't trust her.

I looked past her at where Lancelet leaned against a pillar a ways down the hall, astutely studying her nails.

"No, there's nothing else." I forced a smile. "Thank you for setting me free from that room, however. You were right. I did need a break."

We walked towards Lancelet.

"Draven's gone back to your room," she announced as we drew near. "I can walk you back, then see Guinevere to her chamber."

I shook my head. "There's no need for that. I can find my own way. Take care of your—" I stopped myself. I had almost said "Take care of your lady." "Take care of the High Priestess," I said firmly. "I'll speak with you both again soon."

When I entered our rooms, Draven was sitting on a seat by the window, speaking to two men.

The four of us spoke for a while, discussing the plans that had to be made.

Then the two men left, and Draven and I were alone.

"I didn't think you'd want to go down to the main hall for supper. So I had food brought up for us." He gestured to a table across the room that had been set with two chairs and a lavish tray atop it, holding a mix of grilled seafood, roasted vegetables, and an assortment of fresh fruits.

"You were right." I threw myself backwards onto the large, four-poster bed and then flipped onto one side, looking out the window. Sea birds flew past, and even from here, I could hear the ocean waves.

"It must be nice to live by the sea all of the time," I mused dreamily.

"A little cold, too, though," Draven observed as the wind rattled against the window pane.

He crossed over to the large stone hearth and, crouching down, began to make a fire. I watched him as his hands skillfully arranged the logs, placed the tinder, then coaxed the flames to life. He moved with purpose, not bothering to summon a servant to do what might easily be done himself.

When the fire was blazing hot, he rose and crossed over to the table. Uncorking a bottle of glistening ruby red wine, he filled two goblets and carried one to me.

I sat up, took a sip, and closed my eyes. "Mmm. That's good."

"The waves, the views, the wine. Are we moving to Tintagel?" Draven jested. He sat down on the bed beside me and eyed the tight-fitting red corset I wore laced up over my black tunic.

"I've been wanting to unlace this all day," he said, moving his hands over the planes of my stomach. I sucked in a breath. "All through that meeting."

"Well, why didn't you?" I teased. "Right there in the council room? It's not like you haven't broken with convention in such a place before." I thought of the throne room, and a quiver of hot memory went through me.

"I thought you might prefer... privacy. This time." Leaning forward, he moved his face up over my stomach, hot breath warming my belly until he reached my breasts. Then he grinned. Working his teeth carefully, he pulled out one of the red corset ribbons, holding it in his mouth.

"Are you going to undo the entire thing that way?" I asked with interest.

"I could," he bragged. "But no, too slow."

I watched as his hands moved over me, deft fingers unlacing quickly then sliding the corset top off my body.

"Too many layers," he growled, eyeing the tunic underneath, and I giggled.

His hands slid up and underneath, tugging the tunic over my body.

And then I was bare, lying there as he looked down at me with open admiration.

"Mine," he said, running his fingers over one of my nipples. He cupped my other breast. "Also mine."

"As long as you accept my rule equally," I said softly, arching a little under his hands and gaze.

I reached my hands up and wrapped them around his horns, then drew him down to me, licking the tip of each black, curved piece of bone until he gasped.

"Willingly and eternally," he managed to choke out, his emerald eyes fierce with longing.

He pulled back to trace a line down my stomach with one finger, then stopped at the top of my leather trousers and picked up the goblet of wine he had set down on the bedside table.

He lifted it—not to his mouth as I'd expected, but over me—and let a dribble of the rich, red stuff spill onto my chest, first over one breast then the other.

I gasped. "It's lucky," I breathed, "that the bedspread is red damask."

"Isn't it?" Draven agreed. "I just love a good damask."

Then he lowered his mouth to my wine-soaked breast and sucked.

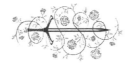

When it was over, I lay staring out the window and listening to the waves crashing against the rocks below as Draven lay with his head resting against my breasts. Slowly, I stroked a hand through his hair. After all we had been through in this place, perhaps it was strange that I felt as relaxed as I did. But the sea drew me. Perhaps Draven was right and we should live by water.

I thought of our cottage in the little forest glade.

"You didn't sleep last night."

I moved, startled. "What do you mean? Yes, I did."

"No, you didn't, Morgan. And you looked terrible today."

I flipped over to face him, narrowing my eyes. "Terrible? I thought we'd just established you thought I looked the opposite of terrible."

He grinned, his eyes moving down my unclothed body with a hunger still clearly unsated. "You always look the opposite of terrible to me. Still, compared to how beautiful you look when well-rested, you looked... well, beautifully unrested."

"What a confusing conversation," I complained. "Of course, I slept. I was just... restless, that's all."

"Hmph," was all he said, but the look he was giving me told me he didn't believe a word. "You need to sleep, Morgan. You're drained."

"What? You think Tintagel is going to be attacked again? Tonight?" I said lightly, tracing my fingers over his chest, over the curling hairs covering his nipples.

Perhaps it wasn't as ridiculous as I made it sound.

He shivered, then squeezed my waist. "Stop, I'm trying to talk to you."

"And I'm trying to talk to you," I said, pushing myself against him. Already, I could feel him stirring. "You want me. Again. Greedy, greedy Siabra prince."

"I'll fuck you again after this if that's what you want. All night long." He bit down on my shoulder, and I gasped. Now I truly was wet again.

"Now," I breathed. "Do it now."

"First tell me you'll sleep after," he growled. "Tell me you won't resist. You need to rest."

Lust subsided momentarily. "I...can't," I admitted.

I pushed myself upright.

"Why not?"

"Because..." I took a deep breath. "He's in my head."

"Who?"

"My father."

Draven sat up and leaned back against the headboard, folding his well-muscled arms over his chest.

"Well, fuck. Tell me."

"He burned our cottage down," I revealed. "I didn't want to tell you... before."

"Before the battle?" Draven scowled. "How long has this been going on, Morgan?"

"Just one night, I swear. The night Ulpheas showed up. The night he died." Did I tell Draven everything? "My father tried to grab me. In the dream. I fought him. When I woke up, Ulpheas was there."

"And what? You think that means something?"

I shrugged helplessly. "I don't know. Part of me wondered..."

"Wondered what?"

"Wondered if I'd somehow... brought Ulpheas to me," I admitted.

"As in, you think you might have stitched him?" Draven stroked his chin. "An interesting thought. Were you trying to save him? Did you sense what was going on?"

"Either way, it was too late. Pointless. Like everything I do."

Draven's eyes widened slightly. "Pardon me?"

"Do I make things better, Draven? Or do I make them worse?" I burst out. "This power I have. Excalibur, the grail. Why do I have it? Why did Excalibur bond to me in the first place?"

"I thought we already knew that. Your blood..."

"Yes, my Three-cursed fae blood," I spat. "But is that all it is? I don't know..."

"What is it you're really trying to say? What are you afraid of, Morgan?"

"I killed my own fucking brother, Draven," I said. "That's kind of... a big deal."

The raven-haired fae prince smiled slightly. "Is it?"

"Very well, so you killed yours, too," I acknowledged. "But..."

"But what? But absolutely nothing. He was trying to *kill* you, Morgan. I don't care who he was. He deserved to die. Just like Tabor did. You gave him a chance. You did more than I would have. You nearly spared his life."

"Yes," I acknowledged. "But..."

"There is nothing to regret, Morgan. And you know that. This still isn't what it's about. What is it really about?"

I stared at him. He was right. Daegen would have killed me. I had been weak when I'd offered to let him go. He would have run right back to my father and then what? He would simply have lived to come against me another day.

"I'm afraid my father will get me. Take me back. That he'll… I don't know… use me somehow. That I'll wind up doing terrible things for him, Draven. He says he loves me. He says I'm part of his family."

Draven laughed wryly. "Family. Right. Fae fucking family."

"They can't all be like this," I said desperately. "Not all of them."

"Not all. Just the royal ones." He touched my cheek. "Ours won't be. I swear to you, Morgan."

"No," I agreed. "Ours will be completely normal. Just you, me, our little niece Medra who was literally born and bred to bring down kings, and my perpetually sleeping younger brother. It'll be a perfect fairytale."

Draven looked slightly hurt by this. "Who wants fucking perfection?"

"What?"

"Families aren't meant to be perfect, Morgan. Anyone who ever claims to have a perfect family is lying. Have you seen mortal families? They squabble and hit and lie and…"

"Very well, I get the picture." I wrinkled my brow. "Do they all hit?"

"Well, the children do." He grinned. "But it's not all bad."

"No?" I asked dubiously.

"No. Think of Lancelet's. Have you ever been to her parents' house? It's a madhouse." He shook his head, smiling, and I could tell he'd kept a good memory of what he'd seen there. "I went to thank Lancelet's mother for the baby carrier. At least three children were fighting in the dirt outside. Noble children, too! And then two more ran by arguing. Another ran up, snot-nosed and crying, saying she'd fallen into the pig pen."

"And? What did Lancelet's mother do?"

"Oh, it was her father, actually. He came outside—he'd been inside reading—and picked up the snotty one and took her inside for a bath. Nothing more. No big fuss."

"And Lancelet's mother?" I prodded. "Did she stop the children from fighting?" I hadn't been to Lancelet's family home in years. Arthur had so rarely permitted me to visit.

"No, she just ignored them, and in a few moments, they were playing and laughing again. Like children. Like ordinary brothers and sisters. She apologized for the noise, and I said it was fine, and"—he shrugged—"it was fine."

"And that's what you want?" I guessed. "A bevy of children? A pig pen?"

I had to admit, I wasn't sure I was ready for any of that. I didn't know if I wanted to be a mother. Ever.

He chortled. "Children? We already have it, Morgan. All of it."

"What do you mean?"

"I mean, look around. Who came to Brightwind? Hawl, Lancelet, Galahad, Gawain, Guinevere..."

"A lot of 'G' names," I observed. "We ought to have named our children better."

"Not to mention Crescent, Sir Ector, Dame Halyna," he went on, grinning. "And yes, Medra and Kaye. And then there's Lyrastra and Odessa back in Myntra. And others I'm sure I've forgotten. We don't need a mortal family or a fucked up fae one. We already have our own. Mortal and fae. A little fucked up, sure. But ours."

He was right.

"We have to protect them," I said, hands tightening in the sheets. "If my father ever hurt them... If he ever used me to get at them..."

"Ah, now that's your true fear, isn't it? Not any guilt or shame you may or may not feel for killing a murderous, treacherous brother you hardly knew. But this. Becoming like your father."

A lump formed in my throat. "He scares me more than Uther did."

"But you never let Uther bring you down," Draven said softly. "You survived. You made sure your family survived, too."

I nodded.

"You'll survive Gorlois le Fay, too. We all will."

"You can't possibly know that," I said.

He ran his hands through his hair. "Fine. You're right. I don't. Some of us won't. But most of us will, Morgan. You will."

"I won't have you dying for me."

"That's not your choice to make," he said shortly. "And if the gods are willing, we'll both come out of this. But if I die saving your life, then it's a choice I'm ready to make."

"And I for you, you stubborn fucking fae," I spat.

He shrugged. "We can fight over it. Who dies for who."

"Very romantic."

He grinned. "I aim to please."

"What does he want?" I said out loud.

"He wants you, clearly. And besides you, he wants everything. Everything, Morgan. And we can't let him have it."

"Total dominion." I nodded. That was what Daegen had essentially confirmed. I hesitated. "Do you really think Medra is the key to my father's downfall as Orcades believed?"

"Not at all," Draven said almost instantly. "The prophecy is bunk."

"But Arthur..."

He laughed. "A coincidence. Oh, it chimed very nicely with the prophecy, I'll give you that."

"But he did die the day she was born," I insisted. "Just as the prophecy said."

"That's one interpretation. Doesn't the prophecy also say she'll bring about the end of the world?"

"'In the child's hands, lies the end of the world,'" I quoted. "Not my favorite line."

"Well, we just need to keep her far away from her grandfather."

I nodded. "Just as I promised her mother I'd do." I'd sworn to Orcades I would kill our father myself.

"You may not believe this, Morgan," Draven said, pulling me against him. "But you're stronger than he is."

He was right. I didn't believe that. It seemed impossible.

"If I am, it's only because I have Excalibur. And what happens when I destroy the sword?"

"Perhaps your father's power will break," Draven suggested. "Don't forget we have the grail, too."

"It can't be that easy." I yawned.

"All of this talk of world doom making you sleepy, my silver one?" He stroked my hair, then kissed the top of my head. "Rest now. I'll guard you."

It went unspoken between us that he could guard my body. But could he guard my mind?

"The true dreamings... Those I might be able to teach you to block eventually if they become a burden. But the world you brought us both to? Our cottage?" I felt Draven sigh. "That's something else entirely. Try to stay away from that place, Morgan. Can you do that?"

I hoped I could. "I'll try."

"Good. And I'll be here. I mean it. I'll keep watch. Just sleep now. Relax your body and rest." He ran his hand over my back again and again, rubbing my tired muscles. It was bliss.

My eyes closed. I thought of Medra. Little Medra. My niece.

Did even babies dream?

It was the last thing I wondered as I fell asleep.

CHAPTER 14 - MORGAN

All of the wise ones were gone.

Merlin. Caspar. Yes, even bloody Tyre.

There was no one to teach me how to shield my mind completely or to explain the dream world I visited when I closed my eyes—to explain just where it was, what it was.

I knew only one other true dreamer. My mate. And I knew even he had struggled to fully block his dreams when his father had tried to use them to his own advantage.

So when I wound up in the exact place I didn't want to be, it should really have been no surprise.

I was an ignorant girl, just as Daegen had said, in many ways.

The cottage was ash and ruins now.

I walked down the little path towards the pile of rubble. Blackened pieces of wood and charred stone were all that remained.

I thought of the pretty cookware in the kitchen. The colorful rugs strewn over the cottage floors. Then I thought of the paintings. Draven's paintings. They had covered an entire wall, copies of sketches and paintings that he had made in the waking world.

Nimue. My heart ached as I thought of the charcoal drawing of Nimue, Draven's daughter, that had hung in the cottage. The real one would be back in Myntra somewhere. Even so, it meant something to me—to have the copy destroyed, to have the cottage and everything within it destroyed so viciously by someone who claimed to love me.

I heard the crunch of pebbles on the path behind me.

"Your own brother, Morgan." The tone was reproachful. Yet something else lay hidden behind it. Dreadful though it was, I thought I sensed mirth.

Slowly, I turned to face my father. "You sent Daegen against me. You knew what could happen."

"Oh, I suspected. But until you slew him, I had no idea just how ruthless you could be. Or how powerful." A jubilant expression crossed his bearded face.

"I'm not ruthless," I said sharply. "I gave him a chance to live."

"Did you? Then you did more than I would have."

"I have no doubt," I said disdainfully. "Are you even mourning for your son?"

He stroked his beard as if he had not given it much thought until then. "Daegen. He was a good weapon. An asset, yes." He smiled. "Fortunately, I have other sons."

"And daughters, I'm sure. So you don't need me," I snapped.

"I have only one daughter like you, Morgan," Gorlois le Fay said. "Only one child who is the true child of my heart."

"The child of your ambition."

"Ambition. An interesting word. Is it something we share, I wonder? I imagine you to be a true woman of ambition. Ambition and daring. Why, the way you turned the tide of that battle." He made an appreciative sound. "Truly impressive."

"If it was so impressive, why didn't you expect it?" I shook my head. "You had no idea what I would do until it was too late."

His eyes narrowed slightly, and it was my turn to smile in triumph.

"I drew from you, Father. I pillaged your power. That storm—you had no idea I could stop it, did you? It would have killed me. Would you have cared?"

He waved a hand. "The rest would have died, yes. But you? No. You would have survived."

"I would have been the only one," I shouted. "The only one left alive. Is that what you wanted?"

Flames erupted around me on the grass. A circle of fire. I made no attempt to put them out.

"You lured me there," I accused him. "Thousands died needlessly. Your people and mine."

"People?" My father laughed. "What do I care for people?"

"You could have found me when I was a child. Brought me back then," I said, following up on what Daegen had claimed. "Why didn't you do it then? Before I even knew what I was?"

My father frowned. "You were shielded from me."

"Until when?" I pushed. "When did you first sense me?"

I had many guesses. When I first used magic? When I touched Excalibur? When I stitched to Camelot into the Temple of the Three?

"I told you before. I sensed you more than once, caught glimpses of your presence. Once, it was a very strong telling. I had an inkling you might be connected to Pendrath then."

When I stitched through the portal.

"You sent the grail to Arthur," I guessed. "To try to lure me out."

He smiled. "I had many things in mind when I sent that insipid young ruler my grail."

I gnashed my teeth, remembering Arthur's plan. To use the grail to charge the sword—if not with Medra then with Kaye.

"In the end, there was no need to charge the sword or give your mortal brother any opportunity to use it," Gorlois observed. "He died. He was not needed. The sword chose you. You bind yourself to it more every day. And here we are."

"Now what?" I demanded.

"A war has begun. Your allies are angry. They've just been attacked. And what do mortals do when they're unfairly attacked? They gather and rally and then they go on the offensive." He rubbed his hands together. "I'm sure even now they're strategizing and plotting and gathering the largest army they can. Perhaps you'll even lead it."

"You'd like that, wouldn't you?" I said scornfully.

I looked into my father's cold, gray eyes and saw the bloodlust there. Perhaps it was the only thing which warmed him after millennia of boredom.

He *expected* us to come against him with our armies, for there to be battle after battle.

He was eager for it. Eager to watch thousands upon thousands of mortals and fae die trying to reach him and fail.

"You think you're invincible," I said aloud. "You truly must be in an impervious place, Father."

I caught a look of satisfaction in the fae patriarch's eyes, and as I did, I knew what I had to do.

"You are a part of me," my father intoned, mistaking my expression for one of temptation. "As much as I am a part of you. Come back to us. Come back to your rightful place. Cease these valiant but futile struggles."

I hesitated, purposely allowing him to glimpse indecision.

When he extended his hand to me, I was expecting it, and this time, I grasped it willingly.

In an instant, my vision warped and contorted.

A whirlwind of ancient memories and deific aspirations I could hardly comprehend flooding my consciousness. I felt the weight of ages, the burden of millennia of knowledge, battles fought in realms beyond mortal ken, the echoes of long-forgotten and broken oaths, and the cosmic majesty of a truly inhuman being.

For a moment, I was a vessel adrift in the vast ocean of my father's mind. Then I swam within the sea, searching for the insight I desired.

I glimpsed fragments. Fleeting images that hinted at what I sought.

I grasped them to me, clutching them like a drowning person might hold tight to floating pieces of debris.

Meanwhile, my own mind was being rummaged through. It was as if my thoughts were an open library and my father an austere scholar, sifting through the volumes, tossing aside what was of no interest to him.

I struggled to maintain my focus as snippets of my childhood, faces of the ones I loved, and vistas of the places I had seen and things I had done flickered in a disorienting sequence. Emotions surged and receded. Joy, pain, heartbreak, my father ruthlessly riddled through them all.

I delved deeper into him, trying to ignore the sense of invasion as the sacred sanctuary that was my essence was trampled on.

Shadowlike, I traversed the labyrinths of his mind like a mouse, nimble and silent, darting between the towering structures of memories and the more terrifying edifices of his desires. I slipped through the gaps, small and unobtrusive, avoiding his scrutiny while he was distracted with his own search.

And as I slipped through the cracks unnoticed, I found what I was looking for.

With relief, I grasped it like a crumb, then slipped it behind my back, a subtle intruder turned thief.

It was time to go.

I moved to leave... only to find myself chained. Each link tightened with every attempt I made to free myself.

Locked in, the assault continued. My father's consciousness hammered against mine like a barrage of thunderous waves. Consumed by his own pursuits, he seemed oblivious to my struggle.

Desperation clawed at me as he delved deeper and deeper, penetrating the recesses of my mind with pitiless calculation.

I was unfortified. Untrained. Untaught. A fledgling flapping against a probing storm. There!

I felt his triumph as he found what he sought. Some confirmation. It was me. I was the one. The true daughter. Not another mere copy, but the source.

I couldn't have cared less. All I wanted was for him to let me go. I hurled myself against the ramparts of my own mind, my consciousness in anguish, teetering on the brink.

And then I felt him turn. Not to withdraw, but to glance over at a small, secret recess I had buried deep.

No, I screamed silently. You cannot have that.

He pushed past me as if I were nothing.

I sensed astonishment as he lifted the curtain and peered inside.

Frantically, I pushed against the chains constricting me, only to feel them tighten once again, squeezing around me like a ruthless serpent.

My father was unsettled. A chord had been struck deep within him, shaking the foundations of his composure.

I launched myself against him as he balanced on the edge of something very much like fear. I was a desperate guardian, futilely trying to seal the breach before he could fully comprehend the depth of what he had seen.

But it was too late. The tide surged over me, pulling me down, chains and all, as the very fabric of all I held dear was swept asunder.

CHAPTER 15 - MORGAN

I woke up gasping like a woman who had been washed ashore on a beach after a tempest.

Guinevere stood over me, her face drawn and pale.

Letting out a breath, she released me—dropping an arm I hadn't even realized she'd been holding—and stepped back from the bed.

Behind her stood Draven.

"What happened?" he demanded. "Morgan, where did you go? What did you see?"

I sat up slowly, feeling groggy and weak, then looked at Guinevere without answering. "What did you do?"

"I got you out," she said simply. "You were trapped."

Draven shook his head. "That's an understatement. You were *dying*, Morgan."

"Dying?" I tried to take stock of myself. My body was trembling but whole. "I highly doubt that." I tried to smile at him, but he wouldn't return it.

"You were gasping for air. Your eyes were open but you couldn't see me. You wouldn't answer. I couldn't wake you."

I caught the edge of fear in his voice and understood.

"Like Kaye," I said softly. "You thought it was going to be like Kaye."

He said nothing.

"It was not the same thing," Guinevere said, turning towards Draven and putting a hand briefly on his arm. "But she was very weak. You did the right thing."

"Could I really..." I cleared my throat. "Could I really have died, Guinevere? In there?" Somehow I knew she already understood where I had been.

"You are drained, are you not? He did that." She looked back at me steadily from beneath long, dark lashes.

"*He*?" My voice was sharp. "I didn't mention a 'he.'"

"Your father was there in your dream, was he not?"

I stared at her. My desire for the wisdom and knowledge she might possess at war with my reluctance to trust her, to share more than I had to—for all our sakes.

Her hair had grown, I noticed. When I had first met her, it had been chopped roughly, as if she had cut it with a dull knife. Now the curly, brown locks nearly touched her shoulders. She was not the broken girl who had first come to the temple, running from my brother's assaults.

"I need to talk to Draven alone now," I said slowly.

She nodded and turned to go. Guiltily, I saw her touch a hand to one of the bed posts and wince. If I had been drained, so had she.

"Thank you. For whatever you did. Thank you, Guinevere."

She smiled briefly. "I am here to serve," was all she said before she left the room.

I turned to Draven, trying to dismiss the disconcerted feeling Guinevere had left behind.

"He knows. We need to go. Tonight."

I might have summoned Nightclaw to our window. We could have flown into the night without the need to sneak past guards or creep down dark corridors.

But after the Battle of Brightwind, after all we had already put the exmoors through, and more importantly, after Sunstrike had been injured, there was no way in hell I was going to ask the battlecats for anything else.

They would join us on this journey as companions. And that would be enough.

But to use them again as my father and his people used the exmoors, as mere mounts rather than sentient partners? No. Perhaps not ever again.

Besides, it was not so difficult to make our way past the guards King Mark had stationed around the palace.

Draven veiled us so that we blended with the dark shadows along every hall. He made us appear disinteresting, dull, and dark. Guards marched past us, talking without sparing a single glance.

We wound our way down through the levels of the seaside castle, reaching the under-croft, and then finally emerging through a passage beyond the palace walls.

The moon cast a silvery glow upon the sand as we stepped out onto the quiet beach.

A horse whinnied, and I turned, expecting to see the two mounts Draven had arranged to have left there.

Instead, I saw a hulking, dark shape break away from the castle walls, the towering figure a looming silhouette against the night sky.

Another figure stepped away from the wall. Then another and another.

"I told you this is what they would do." The Bearkin's voice rumbled across the beach. Hawl still wore the leather breastplate they had equipped for the Brightwind battle. "Didn't I tell you? Didn't I?"

"Crescent!" I narrowed my eyes as the dark-skinned slender man stepped up beside Hawl, looking sheepish. "You told them?"

"They already knew," he said.

I looked around. Crescent and Galahad, we had expected to be there.

Hawl, Lancelet, Guinevere, Gawain, Sir Ector, and Dame Halyna, however...

"You cannot all come," I exclaimed. "There are reasons..."

Draven stepped up beside me, a hand on my shoulder. "I thought we'd already discussed this. Crescent, Galahad, we've made plans..."

"And those plans are not changing." Galahad held up his hands. "We didn't invite them here, Morgan."

Lancelet moved to stand beside Hawl. "No, he certainly didn't." The look she gave me was painfully accusatory. "Nor did you, Morgan. Just tell me why."

"I..." I struggled to put the right words in order. "You can't come with us. It's too dangerous."

"Dangerous?" Lancelet rolled her eyes. "It's like she forgets we all just fought a battle two days ago."

"I know," I said desperately. "And you survived. Again. Incredibly. But before that? What my brother put you through? Your arm is hardly healed."

"My arm is fine," she shot back. "I held a sword easily enough when I fought against your father's forces." She stressed the words "your father."

"I believe it. I'm sure you did. But that's just it," I protested. "He's my father. This is my..."

"Your what?" Lancelet interjected. "Your battle? Your land? Your what, Morgan?"

I licked my lips. "My responsibility. I don't want any of you dying. No one else has to die over this."

"No? Only you and Draven? And what happens if you fail? What happens if you don't make it because you were too stubborn and stupid to take backup along?" Lancelet demanded.

"The woman has a point," Hawl growled. "Seems foolish to go alone. There will be dangers. We shall face them readily, by your side."

"Besides, you can't exactly say no," Lancelet countered. "Not when you've already said yes. Did you lie to us Morgan, when you promised you wouldn't do this? Exactly what you're now trying to do. Sneaking off into the night." She shook her head in disgust. "Do promises mean nothing to you?"

"Friendships mean everything to me," I cried. "Yours. Hawl's. All of you mean everything to me. I need you here. I need you to be alive when we return."

"*If* you return," Lancelet said coolly.

A petite figure in pale blue robes brushed past Hawl and Lancelet.

"There's no need to fight," Guinevere said quietly. "You've made your decision, Morgan. And we've made ours. Where you go, I will follow. I have no other choice."

I looked at the High Priestess uncomfortably. "What do you mean?"

She met my eyes. "I mean without me, you will fail."

My temper rose. "That seems rather presumptuous, even for you, Guinevere."

She did not break my gaze. "Your dreams, Morgan. Your father's attacks on your mind will only grow worse. What did he see tonight?"

I looked around the group, scanning the familiar faces.

"He saw Medra," I confessed. "He knows she exists. I don't know what he made of what he saw. Whether he knows of the prophecy or if he simply saw a baby and that she was important to me somehow. But it was enough. Draven and I need to leave now."

"We all need to leave now," Hawl agreed.

"No," I said, still trying to argue. "That's not what I mean."

"We know what you mean. We also know you can't stop us," Guinevere said tranquilly. "Unless you plan to use force?"

The owl on her shoulder suddenly hooted and swiveled her head to look at me.

"No, of course not," I said, with shock. "I would never..."

"Good," the High Priestess said. "Then the matter is settled."

"Wait. There's still more." I took a deep breath. "You won't want to come. There will be no way out. We can't stitch. We won't. We're not bringing Crescent. No one will be permitted to try to stitch to us either. Even if they could manage to find us. We've... decided that."

"It may alert your father," Guinevere said. "I understand. No stitching. We will get by without it."

"Stitching. Bah. Long days on the road—that is what I look forward to. Dust-coated fur. The sweet taste of fresh meat on a fire at the end of the day. And moths. Delicious moths waiting to be swallowed, fresh and sweet in the cool evening air." Hawl snapped their jaw enthusiastically.

I looked at Gawain. "Crescent is staying behind. Do you understand this?"

The red-headed man nodded. "He'll act as regent for you in Pendrath."

"And he'll take care of Medra," Draven said quietly, looking at Crescent who gave a reassuring nod.

"She'll be like a second daughter to me. And I'll keep in close contact with Lyrastra and Odessa back in Myntra, of course. Odessa will visit from time to time to assess the state of our forces. Who will continue to be maintained by our noble Master-at-Arms." Crescent glanced at Sir Ector.

"Oh, I'm just here to say good-bye," the older knight said, looking at me with a sad fondness. "I won't burden you with my presence, Morgan. Never fear."

I felt my throat constricting. "Never. You could never be a burden. I would have been honored..."

He smiled. "It's all right, Morgan. Quests are best left for the young."

"I'll stay as well," Dame Halyna said. The stout-hearted blonde woman met my eyes. "I'll stay, and I'll pray. For your success, Morgan."

"Thank you," I said softly. "We can use all the prayers we can get."

Especially as I wouldn't be making any of them.

"Nothing's changed on my part," Galahad promised, looking at Draven and me. "I'll remain here in Tintagel, liaising with King Mark. I'll give him an explanation of where you've gone." He smiled ruefully. "At least a partial one."

I nodded. I knew I could trust him.

"I'll work with my father and Dame Halyna as well as Odessa," Galahad continued. "We'll bolster Tintagel's forces, if they'll allow it. And as we discussed, I'll keep in touch with Crescent in Camelot."

Draven nodded and clapped him on the shoulder.

"We'll miss you," I said softly. It would be strange not to be able to communicate with any of them. Not to have anyone following our journey. Even in such a short time amongst the fae, I had become spoiled by such marvels as stitching and portal arches. But as Guinevere had said, we would make do.

I turned to Hawl, Lancelet, Guinevere, and Gawain. "No one can follow us once we leave. No one can try to find us. We'll be completely out of touch. In the dark. Do you truly understand? Gawain, you'll be away from Taina and Crescent and…" I lamely trailed off.

"I might not ever see them again," Gawain finished. "Is that what you're trying to say? I understand. I'm coming. And I have no plans of dying along the way. Or on the way back." He quirked a smile that I had to meet. Gawain's smiles tended to do that. They were contagious.

"Guinevere," I said, trying again. "You're already weak from helping me this evening."

"But I'll get stronger," the High Priestess said calmly. "The more I do it."

"The more you do what?"

"The more I shield you from your dreams, Morgan."

Lancelet shot me an annoyed look. "I don't think you quite appreciate what Guinevere is giving up, Morgan. What she's offering."

"I do," I insisted. "She's offering to leave the Temple of the Three. For an extended period of time. But she's our High Priestess. The people need you, Guinevere."

"Not for an extended period of time," Guinevere corrected gently. "Forever."

I stared. "Forever? You can't be serious."

"I serve the Three. My service goes beyond the temple walls."

"We just lost Merlin," I exploded. "You're already the youngest High Priestess I've ever heard of. Perhaps this is your inexperience speaking. You were just appointed successor, Guinevere. You can't leave now."

"I can. I must." She paused. "I've already appointed a successor of my own."

I threw up my hands. "Let me guess. Kasie. She wasn't even trained for the role."

"Neither was I," Guinevere reminded me. "She'll be fine. She's exactly what the land needs."

"A healing touch," I grumbled. "Very literal of you."

"I am no longer High Priestess," Guinevere went on. "I am handmaiden to the goddesses. I go where they lead me. My path is with you."

"And the owl?" I asked, pointing to Tuva. "Does she fly back to Kasie?"

"No," Guinevere answered. "Merlin left me a choice. Tuva made one as well. She comes with us."

"You don't need to do this," I said quietly. "I don't want you to give this up, Guinevere. You should be High Priestess. It is an incredible honor."

"One I will always remember. I was High Priestess. But that is not all that I am." She touched a hand to my brow lightly. "Morgan, can you sleep?"

I wrinkled my brow. "Can I sleep? Of course I can sleep."

But I knew what she was getting at.

"Can you sleep without dreaming? Can you shield your mind unaided?"

I was silent.

"You cannot. And so I will be your shield. Along the way, I will guard your mind. You need to be able to sleep untroubled. Avoiding stitching—yes, that's a good start. But he will follow you however he can. You know this."

"Fine," I said tersely. I swept my arm out. "Fine. All of you. I suppose we can't stop you. Even though none of you know where we're even going."

"To the heart of evil," Hawl boomed out. "To the peak of doom."

"Well, that's certainly one way of putting it," Draven observed, trying to hide a wry smile.

"There will be dangers," Guinevere said. "But you have guides."

"And friends," Lancelet said, her face finally softening as she looked at me.

"The most persistent kind," I said, forcing a smile and grabbing her hand to squeeze.

Gawain gave Draven a playful shove. "You have no idea how persistent." He glanced at Hawl. "Of course, what I'm most looking forward to is Hawl's cooking."

"It's a treat," Draven agreed.

"Especially if they cook up that special recipe they once promised," Gawain said, a glimmer of mischief in his eyes. "Bugs have a lot of protein don't they, Hawl?"

"Oodles," Hawl agreed.

Draven groaned.

"Will you eat insects on the road, Guinevere?" I asked conversationally, seeing how far I could push the High Priestess. Former High Priestess, I corrected myself.

"I'll eat whatever the Three see fit to provide," she said calmly.

Lancelet blanched but said nothing.

"Well, we'd better get going," I said, forcing a cheerful tone. "Dawn will arrive soon."

"Better than breakfast," Lancelet muttered.

We were on our way.

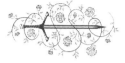

We crossed into Rheged just before dusk the next day.

Skirting the vast plains on which we had fought only days before, we had traveled along crumbling coastal roads to the north, following seaside cliffs and sandy beaches for the better part of the day.

At times, we came near the edge of the battlefield where huge piles of charred remains still smoked.

There had been too many bodies to bury. So those honors had been reserved for those loyal to Tintagel. The others had been burnt.

Guinevere discreetly slipped a scarf over her face when we drew too near the pyres. The rest of us simply stared grimly ahead.

As we crossed over into farmland, it seemed as if we might have passed through the worst of it and were leaving the battlefield and its bloody memories behind.

The first village we encountered was still bathed in the soft glow of the sun. At first glance, it appeared to be a typical farming community.

Only an eerie silence hanging in the air hinted at the truth.

The village, while small, seemed unusually abandoned. We rode past modest cottages, their doors hanging ajar, and glimpsed dishes still set on the table, food left in pots on the hearth.

Dark red stains covered the floors of many homes.

But I saw no bodies.

One of our horses whinnied uneasily. A noise from ahead had drawn the animal's attention.

Near a simple wooden house, a woman sat on the steps outside with a little boy crouched morosely beside her, scratching lines in the dirt with a stick.

In front of the woman lay a fallen soldier. At first glance, I assumed the man had been brought back from the battlefield, a conscript in my father's war.

I peered at the body curiously. So not all of the foot soldiers had been fae.

Previously obscured by the anonymity of his dark armor and the black metal mask all of the infantry had worn, now the man's face lay exposed. His mask rested a few feet away from him, as if it had rolled there when the woman pulled it off her loved one's body.

We rode quietly closer. As we neared, a chill went through me.

The soldier was no man. At least not any longer.

The man lying on the ground had been grotesquely transformed. What lay before the woman was a fusion of humanity and something else entirely.

The figure's skin was a sickly shade of olive, its brutish features contorted into a grimace of eternal agony. Ragged gashes and lacerations criss-crossed the creature's face, as if it had been whipped before being sent out into the battle. Tufts of coarse hair covered a misshapen skull, matted with blood and dirt.

Beside me, I heard Lancelet make a sharp, whimpering sound. I knew what she was being reminded of.

I slid from my horse and forced myself towards the woman.

"What happened here?"

For a moment, she didn't answer. Finally she lifted her face.

"We hid when they came home."

"Home?" I shook my head, not understanding. "Was this man your husband?"

"Was."

I looked at the man again and, for the first time, realized how he had died.

A pitchfork had been thrust through his chest, pinning him to the ground.

"There's a hole in the cellar. We hid there. But he came again. You don't know what you can do until you have to protect your child." Her voice dropped to a whisper. "Even from his own father." She placed a hand on the little boy's head who still played by her side, as if he were oblivious to the gruesome sight nearby.

I nodded, then reached into my pocket and pulled out a small leather pouch and set it down beside her. "Coin. For the journey."

"Journey?"

"You can't stay here," I said as gently as I could. "It's only a two day journey by foot. Take your child and go to Tintagel. Tell them..." I hesitated upon which title and name to use. Which one would inspire the least fear in this poor woman? "Tell them Morgan Pendragon sent you. Ask for Galahad. When you see him, tell him I said you are to be cared for."

She touched a hand to the purse as if uncertain it was real but made no reply.

I walked back to my horse and took the reins, leading it as we moved slowly through the rest of the village.

Most of the younger men and women from the village must have been taken to form foot soldiers in my father's powerful army.

But that did not explain what had happened to the rest of the village or why this man had returned, twisted in shape, to harm his wife and child.

Only when we reached the village square did I finally understand.

The putrid scent of decay lingered in the air as we neared the remains of what had once been a festive feast.

As the ground beneath the horses' hooves squelched with a sickening wetness, I put a hand to my mouth.

Tables had been dragged out and set up around the square. In the center lay the remnants of a massive bonfire where spits of roasted meat had been cooked.

Human meat.

Only gnawed bones remained now, littering the bloodstained tables.

In my mind, I could hear the echoes of the villagers' final moments. The desperate pleas for mercy for the children. The anguished cries of loved ones as unspeakable acts were committed by those who had returned from battle, corrupted by whatever my father had done to them, transformed beyond recognition.

Draven slid from his horse and came towards me, standing by my side as we bore witness.

At that moment, I couldn't bear to be touched. He must have sensed this for he made no attempt to do so. Simply stood by my side, vigilant and present.

All I could think of was that we had two pack horses.

I looked back at where Gawain rode at the rear of our party. "The pack horses. Take one. Bring it to the woman. Take enough food for her and the child."

Gawain nodded. He must have known how very close I was to demanding—nay, begging—him to return with the woman and not simply give her the horse. To escort her all the way to Brightwind and away from this place that had once been her happy home and was now cursed ground.

And so we spent the first night in the silent kingdom of Rheged.

BOOK 2

CHAPTER 16 - MEDRA

"**I** 'll tell you the truth. I honestly don't know what to do with her."

Crescent was talking to someone about me.

"None of the other children will play with her. I brought Taina over from Noctasia. You know that's been my plan all along. I introduced them, urged them to play together, then left them alone together for a little while. Only half an hour, mind you. But it was a complete disaster. I've never seen Taina so frightened." He hesitated. "She was... rather unkind."

"Taina? I've never known her to be cruel to another child." It was Sir Ector's voice, slow and plodding. He seemed so old to me. Was he the most ancient man in Camelot?

"Nor have I. But with Medra, she was different. I practically begged her to give the girl another chance. I had hoped they would be playmates. But she..." Crescent was hesitating again. "Well, she said Medra was too strange."

She had called me a *freak*.

Stupid little Taina. I didn't want to play with her anyhow. Her and her dumb dolls.

I had ripped her favorite doll's head clean off and tossed it out the window. She hadn't told her father *that*. Was it because she was frightened? Of him? Or of me?

I crept along in the shadows, hiding behind bushes as Crescent and Sir Ector strolled through the cloisters that edged the Queen's Garden.

"The truth is, Sir Ector," Crescent was saying, "she *is* strange. Surely we may admit that, at least to one another. I have never met a child such as her. Not that I don't care about Medra very much, regardless of how different she may be," he hastened to add.

"But she is half-fae." Sir Ector sounded puzzled. "Surely you have seen such things as this. The fae have many features I might find odd or different, but such is your way. Admittedly, perhaps Medra is more unique."

"Unique?" Crescent gave a laugh that sounded strained. "More unique than any other fae child. More unique than any fae child I have read about or heard of. And believe me, I have tried to find one. I've had clerks and librarians scouring the records of Myntra searching for a suitable comparison. A precedent if you will, for, well, for whatever Medra is."

"And what is it exactly that you think she is?" Sir Ector's voice was still very soft, but I detected a slight chill. "She is a half-human, half-fae child. Just as I once believed Morgan to be. But she is still a child, Crescent. A very young, very inexperienced child in need of our protection and care. Let neither of us forget that."

"A child, yes! But a month ago, she was a babe in arms, Sir Ector." Crescent's voice had turned shrill. "And a few weeks later she was a toddling thing, walking, then running, then speaking sooner than any child anyone in Camelot has ever seen. Her nurses would not stay, Sir Ector. They simply would not stay. Have you ever known a woman to leave an infant they nursed? I never have. Usually you have to beg them to leave. I certainly had to with Taina's. Her old nurse still visits at least once a month." He gave a stiff laugh which Sir Ector did not return. "Well, you get the general idea."

"She frightens people," Sir Ector said. I could almost picture him scratching his chin. "Yes. I understand what you are saying, Crescent. I suppose the question is—does she frighten you?"

A pause. A long pause.

"No. She doesn't frighten me," Crescent said finally. "And I care for the child. I would never abandon her. I know my duty."

I had been biting my lower lip hard without even realizing it. Now I let out a breath and let my body relax, sinking down into the soft grass.

My lip hurt. My hands were full of something.

Looking down, I saw I had pulled all of the grass up around me. There was a circle of dirt surrounding the spot where I crouched.

Well, grass would grow back. Unlike Taina's doll's head.

Blood was trickling down my chin from where I had split my lip. I wiped it away with a dirt-smeared hand.

"But doesn't it bother you?" Crescent had lowered his voice. Perhaps another person would not have been able to hear him from where I hid. "She's stronger than she should be. Larger. Smarter."

But I could. I could hear all sorts of things most people couldn't hear.

The mice running through the castle walls. The ants as they scurried through the dirt. And voices. Always the voices. They came in my dreams, and I tried to shut them out.

"It wouldn't make sense for her to be one thing without the others," Sir Ector answered. "She couldn't be bigger without being stronger. And it would be odd if she looked like an older child without having the comprehension of one."

His voice was calm and soothing. It reminded me of the sparrows who had built a nest outside my window. For days, a female and her mate had brought twigs and twine, grass and feathers, until the nest was complete.

Then the female had laid a clutch of four perfect little eggs.

"It's more than her comprehension, though what she understands is incredible," Crescent replied. "It's her anger."

Crouching in the grass, I shivered and licked the blood from my lips.

"What do you mean?"

"Surely you've heard the servants speak of them. She'll have tantrums. Fits of rage. She loses control, flees from me when I try to calm her. She'll hide. Even break things." Crescent rubbed a hand over his face. "The servants have said she may be taking things."

"Well, it's her castle. She can take what she wants, can't she?" Sir Ector sounded more amused than I'd expected. Not angry with me.

"Yes, but it is my duty to oversee this castle and everyone and everything in it while Medra's aunt and uncle are away. I don't think they'd take kindly to her stealing things. Or worse, stealing and then breaking them."

"Well, I doubt the girl is making off with priceless works of art and destroying them. She's probably snatching little trinkets, that sort of thing. She's troubled. The poor thing has no mother, no father. Isn't it to be expected?"

"In any ordinary child, yes, of course. But in Medra... the anger is so intense."

It was bad to be angry. It was bad to make other people angry.

That was what Crescent was really saying.

Somehow I knew this. Yet I couldn't stop doing it. I couldn't stop what I felt.

As soon as I had discovered what anger *was*, it seemed I had always been filled with it.

I was angry because people were afraid. I was angry because they looked at me as if I were different.

It didn't help to know Crescent thought I was strange and different, too. So different from his daughter. Stupid Taina.

It felt good to frighten people when I wanted to.

Besides, they were mostly frightened anyway.

"I'm afraid…" Crescent began, and I shivered again. "I'm afraid servants will soon start leaving."

Sir Ector was quiet for a while. "Then the girl needs training. Discipline. A tutor."

"I agree." Crescent sounded relieved. "Will you help?"

"Absolutely. Send her to Dame Halyna and me. We'll whip some sense into her."

I froze.

"Not literally whip," Sir Ector said hastily. "You take my meaning. The girl needs a gentle but firm hand."

He made me sound like a horse. Was that what I was? A very special animal? Not like the rest of the people in this castle?

Despite what Sir Ector had offered, I could still sense Crescent's hopelessness.

Soon he would give up on me.

Just like the man I remembered holding me in his arms when I was no more than a squalling baby had done.

My uncle, Draven.

I snuck out of the garden again without being noticed, then crept up the stairs to my room in the tower.

It had been my aunt's when she was a girl. They had moved her things to a larger chamber. She was an empress now, they said.

The sparrows weren't chirping anymore.

I leaned out my window to peer at the cobblestone path below, checking to see if it was still there.

Down on the path, a nest was split open. Four broken eggs lay beside it.

CHAPTER 17 - MORGAN

It couldn't be like the village everywhere. And thank the Three, it wasn't.

There was green beyond the burned-out, hollowed hamlet. Fresh air and trees and a cleansing wind that was blowing in off the sea.

We camped high on a clifftop that evening, in the shelter of a strand of trees.

After helping to set up the tents, I sat on a rock looking out at the great Moring—the sea that touched all of Eskira to the north. Behind me, Gawain was constructing a small wall of rocks to keep the wind out as he began to build the fire.

The thought remained in my mind: What else would we find in Rheged?

A hand touched my shoulder, and I jumped.

"You're still thinking about the village," Draven said. Taking a dagger from his belt, he sat down on a boulder across from me and started to sharpen it.

"She killed her own husband," I said quietly.

"She did," Draven agreed. "To save her child and herself. Very brave."

"I'm not saying she didn't do the right thing. But she should never have had to do it at all." I hesitated. "What if it's like that everywhere? In every village?"

Draven met my eyes. "It could be. It might not. We'll have to find out."

I wasn't sure I could take the sight of more villages like the one we had passed through. But I didn't say it aloud. Draven already knew what I was thinking anyway. He knew I was worried. He also knew I didn't want to seem weak.

Draven was still watching me. "What is it, Morgan? I know you're not afraid of fighting those things. We've fought worse."

I stayed quiet.

"Are you afraid you'll be like the woman? Is that it?" he asked softly. "That you'll have to... what? Put me down?"

I flinched. His words had struck true. "You never know. How can we say it won't happen? We have no idea how my father is making those things."

"We don't. But we have our own defenses. We're not exactly helpless. We're more prepared than those poor people were."

"It's my fault," I said. "My fault that this happened to them."

"You had nothing to do with it."

"But I did! I did, Draven. None of this would be happening right now if it weren't for *me*. He's coming for me. Trying to get to me. The battle at Brightwind would never have happened if it weren't for that. How many innocent men and women died that day because of me? And do they even know that's what they died for? Will we ever tell them? Or will I just keep on hiding?"

"Hiding? You're not hiding."

"Oh, but I am," I said bitterly. "I was *born* into hiding, Draven. All my life I've been hiding from things I never even understood."

"You're not hiding now," he said firmly. "Look at where we are, Morgan. Is this hiding?"

Slowly I shook my head.

"No, it's not. You're going straight towards him. You've nothing to be ashamed of."

"Perhaps not ashamed. But guilty? Yes. I could have given myself up. Gone with him. Just given him the grail and Excalibur."

"And what do you think would have happened then? Peace and harmony throughout the land? No." Draven shook his head. "What's happening right now has been a long time coming, Morgan. Odessa tried to tell me, but I didn't understand then. Your father wants you back because he's weaker without you. He can't truly strike—not fully. Not until he has you back. Going to him willingly and sacrificing yourself would only strengthen him more. And then what? His plans for dominating Aercanum would simply advance more quickly."

"A world ruled by Gorlois le Fay," I murmured with a shudder.

"He wants power and control. And he believes in his total superiority." Draven stood up and slid the dagger back into its sheath. "We were closer to that sort of thing in Myntra. That belief in the superiority of the fae race. And it lingers." He gave me a hard look. "It might be easy to stoke such a belief again. Only too easy for your father."

I understood. Without Draven and me to keep the tide from turning, Myntra could just as easily become an oppressor to the mortals of Eskira.

"Besides," Draven said, "think of the village. Your father has been positioned in Rheged for more than a hundred years, Morgan."

The question lingered in the air. What had he done to this once proud kingdom? What else would we find down this dark road we traveled?

"Whatever we find," Draven said softly. "I'll be there by your side. To the end."

"Will it be?" I whispered. "Our end? I won't let him have me, Draven. No matter what."

My mate leaned forward and brushed his hand over my cheek as softly as a butterfly's wings. "I would never let that happen, silver one. Never."

"No matter what?" I pressed him.

His eyes were steady. "No matter what."

"And what cheerful matters are we discussing over here this evening?"

Lancelet brushed between us, moving to stand at the edge of the cliffs overlooking the rocks below.

"Hawl says dinner is almost ready," she continued.

I glanced over at where Hawl hunched by the fire, stirring something in a large pot. "Hawl is no more than ten feet away and could easily tell us that themselves."

"Yes, well." Lancelet let out a huff. "You looked as if you were being morose and depressing and needed a good interruption."

My lip quirked. "I see. Thank you, then, I suppose."

"Don't mention it," Lancelet said brusquely.

"Any cockroaches on the menu tonight?" Draven inquired seriously, turning towards Hawl.

The Bearkin growled menacingly. "I ought to say yes. It would serve you right."

"So that's a no then?" Draven's eyes twinkled with mirth.

"I should never have told you and Gawain about their nutritional value. You'll never let a day go by without mentioning insects in my cooking," Hawl grumbled. "When I do include them, you can be sure I'll only mention it after you've had second helpings and not before."

"I'd be all right with that," Draven said consideringly. "What you don't know can't hurt you."

He winked at me and I rolled my eyes.

"I'm fairly sure my entire life disproves that saying," I said ironically.

Lancelet snorted.

"Shall we play a good drinking game after supper?" Gawain suggested, coming to sit down on a log by the fire. "Although, Guinevere, I suppose you won't be able to join in."

The former High Priestess had emerged from her tent where she had been resting and now came to stand near the fire.

"Not at all," she said. "I'd be pleased to."

"To drink?" Lancelet sounded so startled, I nearly laughed. "But you're…"

"Not the High Priestess any longer," Guinevere reminded her. "And not bound to any of the rules of the temple."

There was silence around the fire. One might have heard a pin drop. I know I heard at least one cricket chirp.

I held very still, afraid of what I might find if I dared to look at Lancelet's face.

"This is quite new territory for me," Guinevere went on, as if she hadn't noticed the awkward stillness.

"Drinking, you mean?" Gawain joked. He caught my eye and winked. I cringed, hoping he wasn't about to go any further with his teasing.

Guinevere laughed. She had a very pretty laugh. I was sure Lancelet was well aware of it. "Oh, no. As a king's daughter, I am quite familiar with drinking. Not so much personally, but then we always had wine served with every meal."

I tried to imagine Guinevere before she had come to Camelot. A young woman who believed she was being wed to the powerful king of a neighboring kingdom to strengthen alliances between nations. She had been bartered by her family like property and had not chosen Arthur herself. But then, that was nothing new for our two kingdoms.

It would change, however, with our generation. There was no reason to continue such cruel and antiquated traditions.

"You've never drunk to excess is what you're saying," Gawain clarified. "Well, my dear Guinevere, there's a first time for everything. And you know what they say about fae wine…"

"No, what's that?" Guinevere asked with surprising innocence.

"Don't tell me you've actually brought fae wine, Gawain," Draven interrupted.

"Why not?" Gawain replied, unruffled. "For times like these…" He glanced at me, then briefly at Lancelet. "Well, you know what they say about wine and life…"

"What's that? Raise your glass high tonight because tomorrow you might not have a hand to hold it by?" Draven quipped.

I elbowed him. His jest seemed uncomfortably macabre after what we'd witnessed that day.

But I could see what Gawain was trying to do. Bring levity to a party of travelers that had already become uncomfortably subdued. There was a long way to go before we reached the darkest part of the road. It wouldn't do to let our spirits sink already.

Gawain grinned. "The goddess Marzanna is a fickle lady." He reached down beside him and lifted a sizable leather wineskin, then sang, *"Spring is here, the sun is warm, the flowers are in bloom. So drink you must, drink you must, drink to your watery tomb."*

"Your singing voice is an offense to the Three if I ever heard one," Lancelet said drily. "Not to mention, the song makes no sense whatsoever."

"Is that really what we're toasting to?" Guinevere asked, sitting down on the log and looking curiously at Gawain. "A watery grave?"

"I've always thought it strange that Marzanna was the goddess of death but her festival was in the spring," Lancelet observed, moving to stand closer to the fire.

"Well, it's to celebrate the end of winter, I always thought," I said.

I remembered a time when Lancelet and I had stood on the riverbank in the spring alongside Merlin and Galahad and watched as children sang the very same song Gawain had just mangled. The laughing children threw a burning effigy of the goddess into the churning waters. As was tradition every spring for the goddess's festival.

It seemed so long ago now. Another lifetime.

A watery tomb. I had believed I might drown in a watery tomb once. Vesper had pushed me into the pool in Meridium. Instead, I had awoken in my sister's prison.

I pushed the memories away.

"Just what's in that wineskin exactly?" I said, trying to strike a lighter tone.

Gawain hesitated. "Fae wine, as I've said." He looked over at Draven. "Of Rychel's making."

Draven gave a low whistle. "Mermaid's Song."

I remembered the green-blue liquor his little sister had poured into my glass at her home as we all feasted and celebrated Draven's success in the Bloodrise.

"In that case," I said, forcing a smile, "Guinevere is in for quite a treat."

"Do we have enough glasses?" the curly-haired young woman asked cautiously.

"Glasses?" Hawl gave a deep resounding laugh. "Pass that wineskin over here, Gawain."

The red-haired warrior complied quickly. Hawl tipped the wineskin back.

"Excellent stuff, though a tad overly sweet," Hawl observed, brushing a paw across their brown-furred face as they lowered the wineskin. "Here. Pass it along." They handed the flask off to Guinevere who held it a moment then took a small sip.

"Delicious," she remarked, then held it up... to Lancelet who had appeared beside her. I watched their eyes meet.

Silence fell around the campfire for a second time that evening.

The sun was setting in blazing streaks of pink and orange, the fire was crackling, the sea breeze was blowing... and Lancelet and Guinevere were staring at one another as if they were the only two people in the world.

Gawain cleared his throat, and the moment was broken.

Lancelet snatched the wineskin and took a long chug that turned into a sputter.

Draven clapped her on the back as she pulled the skin back with a cough. "Good goddess, this stuff is potent."

Gawain's face was red from laughter. "Rychel's homebrew. Vela only knows what she put into it."

"Phoenix tears and mermaid melodies," I remembered.

"If anyone could find a mermaid, it would be Rychel," Draven murmured. He took the flask from Lancelet and tipped it back.

It was my turn. The Mermaid's Song wasn't cloyingly sweet. There was a savory hint of something nutty to it. As the liquid spread down my throat, a golden warmth went through me, and almost instinctively, I looked over at Draven.

"Do try not to set the tent on fire tonight," he murmured.

I blushed, remembering our wild coupling the night of Rychel's feast and the scorched sheets the morning after.

"The stew is ready," Hawl announced suddenly. There was a stack of wooden bowls beside the Bearkin which they began ladling stew in.

I stared at the pot, abruptly unsure of whether my stomach wished to be filled with anything but the pure, sweet liquor Rychel had crafted. Not after what I had seen today.

"It is a vegetable stew," Hawl said, looking over at me. "Barley, potatoes, carrots, and fresh herbs. No meat."

"Well, that's a relief," Lancelet muttered, coming forward for a bowl. "Never thought I'd be so happy to hear that."

She'd come a long way, I thought, if she could say such a thing in jest. I couldn't even begin to imagine how triggering today must have been for her.

But whatever she was feeling at seeing the similarities between the children of Meridium and what had been done to the people of the village we'd passed through, she seemed determined to grit her teeth and get through it.

"We should do this more often," Gawain said brightly as we sat around the fire, eating Hawl's vegetable stew and passing the wineskin around from time to time. "Dining outdoors, beside the sea. Why, Draven, you and I used to do this all the time when we were younger."

"We would sneak out of the palace," Draven recalled. "Go up to Noctasia, then catch a ride with some peasant farmer on the back of his cart. We had our bedrolls strapped to our back, our bows, and enough food to last us a few days."

"We would hunt and swim and fish," Gawain added. "And as we grew older…" He grinned at Draven.

"We'd drink," Draven said, carefully avoiding my eyes.

"Copiously, I presume," I said, elbowing him with a grin.

"At times. Better to vomit into the grass than at one of my father's parties. We learned our limits."

"Alongside some very pretty boys and girls," Gawain said with a wink. "I won't bore Morgan with the stories."

I flushed. "Crescent wasn't with you then?"

"Oh, no, the Royal Prince would never have been allowed to associate with Crescent back then."

"Why not?" I demanded.

"The di Rhondans were another class, essentially. In service to the emperor and his family. Noble warriors, to be sure. But we weren't permitted to mingle as freely with him and Odessa as Gawain and I could," Draven explained. He smirked. "Of course, eventually, he and Crescent mingled very freely."

Gawain laughed loudly. "Very. My mother was furious. She wanted me to wed one of your cousins. A girl with a viper's tongue. Quite literally. But that was not to be."

"You broke the mold," I noted.

"We had no choice," Gawain said simply. "Just like you and Draven. I couldn't stay away from Crescent. We were meant to be."

Quiet fell again. I glanced around the fire. Lancelet and Guinevere were sitting across from one another. I noticed Lancelet was being very careful not to lift her eyes.

"Do Bearkins choose mates in the same way we do, Hawl?" I inquired. "Do they believe in fidelity?"

"There are very few Bearkins left to believe in anything," Hawl said gruffly. "But no, we do not form bonds the way fae and mortals seem to. With these romantic notions. That is not to say we do not take mates or care for those mates. But an Ursidaur mates for a purpose, and when that purpose is over, they are solitary once more. We prefer it that way."

"You're not so solitary now," Lancelet observed.

"Companionship. Friendship. Now that is different." Hawl rose and lifted the heavy copper pot from where it hung over the fire. "And to fight by a companion's side in a worthy battle. Now that is what all Ursidaur aspire to."

"You're born for battle then?" I asked, curious.

"Most of us. There was a day... well..." Hawl became quiet.

"What?" I urged. "Tell us."

"Once, the Ursidaur had their own court. As fine as any fae, though vastly different. We were famed warriors. Sought after by many kingdoms."

"It's true," Draven said. "My father would speak of the Ursidaur who served in the Court of Umbral Flames before his time. They were legendary."

"I wish I could have seen you fight at the Battle for Brightwind, Hawl," I said softly.

"It was an impressive sight," Lancelet confirmed. She nodded to the Bearkin. "We fought back to back at one point. You covered me when I was most fatigued."

"You fought well," Hawl acknowledged. "For a mortal."

Lancelet grinned and tossed her short blonde hair back. "High praise from an Ursidaur."

"There were rumors after the battle," Gawain said abruptly. "Amongst the Tintagel soldiers. They said many of their comrades' bodies could not be found. While others had... strange markings. Teeth marks." He shook his head. "I thought wild animals must have been at the bodies. Not all could be buried quickly enough."

"We all know what happens to bodies lying out on a battlefield, Gawain," Draven said quietly.

"Yes, but this was different. I hadn't believed the rumors. Not until today. Now what they said makes sense, doesn't it?" Gawain rose to his feet, a little unsteadily. He was holding the wineskin, I noted. Now he took another swig. "Those bastards. They ate them, didn't they?"

The campfire circle had become silent.

"Those poor men and women who my father conscripted by some unnatural means and turned into slavering beasts may have eaten the Tintagel soldiers, yes," I said, rising to my feet. "But, Gawain, we will put a stop to it."

He nodded quickly. "Of course. That is why we embarked on this journey. But how powerful your father must be to have done all of this, even without the sword, without the grail."

He was right. But I did not wish to dwell on it.

"I wonder if he even used any of his own men at all," Lancelet observed. "Or simply drew from the people of Rheged to form the entire force of foot soldiers that came against us."

"He'll have plenty of reserves of his own. I have no doubt of that," Draven said. "But we're not trying to meet them with equal numbers. Our advantage is stealth."

Lancelet nodded.

"All this over a simple cup."

I looked over and, to my shock, saw that Gawain had taken the grail out of Draven's saddlebag and removed the soft velvet cloth we'd wrapped around it. Now he held it aloft, peering at it as if it might explain itself to him.

"I suppose it is a lovely thing," he said consideringly. "All of those rubies."

"Rubies? It's just a simple wooden cup," I said with surprise, just as Lancelet said, "Rubies? You're mad. Those are diamonds."

I stared at her. "But the outside of the cup is wood. Don't you see it?"

"I see a gold and silver exterior with sapphires and diamonds," Draven said. "No wood. And I've had close contact with the thing for quite some time."

I remembered. He had tried to destroy it. I wondered if he'd been the first to ever make the attempt.

"Emeralds with silver," Guinevere said. "That's what I see."

"The thing is made of solid gold," Hawl chipped in. "It's clear as day."

"We all see the cup differently," I said with wonderment. "I've never realized that before. To me, it's not beautiful at all."

Although, even if I had been able to see the diamonds and gold the others saw, I knew the chalice would never have been beautiful in my eyes. Not after what it had done to Kaye.

"It's a bloodthirsty, leeching thing," Draven said with an edge to his voice. "You should put it away, Gawain."

"It's not going to hurt me," his friend protested. He grinned at Draven. "We could make a toast with it. Do you suppose it's ever been used for something so mundane before?"

But when Draven did not return the grin, Gawain gave a reluctant shrug, wrapped the grail up carefully again, and tucked it back into the saddlebag.

"Why can't we just destroy it now?" Lancelet asked grimly. Her tone told me she understood the grail's true power and would be making no jests about drinking from it as Gawain had.

"How would you have us destroy it?" I replied. "Something tells me it won't melt easily over a simple fire or even a blacksmith's forge. We could toss it in the ocean or bury it somewhere, yes. But my father would still sense it out here. I know he would."

"I tried a blacksmith's forge, actually," Draven remarked. "Left not a scratch on the blasted thing."

"Why do you think it was made in the first place?" Lancelet demanded. "They say the goddess Marzanna..."

I snorted. "Do you really believe that?"

"Well, it certainly deals death," she countered. "You have to concede that much."

"Marzanna has never been considered evil by any means. She balances the scales between life and death. She brings a sweet and merciful end to many," Guinevere said thoughtfully.

"Rychel thought the old stories could have some truth to them," I admitted. "But she also thought the grail could be used to heal as well as destroy. Or, at least to perhaps undo the evil it had been used for." I shook my head as I stared at the saddlebag. "I've never seen it used for good though. And it took Rychel away from us."

Possibly forever.

I could have asked my father about her whereabouts. But would that have done any good? Or simply drawn attention to the fact that Rychel was important to me?

I suspected if he still had her, he already knew that. And if he didn't, there was no point in asking. We would find her ourselves.

"We should get some rest," Draven said, standing up. He gave me a pointed look, and I nodded, then glanced at Guinevere.

"I lay down earlier when the rest of you were still making camp," Guinevere said, seeing my expression. "I've had a few hours of sleep. It's your turn, Morgan."

I knew she was vastly overestimating the amount of sleep she'd gotten.

The night before, I had stubbornly refused to shut my eyes... tossing and turning for hours, trying to stay awake until finally I had been unable to fight the weariness any longer and had fallen into a restless slumber.

When I awoke near dawn, I felt panicked at first, then filled with relief as I realized I had not dreamed.

I'd emerged from the small tent I shared with Draven to find Guinevere sitting quietly outside, watching the sunrise.

She had shielded me somehow. Sat in a state of vigilance and guarded me in some way I didn't understand.

"We both need rest. Equal amounts," I said stubbornly.

"I agree." Lancelet came up beside me. "I'll make sure she gets it."

When it came to protecting Guinevere, I knew I could count on Lancelet. Even if it meant my own sleep would be short. Better than nothing.

"How are you doing it, anyhow?" I asked, as I passed Guinevere on the way to my tent. "How are you making the dreams stop?"

Guinevere smiled slightly. "One of the many mysteries of the temple, Morgan."

I knew that meant I wasn't going to get an answer.

A hooting sound came from a nearby tree, and I looked up to see Tuva sitting peacefully on a high branch.

"She hunts at night," Guinevere explained. "Sometimes she'll bring me gifts."

"Gifts?"

"She means the kind a cat drags in," Lancelet said sourly. "Dead mice and things like that."

"Ew," I said, wrinkling my nose. "How sweet."

And for once, we all laughed together.

CHAPTER 18 – MORGAN

I woke to a familiar smell. Flapjacks cooking over an open fire.

There was a time the scent would simply have filled me with hunger. And indeed, my stomach rumbled in response to the sweet fragrance.

But my mind had gone elsewhere. Flashing back in an instant to memories of Vesper and the woods of Cerunnos.

I felt a stab of pain as I remembered the feeling of Vesper's dagger sliding into my belly. Sitting up in the tent, I instinctively touched a hand to the scar on my stomach.

A strong hand was placed atop mine. "He's not here, Morgan. I am."

I turned my head towards Draven's dark one, feeling a multitude of emotions rush over me. Relief, gratitude, and over all of it, pure, intense, heartfelt love.

My mouth was on his before he had time to react, and I reached out my arms, pulling him tight against me, reveling in the warm, comforting sensation of his bare chest against my own.

He tasted like the mint leaves he'd been chewing. Evidently, he'd been up before me.

I pulled back, a little embarrassed. "You taste very fresh."

Whereas I knew I did not.

He grinned and yanked me back against him. "And what? You don't and you think I'd care?"

He buried his mouth against mine, biting down gently on my bottom lip until I gasped.

A hand slipped between my legs, and I groaned, then pushed it away.

"No, no, no."

"Yes, yes, yes," he murmured. "This is the perfect way to wake up in the morning."

"It would be, yes. If it weren't for the fact that everyone else is probably up already, listening to us right now," I hissed.

He smirked. "Let them listen. What? Do you think we were so silent last night?"

I glanced up and saw the burn marks on the sides of our canvas tent. "Oh, gods." I glared at him. "That was the Mermaid Song."

"Sure it was," he teased. "You tell yourself whatever you need to in order to look our friends in the face as you crawl out of that tent flap."

"Damnable man! Detestable Siabra bastard," I swore, beginning to rifle through the clothes strewn on one side of the tent, pulling out what I planned to wear that day and shoving the rest back into my saddlebag.

Draven lay there, grinning with his arms folded behind his head, evidently in no rush to get up as I yanked a forest-green tunic over my head, then pulled on trousers and finished up with the comfortable pair of knee-high leather riding boots I'd been wearing the day before.

Everything smelled like campfire smoke and horses. Fortunately, that was a combination I'd grown rather fond of.

I pushed open the tent flap and crawled out, then darted a hand back in to pull a cloak out with me. It was chilly by the sea in the mornings. A coating of dew still covered the grass.

Across from our tent, by the fire, Hawl was hunched over a large, cast-iron pan.

Fastening my cloak, I walked over to them slowly and peered into the pan, expecting to see the most delectable griddle cakes known to mortal or fae.

Instead, I covered my mouth. "Are those...moths?"

Hawl looked up. Ursidaur expressions could be difficult to read at times, but right now, I'd have sworn Hawl looked guilty.

"Good morning, Morgan."

"Good morning, Hawl. Are those moths?" I repeated, stressing the last word.

"They're packed full of protein and taste like butter," Hawl assured me. "In fact, I've greased the pan with some of them."

I sat down on the log across from the fire, watched as Hawl flipped one of the moth-cakes, and tried to quell my queasy reaction. "I suppose they're no different from any other meats we consume."

"Of course they aren't. It's all about what you become used to," Hawl assured me.

The Bearkin lifted the lid of a covered mug beside them, and as they did, a moth flew out, beating its wings frantically and flapping off into the morning.

"Oh, gods," I groaned. "They're still alive?"

"Not for long," Hawl promised, dumping the rest of the contents of the mug into a new, separate pan and squashing the moths down with a utensil. "There. Like butter. Just as I said."

The Bearkin may have been right. The smells emanating from the pans were not entirely repulsive.

Even so. "I don't think I can eat that, Hawl. I'm sorry."

"Not to worry." The Bearkin gestured to a covered plate resting outside the ring of hot stones. "I took the liberty of preparing simpler refreshments for the rest of you."

I lifted the cover and looked down at the plain, moth-free griddle-cakes in relief. "Thank you."

"Of course..." The Bearkin looked at me conspiratorially. "Gawain and I will enjoy these together. Have you noticed how the man prefers his food piping hot?"

"As do I," Draven said, striding over. He finished strapping on his belt and looked down at the campfire. "Mmm. Those look incredible, Hawl."

Hawl's eyes met mine over the frying pan.

Behind his back, I put a finger to my lips. The Ursidaur nodded.

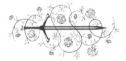

We started passing refugees on the road later that day.

They were moving from Rheged towards the Tintagel border. They seemed to have no interest in us. Dust-covered and weary, they carried small bundles of clothes and possessions and led children by the hands.

Most were not injured, I saw, to my great relief. But they looked haunted, hopeless.

Eventually, Draven stopped his horse, and dismounting, he approached a man driving a wagon with his family behind him.

"What news from Dornum? What news of Nerov?" Draven asked, coming up to the man slowly, his hands raised in the air to show he meant no harm.

Dornum was the capital of Rheged, and Nerov its king. Long ago, a tale had been told to me of Draven's role in placing Nerov on that throne.

Draven had told me Nerov was not a bad man—and had been replacing a much worse ruler.

"No news at all," the man in the wagon said, seeming surprised at our ignorance. "There's been no news from the city for months. Shut up tight and full of ghosts, it's said to be."

"Why are you all leaving? Where are you going?" Gawain called from his horse. "What lies ahead?"

The man spat beside his wagon as if to ward off evil. "I won't be made into a monster. Nor a soldier either. Nor my children."

Behind him, three children huddled beside their mother. A boy and two girls.

"Is that what's happening? Are villages being conscripted?" Draven asked.

The man had slowed his speed. Now he pulled his wagon to a halt, as he realized we expected more answers. "Conscripted? Would be more honest to say vanished. Entire towns taken up and into the Black Mountain."

I shivered.

"The Black Mountain?" Draven glanced back at me. "Where does it lie?"

"Behind Dornum. In the Mountains of Mist as they've always been called."

Rheged was a rough land, famed for its huge, vaulted peaks and the icy glaciers and vast chasms that lay to its north, beyond the capital.

We had been following the coastline from Brightwind. Eventually, our path would lead us directly into those mountains, provided we did not skirt them by continuing along the sea.

"I've never heard of the place, but then, there are many mountains," Draven remarked.

"Aye. Too many in the mist to count or name. And few who have traversed there. But none such as this. Appearing as it did one day."

"What do you mean?" Lancelet demanded from her horse, leaning down a little. "Appeared? Appeared how? Mountains don't just appear."

"Appeared from nowhere. Towering over all of the others with a summit that one can see even over the clouds of mist."

"That is high indeed," Draven murmured, his gaze thoughtful.

"Perhaps it was always there. Some say so. Perhaps it grew."

Behind me, Gawain gave a chuckle. "I've never heard of such a thing, my good man. Mountains usually stay where they are."

The man cast Gawain a sour look. "Once, I would have said the same."

"We've seen many strange things already," I murmured to Gawain.

He shrugged. "I suppose. What's one more?"

"Has anyone gone to the Black Mountain? Tried to explore it?" Hawl challenged in their thundering rumble.

The man's eyes widened, taking in the Bearkin mounted on the oversized black stallion.

"An Ursidaur," I explained quickly. "You may have heard them called Bearkins. Hawl hails from Myntra."

"Myntra?" I heard the woman in the wagon murmur. "So far."

"You're fae," said the man suddenly, looking at Draven, then me, then Gawain. "Fae and a talking bear."

I smiled encouragingly at him. "We're here to help."

"There's fae in that mountain. Fae treachery at the heart of it all, and worse," the man said darkly, his eyes narrowing as he looked at me more carefully, taking in the markings on my wrists and hands that peeked out from my tunic, then seeming to note Draven's small black horns for the first time.

I sensed him turning against us and becoming fearful.

"There was a battle at Brightwind," I said swiftly. "Did you know?"

"Brightwind? A battle?" The man glanced back at the woman in the wagon. Both seemed surprised.

"The soldiers appeared to come from Rheged. Brightwind was under total attack." I gestured to my companions. "I come from Pendrath and some of my friends from Myntra. We fought with the Tintagel forces at Brightwind."

There was no need to tell the man exactly who we were or how we'd fought.

"Rheged attacking Tintagel?" The man shook his head. "There were battles last year. Attacks on Pendrath. We were spared from that. Our village was too far north. But now... no one is spared."

I decided we'd bothered the man and his family enough. Besides, hearing him speak of the Black Mountain had told me all I needed to know about where we should head.

"You'll find safety in Tintagel," I promised the man. "King Mark is a fair ruler. He doesn't blame the people of Rheged for the attack. He knows it came from... somewhere else."

"The Black Mountain," the woman in the wagon whispered.

I nodded. "As you say. Good luck on your journey."

"May the Three watch over you," Guinevere murmured as the wagon rolled past.

We rode in silence a few moments until the road was clear once more.

Then Gawain came up beside where Draven and I rode at the front. "I take it we're heading for that mountain?"

I nodded. From my father's mind, I had seen the general region I had to move towards. I had known the direction and that there would be mountains but not much else. Now we had a name.

"I doubt we'll have to ask for anything more specific," Draven remarked. "Not if this thing towers above the mist as the man claimed." He looked over at me. "A few more days along the coastal road, then we'll turn inland to the west. A few days after that, we should come to the Mountains of Mist. The riding will be hard. We'll skirt around Dornum. There's no reason to go there based on what you've shared with me already. When we reach the mountains, the terrain will turn rocky and treacherous. We may have to leave the horses."

I nodded. "The exmoors should be fine."

Even now, Nightclaw and Sunstrike traveled with us, staying close but keeping out of sight. At times, they prowled along the beach below the cliff road. At others, they rested and caught up with us at night.

When they flew, they flew low and slow. Sunstrike's wing could not tolerate anything more strenuous than that yet.

We rode throughout the rest of the day, stopping only to water the horses. All afternoon, I imagined a black mountain rising out of the mist.

CHAPTER 19 - MEDRA

I passed a cold and lonely night hiding from Crescent atop a turret watchtower.

Crouched beside a stone guardrail, I drifted in and out of sleep as above me the stars rose and set in the sky. They seemed very distant. As cold and lonely as I felt.

Things with Sir Ector had not gone well. I had realized too late that I was not supposed to beat him.

Twelve-year-old girls were not supposed to beat grown men in feats of arms.

Or, at least, girls who looked twelve-years-old.

For I was not twelve, was I? I was not even a year.

And yet when I saw other children, I *felt* older than them all. How easily they laughed and smiled and played. They felt a happiness I could not.

I'd hurt Sir Ector.

Sent him tumbling down. He'd broken his hip. A healer had to be called. Dame Halyna had chided me angrily and sent me away.

I think she thought I'd done it on purpose.

I hadn't, of course, not really. Though I could have if I'd wanted to.

But I hadn't. I liked Dame Halyna and Sir Ector. Until then.

I simply lacked an adequate understanding of my own strength. I'd *wanted* Sir Ector to be stronger than me. I'd wanted to believe he could beat me no matter how far I let myself go—and so I had given myself permission to go far.

And then he had fallen.

I was stronger than they thought. Stronger than I still knew.

They had been the last of my tutors. Somehow I knew there would not be any others, no matter how Crescent beseeched for more to come.

He was alone. I was alone. And the castle grew emptier and emptier by the day.

Taina had been sent home. Crescent didn't want me near her anymore.

Dame Halyna had come searching for me. She had seemed to expect me to make some kind of apology. When I'd stood there stubborn and sullen, eventually, she had gone away.

I hadn't gone to visit Sir Ector. I didn't think he'd want to see me. They said his hip was very bad. An infection in the bone.

Perhaps he would die.

Would it have been my fault if he did? Would I be... a murderer?

There was more to what I could do. So much more than strength.

But I would never let them see it. It would only make them more afraid.

Sometimes I was afraid of myself.

Of how fast I grew.

Of the voices in my head.

Of my dreams.

There had been a man in my dream once. Grey-haired and ancient as the wind.

But I'd closed the door on him, and after that, I had never seen him again.

A light rain had begun to fall. In the distance, thunder boomed.

Soon, the cloak I had wrapped around me was soaked through.

I let it fall to the ground and walked to the edge of the watchtower.

The height was dizzying. A shiver of apprehension went through me as I ran my hands over the cool, wet stone of the guardrail.

A wild wind blew through my hair, tangling the strands.

Heavier drops of rain were falling around me now, splattering the stones. The building storm mirrored the turmoil inside of me.

The rumbling of thunder came again in the distance. I had always hated the sound. Now I welcomed it.

The taste of my loneliness was bitter on my tongue.

I knew this was not a feeling ordinary children had. This sense of dark disquiet that seeped into my very being, casting a shadow on my heart.

My fingers curled around the stone edge as I pushed myself up and slowly stood.

A gust of wind swept over the watchtower.

For a moment, I swayed, teetering on the edge. Far down below, the landscape unfolded like a tapestry. Miniature figures scurried through the castle grounds, seeking shelter from the rain.

The perspective was vertigo-inducing. A tingling sensation crept through my limbs the longer I stood balancing on the edge looking down.

Another gust of wind buffeted the tower, and for a heart-stopping moment, I teetered. With a gasp, I crouched down, digging my fingers into the cold stone of the guardrail for support.

A choked sob broke from my throat as I steadied myself, muscles tense with the effort.

It was all so much trouble. This business of being alive.

I dared to glance down once more. The ground seemed to swirl and shift as the rain and mist clouded my view of the castle grounds.

What was the point of any of it? No one had ever explained it to me.

There was no one down there who mattered to me, and I mattered to no one.

No one would miss me if I were gone. They would be glad.

Crescent wouldn't have to worry about me anymore.

The servants could come back. They wouldn't have to be afraid.

Maybe there was one who would care. The man who had held me in his arms. He had smiled down at me. Even his eyes had seemed to smile. They had been a brilliant green.

He'd talked to me, sang to me, cradled me.

Was that love? The feeling I'd had when he'd held me, knowing I was safe?

Had he loved me?

My heart hardened.

He hadn't loved me.

If he had, he would have stayed here forever and never left. He hadn't kept me safe. He had been selfish. He had gone away.

"Feeling sorry for yourself, little one?"

Had I not been crouched on a slippery ledge, I would have whirled around in a blinding fury.

Perhaps I would even have run past the person, showing just how quick I could be, shoving them hard on the way out. Then I'd have escaped their knowing gaze and smirking mouth.

But for the moment, I was stuck. Afraid to make any false move in the pounding rain.

I turned slowly, moving my body towards the speaker who had mounted the tower stairs and dared to speak.

A tall and imposing woman stood there. Her skin was a dark, rich brown. Long black hair had been swept back and twisted into a heavy knot made up of many small braids.

I examined her features. Scars criss-crossed her face. Otherwise, she might have been pretty.

But the scars weren't what drew my eye the most.

Two blades were strapped to her back, the hilts wrapped in worn leather.

The woman had a warrior's build. Broad shoulders, a muscular physique. Her well-formed arms were crossed over her chest as she looked at me.

There were many things I might have said in reply to her. Rude things. Cruel things.

But with my tutors, I had quickly learned the best way to provoke someone was to simply say nothing at all.

So I sat on the ledge, fingers clenched but unmoving, staring stonily back at the strange woman in silence.

Until finally she nodded. As if she understood.

"I'm Odessa. Crescent's sister. I promise you here and now, Medra, that no matter what you do—or don't do—you won't be able to frighten me away."

I flinched, as if she had penetrated my mind.

"I'm not going anywhere," she continued. "I'm here to stay. Now why don't you come down off that ledge and tell me about yourself?"

When I made no move to come down to her, she sank onto the watchtower floor and crossed her legs, paying no heed to the wetness of the stones.

"Very well. We can speak out here in the rain as easily as anywhere else if that's what you prefer." She tilted her head. "Why don't we start with why you were thinking of jumping?"

CHAPTER 20 - MORGAN

In times of desperation, some fled, some fought.

In between the two groups were the worst sort. The leeches, the parasites. In the midst of chaos, they fed on others for their own survival.

We were attacked in the middle of the night.

The exmoors had left to hunt or we would have been alerted sooner.

As it was, the campfire had been put out and everyone had retired.

I was lying in our tent, just beginning to close my eyes and drift off, when Draven's hand clamped down on my arm. A warning. I looked over and saw him sitting up, an unsheathed dagger already in his other hand.

At the same moment, the tent flap rustled and Guinevere's head popped into sight, eyes wide and frightened.

She had just enough time to open her mouth and whisper a single word—"Bandits!"—before there was a whistling sound over our tent. One all-too familiar.

In the next instant, our tent lit up, flames dancing in wild patterns along the canvas.

A tent was on fire. But it wasn't ours.

Draven was rolling out of the shelter in an instant, swift and decisive, then reaching a hand back to pull me out behind him.

I had just enough time to drag Excalibur along. Strapping the leather belt it hung from around my waist, I looked about, my eyes struggling to adjust to the chaotic scene—just as the tent beside us erupted in a thunderous explosion of fur and canvas.

A furious roar echoed through the night.

Having never been stupid enough to ever really annoy Hawl, I had never seen the Bearkin look as they did now.

The entire camp—friends and foes alike—seemed to freeze in unison as Hawl rose to their full height from the wreckage of their tent, revealing themselves in all their primal splendor, an embodiment of untamed, terrifying power.

Bared jaws showcased rows of formidable teeth glinting in the fiery glow of the flaming tent behind them. The Bearkin's eyes blazed with fury as they lifted their massive paws, sharp claws extending.

Slowly, Hawl looked around them.

"Bandits," they bellowed. "I hate bandits. Which one of you sniveling, thieving insects dared to wake me?"

I found myself trembling—and I wasn't even a bandit.

I caught the eye of the attacker closest to us. The bandit's face was the picture of panic. I assumed this was the man who had disturbed Hawl in their tent.

And then the bear exploded into action. Snatching the bandit with one colossal paw, Hawl lifted him effortlessly into the air.

The bandit had just enough time to scream before the grizzly tossed him over the nearby cliff. For a moment, his cries echoed back to us as he fell, then there was a crunch as he presumably hit the rocks below and they abruptly ceased.

With a speed that surprised me, the Bearkin turned their attention to the next bandit—a man standing near the edge of Hawl's tent. Closing the distance between them in a single thunderous step, Hawl seized the hapless man by the throat.

There was a sickening crack of breaking bones as the grizzly snapped the bandit's neck then dropped him to the dirt.

A shout went up behind me. The remaining bandits, shaken from their initial shock, were trying to rally.

I looked around me wildly, my hand on Excalibur's hilt.

We were better armed than our attackers. Better than they could possibly know if one took into account what Draven and I could do. Not to mention the Bearkin.

But there were only six of us. And of the six, only five of us were fighters.

Whereas the bandits had numbers. There were at least twenty or more scurrying around the camp and forest edges that I could see. I prayed no more were waiting deeper in the forest.

I scanned swiftly until I found Guinevere. She stood behind Lancelet, her eyes wide and frightened. For once, the owl was not on her shoulder. Tuva was off hunting, I supposed, like the exmoors.

The sound of steel on steel. I turned towards it as Gawain's earsplitting bellow broke through the air. The towering, red-haired warrior was moving like a force of nature. Bearing a massive battle-ax that gleamed in the moonlight, he swung it effortlessly as he faced a ring of bandits.

I had never seen the big man fight in real combat before. He had no shadows to coil or flames to throw. But his skill was enough. Each time his ax carved through the air, it cut through his foes one by one with merciless grace. His wild, red mane of hair flew around him as he moved with an innate understanding of his enemies, positioning himself strategically to intercept each attack. And since it was Gawain after all, he grinned the entire time.

"He'll be fine, Morgan," Draven shouted, mistaking my awe for concern. "Stand with me now. Back to back. Here they come."

I had trained in Sir Ector's combat ring. I had fought from the skies on the exmoor. I had dueled my brother face to face.

But now, as I looked at the leering faces of four bandits as they approached us, I felt suddenly unprepared.

I could not use flames, that much was clear. The horses were too near, as were Lancelet, Guinevere, and Hawl. I could not risk them.

Even now, Lancelet fought, one against two, pushing Guinevere back behind her, then back still more as her blade whirled through the air, shielding them both.

But then I had no time to think of our friends, their safety, or our horses. Excalibur was in my hand. My mate was at my back. And we were fighting where we stood as the group of bandits, looks of hunger and desperation in their eyes, rushed towards us.

As the first one approached me, a rusted dagger raised high, I pivoted on one heel. Metal clashed against metal as vibrations from the blow reverberated up my arm. I had just enough time to see the bandit's eyes widen as Excalibur began to glow with its battlelight before the sword thrust through the man's chest and he fell.

I turned to my next foe, breathing hard. A woman armed with a serrated blade charged towards me, looking furious. Had the man I'd just killed been her brother? Her husband?

I shoved pity aside. These people had expected us to be sleeping in our beds, unsuspecting and unarmed. We might have had children with us. Would they have cared? Or would they have slit our throats while we slept without a second thought and simply taken what they wanted?

Baring my teeth as Hawl had done, I sidestepped the woman's thrust easily, feeling the rush of air as her weapon narrowly missed. A quick counterattack. The woman staggered back, the metallic scent of her blood joining the tang of sweat and fear.

Beside me, Draven's dagger danced. His swift, precise strikes easily parried much larger weapons. With a deft flick of his wrist, he tossed aside a bandit's wooden club, then darted his blade out again and again until the man fell to his knees, blood streaming from his mouth.

Our last adversary was a cautious but stupid man. Armed with a makeshift slingshot, he attempted to launch a stone projectile.

Ducking smoothly, Draven lifted his left hand and almost lazily let a band of shadow extend, yanking the slingshot from the man's hand and tossing it aside before wrapping it around the bandit's neck and twisting.

Shouts came up from around us. Other bandits had noticed what Draven had done.

I grinned as a few ran back towards the main road, probably to clamber up onto their horses as quickly as they could and flee.

But the majority stayed.

Still, the numbers were becoming more balanced.

"Morgan!"

I whirled at the sound of Lancelet's cry. She was fighting another woman in single combat, but her eyes were frantic, darting to where Guinevere fled towards the treeline, pursued by a tall man.

I was already running as the man reached out a hand and ripped at Guinevere's gown, tearing her sleeve as he laughed.

She let out a cry of fear that pierced the night. Fury filled my veins.

It would be my honor to slide Excalibur right through the man's heart, I decided.

But as it turned out, the former high priestess did not need me for her champion.

A shrill hoot pierced through the air. The sound of an owl on the hunt.

The man was closing the distance, oblivious to the cry of the bird or what it might mean.

I slowed my pace slightly as I watched the owl's descent, swift and purposeful, body of gold and brown slicing through the air with divine grace.

The man lifted his head at the sound of rustling feathers but it was too late. A guttural cry escaped his lips as the bird's beak found its mark, piercing into his right eye.

The man screamed.

The owl lifted into the air once more, ascending and circling before diving again.

The bandit thrashed wildly as blood poured from his eye and he tried to fend off the vengeful owl, but Tuva's attack was unyielding.

I reached the scene just in time to witness the man collapsing to the ground, his face a mess of torn flesh, hands still raised to futilely shield his battered face.

Tuva, wings spread, let out one last hoot, then took to the skies.

Draven brushed past me, striding up to where the man kneeled, quivering. With a thrust of his dagger, the bandit was left lifeless in the dirt.

I turned to Guinevere. "Are you all right?"

But she was pointing at something behind me. "Morgan, look!"

I turned to see a bandit near our tethered horses. He was rooting around in the saddlebags. My saddlebags.

The man's eyes lit up greedily as he snatched up an object and held it aloft in the moonlight.

The grail.

From the look in the bandit's eyes, it was clear he saw more than a mere wooden chalice.

I ran towards him, ignoring Draven's shouts from behind me.

The man was too focused on the grail to even notice as I charged. Reaching him, I knocked the grail from his hand. It clattered to the ground as the man looked up at me, enraged, and drew a needlelike dagger from his belt.

The man was quick. Quicker than the others had been.

The blade darted forward like a viper seeking vulnerable flesh.

I danced around his strikes, searching for an opening to thrust Excalibur forward. But the man blocked me each time, then moved back between our horses, shielding himself with their bodies. I clenched my jaw, limited by the necessity of not hurting a horse, and followed him in between the tethered mounts.

A sudden flash of pain cut through my hand as the man darted out from between two of the horses, his stiletto finding its mark as it carved a crimson tribute on my palm.

A look of triumph lit up his face. Then he crumpled like a marionette, falling to the ground as Draven's longsword appeared through the center of his chest.

"You should have waited for me," my mate said mildly, looking down at the man's body as the horses whinnied nervously and sidestepped the pool of blood.

"I was fine. I had him." I gestured to the sword. "You fetched your other blade I see."

He shrugged. "I was tired of the daggers. You were holding your own." He gestured to my hand.

"Just a scratch."

I turned back to my horse, searching the ground for where the grail had fallen.

It was gone.

Panic welled in me.

Then I noticed Gawain standing a little distance away.

He had the grail in his hand and was raising it to the light, turning it this way then that, admiring it as the bandit had done.

"Gawain," I called sharply. "Give it back."

He looked towards me, a scowl disfiguring his normally pleasant face, and I blinked in surprise.

Then he tossed it. "Catch it then."

The chalice flew through the air, spiraling over and over.

Without thinking, I reached upwards and caught the cup.

Instantly, a pain went through me. I dropped the chalice as if it were a hot coal and gasped.

"What is it?" Draven appeared at my shoulder. "Fuck."

Reaching into my saddlebag, he retrieved the leather bag we'd been keeping the cup in, then pulled out the velvet cloth it had been wrapped in.

Wrapping the cloth around his hand, he carefully lifted the grail from the dirt and wiped the traces of my blood off it.

Shooting Gawain a displeased stare, he folded the grail into the cloth and packed it back into the saddlebag.

"Fucking humans," Hawl grumbled. The Bearkin was nursing a cut over one eye, but other than that, seemed none the worse for wear.

"Fucking bandits," Lancelet corrected. "Not all humans are bad."

Hawl looked at Lancelet for a moment then grunted. "I suppose not."

"They were desperate men," Guinevere said quietly. She still looked shaken from the attack. Lancelet had draped a heavy wool cloak around her shoulders. Now she pulled it more tightly around her throat.

The campfire crackled. The moon shone overhead. It might have been any other night on the road. Were it not for the scent of burnt wood mingled with the lingering scent of blood. An unpleasantly aromatic reminder of our recent battle.

Draven sat beside me. With practiced care, he wound a strip of linen around my hand, his touch firm but gentle.

There was a soft whooshing sound, and the ground shook momentarily. The campfire flickered, casting its amber glow on the two battlecats as they landed and lumbered towards us.

Nightclaw, his fur obsidian velvet beneath the moon, padded over to me, his golden eyes reflecting the firelight. Folding his wings along his sides, he looked down at my hand, then lowered his massive head and nuzzled me, gently but a little reproachfully, too.

"What would you have had me do?" I said, lifting my free hand to run it over his head. "Summon you back?"

A low rumble came from his chest. An unmistakable growl of disapproval.

I shook my head. "You know I'm not going to do that. Besides, you were hunting. Probably too far away to come back in time."

Another low growl, but softer this time.

"I know," I said, leaning my head down to rest atop his. "I know you would have come back. But it's just a scratch. Nothing more. We were fine. I promise you."

I glanced over at where Sunstrike sat watching and cleaning her paws.

"Besides, you have your own mate to take care of now," I said quietly. "She has to come first. She has to heal. You had her back. And my mate had mine."

I looked up at Draven. He finished knotting the bandage, then pulled me tight against him.

"Remind you of another night?" I murmured. "Far from here?"

He smiled slightly. "It was your back that time."

"Fenrirs." I shuddered.

I glanced at where Gawain sat on a rock nearby. The big man was staring into the fire.

"You fought well tonight, Gawain," I said softly, feeling the need to somehow reassure him.

He looked over at me and forced a smile. "Thank you, Morgan." His smile fell away. "But the grail. I'm sorry. I don't know what came over me."

"It's a powerful object. Hard to describe the pull it can have," I said, even while I knew I had never felt that same pull.

"Do you think they came for it? Specifically for the grail, I mean?" Gawain queried.

I shook my head. "I don't think that man had any idea that it was even there or what it was. He just saw a precious treasure. Something he could sell."

Gawain nodded. A few moments later, he had drifted off to his own tent for the night.

Across the fire, Guinevere was rising to her feet. "I think I'll lie down. Morgan..." She gave me a questioning look.

"Rest, Guinevere," I said firmly. "There's no way I'll be able to sleep after that. One of us should get some rest tonight."

To my surprise, Draven rose and escorted Guinevere to her tent, making sure she was safe inside before walking over to our own. Then, crouching by the tent flap, he gave me a meaningful look and darted his eyes towards Lancelet before slipping inside.

Hawl was the next to leave. "I shall dream of blood and snapping bones," they said, sounding happier than they had all week. "A satisfying battle."

"Delightful," Lancelet muttered as the Bearkin stomped away. "I'll be dreaming of that crunch the rest of my days, too."

She threw another log onto the fire, and sparks flew upwards. "Guess it's just us then."

I walked over to my saddlebag and pulled out a silver flask. "Gawain's not the only one prepared. It's not Mermaid Song, but want some?"

"What is it?" Lancelet asked, perking up.

"Try it and find out," I suggested, taking a swig myself.

She tipped the flask back for a long swallow then immediately started to cough. "Whisky!" She shot me an accusing look. "Disgusting, Morgan. Whisky? Really?"

"Draven's developed a taste for it." I preferred spiced rum. There was a clove and orange one from Lyonesse I particularly loved. But even I had to admit there was something about the way whisky flowed through one like molten lava that could be rather bracing.

She passed back the flask. "My throat is on fire. What I wouldn't give for a tankard of ale from The Bear and Mermaid right now."

"Perhaps more liquid courage is just what you need," I said, holding the flask out towards her again with a meaningful look.

"What's that supposed to mean?"

"It means Guinevere is sleeping alone."

"Of course she is. She always does. So what?"

"So perhaps she doesn't have to." I was hesitant as to how far to go, how blatant to be.

Lancelet stared. "She was just attacked by a bandit."

I sighed. "We're always going to have just been attacked by something or other, Lancelet. Look where we are. Look where we're headed. Do you think things are really going to improve from here on out?"

Lancelet snorted. "I suppose that's true."

"It is. So seize the moment."

"Seize the moment?" Lancelet laughed. "That doesn't sound like the Morgan I used to know. At least, not when it comes to taking lovers."

"I've changed," I said, blushing slightly.

Lancelet looked at me thoughtfully. "You certainly have. And it's Draven who did it."

"Is that a bad thing?" I asked, not sure I was ready for the answer.

"No. He's been good for you. The two of you..." She shook her head and looked up at the moon.

"What? Tell me."

"The two of you are equal parts disgusting and inspiring."

I choked. "Disgusting?"

"Disgustingly in love, Morgan. Oh, you're not all over each other constantly. Thank the Three for that. But the looks you give one another. The little touches—when I catch them. The way you talk about one another. The way he shields you."

"Just as you do with Guinevere," I interjected.

"Right. I have no choice."

"Because you feel the same way about her as Draven and I do about each other," I pointed out.

"If I do, I'm alone. It's one-sided, Morgan."

I stared at her. "Do you really believe that?"

"Of course. Don't you?"

I thought about it carefully for a moment. "No. I don't. At least, I think there's a real chance that... that your feelings are not at all one-sided."

Lancelet had paled. "Truly?"

"Truly. You really had no idea?"

"I know she cares for me as a friend and... well, tolerates me as a guardian. I'm in her way, but she never complains."

"Is that what you think?" I shook my head. "I see something different. But even if I didn't... you love her. I know you do. Will you go your whole life without ever expressing that? Simply being a silent guardian?"

"I could. Easily. And die happy," Lancelet claimed.

"Happy?" I shook my head. "I don't know if that's happiness, Lancelet. When I think of you before..." I paused. "Well, I'm not the only one who's changed."

"Yes, well, being ravaged and nearly killed by flesh-eating children can tend to do that to one," she snapped. She looked at me. "Besides, did you think I would simply hop from one dalliance to another forever?"

"I honestly had no idea what you would do," I said. "I certainly never expected you to fall for a celibate priestess."

Our eyes met, and we burst out laughing.

"Neither did I," Lancelet managed between choked laughter. "Oh, gods, it's unbelievable in some ways, isn't it? What a curse."

"But she was always more than a priestess, I suppose," I said as our laughter died off.

"She was meant to be your brother's bride. The fucking bastard."

I nodded. "She's complex. I can't read Guinevere."

"Nor can I," Lancelet said morosely. "She's a mystery. Like the goddesses themselves."

I bit my lip, knowing that to her, Guinevere was a goddess as much as I was one in Draven's love-blinded eyes.

"And yet here you sit telling me to do what?" Lancelet complained. "You want me to do what? Go and knock on the flap of her tent?"

"Something like that. Yes, maybe precisely that. Why not? Lancelet, she doesn't belong to the temple anymore. She made that clear."

"So? That doesn't mean she wants me bothering her."

"It's not as if you won't go away if she says no. But to never give her a chance to say yes?"

Lancelet was quiet for a while. "I'm not sure what I'd do if she did say no. How could I face her?"

"You'd do what you're doing now. Continue guarding her, protecting her. At least for the rest of our journey. But at least you'd know."

"My path lies with her, whether she wants me or not," Lancelet said quietly.

"Fine. I won't argue with that. But go to her, Lancelet. At least try."

Lancelet shook her head.

"You've never been afraid of a woman before. You've never hesitated to approach one before," I reminded her. "Why, you might have had any girl you chose back in Camelot." At least, any girl of a certain persuasion.

"This is different. *She's* so different. She's... practically celestial."

"No," I said bluntly. "She's not. She's very human and all alone. She has no one. No one but you and that fucking bird."

Lancelet snickered.

"A fucking amazing bird," I conceded, glancing around just in case the owl was listening to us from the trees. I wouldn't have put it past it. "But still, just a bird, Lancelet. Guinevere has no family. Not really. At least, not any that seem to particularly care for her. And now she's given up the temple, too."

"I still can't believe she did that," Lancelet muttered, staring into the fire.

"She could have been one of the most powerful women in the land," I acknowledged. "But she gave that up. And with it, she gave up the rules. She's free." I glanced at Guinevere's tent. "Think of what she went through tonight. I know if that had happened to me, I might want arms around me. Even if they were simply the arms of a friend."

Lancelet's eyes met mine across the fire. "I can do that. I think I can."

"Why not start there?" I said gently. "Ask if she wants company. Simply be with her."

"Fucking hell." Lancelet shook her head. "Pass me that flask."

I did as she asked and watched as she took a swig. "What?"

"I never thought I'd be taking advice on women from you, Morgan," she said, smirking in that cocky way I loved about her.

I laughed. "Neither did I. But if you take it, I'll never give you any again. I promise."

I thought of something and, rising to my feet, went over to my saddlebag again and fished around.

"Here," I said, passing her a small wad of green leaves.

"Mint." Lancelet grinned. "You're a lifesaver."

"Whisky might not be the best thing to smell of." Especially considering what Guinevere had been through.

Lancelet was already chewing and standing. "Well, if I'm sobbing on my horse tomorrow, you'll know why."

"You'd never do that," I said immediately. "You'd hide it like the ridiculous stoic you've become. But I'm here, Lancelet. No matter what happens. You can talk to me about anything. You know I'll be here."

She nodded seriously. "I know."

I stood up. "Get over here, woman."

She grinned, then did as I'd demanded.

And standing by the fire, with the fresh scents of whisky, blood, and mint around us, I embraced my best friend.

CHAPTER 21 - MORGAN

We left the coastal road the next day, turning inland to the west. As the sound of the sea gradually faded behind us, the landscape transformed. Rolling hills and sporadic clusters of small trees dotted the scenery.

The soil beneath our horses' hooves changed from a sandy soil to a rockier mixture with patches of hardy grass.

As we moved along the road, abandoned farmsteads stood silent, their once-thriving fields now becoming overgrown with vegetation.

Had the people who lived in them fled before they could be taken? Or had the families who had once lived in these places already been swept away by my father and his cruel powers?

With each league we traveled, the air carried an increasing chill, reminding us of the colder realms that awaited us to the northwest. Far off in the distance lay the rugged peaks and mountain passes we would need to traverse before arriving at the Black Mountain.

I'd thought a lot about Rheged and its place as the host kingdom for my father's secret court. Long ago, had Rheged been greedy? Had they invited my father and his people in, granting them secret sanctuary after being lured with promises of power and riches? Or had my father given them no other choice?

For how long, I wondered, had Rheged been little more than a puppet state? Ruled from behind the throne, quite literally, by the Black Mountain and Gorlois le Fay.

And for what purpose overall? To send Eskira spiraling into chaos. Kingdom against kingdom, until finally, after lands had been ruined and peoples destroyed, my father's court would surface and take the entire continent as his prize.

It was a chilling vision of an all-too possible future.

One that awaited us if we failed.

Yet the self-doubt was equally agonizing. Was I doing the opposite of what my father expected by refusing to meet him again on the battlefield? Or was I playing right into his hands by bringing the sword and the grail into the heart of his dark territory?

I glanced around at the five riders accompanying me, and my eyes lit upon Lancelet.

She rode beside Guinevere. They were holding hands between their horses.

I smiled. Not an easy feat. But I admired the attempt, even though if they kept it up for much longer, their horses might become rather annoyed.

The looks between them were as muted and subtle as the two women could make them. But they were not invisible. Not to me.

Lancelet radiated a quiet joy. While Guinevere... Well, she was less readable. But she seemed happy. More relaxed than I had ever seen her. Not simply the superficial calm she always seemed to possess, but something that went below that tranquil surface.

I wondered now if the tranquility had been a mask she had been forced to wear all these long months, through her ordeal with my brother, the loss of Merlin, and then her great responsibility in overseeing the temple.

Was this the closest thing to a holiday she might ever have? I pursed my lips together.

"What's so funny?" Draven asked, riding up beside me.

I looked at him and felt wicked. "I was simply thinking about the way your cock felt in my mouth this morning. So long and hard and thick."

I watched as my mate's eyes widened slightly.

Then something incredible happened.

"By the Three, Draven," I said with delight. "Are you actually blushing?"

"Fae don't blush." His jaw clenched tightly.

I hooted. "That's absolutely untrue. I blush all the time." I peered at his warm, brown skin. "Yes, I definitely detect the hint of a blush there behind my husband's beautiful, golden-brown cheeks."

"Impossible," he scoffed, tossing his head. "Perhaps Valtain fae blush, but Siabra don't."

I narrowed my eyes. "Oooh, that's a low blow."

I glanced back at Gawain and Hawl who were riding behind us.

"Shall I speak in more detail of not just the feel of your cock in my mouth, but the taste?" I made my voice become a throaty purr. "The taste of you as you spilled into my mouth and poured your rich seed down my throat as I hungrily sucked, desperate for more, more, more?"

Draven's hand shot out like a flash and wrapped around my wrist.

I squeaked.

"Not unless," he said through gritted teeth, "you wish for me to pull you from your horse, toss you over my shoulder, and take you in that rocky field over there while the rest of our friends blush and look away. Not unless you wish for your cries of pleasure to fill the air from here to the Black Mountain itself."

I gasped as his green eyes pierced through me, rendering me naked with a single glance, undressing me from head to toe.

"Stop that," I accused. "It's not fair. It's too easy for you."

"Not fair?" He laughed. "But what you just did to me was?"

"There are many things not fair about you," I grumbled. "Another one is your smell."

He raised his eyebrows. "My smell? You've never complained before."

"It's not a complaint so much as an accusation. You smell ridiculously good. Even when you've been in a saddle all day. Even when you haven't bathed in a week."

It was true. Even from here I could smell the mix of musk and spice.

"Cinnamon and sandalwood." I narrowed my eyes suspiciously. "You rub it all over yourself when I'm not looking, don't you?"

He grinned. "I'll never tell."

My heart flip-flopped. He'd slicked his black hair back that morning. Now his horns were more noticeable, black and sharp and alluring.

"Would you like me to lick your horns tonight?" I asked, trying to sound casual.

"My horns?"

Was I mistaking it, or had he jumped a little?

I took a deep breath, hoping for a deeper whiff of his scent, hoping he wouldn't notice. "Yes, your horns. Would you like me to wrap my hands around them as you thrust deep within me?"

He was watching me with a strange expression. "What are you doing, Morgan?"

"What?"

"You look like you're tracking an animal."

I felt a blush spreading across my cheeks.

"Aha, the Valtain blushes," he crowed, just as Gawain rode up and clapped him on the shoulder.

The red-haired man grinned at us. "Well, you two look as if you're enjoying yourselves on this long and lonely road. What are you talking about?"

"Oh, nothing," I said swiftly. "Nothing at all."

Gawain raised his brows. "Nothing? C'mon. It has to be more interesting than what Hawl was just telling me about."

"What's that? How many more moths they plan to put in your pancakes?" I quipped.

Gawain grimaced while Draven chortled. My mate hadn't minded the taste of the flapjacks. Once he'd found out what Hawl had done, he'd laughed his head off then asked for another helping... while Gawain had run to rinse out his mouth with seawater.

"Something like that. Not to mention their hope that we'll run into more bandits soon." Gawain snuck a look back at the Bearkin. "Honestly, part of me wonders..."

"Wonders what?" Draven asked.

"If we weren't here... would Hawl have... you know." Gawain lowered his voice. "Would they have eaten those bandits?"

I choked back a laugh. "I suppose to bears, it was rather a waste of meat."

Gawain shuddered. "Gruesome."

"Well, it's no less gruesome than us eating a fish," I said.

"Though the bandits were sentient," Draven reminded me.

"I suppose there is that," I admitted. "Perhaps that changes things." I grinned at Gawain. "I'm sure they wouldn't have done it. I'm sure they wouldn't eat *you*. Is that what you're really worrying about?"

Gawain made a face at me. "You're probably right. Though all of their talk of crunching bones and rending flesh..."

"Well, you love to fight, too," I pointed out. "It's not much different."

"I love to fight, yes," he said grumpily. "But I don't go on and on about how many people I hope to kill each day."

"Just tell the Ursidaur to tone it down with the battle talk," Draven suggested. "Or I can, if you're afraid to talk to them." He grinned.

"Afraid?" Gawain glared playfully. "Not of that damned bear, if that's what you're suggesting." He looked between us thoughtfully. "I suppose you aren't going to tell me what you were actually talking about."

I couldn't help it. I felt my face flushing again.

"Oh, ho!" Gawain tipped his head back and chuckled. "I suppose I don't need the details after all." He nodded ahead to where Lancelet and Guinevere rode. "And what about those two?"

"What about them?" I said.

Gawain gave me a shrewd glance. "Very well. Don't tell me then. But it's clear to see that something's changed. I suppose if some people find happiness on this journey, so much the better."

"I agree," I said quietly, looking ahead at my friend and the woman I believed was now her lover.

Just at that moment, Lancelet turned in her saddle. "There's something ahead," she called back. "An encampment."

Draven spurred his horse forward with Gawain and I close behind.

Twilight was falling as we entered a makeshift refugee camp nestled within a valley. A sea of tents bordered a green forest. Patched and weathered, they stretched across the plain as people bundled in worn garments walked between them or huddled around small fires.

We rode into the camp slowly, trying not to startle anyone with our arrival. Moving down the main row of tents, we passed families clustered together, their possessions packed into humble carts or tied in rough bundles.

Children played in the small spaces between the tents, their laughter sharply contrasting with the looks of worry and despair in their parents' eyes.

The scent of simple meals being prepared wafted through the air. Boiled potatoes and rabbits in pots mixed with the fresh scents of pine trees and horses.

My horse shied as someone almost stumbled into us. I looked down to see an elderly woman, stooped with age, her eyes misted to near-blindness. Beside her walked a young girl of perhaps ten or so in ragged clothes. Her arm was linked through the old woman's as she helped to guide her along the row of tents.

The child looked up at me briefly, as if momentarily curious, then looked away. I glimpsed irises almost white in a pale, thin face.

"Hey, now!" A man was pushing through the people walking ahead of our horses. Grey-haired and dark-skinned, he had the look of more than a simple farmer and reminded me immediately of Sir Ector.

Nevertheless, I glanced at Draven in concern. Was this man about to make trouble for us?

"Watch out," the man shouted again. His eyes were not on Draven or me, I realized. "There. Your companion. Catch her."

I turned to my right to see in horror the man was correct.

But before I could move to do anything, Guinevere slipped from her horse and fell to the ground, her eyes closed.

CHAPTER 22 - MEDRA

The horse was screaming.

The tree was on fire, and my horse was screaming.

From a long way away, I could hear someone shouting.

The horse reared, tossing me from its back. I fell to the ground, wincing in pain, my eyes never once leaving the tree.

The fire was spreading from one tree to another. A heavy rain fell. But it was not enough to put the fire out.

Branches crackled overhead, tongues of orange and red consuming them alive. I leaned back and watched them die, fascinated.

Around me, the grove was thick with smoke and the scent of burning wood. Fiery tendrils were spreading through the canopy, reaching skyward, a vivid blaze of red against the stormy night sky.

A trampling of hooves came from the underbrush.

My horse had fled. I was alone.

I breathed in deep, letting the smoke fill my lungs.

Another thunderclap. Closer this time. The ground beneath me shook, and involuntarily, I shuddered.

Hands, firm and unyielding, suddenly seized me, dragging me from my stupor and lifting me off the ground.

Hoisted to my feet, I was dragged, stumbling forward, a strong arm wrapping around my waist to guide me.

Odessa.

She did not speak.

Billowing smoke curled and twisted around us. I coughed, tasting ash in the air.

Odessa moved forward, dragging me with her, pulling me between raining embers and falling branches.

I stumbled.

A cracking sound above.

I lifted my face to see a flaming branch descending like an incandescent meteor.

I closed my eyes.

There was a sizzling hiss, a grunt of pain.

The unfamiliar but unmistakable scent of burning flesh.

I opened my eyes. Odessa's arm was still raised, her teeth gritted.

She had shielded me.

The sight of her arm was what forced fear into me at last. Torn cloth and melted flesh, blood dripping to the forest floor.

We flew between the trees, running together, hand in hand, until finally the smoke and the flames were far behind us.

The thunder had passed.

Only the rain remained.

Odessa was already binding her wound. Standing there in the shadows with only the burning grove behind us for light, I watched as she tore a strip of cloth from the hem of her tunic, then stooped to pluck some large leaves from a nearby bush. Pressing them against her arm, she winced.

I made a motion as if to help, then forced my arms to my sides. Everything I touched I destroyed. It was better not to try.

Winding the torn strip of cloth around the makeshift dressing, she secured it in place with practiced precision.

As she finished, she met my gaze. I tried not to look away. Tried. Failed.

I waited for the inevitable questions.

What happened?

What did you do?

Why were you there?

Why why why why.

But the questions never came.

"Your mother loved you."

My head jerked up as if I had been slapped.

Odessa's eyes were still on me, dark and unflinching.

"You've never asked. But you must have wondered. Did Crescent ever speak of her to you?"

Mutely, I shook my head.

"He never knew her. I didn't either," Odessa said.

I tried to form words. To part my dry lips. My mouth felt full of smoke.

"Then how..." I tried.

"How do I know?"

I nodded.

"Your aunt. Morgan was there when your mother died."

I cleared my throat. "Orcades."

"Yes. Orcades. Orcades le Fay. Or Pendragon."

"Morgan... told you?"

"Yes. Your aunt told Crescent before she left. In case she never made it back. And Crescent told me."

A blaze ripped through me. Odessa saw.

"I know," she said. "He should have told you. Over and over again. A child needs to be told. It's not like Crescent to be so thoughtless. You were old enough to be told. I'm sorry, Medra."

I lifted my chin. "He's never liked me."

"That's not true." Odessa's voice was gentle. "He doesn't understand you, which is very different from not caring about you." She was quiet for a moment. "I think he thought it would be easy. He's always been good with children, you see. He's always wanted more."

"More like Taina," I said bitterly.

"Taina is... Well, she was easy for Crescent to connect with. She's an easy child."

"Easy? Ordinary," I spat. "Normal."

Odessa smiled. "There's nothing wrong with being extraordinary. Or with not being easy to get along with. The same has been said about me."

I felt surprised to hear we were alike in some small way. Pleased, for a moment. But then my temper rose. "Not extraordinary. A freak."

"Oh, Medra." Odessa sounded tired. "Is that what you really believe?"

I said nothing.

"Your mother did not believe that. She thought you were the most beautiful thing in the world."

I couldn't help it. My heart sped up. "How do you know?"

"Your aunt was there with her when she died. You don't forget a thing like that, Medra. A dying woman's last words to her child."

I felt something stinging in my eyes. Rain most likely.

"What were they?" I demanded, making my voice hard and tough. "Her words? Tell me."

I wanted them. I was *owed* them. I should have been given them long ago. The only thing my mother had left me.

Beyond this cruel birthright. *My self.* This life.

Odessa had begun to walk slowly back in the direction of the castle. She seemed heedless of the pain her arm must have been in. Heedless of the falling rain. The dark. The roots at our feet that might have dragged us down.

"Orcades said you were the most beautiful thing she had ever seen. And she said she loved you."

"That's all?" I tried to sound dismissive. But the rain on my face had become a flood.

"'Who meets their death devoid of love shall surely face their end,'" Odessa murmured. "'But one who gives their soul away, eternity extends.'"

"What's that?" I curled my lip. "Some kind of riddle?"

"Morgan said it was something your mother said as she was dying. I'm not entirely sure what it means. But it's clear she loved you, right from the start."

"But she didn't stay."

"She *couldn't* stay," Odessa corrected. "That doesn't mean she didn't want to. She seemed to believe she was giving you something important though. She died giving you life after all."

"No more than most mothers do," I muttered, viciously kicking at a tree branch. "Lots of women die in childbirth."

"That's true." Odessa sighed. "My own mother did. Giving birth to Crescent."

I hadn't known that. It was something else we shared.

"You must have hated him," I guessed.

"A little. At first." I could almost hear her smiling in the dark. "Then I was glad to have him."

"I don't have anyone." The words spilled out. I detested how they sounded. Pathetic. Weak.

Odessa stopped abruptly. Turned to face me.

"Now that's just not true, Medra." She moved her arm, the burned one, then grimaced.

"I did that to you," I said. "You should hate me."

"But I don't," she snapped. "Stop trying to make me. It won't work."

I looked away. "It worked with everyone else."

"Is that what you think? That you succeeded?"

I wouldn't face her. "They left, didn't they?"

"Your aunt? Draven? They left to *save* you, Medra. Not because they didn't care."

I frowned. "Save?"

"Perhaps save was the wrong word," Odessa said quickly. "But to protect. They left to protect you. They left to do something important. Something that will protect not just you but so many people. Everyone in Pendrath. Perhaps everyone in Eskira."

I didn't want to hear this. Crescent had given me some version of it before.

"So they didn't care about me. They cared about everyone," I shot back.

"To you, that's worse, isn't it?" Odessa shook her head. "Oh, to be a child again. I don't envy you the experience a bit."

"I'm hardly a child," I said, tossing my head.

A stable boy certainly hadn't thought so. He had flashed me a wink when I'd led my horse out that afternoon and asked me to meet him at the tavern tonight.

I wouldn't, of course. Stupid boy.

"You may look like a fourteen-year-old girl, Medra, but you most certainly *are* just a child. You've been alive for less than a year. That's the tragedy."

"Tragedy?"

Odessa looked at me with pity. "Don't you see? They don't even know."

I shook my head, still not understanding.

"Your aunt and uncle. They're expecting you to still be a baby when they get back."

If they got back. But I kept my mouth shut.

"But you'll be a woman," she continued. "Or close to it. They're missing everything. It will break their hearts."

Like it had broken mine.

I wouldn't say that though. Weak and pitiful. They were the worst things to be.

Like my other uncle. Resting in a bed chamber, so silent and still. So alone. Everyone pitied him. No one really thought Kaye Pendragon would ever rise again.

We had stopped near the edge of the castle grounds.

"They love you, Medra," Odessa said softly. "You are loved."

She reached out her unhurt hand to touch my arm, and I recoiled. Quickly, she held up her hand.

"It's all right. Slow moves."

No one had tried to touch me with affection in so long. I couldn't remember the last time.

Crescent had tried to embrace me once. I had hissed at him then watched his eyes widen. In fright, disgust, or horror—I was never sure which. But he hadn't tried it again. Touching me just once—that had been enough for him.

"But I won't stop trying," Odessa said now. "And I promise you, neither will your aunt or uncle when they return. We are your family, Medra. There is no pushing us away. No matter how hard you try."

"You're not my family," I spat. "We're nothing alike."

I wanted to wound her. To be cruel. But suddenly, I felt so tired. I couldn't force out more bitter words.

I looked at her arm. She had already done so much for me. She had stayed. She had trained me. Taught me to fight. Taught me so many skills Sir Ector could not have.

She had silenced any servant who dared to speak ill of me. Sent them all packing.

She didn't know I knew, but I did. I watched. I listened.

Even Crescent. She had given him an earful. A few days after she'd arrived, I'd come across them. She'd told him everything he'd done wrong, every way he'd failed me.

And then she'd stayed.

"You don't have to consider me your family," Odessa said quietly. If she was hurt, I couldn't tell. "I can still consider you mine."

The stinging filled my eyes again. Blast the rain.

But when I looked up, it wasn't raining any longer. The sky was clearing. The stars were out.

"You've been having the dreams again." It was a statement, not a question. "They frighten you," Odessa went on. "Make you feel even more alone. You worry about yourself. About what you'll turn out to be. What will become of you."

There was more. But what she'd guessed was enough. More than enough.

Slowly, I nodded.

"There is darkness in all of our souls. But there is also light. Just because the darkness threatens doesn't mean the light won't win out in the end." She raised her hand and very carefully touched my cheek. This time, I didn't pull away. "You've known the dark more than most children have. No one can imagine or say what you've experienced. You are truly unique. Truly extraordinary. And, this I swear to you, truly loved."

A sob wrenched through my chest.

And then Odessa was pulling me towards her, wrapping me in her arms, and telling me I was loved more than I knew over and over and over.

CHAPTER 23 - MORGAN

A healer had been called. There was one among the refugees.

Lancelet had lifted Guinevere and carried her into the healer's tent.

The healer's name was Amara. A petite woman with golden skin and long black hair, she had declared Guinevere was suffering from nervous exhaustion. Before anyone could stop her, she'd poured a sleeping draught down Guinevere's throat, announcing the best thing for her was total rest.

I tried to mask my look of panic from Lancelet but could not hide it fully from Draven.

Outside the tent, we all conferred.

"We'll stay however long it takes for Guinevere to get back on her feet," Draven assured Lancelet.

Lancelet's eyes were troubled. "How could she have been hiding this from me?" She glanced at me and then quickly looked away, but I knew what she was thinking.

"It's not your fault. If you're blaming yourself, stop. She could have told you or any of us if she was growing weak." I hesitated then went on. "If anyone should feel guilty right now, it's me. She must have drained herself shielding me. Staying awake too long."

We had been riding hard, but not to the point of this kind of fatigue—or so I had thought. We camped each night at dusk and rose a little after dawn. We spent at least eight hours on the road, but paused for a midday meal. And usually Guinevere would sleep for an hour or two at that time.

At night, she made me sleep for at least six uninterrupted, blissful hours after taking five or six for herself.

But perhaps she had not been sleeping. Or had not been able to.

I hesitated, then asked, "Has she been sleeping? Truly sleeping? Do you think you could tell?"

Lancelet shook her head, her eyes anxious. "I'm not sure. I thought she was. But perhaps she was pretending. Why would she do that?"

"Or perhaps she was sleeping," Draven said. "But perhaps shielding Morgan has been draining Guinevere much more than we realized."

"Clearly it has been," Gawain agreed. "We must rest here however long she needs."

I nodded. But my mind was already on the night ahead. How long would Guinevere be out because of the draught? A night? A night and a day? Longer?

I thought I could last the night, but suddenly found myself wishing I had availed myself of the chance to sleep when I had it the night before instead of lying there worrying about the road ahead.

But perhaps I could take those same sleep-stealing anxieties and turn them to my advantage, I thought grimly. If they could leave me sleepless one night, they could surely help to do so the next.

We set up our tents at the edge of the refugee camp, on the outskirts of a field that led into the nearby forest.

"At the very least, maybe we can help these people while we're here," Draven said quietly to Gawain and Hawl and me as we unpacked. "Provide some extra protection."

Hawl nodded. "There must be many bandits roaming these lands. These people are easy pickings."

"I wonder if they've been attacked before. There can be safety in numbers," Gawain observed. "We could offer to help keep watch."

"Their leader—or whoever that man was—seemed to have a solid look to him," I said.

Draven nodded. "I'll speak with him later. See if there's anything he needs. There aren't many of us, but..."

I smiled slightly. But my mate hated to be useless. And staying put, even while our friend recovered, would drive him to distraction.

Hawl and I set up our tents. Then I helped the Bearkin prepare a simple meal while Draven and Gawain went to find the leader of the refugee camp.

Madoc was the man's name. His wife, Amara, was the healer.

The camp was on the move. They had stopped only to rest a night or two before advancing westward. The same direction we were going—westward, then north into the mountains.

Extra help keeping watch was welcomed. Draven had already volunteered to take the first shift, Gawain informed me when he returned. Gawain would take the second.

By the time Draven returned, most of the camp was asleep. Of our group, I was the only one who remained sitting by the fire. Lancelet had gone to bed early, crawling into the tent she'd begun sharing with Guinevere.

I'd stayed awake with Hawl, cleaning up after the meal, then sitting alone with one of the books I had brought, reading by firelight.

My eyes were heavy, but I was determined to stay awake.

Draven kissed me, but I could see from his eyes he was weary. It had been a long day. And we were all worried about Guinevere.

I crawled into the tent after him, helping him undress, then pulling a blanket over him as his eyes closed.

For a while, I simply watched him sleep, smoothing his dark hair off his forehead and listening to the comforting sound of his breathing.

I thought of Medra. Just a tiny babe, slumbering back in her cradle in Camelot. Or had she outgrown the cradle? Perhaps she was in a crib now. Was it the same one Kaye had used?

I thought of the path we were on and the destination it led to. The Black Mountain. My father and siblings. My father's court.

The spear. Rychel. Would they be easy to find?

What sort of a court could exist within a mountain? I couldn't imagine.

But I must have tried. Perhaps I tried too hard.

Because some time later, Lancelet was shaking me awake.

"You fell asleep." Her eyes were wide. "Did you...? You know."

Dream.

I sat up groggily. Beside me, Draven was still asleep.

Lancelet glanced at him. "I'm sorry. I wouldn't have come into your tent, but it was so quiet..."

"What time is it?" I demanded.

"Dawn. Guinevere's still asleep. Gawain's on watch. Hawl was just about to start breakfast."

She was still eyeing me nervously.

"No," I assured her. "I didn't. Dream that is."

Her face filled with relief. "Thank the Three for small miracles."

I tried to smile, but inside, I was confused. Why hadn't I dreamed? It had been the perfect opportunity.

Perhaps I'd slept for less time than I thought. I'd been lying by Draven thinking for what had felt like hours.

Lancelet disappeared, the tent flap falling back into place, and I quickly pulled clothes on.

I would let Draven sleep, I decided. While I checked on Gawain. I'd bring him some breakfast if his watch wasn't over.

Dawn's light was spilling timidly over the valley as I walked through the quiet camp. I pulled my cloak tighter around myself as the chill morning air greeted my senses.

The dew-laden grass was soft beneath my boots as I moved between rows of tents towards the spot Gawain was keeping watch at the edge of the camp near the treeline.

But when I reached the place he was supposed to be, no one was there.

Assuming he was strolling the perimeter, I decided to take up my own position, holding his place for him until he returned.

A meadow lay just beyond the camp, between the rows of tents and the treeline. I turned towards it, enjoying the feel of the cool breeze whispering through my hair. As I did, a flash of movement near the edge of the forest caught my eye.

Gawain was standing in the field, close to where the trees began, his figure cast in shadows.

As I watched, he stepped into the light, his hair glowing orange and crimson.

My breath caught. There was someone beside him.

A woman was emerging from the trees. Even from a distance, she stood like a specter of beauty, her silken gown shimmering in the soft morning light. Her hair, a mesmerizing blend of rich black and deep velvety blue, cascaded in silky waves down her back.

As I watched, wondering who she could be, the woman extended her hand and held out a small, golden object to Gawain.

It radiated, glowing like a tiny beacon of celestial light. For a moment, I was as transfixed as Gawain, staring at the object, whatever it was, so glowing and full of allure.

Then Gawain raised the object to his lips.

"Gawain, no!" I screamed.

Gawain paused and looked towards me, his face shifting into surprise then delight, he smiled radiantly. "It's all right, Morgan," he called. "It's beautiful. A beautiful gift."

And then Gawain swallowed the gift he'd been given.

I sprinted forward into the field, panic surging through me as swiftly as understanding.

But it was too late.

The woman turned towards me, a smile on her lips. "A gift, Sister." Her voice was lilting and melodious. Like Orcades's had been. "From our father."

I stopped a few feet away as Gawain's entire body began to tremble. Shudders rippled through him as the ghastly metamorphosis my sister had induced took hold.

His skin took on a sickly pallor. A familiar greenish hue. His features began to sharpen. Eyes lost their luster as an unholy shadow eclipsed their life and spark.

His limbs convulsed, undergoing a twisted reconstruction that defied nature itself.

A choked sound came from my throat as Gawain's fingers elongated into gnarled claws and a guttural snarl escaped from his lips.

"Gawain."

I whirled around to the source of the familiar voice.

"Draven," I said desperately, lifting my hands to try to shield him, knowing it was far too late. "Draven, no." A sob escaped my lips. "Draven. Please. Don't look."

"Don't worry, Morgan," my nameless sister called from behind me. "There's enough for all of your little friends."

I ignored her.

From a few feet beside me, Draven let out a low growl of pain and fury. "Gawain."

His hands were curled into fists by his side. He hadn't even reached for his blade.

I closed my eyes, knowing what I might have to do.

And then the choices were removed from the table.

Gawain sprinted towards Draven like a feral beast, snapping and snarling, spit dribbling down a ravenous face that was no longer close to human.

Like a flash, Draven had moved, letting Gawain barrel past him.

But the man-turned-beast would not be put off. He was slower, more awkward, but nonetheless deadly.

We could not let him return to the camp like this. This... This was beyond any healer. I knew Draven knew it, too.

I turned to my sister. "Is there a cure?" I shouted towards her. "Give it to me, and I swear I will return with you."

But she just smiled, her hands clasped in front of her pristine white gown, looking beautiful and innocent as if she hadn't just murdered my mate's best friend.

Swearing, I turned back to Draven.

Gawain was hurtling towards him again.

Draven glanced at me. Just once. It was enough. My heart tore apart at the look in his eyes.

He knew what he had to do.

I lifted my hands. I could use fire. But a blade would be quicker. Kinder.

Draven's claws were out, I now saw. As Gawain ran towards him, Draven caught him by the shoulders, digging his claws in to hold his friend at a distance.Gawain howled. A cold shiver went through me.

Our friend was gone. In his place was something worse than an animal. There was nothing in his eyes. Nothing but blind rage and hunger.

I watched as Draven released Gawain with one hand, holding him back with the other as Gawain spit and clawed, tearing at Draven's clothes, narrowly missing his face.

There was a blade at Draven's side. He slid it out slowly.

I refused to close my eyes, to look away. I stayed where I was, watching, witnessing.

Gawain let out another howl of rage as Draven's claws dug further into his shoulder, holding him captive, holding him steady.

And then to my shock, a second howl joined the first, and I saw my mate's lips were parted.

He howled with Gawain, a sound of grief and rage and torment like nothing I had ever heard.

Their voices joined in an incongruous harmony. A death song.

Then the blade slid home, hard and true.

An expression of pure shock came over Gawain's face, and for a moment, just an instant, he looked almost human again.

I let out a gulping, heaving sob and ran forward as the big man slumped to his knees with Draven's arms around him.

Gawain's eyes were already vacant.

His lips parted, as if in shock, as his chest lifted and fell once, then twice, then one last time. And then he was gone.

All I could think of was how were we going to tell Crescent? How were we going to tell Taina?

"Where is she?"

I looked down, hardly seeing Draven.

"Where is she, Morgan?" he repeated, his voice cold and hard.

For a moment, I had no idea who he was talking about. Then I remembered.

My sister.

"She was just there..." Dazedly, I turned back towards the forest line.

She was gone.

"Who was she?"

I shook my head, feeling dazed. "I don't even know her name. My sister. I think she was my sister."

Draven growled. "She's dead. She's mine. Do you understand?"

I nodded. It wasn't as if I'd have tried to defend her. Sister or not.

I was starting to think Orcades had been the only worthwhile person out of a rotten and poisonous bunch. So much for fucking family.

A scream. One, then another. Then a wave of screams.

I turned towards the sea of tents behind us, my heart pounding. "The camp. The refugees."

I started towards the camp, then paused to wait for Draven, who was gently arranging Gawain's body on the grass.

He had just gotten to his feet and was coming towards me when the first arrow hit.

A jolt of searing pain shot through me, stealing my breath.

For a moment, I was frozen, looking down at the arrowhead protruding from my shoulder without fully understanding what I was seeing.

Then a second arrow found its mark.

I screamed, my left leg going out from under me, an arrow buried deep in my calf.

"Morgan!"

I turned towards Draven just as the wolves broke through the line of trees.

My breath hitched in shock as I saw the rider who led them.

He sat on the largest of the wolves, a bow in one hand, a golden spear in the other. His skin was a deep shade of obsidian. Dark, braided hair hung around his shoulders and framed a diamond-shaped face. He did not smile as my sister and Daegen had done. There was no mirth in his eyes. Only a commanding resolve that spoke of centuries of experience. His chiseled jaw was locked and resolute.

My heart was hammering. I knew who this must be.

"Lorion," I murmured to Draven. The most brutal of our father's generals. And he carried my father's spear.

Could it be this easy? Was the spear truly so close? And yet, as I felt my leg give way and I sank to the ground, I knew it was not going to be easy at all.

The screams from the refugee camp were growing louder now.

"I see you've already met our sister," Lorion shouted. "Tempest has no patience."

My shoulder and leg were burning with agony. I gritted my teeth, trying to focus.

"Fucking coward. You'll die today. As will she." Draven's voice was more menacing than any wolf's.

Draven had reached me. He was holding me upright. His face was filled with concern. I tried to smile, to reassure him, but the pain was bad. So bad. Worse than anything I had felt with Fenyx. How could it be this bad, I wondered?

Something was on the arrowheads, seeping through me. Poison.

Was it the same stuff my sister had put in the food she had given Gawain? Was I turning into a monster like him, even now?

Lorion's bow was raised to his shoulder, an arrow notched.

"Draven," I tried to say.

"Don't worry about it." His voice was short.

He moved his arm to his side.

A blade whistled through the air.

Before Lorion could even loose his next arrow, the bow was wrenched from his hands. It fell into the trees behind him.

Lorion looked at Draven, a small, tight smile on his face.

Then he raised his arms over his head.

The wolves surged forth.

They ran, not to us, but around us. Foaming and frothing, they raced eagerly towards the camp.

"No," I moaned, thinking of the children, the families, the elderly. What had we brought down on these innocent people who had lost so much already? "No, Draven, no. We have to stop them."

My sister was already there, no doubt leaving a trail of blood and destruction in her wake.

I knew what she was doing, what she must be looking for.

The sword. The grail.

And when she found them? What would she do with the people left behind?

The camp would be a ruin of blood and ashes.

Guinevere. Lancelet. Hawl. They were still back in the camp.

"You fucking coward, Lorion," Draven bellowed. "Shooting her from behind. What kind of a warrior does that? You couldn't face her on equal ground after what she'd done to your brother, could you? You were too afraid she'd best you. The lot of you, you're all pathetic."

He was lowering me to the ground. I knew he had to. There was nothing else he could do.

He met my eyes. "I have to leave you here now, Morgan," he murmured. "I'll be back. You know I'll be right back. Just let me finish this bastard."

I nodded and tried to look encouraging, but all I really wanted to do was lie in the soft grass and close my eyes, shut out the pain, shut out the screams.

Lorion was saying something to Draven.

"This is not my day to die, Siabra," I heard him call out. "Honor has nothing to do with it. I perform my duty, nothing more. My father wishes you dead, so here I am to see his will carried out. If it weren't for you, our sister would have returned home willingly. You're a disease. A curse, like all your people. Now you and she will die here together. Let this be the end of it."

And then, spear held high, his wolf raced forward.

Pulling his sword from its sheath, Draven maneuvered away from where I sat in the grass, leading Lorion to the left and further across the empty field.

My legs felt very cold now. My eyes were blurring. Still, I looked towards the camp.

A red fog seemed to hang over the sea of tents. Tendrils of crimson, like putrescent vines, covered some of the canvas shelters themselves. And between them all ran the wolves.

I could hear the howling, the growls, and amongst the sounds of the beasts, the screams of children.

Gritting my teeth, I shoved my leg out in front of me and looked down at the arrow embedded in my calf. Pain seared through me. I took a deep, steadying breath.

Wrapping my hand around the arrow, my fingers closed around the shaft. My teeth clenched, the taste of metal flooding my mouth as I braced for what came next.

In a deliberate motion, I swiftly pulled. The barbed arrowhead caught, lingering on flesh and sinew, resisting removal.

I could feel the blood draining from my face. Praying I wasn't about to pass out, I tugged harder. The arrowhead gave up its hold. I gasped as an intense burning surged up my leg.

I leaned over into the grass and emptied the contents of my stomach, then pushed myself up again and clenched my teeth. It wasn't over.

Exhaling shakily, I turned my attention to the arrow in my shoulder. Gingerly, my fingers traced the shaft. Then, taking a deep breath, I grasped it hard. Drawing on every ounce of willpower I had, I yanked the arrow from my shoulder, feeling muscles and sinew rip and tear as I pulled.

For a moment, there was some relief. Then agony swept back over me.

I fell backwards onto the grass, waves of nausea and dizziness filling my body.

Across the field, Draven and Lorion were still fighting. I turned my head, trying to focus my eyes enough to see.

Lorion's wolf was already dead. The massive beast lay lifeless in the grass, its eyes glazed over.

I hoped the wolf had meant a great deal to my brother. But I doubted it had.

The men paid the dead wolf no need. They were engaged in a deadly waltz. Draven's steel blade against Lorion's golden spear.

My mate moved with calculation, parrying my brother's thrusts. I could see that both were deadly fighters.

As Lorion moved, I thought of the countless battles he must have fought by my father's side. He was older than Draven. Perhaps more experienced.

The battle was intensifying in a flurry of close combat. Lorion seemed to be giving ground. My heart sped up as I realized he was luring my mate in with a false sense of advantage. Would Draven fall for it?

Draven pressed his attack, swinging his longsword. I could see the cold fury in his eyes as he danced in battle with my brother mere steps from where Gawain had fallen.

Gawain. And now me.

I closed my eyes, listening to the sounds of clashing weapons and the cries of desperation coming from the camp. My mind felt urged to action. But my body felt weighed down with weakness, as if heavy chains bound me to the earth.

I opened my eyes. A bird spun overhead.

A carrion bird. A harbinger of death.

Was it waiting to feast upon Gawain? Or upon me?

It circled as if assessing me, then evidently deciding I was no threat, swooped down with purpose.

I closed my eyes, preparing to beat away the cursed bird with my fists if I had to.

Then to my shock, a heavy weight landed upon my chest.

I opened my eyes to see Tuva sitting there, fixing me with her keen, luminous eyes.

A connection sparked between us. I could feel a profound intelligence emanating from the owl.

She pecked me. Hard. Digging her curved beak into my forehead and raking downwards.

"Ouch!" Touching a hand to my forehead, I felt blood running down.

The bird's expression, if it could be called that, was one of ample frustration. As if I were not doing what she thought I should be.

My pulse quickened. Pain and clarity converged.

I held my breath, looking into the owl's golden eyes.

Why was I lying here?

Was I merely a pawn in my father's game? A prize to be won or a trinket to be broken and discarded?

An awakening was taking place within me.

My vision spun, but this time, I could glimpse the threads hanging between the fabric of reality. Threads I could almost reach out and touch. A wellspring of energy waiting to be harnessed.

And I had never truly tapped its full potential. Not really.

I had used what seeped out of me. The power I could not contain. I had used Draven's power out of necessity. I had tapped into him, into Nightclaw, even into Excalibur—believing my own powers were so limited, so drained, that I had no other choice.

I had healed Draven when he was wounded and believed myself clever for pushing myself to the edge of my limits. For healing him with my will.

Now a surge of determination flooded my weakened limbs.

Closing my eyes, I delved. Delved into the well of power within. Saw how deep it went. How vast the pool truly was.

I navigated the currents of my magic, saw the poison trapped inside my body, and rushed to meet its insidious advance head-on.

The grass beneath me seemed to shiver. Silently, Tuva lifted off and flew away.

My eyes remained closed, watching the poison recoil from my advance as if scorched by an inner sun.

I turned my attention to my wounds, envisioning the knitting of flesh.

I *felt* the moment the arrow wounds closed and the poison's malevolence dissipated.

I rose to my feet, no longer bound by weakness.

The battleground awaited me, and with every heartbeat, I knew I stood at the threshold of destiny.

Across the field, my mate fought on.

He fought alone.

But he did not have to.

Dark coils shot from my hands, weaving across the field like vines and catching my brother by the ankles.

He stumbled, then fell with a shout.

The coils continued wrapping, winding up Lorion's legs, over his chest, binding his arms to his sides, then sliding over his face, into his mouth.

He was rendered silent. Contained. Just the way he and our sister had hoped to make me.

I walked slowly towards the two men. Draven had lowered his sword.

He stared at me, taking in my closed wounds, my unimpeded gait.

"Once, you did the same for me," I said quietly as I reached my mate. "Do you remember?"

Beside us, my brother writhed in his shadowy bonds. Like Fenyx on the wall of the dungeon in Camelot where Draven had held him.

Draven slowly nodded.

"Let me do this for you now. Finish him. So we can find my sister."

Lorion writhed harder, squirming and twisting against the black coils.

I knew what he would say if I were to release him, unstop his mouth. He would call us cowards. Say Draven owed him a fight—single combat to the death. He would demand honorable terms. He who had been so dishonorable.

And if he lost to Draven, he would behave just as Daegen had. He would crawl through the earth on his hands and knees if he had to, and he would not stop coming. None of them would. Until they had reached me, finished me. All to gain the honor of returning to our father with my head in their hands.

So there would be no more speeches.

I had no need for Lorion's words.

We owed him nothing. *Nothing.*

The only one we owed lay dead in the field already.

We owed Gawain revenge.

Lorion's golden spear had slipped from his fingers. Now it lay gleaming in the grass beside him.

Draven picked it up, then planted his feet firmly in the earth.

The spear's blade glinted menacingly.

I watched as Draven lifted the spear, his muscles rippling beneath his tunic, his eyes locking onto my brother's face.

Then with a powerful rotation of his torso, he released the spear.

It hurtled forward and found its mark, lodging itself in Lorion's chest with ruthless efficiency.

Then, to my surprise, Draven leaned forward and wrenched the spear out again.

It dripped with my brother's heart blood as he held it in both hands, then he shifted his weight, brought the weapon against his knee, and tensed his muscles.

The spear bent and snapped with a loud crack.

I stared in shock as Draven tossed the jagged halves of the weapon aside without ceremony.

"Only gilded wood after all," he observed as he walked away from the broken spear and the dead fae general lying dead in the grass.

I gave my brother one last glance.

Lorion le Fay. Long may he lie forgotten. The insects would have him. He would lie unburied. Decaying and festering until the worms devoured his flesh and left his bones polished and white.

"It wasn't the spear." I couldn't keep the disappointment from my voice.

Draven shook his head. "Not *the* one."

"How did you know?"

"I had no idea. Not until it broke."

The refugee camp was in turmoil as we entered.

Above the camp, a red fog hung in patches, casting an eerie canopy of light.

We passed between the tents, stepping carefully over tangled bodies. Red tendrils spilled from lifeless mouths.

Poison, it seemed, was my sister's weapon of choice. Perhaps she had poisoned the arrows Lorion had used. If so, she was sure to be surprised to see me.

A lone wolf ran between the tents in front of us. In a heartbeat, Draven had darted ahead, and with a flying leap and heavy blow, the wolf's head rolled on the ground.

Across the makeshift road, more wolves snarled, chasing fleeing refugees. Draven looked towards the wolves. I knew he longed to go after them and stop their slaughter.

But he would not willingly leave my side. Nor give up his chance of vengeance upon my sister.

I touched his shoulder. "Look."

Amidst the horror, some refugees were fighting back. Men and women, their faces lined with defiance, were battling the wolves, using small knives, clubs, and other makeshift weapons.

A crackle of magic sparked through the air, and I whirled in the direction where our tents lay.

"First Tempest," I said, my voice low. "Then the wolves. We'll finish this then aid the camp."

Draven nodded grimly.

We moved towards the source of the spark, dashing through the maze of tents.

As we reached the place where we had made our camp, a chaotic scene unfolded.

Hawl lay on the ground, blood soaking their fur. Guinevere crouched beside the Bearkin, trying with great difficulty to wrap a bandage around one of the creature's huge arms that had been lashed to ribbons while Hawl struggled to rise to their feet and rejoin the fray.

Meanwhile, dancing around the small stone circle where we had made our fire the night before were Lancelet and Tempest.

Lancelet held Excalibur. That was enough to shock me to my core. The blade had fought for her once, yes, but only at my urging.

Tempest held the grail. She gripped it tightly in one hand as, with her other, she split the air with her poisonous red tendrils.

As my sister's venomous vines slashed out, Lancelet employed the sword with impressive finesse, bouncing the long stems off the blade.

I felt a surge of affection towards the sword as well as panic at the idea that Tempest had gotten this close to it. Excalibur must have been so desperate to avoid my sister that it had allowed Lancelet to wield it.

Beside me, Draven moved restlessly. Lancelet, I saw, was struggling. Excalibur was allowing her to wield it, yes, but there was a difference between wielding the sword and surviving, and wielding it and succeeding.

Lancelet's movements were becoming more and more labored as she tried to keep pace with Tempest's assault.

Just as the thought left my mind, a coil of red snaked through the air, moving past the sword and grazing Lancelet's armor, leaving a sickly residue in its wake. She yelped and twisted, Excalibur's light flickering as the pain from her wound washed over her.

In an instant, Draven was in front of her, his own longsword out, shadows wrapped around its hilt.

"Lancelet, this woman is mine," he said without looking at her. "Stand down."

For a moment, Lancelet seemed prepared to argue. Then she glanced at me—and to the empty space beside me. Her eyes scanned the camp. I knew who she was looking for. Gawain.

When her eyes moved back to my face, I nodded tersely.

Draven was already in the throes of combat, his sword and shadows moving to meet every red tendril Tempest was throwing out.

He was giving everything to the fight.

Together, he and my sister moved faster than I could track, faster than I could see.

"Your mate fights well, little sister," Tempest screeched. She sounded delighted, as if she were relishing the battle. Clearly she did not fear Draven. Not as she should.

"Our sister Orcades spoke of you with fondness, Tempest," I called to her. "I had foolishly hoped that meant there was something good in you as there was in her."

Tempest laughed. A tinkling sound that reminded me of Orcades's melodic laughter.

"Foolish indeed. Your idea of goodness is as silly as a child's." She whipped red vines towards Draven, and he jumped back just in time. "With Orcades gone, a place opened up by our father's side. Lorion and I won't fail him as Daegen did."

"Really? But Lorion already has," I informed her.

Tempest's eyes shot to my face incredulously. "You lie." But she was already scanning the camp around me, just as Lancelet had done moments before, as if expecting to see Lorion approach at any moment.

"He's not coming, Tempest. He's dead."

She paled slightly, distracted. Draven took advantage of it.

One of his shadow coils shot out, seizing her around the waist and lifting her into the air.

She screamed and sliced through the dark coil with a red tendril of her own.

I pressed my hands against my sides. My fingers itched to help my mate, to join him in this fight. I could cast flames. Take Excalibur and fight by his side.

But he had said she was his to finish.

She had killed his best friend.

I would not intervene.

But words—those were another matter. I could still distract her with my words, give him the opening he needed, just as he had always done for me.

"You're all alone, Tempest," I called. "Lorion is dead and no one is coming to help you."

In answer, she shrieked and spun, throwing vine after vine of scarlet around her.

Lancelet and I ducked aside just in time.

It was working. I shot a meaningful look at Lancelet, and with a nod of understanding, she passed me Excalibur, then ran towards Hawl. Together, she and Guinevere grasped the Bearkin by the shoulders and began dragging them kicking and protesting away from the vicinity of the camp.

"Do you have any idea what you've done, Morgan?" Tempest's voice was shrill. Was she frightened? Or simply furious?

"I'm sorry, Sister. Was Lorion your favorite brother? Were you very close?" I drawled.

In answer, she tossed a long red thread my way. I blocked it almost lazily with Excalibur, bouncing it back towards her.

"Our father," she hissed, "will be furious. Daegen, he could forgive. Daegen was a fuckup. Sent out only because you were underestimated. I told Father to let Lorion and me accompany him."

"Oh, yes, and look how much better you and Lorion are doing." I lifted Excalibur and studied the blade's rose-studded hilt as if everything she said bored me to tears. As if I had all the confidence in the world. "One dead. One almost down. Right, Draven?"

"I am not dead," Tempest screamed. "You believe it is so easy to destroy the daughter of a god?"

I went very still. Behind her, Draven froze, momentarily pausing his attack.

Tempest's vines wavered around her.

"What are you talking about?" I breathed. "A fae high king is not a god."

Her eyes flashed, and for a moment, I could see just how easily Gawain had been bewitched. She was beautiful, yes. Incredibly so. And her beauty was more terrifying than any sword.

"You don't know everything, Sister." The look of triumph on her face made me gasp. "Even now, our father moves to strike the thing you hold most dear."

My mind raced.

Medra. She meant Medra.

"I have no idea what you're talking about," I replied, trying to keep my tone cool. "My mate is behind you. Perfectly safe."

In answer, she tossed tendril after tendril over her shoulder, forcing Draven to block and dive.

"Not him, you fool." A cunning smile crossed her face. "The baby. *Your* baby."

She stepped towards me. Behind her, I saw Draven moving slowly into position.

"He saw her in your dreams. The little girl." She dropped her voice to a whisper. "She's probably dead already. The poor little thing. She won't have had a chance."

My hands twitched at my sides, longing to set her face alight, to see that lovely smile melt.

But I did nothing. She was not mine to take.

And I refused to show her just how terrified her words had made me for Medra's sake.

"Lorion shot me from behind," I announced, disregarding her attempts to frighten me and forcing thoughts of Medra aside for the moment.

She frowned, confused. For a moment, the red flurry of tendrils she had woven around her fell away.

"Here." I touched my shoulder. "And here." I gestured to my calf.

Tempest looked at where I'd indicated, but her expression suggested she thought I was a fool.

"So don't expect my pity," I explained, as Draven's coils of black night wrapped suddenly around my sister's exposed throat and tightened.

She gave a strangled gasp and dropped the grail, raising her hands to her throat, trying desperately to slice through the shadowy binding with her crimson vines.

The wooden chalice rolled towards my feet. I looked down at it with distaste.

"We have no child," I told Tempest as the breath left her lungs. "There is no baby. Our father is wrong. Just like he has been about everything. You're not a child of a god. You're a simple fae. And just like a mortal"—I leaned in and lowered my voice—"you can *die*."

The coils strained and constricted, and my sister's lovely eyes bulged wide.

CHAPTER 24 - MEDRA

S omeone was singing.

I pushed back the blankets and slid out of my bed.

Along the walls, candles flickered in their iron sconces as I wandered through the castle, straining my ears towards the source of the sound.

Meandering slowly through corridor after corridor, the voice gradually grew clearer.

I trailed my fingers over a tapestry, feeling it flutter with an unseen breeze.

As I walked, I began to catch some of the words of the song. A plaintive tale of a child stolen away at night by her mother the queen, leaving her father the king to bitter heartbreak.

"A king revered," the woman's beautiful voice sang sorrowfully, as if the loss had been her own. "A daughter's tears. A mother feared."

A chill ran through me at the inhuman beauty of the voice.

Quickly, I ran up narrow stone steps towards the sound, my footsteps echoing off the walls of the tower.

At the top of the tower, I turned a corner and entered a small chamber bathed in moonlight.

A woman sat alone by the window. She was turned away from me, her face in profile.

A cascade of dark red tresses framed her face, glinting like strands of rubies in the moonlight. The hair fell in graceful waves, gently brushing across her slender shoulders and over the gown of black and emerald she wore.

Ruby-red lips, like the petals of a rose, parted as she continued her haunting melody,

"Through veil of night, a stolen bond,

A secret guise in shadows veiled,

As darkened queen took flight with dreams,

And left behind a shattered scene."

As I watched, the woman lifted a delicate hand and pushed strands of her hair aside, revealing the subtle pointed tips of her ears.

My heart sped up. She was fae. But I had never seen her in the castle before.

Was she a friend of Crescent? Or Odessa?

I took a step closer, and the woman whirled towards me.

My heart pounded. I held up my hands, not wanting to frighten her away. "Forgive me, lady."

She put a hand to her heart. "You startled me, child."

"You have the most beautiful voice," I said, not wanting her to stop singing.

She smiled. A breathtaking sight. I caught my breath. "Perhaps I'll sing for you again sometime. Would you like that?"

I nodded eagerly, still intoxicated from the sound of her voice.

She beckoned. "Come closer, my dear one. Let me look upon you."

I did as she said, steeling myself. I was not pretty. I was unusual and plain. I knew that. In a moment, she would, too.

But she looked at me silently without revealing anything in her expression.

Then, she touched my arm gently. To my surprise, I did not shy away.

"You have your mother's features. She was very beautiful, you know."

"That can't be," I said, disbelieving but not wanting to call this lovely fae woman a liar. "She had amethyst hair and violet eyes. Mine are only black."

The woman smiled sweetly. "But the shape of them is all Orcades."

"You knew her then? You knew my mother?"

"Of course I did." The lady laughed. "She was my sister."

I took a step back, my mouth falling open.

"That's right, Medra. I am your aunt. Sarrasine is my name."

"I didn't know I had any other aunts," I said, feeling as if the room were spinning around me. "No one told me."

Sarrasine looked sad. "Of course not. Why would they? Why would your Aunt Morgan speak to you about the rest of her family when she hardly knows us herself?"

"She doesn't?"

The crimson-haired beauty shook her head. "She doesn't. Not yet. But she will soon. And how happy she will be to see you have already taken up your place with us, Medra."

"With you?" I croaked. "Does that mean…"

"Yes." Sarrasine clapped her hands together joyfully. "I'm here to take you back with me, Medra. Would you like that? To join me and meet your grandfather and the rest of your family?"

"But this is my home. I've always lived here."

"Always is a very short time when one is a child, isn't it?" she said gently, lifting her hand to push a strand of my hair behind my ear.

I wanted to argue and say I wasn't a child. Not really. But then I realized she might know what I really was. And perhaps she could explain it all to me if I went with her.

"It must feel very strange to think of leaving. But your grandfather very much wishes to see you, Medra. He sent me to fetch you."

I thought of Odessa. The way she had stayed with me. Cared for me. Trained me when Sir Ector had given up on me.

Then I thought of all the things I hadn't told Odessa. The things I couldn't say. For fear she'd run the other way, despite her claims she'd always stay.

I looked at my aunt with the ruby hair and lips and said, "My eyes aren't always black."

"Oh, no?" She looked curious, interested. In no way frightened by my revelation.

I shook my head. "No."

I looked at the window beyond her. Outside, a hawk was flying past.

I took a deep breath, then let my eyes flare red.

The hawk burst into flames and plummeted to the ground.

My aunt watched as the bird fell. She did not run. She did not flinch.

"Incredible," she said, finally. "You have incredible power, Medra. Such a thing is not uncommon amongst the fae. Surely, you know this? You have been told?"

I nodded. "But my power is different."

"Different how?" She leaned forward, peering at me closely. "Tell me."

I hesitated. "Sometimes I hear voices."

"Yes? And what do they say?"

I bit my lip.

"Go on, Child," she encouraged. "It's all right. You may tell me."

"They tell me to kill. To destroy." Not just a bird. No, not just a bird.

Sarrasine smiled. It was a true smile. Not one hiding fear. "It's very good I came then. Your grandfather will be so pleased to see how far you've already progressed."

"He will?"

"Yes, he certainly will. We left you too long. It was nearly too late."

"Too late? Too late for what?"

"Why, you might have harmed yourself. Or harmed someone else. And we wouldn't want that, would we, Medra? You wouldn't want to stay here and hurt someone you cared about, would you?"

I thought of Odessa and her burned arm. "No. I wouldn't."

"Your grandfather will help you from harming anyone ever again. Wouldn't you like that? To be taught and properly trained? Everyone in your family is special. We are of royal blood, you see. The oldest of all the fae. But you, Medra, may be the most gifted one of all. The most special child. And it's my job to bring you straight to him, to your grandfather."

Sarrasine rose from the seat by the window and smoothed down her gown. "Gorlois le Fay. My father. Our most extraordinary, most powerful king. Only he is worthy of our full devotion. Soon, he'll rule over all of the world. Just as he did once before."

I was impressed. What child wouldn't have been? "Truly?"

"Truly. And you'll be there by his side, helping him along the way."

She made a gesture with her hands, and suddenly two figures appeared from the shadows to her right and to her left. Fae guards.

Alarmed, I moved impulsively towards the door.

"They're only here to help me, Medra," she said quickly. "We're ready to go now, aren't we? There's no need for guards. They were only here to protect me. I wasn't sure what I might find here, you see. But everything has gone exactly as I'd hoped. For you found me before I even had to search for you. You came right to me. My dear, dear niece."

I looked between her and the guards in their black masks and shining black metal armor. I wanted to ask her what she needed protection from.

"Can't you come and meet Odessa and Crescent? Can't I tell them that I'm leaving first?"

Sarrasine shook her head sadly. "That wouldn't be a good idea, I'm afraid. They won't want you to leave. It's their job to keep you here, Medra. To keep you captive."

Captive? Was that what I was? Was that what I'd been all this time? The thought startled me.

"I need time to think," I said fretfully. "Can you come back tomorrow? I need to say good-bye to them."

At least to Odessa. I couldn't leave without saying good-bye to Odessa.

"We have to go *now*, Medra," Sarrasine said firmly. "We're out of time." She looked between the two guards, then back at me consideringly, and I took a step closer towards the steps.

"Here now," she said, her tone becoming sharper. "What are you doing? Stay close. I need to be touching you for it to work."

"For what to work?"

"The stitching, of course. Not many can do it, even in our family." She smiled brilliantly at me. "Won't it be fun? Have you ever stitched before? We'll be gone in a flash."

She was speaking to me as if I were a child, I realized. A much younger, much more naive child.

And perhaps I was one. In part.

But I was something else, too.

"No," I said stubbornly. "Come back tomorrow. I do want to come with you, but I can't go yet. I need to say good-bye to Odessa."

"How ridiculous," my aunt said impatiently. "Medra, please. You won't like it if I lose my temper with you."

My eyes must have widened at the sharpness in her voice, for abruptly, her face relaxed. She shook her head, letting her lovely hair cascade around her shoulders. "Come, my dear, take my hand. This will only take a moment."

Her voice had changed. It was becoming sweet once again. I could feel myself being drawn in. I took a step towards her instinctively.

"Step away from her, Medra," a hard voice said. "Quickly now."

I whipped around to see Odessa poised at the top of the tower stairs. She was barefoot. Clearly she had been sleeping. But her swords were strapped to her back, as they always were.

"Come towards me, Medra. Very carefully."

"This is my aunt," I explained, knowing they were already getting off on the wrong foot, desperate to fix it. "Her name is Sarrasine. She wants me to go with her. But I've told her I can't. Not yet. But tomorrow. I've told her to come back tomorrow. Then she can take me to meet the rest of my family. I have a grandfather. Why didn't you tell me, Odessa?"

"It wasn't my place," she said quietly. "You have a large family, yes, Medra. But there are only a few within it who truly care about you and want to keep you safe."

"How silly. And I suppose you're one of those people?" Sarrasine said disdainfully. "Or perhaps Morgan? We have as much right to this child as anyone does."

"Medra is her own person. And we both know what you plan to do with her as soon as your father has her within his grasp," Odessa replied.

I had never heard her sound this way before. So cold and full of rage. And more than rage. She was frightened—not of me, but for me.

"What do you mean?" I demanded.

Odessa met my eyes. "Your grandfather is afraid of you, Medra. That's why your aunt has come. Not out of love, but out of fear."

I thought of the hawk and flinched.

"That's not true," Sarrasine said, her sweet voice turning sharp again with annoyance. "We love the girl. Of course we do."

"Love her as you did her mother?" Odessa challenged. "The mother your father had locked up? Imprisoned?"

I looked at Sarrasine. "Is that true? Did he do that to her?"

"There was a reason for it. I'll explain it all to you later. Come now. There's no time for this." My aunt reached towards me.

I darted backwards behind Odessa.

"Stay there, Medra," the warrior murmured. "No matter what happens next."

"We understand what Medra truly is. We can hone her powers. Teach her to use them properly. There's no need for fear," my aunt said.

"Use them? For what purpose? And if she won't do as you or your father wish, what will happen to her next? Will he kill her?"

I caught something in my aunt's eyes. A look of guilt perhaps. Odessa had touched something there. Something close to the truth.

"You have a choice to make, Medra," Odessa said quietly. "You could choose to go with this woman, your aunt. But I don't think you'll like the place she'll take you or the people you'll meet there, even if they are your family. You aren't a cruel child, Medra. You've never been cruel. You long for the light. Don't turn away from it now. Stay with me here. Stay with me until your aunt and uncle return to us."

"They won't return." Sarrasine sneered, and instantly, her elegant face was transformed into something cruel and spiteful. "They'll never return. Don't fill her head with stupid hopes that are doomed to fail." She looked down at me. "There are winners and there are losers, Medra. These fae and mortals you stand with now will not prevail against your grandfather. Soon, all of Eskira will be his dominion. Your family will rule these lands. We will control these people. The woman you see standing before you will be a slave—like many others. Is that what you want? To be a slave, Medra? Or do you want to rule by your family's side and be the princess you were meant to be?"

She held out a slender hand. "Come with me now, sweet child. Come home."

"Odessa will never be a slave," I shouted, my eyes flaring to life.

They flashed, and the guard to Sarrasine's left fell to the ground, writhing in pain.

Another flash, and the guard to her right fell, rolling on the ground as if invisible flames were wrapped around him.

"Then bring her with you," my aunt hissed. "And keep her as your pet, if that is what you desire. Either way, you are coming with me. Now."

And then she moved towards me.

In a flash, Odessa had blocked her way. Both her blades were out. "You shall not have her."

"Do you really think you can challenge me, Siabra?" Sarrasine said, her lovely lips twisting in a cruel smirk. "With steel of all things?" She looked at me. "Come here, Medra. No more games."

Her voice was sweet. So sweet. I *moved*. Not because I wanted to. But because I was compelled.

I stepped out of Odessa's protective shadow and walked slowly towards Sarrasine. One step, then another, before coming to a halt in the middle of the tower.

"Closer," Sarrasine demanded, her eyes narrowing, her voice still as sweet as the nectar of a blossom.

I gripped the floor, digging my heels in with everything I had, feeling my aunt's voice pressing into my mind and urging me on even as I refused her saccharine-infused command.

Odessa let out a battlecry and lunged forward, twirling around me and slashing out at my aunt.

My aunt lifted her hands protectively, and Odessa's blade ripped across them.

Blood dripped to the floor.

Fury flashed in my aunt's eyes. Before Odessa could move towards her a second time, Sarrasine screeched, "Lift your blades to your own throat and cut it, you Siabra bitch."

"No," I screamed. "No, Odessa."

The room shook with power as the words rang out, countering my aunt's command.

But Odessa was fast.

She had always been faster than me with her blades.

I had always aspired to be as good as she was.

Now I wished she were slow.

The two blades swept across the air. She had started to lower them slightly when I screamed out but they still sliced through flesh, cutting across her chest.

She fell to the ground, her body shredded and torn, gasping for air.

I whirled towards my aunt.

"It's all right, Medra," Sarrasine said, raising a hand to soothe me. There was no compulsion in her voice now. "She was nothing. No one. I'm here. I'll take care of you."

All I could think of was that I might have gone with her.

I had truly been considering it. To go to a place where people might understand and accept me exactly as I was. It had seemed almost too good to be true.

But she had hurt Odessa.

I wasn't going to waste another word on my aunt.

My eyes flashed. For a split second, I caught the look of fear on Sarrasine's face.

Then she was gone.

I turned to the left and then the right. In another instant, the guards were gone, too.

All that remained were ash piles. Litter on the floor for a servant to sweep up the next morning.

I fell on my knees beside Odessa. She was clasping her hands to her chest. Blood flowed between her fingers. She looked down at them and let her hands fall away with a sigh. Then she smiled at me. The tenderness in that smile made me want to weep.

"Odessa." I looked at her, shaking my head as I fought back tears. Tears were for the weak. "I'll go for a healer. Stay here."

"No." Her voice was surprisingly strong. "No, Medra. Come. Sit with me."

I sat down beside her, trying not to look at her wounds. Knowing I would never forget the sight of them for as long as I lived.

"Come closer," she said. Her voice wasn't sweet. That wasn't Odessa's way. Odessa was never sweet. But she was gentle. Tender. She loved me. I knew that now. "Closer, dear one."

With a choked sob, I scooted forward, wrapping my arms around her.

Wearily, she lifted a hand and squeezed my arm.

"Oh, my little Medra."

"You're dying." I hiccuped. "You're dying, and it's all because of me."

"No." Her voice was sharp. "Don't ever say that. Don't ever think that. Not because of you. Because of them."

"My grandfather?"

"Yes."

"He's the one my aunt and uncle went to stop," I guessed.

She nodded. "I should have told you sooner. But no one expected you to grow so fast, Medra. You're a miracle." She squeezed my arm again. Her grip was not as strong as it should have been. I leaned against her, feeling her warmth, knowing it would soon be gone. "My precious miracle."

She coughed, and I saw blood trickle down her face. She wiped it away with the back of her hand.

"There is a prophecy, Medra. One that Morgan would have told you about when she returned. But she's not here now. I am. And... I don't know. Perhaps it's time you knew all of it."

"What kind of a prophecy?" I asked, my heart speeding up.

"A prophecy that claims you will be the killer of kings. A prophecy that, interpreted one way, suggests you could be your grandfather's downfall."

"That's why Sarrasine came for me," I whispered. "Not because they actually wanted me. Because they want me dead."

Odessa was silent for a long moment. "Probably. I think so. Or maybe your grandfather truly does hope he can use your powers to his own advantage. That's the thing about prophecies, Medra."

"What's that?"

"They don't have to come true. Your mother hoped you would spell her father's downfall. She hoped for that with all her heart."

Had she loved me because of it, I wondered? Only because of it?

"But your aunt refused to accept that it was the reason you existed," Odessa went on. "She refused to let the prophecy determine your fate, your future."

"And you?" I demanded, suddenly furious at my mother, furious at my aunt.

"The choice should be yours," Odessa said, her voice heavy with fatigue. "The choice should always have been yours. But no one knew you'd be ready to make it so soon. How could they have?"

It was a fair point. I said nothing.

Odessa coughed again. "I think I need to lie down."

I helped her recline, then closed my eyes as her breathing grew more and more ragged.

"I love you, Medra. You know that."

"I love you, too," I whispered. "Please don't go. Please don't leave me."

"I know you'll make the right choice, my dear one. I'll always be so proud of you."

She lifted a hand and touched my face with a finger stained with her own blood.

Then her hand fell. She did not lift it again.

I sat at the top of the tower and finally let the tears fall. There was no one left to see.

CHAPTER 25 - MORGAN

D eath surrounded me. Followed me. It always had.

First my mother, whose death I would always feel partly responsible for. If she had not given me her magic, would she have been able to defend herself? Would she have tried?

Then Uther, that dark tormenter who had left so much to be desired as a father. My first kill.

I had spared Arthur only to have him discharge death upon so many innocents.

Then Florian.

Vesper.

I had believed Lancelet was dead. It was a miracle she had survived and due to no feat of mine. I had left her.

The children of Meridium. Could their fates be traced back to me? My father had desired their souls to fuel his own power. Was it because he had lost me that he needed them?

All through the Court of Umbral Flames, I had courted death, walked with it, delivered it, narrowly avoided it.

Beks's death. I had not seen it coming, had done nothing to stop it.

Javer had sacrificed himself for me. Literally throwing himself towards my father's altar.

Kaye. Lifeless but alive. I had not been able to save him.

Now I had brought death into the heart of these people of Rheged who had already been filled with so much sorrow.

And Gawain... Gawain was gone.

I could not bear to look around me. Mine, I knew, was not the only heavy heart.

The pyres that scattered the field bore the remains of mothers, fathers, children, grandparents. And in the center, a little larger than all the rest, lay Gawain's. His final resting place would not be by Crescent's side or with Taina holding his hand, but instead on a bed of wood and kindling.

They were lighting the pyres now.

A woman in the crowd behind me broke out wailing as a small pyre near the front was lit. A child's.

I kept my eyes straight ahead. If I looked back at her, I knew I would break.

Draven brushed his hand against mine briefly, then moved forward and accepted a torch from a man with a soot-streaked face.

Touching the torch to each side of Gawain's pyre, he stood back until the flames grew into a crackling blossom of crimson and orange.

All of the pyres were alight now. The heat emanating from the field was almost unbearable, but still we stayed. Around me, mourners bowed their heads, some whispering prayers, others quietly crying.

Tendrils of smoke rose into the night as the scent of burning wood became more pronounced.

To my left, Lancelet and Guinevere stood motionless. Hawl was not present. The Bearkin had gone to visit the exmoors. In truth, I believed the Bearkin had no wish to participate in one of our death rituals, no matter how respectful and well-intended. In Ursidaur culture, a body was left to decay where it fell, feeding back into Aercanum as nature had intended. They did not burn or bury their dead as we did.

Draven's arm slid around my waist, pulling me against him. I stiffened, then forced myself to relax.

"Can we go back now?" he murmured into my hair.

I nearly sagged in relief.

I nodded, and together, our small group turned away from the burning pyres and chanted prayers.

Slowly, we made our way through the remains of the refugee camp, past burned husks of tents and scuff marks in the dirt from yesterday's fighting to our small cluster of tents.

The fire was out. I sank down beside the little ring of stones anyway and wrapped my arms around my knees, resisting the urge to bury my head in my hands.

Guinevere moved to my side to gently touch my shoulder. "You need rest, Morgan."

I yanked away. "So do you." I ran my hands over my face. "I'm sorry." I knew she meant well. I knew she simply wanted the best for me. "But it's true. You're the one who was ill."

We would never know what had brought my brother and sister down upon us.

Was it the fact I had dozed off while Guinevere was sleeping?

Or was it because of the grail? I had touched it with my bleeding hand after the bandit attack. Could my father have sensed that somehow? Had the grail drawn Tempest and Lorion down upon us?

For my part, I was inclined to blame the grail. I hated the chalice. It had destroyed Gawain. Touching it had corrupted his soul in some way. Weakened him to Tempest's magic. Allowed her a foothold for her poison.

But either way, it all came back to me. I was the poisoned source that had led Gawain to his death, whether through my dreams or through my father's dark creations.

There was no way around it. Gawain would still be alive if I had made him stay behind.

Now I looked up at Guinevere and saw only death. Her death.

I turned away. "No matter what happens next, none of you are to touch the grail. Ever. Do you understand?"

Lancelet and Hawl had wandered back to the tents. Now Lancelet looked across at me.

"We understand," she said quietly.

Hawl nodded. "You believe that contributed to Gawain's..." The Bearkin cleared their throat loudly. "That he was bewitched somehow because of the cup?"

I nodded.

"Morgan believes he saw more than he was letting on when he touched the grail," Draven said, coming to crouch beside me.

"But you've touched it before, haven't you, Draven?" Lancelet pointed out. "And nothing terrible has happened."

He shrugged. "Perhaps I'm immune somehow. I'm bonded to Morgan. I'm not sure the cup recognizes I'm separate from her. In any case, it doesn't seem interested in me."

I thought it was something else. Draven was stronger than Gawain had ever been. Oh, not physically. But inside, mentally. If the grail had a pull, then Draven and I had never felt it. We were able to resist its lure.

"We'll be leaving tomorrow at dawn then?" Lancelet said, changing the subject.

Draven nodded. "We'll help to escort the refugees on the next leg of their journey." He glanced at me. "At least, until we need to turn north."

I stared straight ahead without speaking.

"I'm surprised they want our help," Lancelet said quietly.

So was I.

"Madoc understands that we didn't intend to..." Draven began. He stopped. "He understands. We did what we could to stop it. As soon as we had the chance."

We had killed the wolves, Draven meant. We had killed Lorion and Tempest. But not before they had slain refugees.

"I don't understand it either. They should want us gone," I said bitterly. "We brought misfortune upon them."

I had seen the looks some of the refugees were giving me. Their leader, Madoc, might be a liberal-minded man, but others were not so forgiving. I was sure they would be glad when we all parted ways.

"We'll give them a little support and then leave them," Draven said. "They know who you are, Morgan. Yes, terrible things befell them here. But it was not your fault. And you are doing what you can to make up for what's happened."

He meant by providing a letter.

Madoc and his wife, Amara, the healer, would carry it with them all the way to Pendrath. When they reached the border, they would give it to the first soldiers they found who would then escort them and the rest of the refugees to Camelot where they would be put in Dame Halyna's capable hands.

The letter ensured they would not be turned away when they reached our border, that they would be accepted and provided for.

I owed them all that much.

Rising to my feet, I looked at Guinevere. "I've changed my mind. I'm turning in. If you're sure...?"

She nodded quickly. "Please. Rest, Morgan. I can sleep tomorrow. Even on horseback if I need to."

"It's true. I can strap her on behind me if I have to." Lancelet grinned at me, as if trying to urge me to smile. But I couldn't do it.

I nodded and went towards the tent.

Draven joined me a few moments later.

He crawled in, then sat, looking at me in silence.

"I lost him, too, Morgan," he said finally.

I closed my eyes, hands tightening on the trousers I had been folding. "I know. That's why you should hate me the most."

I lay down on the bedroll we shared and turned away from him.

The tent was very quiet that night.

CHAPTER 26 - MORGAN

Twilight was descending upon the rocky landscape as we reached the remains of a small village. The abandoned community lay in the shadow of the first true mountain we had encountered on our journey. Skeletal, burnt-out remnants of little huts and barns whispered of a forgotten past. One where simple people had lived simple lives.

I could sense the wistfulness and sadness among the caravan of refugees as they looked at the village, perhaps reminded of all they, too, had lost and left behind.

Madoc, their leader, had a loud, carrying voice. Turning his horse to face the train of wagons and people on foot, he announced we would spend the night here.

I looked towards the north where jagged peaks loomed in the distance, shadowed against the darkening sky. Bathed in deep hues of purple and pink, they created a breathtaking backdrop as we began to set up camp. Tomorrow, we would turn off the western road and go towards those forbidding mountains, searching for my father's concealed court.

At the foot of the mountain that towered over the village, something caught my eye. Hewn into the side of the cliffside were the crumbling remains of an ancient stone building. The entrance, marked by an eroded archway, was surrounded by rocks and debris.

"A temple."

It was Madoc. The gray-haired patriarch of the displaced. He was much shorter and stockier, but I was still reminded of Sir Ector each time I saw him.

"I remind you of someone," he said, seeing my expression.

I nodded. "A very dear friend back in Pendrath."

"Ah. I'm glad it is a friend and not an enemy," he said, smiling.

"You'll meet him in Camelot," I said a little stiffly, not wishing to speak of enemies. "Sir Ector Prennell."

Madoc raised his eyebrows. "A 'sir' is he?"

"He'll welcome you with open arms. No matter your rank," I said. "Especially with the letter you bring."

"We'll bring him news of your friend, too," Madoc said. "I hope we can soften the blow a little."

I winced, thinking of how Crescent would react, hearing the news of Gawain's death from strangers. It was cowardly, but part of me had to admit I was glad I wouldn't be there when it was delivered.

Would I ever return home to tell Crescent face to face exactly what had happened to his husband? To explain in detail just how Gawain had died? Would he even want to know?

"It's a temple," Madoc said again. He pointed to the ruins on the side of the mountain. "Abandoned long ago from the look of it. Probably not safe to venture into either. I'll have to let the people know not to let the children wander off too far."

"A temple to whom?" I asked, my skin tingling. "To the Three?"

"The Three?" Madoc shook his head. "No, the closer you get to Dornum, the less you'll see of the Three. Most people in Rheged are ambivalent towards the gods these days. But when they used to worship, the god we traditionally turned to was a fierce one."

I already knew what he was going to say. Still, I cringed as the words left his mouth.

"That temple was devoted to Perun. You can tell by the symbols on the stone pedestal." He pointed again, and this time, I saw them. Crude signs for thunder and lightning carved into the stone.

The lie I had told my sister coalesced in my mind. She was *the daughter of a god*, Tempest had claimed.

So then, so was I.

Madoc slapped his thighs. "I came to deliver a message but nearly forgot what it was. My wife wants to see you."

I was surprised. "Your wife? The healer?"

He nodded. "Amara and I have set up our camp over there by the stream. Will you come?"

I glanced around. We'd finished setting up our tents. Draven had gone to tether the horses. Guinevere was resting. Lancelet had gone to the stream to see if she could catch some trout. Hawl, as usual, was about to make dinner. We were spoiled, having the Bearkin with us.

The exmoors, I knew, would be somewhere nearby. They were close enough that I could sense Nightclaw. He was prowling. I smiled to myself as I caught a flash of sensation. Prowling for trout and half-wet already.

But the exmoors were far enough away that none of the refugees would catch sight of them and become afraid.

I followed Madoc through groups of refugees settling in for the night, keeping my head down as the genial man stopped over and over again to say hello to this one and ask another if they needed anything, to bop a child on the nose, to touch a baby's cheek.

"How did you come to lead these people?" I asked quietly as we finally neared the stream. I could see his wife standing outside a large tent, hands clasped in front of her. A smaller tent had been erected nearby. One was her healer's tent, I realized. Of course she still had the sick and injured to treat, even as the refugees traveled.

"I was a farmer before this," he answered. "Not even an elder on the village council. Can you believe it? And yet somehow, here I am. Sometimes you step forward because there's no one else who will. So many have given up hope." He shook his head. "Amara and I have no plans of doing that."

His wife smiled at me as I approached, then tilted her shining dark head questioningly at her husband. "I thought I told you to bring them both."

"He wasn't at their camp. I'll go and find him now," Madoc assured her.

"Who? Do you mean Draven?" I asked with a frown. "Why did you wish to see us?"

"It's all right," Amara said soothingly. "We aren't the ones who wish to see you. Here, step inside. Someone has been asking for you and your husband." She lifted the flap of the large tent, and I saw someone lying on a pallet inside. "I believe you already know her?"

I said nothing as I followed Amara into the tent. A lantern sat on a little table, illuminating the space.

An old woman lay on a low pallet. A child was crouched beside her.

"I've never seen this woman before," I started to say in answer to Amara's question.

Then I paused, realizing I *had* seen the old woman before.

On the road, as we had met up with the refugees. I had looked down to see this same woman walking with a young girl. The same girl who now sat beside the old woman's bedside.

"I've seen this woman before, yes. Amongst the other refugees. But I don't know her," I said, turning to look at Amara. "Why have you called me here?"

Amara looked surprised. "The woman asked for you. She was very specific in her description of you and your husband."

I glanced at the pallet and lowered my voice. "What's wrong with her?"

"Nothing but old age," Amara said softly. "Old age catching up to her. The road is even harder for the elderly. She had a place in a wagon with a kind farmer's family. But even that wasn't enough."

"She wasn't injured in the attack? Or poisoned?" I demanded sharply.

Amara shook her head. "No, nothing like that. She's simply old. She was frail even before this. Her body was under tremendous strain, and now... Well, it's simply breaking down." She glanced past me at the woman. "She doesn't have much time. Perhaps a few hours. I suppose she was muddled when she thought she knew you. Perhaps you reminded her of someone." Amara smiled and took my arm as if to lead me out.

"Wait," I said suddenly. "I'll sit by her for a while."

If Madoc really had gone to get Draven, the least I could do was make sure we didn't know the woman somehow.

"Is she... sleeping?" I whispered to Amara as I moved towards the pallet. "Her eyes are closed."

"Just resting a little, I think. If you speak to her, she should hear you."

"And this girl by her side? Who is she?" I asked, glancing downwards. The child remained unspeaking, her eyes on the old woman.

Amara shrugged. "A granddaughter perhaps? She doesn't seem to talk. I've tried to ask her questions. Only the old woman will answer them."

I wondered who was going to care for the child if the old woman she seemed so attached to was about to pass on.

But then, I thought, trying to harden myself, it was none of my concern.

I kneeled down beside the low cot.

"Do we know her name?" I asked, looking back at Amara.

The healer had already lifted the tent flap to wait outside. Now she paused. "I believe she said Rachel, but I may have misheard her."

My heart began to hammer.

No. It wasn't possible.

"Do you mean Rychel?" I said slowly.

Amara tilted her head. "That may have been it. I'm sorry. Perhaps you can ask her again if she awakens."

"I'll do that," I said.

I looked down at the elderly woman and softly placed my hand on her arm, noticing the fragile feel of her skin under my touch. Though a few streaks of black remained, her hair was mostly white. Her face bore the marks of countless years, with fine wrinkles tracing her features. She appeared ancient, her frail form seeming almost translucent against the bed.

"Rychel," I said quietly. "Is that your name?"

The elderly woman opened her eyes. Beneath the mist of white, the veil of near-blindness, I spotted green in them.

My heart caught in my throat.

"Rychel," I breathed. "Is it you?"

Eyes that had once been a vivid emerald looked back at me, full of pain and regret.

Her glasses were gone. As were the small horns that had matched Draven's.

But the dainty, heart-shaped face. The sun-kissed, golden-brown skin. Those were the same.

The more I looked at her, the more that was familiar.

"What happened to you?" I could hardly get the words out. "Who did this to you?"

Cracked, wrinkled lips parted slowly into a small smile.

"I did," the woman in the bed whispered.

"What do you mean?" I whispered back. I looked across the bed at the little girl crouched there so silently. "And who is she? Who is this girl?"

"My... daughter."

"Your daughter?" I shook my head. "That's not possible."

"Think of her as my daughter." Rychel's eyes were passionate and pleading, just as I remembered them. "I beg you to. Please."

I shook my head in frustration. All I could think about was how Draven would be striding into the tent at any moment. "What do you mean?"

"She is my child. She has no one else. Take her with you. Please."

"That's impossible," I said flatly. "You don't even know where we're going."

"Then send her somewhere safe," Rychel breathed.

I nodded. "I can do that. If you tell me first what happened to you. Tell me you're really Rychel." I clenched my fists. "None of this makes any sense."

"Did you ever expect me to make sense, Morgan?" Rychel whispered. There was a twinkle in her faded eyes.

The answer was so very Rychel that I couldn't help but laugh.

"I took the grail," she continued, her voice strained. "I went... to your father."

I froze.

Behind me, the tent flap opened.

Draven.

"What's all this about?" he asked quietly, taking in the elderly woman and child. He crouched down beside me. "Hello, my lady. I understand you are not well. Is there anything we can do for you?"

"Hello, brother," Rychel said—and I felt my heart crack and break. "I believe I shall die tonight. No, I don't believe there is much you can do. Not now. Besides put my mind at rest."

I watched Draven's face as it transformed. As he took in the small form, the wrinkled skin. As he told himself he didn't know this woman, then took in the once-luminous green eyes, the heart-shaped face.

"No. It can't be." He looked at me, his eyes wide and helpless like a boy's, and I pitied him. I wished I could have lied. I wished I could have told him the old woman dying in the bed was not his little sister.

Instead, I nodded slowly.

"Rychel?" he asked, looking down at the old woman. "What happened to you?" His voice was a plea.

"I'm sorry," she whispered, her milkish eyes transfigured with grief. "I'm sorry, Draven." She lifted a frail arm as if to touch him, then dropped it, shaking, as if the strain of merely lifting it had been too much for her.

She drew a shaky breath. "I took... the grail. Went to the Valtain. To Morgan's father."

"Yes, and then what? Did he do this to you?" The muscles in his jaw tightened.

She shook her head, almost imperceptibly. "Yes... and no."

"What do you mean? How can that be?" he demanded.

"The grail was taken from me. I was... naive... to think he would let me do my work."

I glanced at Draven. That came as no surprise.

"Were you mistreated?" I asked.

"Not... then," came the response.

But she had been. Eventually.

I could almost feel Draven's fury. Hot and palpable. Murderous. And directed entirely at my father. First Gawain, I could almost hear him thinking. Now Rychel. It could not stand. It would not stand.

"Later?" His voice was hard.

She nodded slowly. "After. When he was... angry with me."

"After what?" I asked, trying to keep the impatience from my voice.

There was a rasping sound. I realized she was struggling to draw breath. Glancing at Draven again, I wondered how much Amara had told him. Did he understand this was the end?

"I got past his guards. Got to the grail," Rychel gasped, her frail chest rising and falling.

"Why couldn't you do what needed to be done back in Myntra?" Draven demanded, his face twisting with grief and anger. "Why did you have to leave, Rychel? What good was giving him what he wanted?"

"You don't understand. I had to go. The children... The children were there."

A cold shock jolted through me. "What are you talking about?"

"I was right. They weren't all at Meridium. He had... kept some."

"Kept some?" A shiver ran down my spine. "Why?"

Rychel shifted slightly. "To display. To use. Residual power."

My heart sank. Of course. The despicable man. Of course he had.

"They frightened... the others."

"Those in my father's court, you mean?" I said.

"Yes. I got the grail. And then... I managed to get... a child."

Not a dead specimen like the one she had been dissecting back in the Court of Umbral Flames. But one with unnatural life still flowing through its veins.

I wasn't sure I even wanted to know how she had done that. How she had managed it without coming out looking like Lancelet.

"I used the grail's power," Rychel whispered. "Before he sent it away." To Arthur. My father had passed on the poisoned cup to my brother. But evidently not before Rychel had used it herself. "I knew it would work. I knew it. I was right."

"But it took something from you, didn't it?" Draven demanded, his voice grim. "What happened?"

"It took... all of me." Rychel slowly turned her head towards the little girl beside the bed. "I had... no idea... what it would be like. What it would... feel like. But... it was... worth it. I saved one." She closed her eyes. "Just one. But it was... worth it."

Draven and I both stared at the child. At the girl's pale, nearly colorless eyes. At her vacant expression, as if she were in this world but not entirely of it.

"What's her name?" I asked eventually. "What do you call her?"

"She has no name. None that I knew. I call her Lynette." There was a pause as she gasped for air. "She... answers to it."

Draven stroked Rychel's arm. "Stop. Don't strain yourself. We can speak more tomorrow."

Rychel closed her eyes. "There... won't be... a tomorrow. Not for... me."

"Why did you wait so long? Why not come to us before now?" I shook my head helplessly. "Maybe we could have, I don't know... done something. Tried to undo this. Is it truly too late?"

"Don't cry for me. I saved one life," Rychel said, her voice suddenly strong and familiar. "My only regret..." She broke off coughing. "My only regret was not being able to save them all. He wouldn't let me."

"We'll do what we can for them when we get there," Draven said, rising to his feet decisively. "As for you and Lynette, I'll arrange for you both to be carried in a wagon tomorrow. I'll hire guards to accompany you. I'll make sure Madoc and his wife care for you themselves the rest of the way to Camelot."

"Camelot," Rychel breathed. "Not going to Camelot. Take Lynette."

"Lynette will be taken care of for the rest of her days," I promised. "Don't be concerned for her."

"We'll see to you both," Draven insisted. "Both of you. Not just Lynette."

Rychel smiled slightly as if she knew there was no point in arguing with her stubborn, hard-headed brother.

Hard-headed but soft-hearted.

"I'll go and speak with Madoc now," Draven decided. "Then I'll return with warmer blankets for you both. In fact, you'll take our tent. Mine and Morgan's. We'll move you there. I'll ask Amara..." His voice drifted away as he left the tent.

I looked at Rychel and she looked back at me, then lifted her hand and gripped mine, squeezing gently.

"I'm...going... now."

I bit my lip but nodded.

She let out a shaking, rattling breath. "Oh, my brother... I'm so sorry."

When she was gone, her eyes remained open. Very gently, I touched them, closing each one.

Beside her, the girl Rychel had called Lynette did not cry or move.

I stood slowly then called for Amara. The healer came quickly. When she saw Rychel, she did not look surprised.

"So, she's gone then. It was peaceful at least."

I nodded. "My husband... I don't think he understood that it would be so soon."

"No," Amara said softly. "He's out there now, trying to arrange the very best care for her. What a kind man."

I put a hand to my brow. "Tomorrow, my friends and I will be traveling northward. Back into the mountains." I looked down at Rychel's body. "Where did you find her?"

"She and the girl were in a village near the coast," Amara said. "I assumed they were from there."

I supposed we would never know exactly how Rychel had escaped or managed to get that far. Was there another way to reach my father that we'd missed out on learning about? It was too late to ask now.

"This little girl is named Lynette," I said quietly, looking down at the silent child. "She was very important to my husband's sister. She has no family of her own."

"Sister?" Amara looked shocked. "Is that who she was? The woman seemed so old to be his sister."

"They had different mothers," was all I said. Which was true. "Amara, I want to ask you something."

I looked into the healer's dark eyes and saw the kindness there. She was a woman who could be trusted.

"What do you need?" she asked, looking back at me steadily.

"I need you to watch over Lynette as if she were your own child until you reach Camelot," I said bluntly. "When you arrive there, you may turn her over to the care of Sir Ector and Dame Halyna. Tell them I expect them to do the same."

I could not ask Crescent to watch over this newfound child. Not after we had already made him responsible for Medra. Not when he would be drowning in grief, with Taina to care for as well.

"And what if we don't wish to turn her over when we arrive?" Amara asked.

I stared. "What do you mean?"

"I mean, my husband and I have no children of our own. I've always wanted a little girl. If we get on well with her, perhaps she would wish to remain with us."

"You would do that?" I said slowly. "Take in a strange child as your own?"

Amara smiled slightly. "Look around you. We care for strangers every day here."

It was true. I nodded. "Fine. yes. But I would like to know where you'll be staying so that I may visit when I return to Camelot with my husband, if we wish to."

With Lynette's care arranged, I left the tent to find Draven.

He was outside, talking to Madoc about how to ensure Rychel would be comfortable in the wagon as it rolled and bounced down the unpaved, rocky road that led to Rheged's border.

"Draven," I said, putting a hand on his arm. "That won't be necessary." I glanced at Madoc and saw he had instantly understood. The leader of the refugee camp ducked into his tent, leaving us alone.

Draven looked down at me, unspeaking. I couldn't read his expression. I wondered if he could read mine.

We were so far apart then.

"She's gone," I said simply. "Rychel is gone."

He walked away from me. I did not follow.

"Morgan."

It was Amara. She had come out of the tent, but now stood, hanging back.

"Yes?"

She approached me slowly. "There's something else I wished to speak with you about before you leave tomorrow..." She paused, hesitating.

"What is it?" I encouraged her.

"Your friend. Guinevere. She's very weak."

I was surprised. "I thought she'd recovered. She seems much better after the long rest you... gave her."

Amara smiled ruefully. "Inflicted upon her, you mean. I know I should have asked first before delivering that sleeping draught."

"It's all right. I understand." At least Amara's intentions had been good, which was rare to be able to say about anyone these days.

"She's being drained, Morgan," Amara said hurriedly. "By what, I'm not sure. But the sleep she had was not enough. Not truly."

"Are you a healer or a priestess?" I asked sharply. "Or perhaps part-fae?"

I was being rude. I knew that.

"Neither. None of those. But I have seen strange things before." Amara met my eyes. "Something is draining her life force away."

"What exactly does that mean?"

"It means that what happened to your husband's sister, the woman in the tent—"

"Could be happening to Guinevere?" I was horrified. "No! We would have seen signs before now. We would have noticed."

Amara smiled slightly. "We see what we want to see, when it comes to the ones we love. Sometimes it's only too easy to blind ourselves."

"We'll look after her," I swore. "Now that I know…"

Amara nodded. "I thought you would. That's all I wanted to say."

I walked away, feeling stunned. It wasn't mere sleeplessness that I had inflicted upon Guinevere. She had been shielding me. But did it go beyond that? Had she secretly been battling my father in her mind on my behalf, just as I had done in my true dreamings?

I had barely been able to face him and hold my ground myself. How could Guinevere be doing it?

The ground seemed to be rising up around me as I walked, blindly, aimlessly, crossing a small bridge that led over the stream.

Gawain. Rychel. Now Guinevere.

Would all our friends and loved ones fall around me? Would I lose even Draven at my father's hands?

I walked without caring where I was going.

When I focused my eyes again, I saw I had arrived at the edge of the crumbling temple to Perun.

"You," I said to myself bitterly, looking at the broken arch. "It's always been you, hasn't it?"

I touched a hand to the blade at my side.

"The grail. The spear. The sword. The dread curse of Three." I shook my head. "A curse indeed. I bear the sword. I bear the curse."

Somehow, the blade was in my hand. I stared down at it.

In that moment, I hated the sword. Just as I hated the grail. Just as I would hate the spear—whenever I finally found it.

And yet… I loved Excalibur, too. How could I not? The sword had saved me. It had saved Lancelet for me.

It was a part of me.

But it was also a part of my father. *Forged by the gods under sacred skies.*

I lifted my head to the skies and screamed, the blade twisting beneath my hands.

I screamed in rage, in sorrow. I screamed in guilt.

"Ferrum deae," I screamed to the heavens. *"Ferrum deae."*

Iron of the goddess.

Mine. Not yours, Father.

When I finally looked back down, Excalibur was no longer a sword.

Instead a sickle rested in my hands, curved like a crescent moon.

CHAPTER 27 - MORGAN

I was still standing there, staring at the temple entrance with the curved blade in my hand, when there was a crunch of footsteps on the rocky ground behind me.

"I can go," Draven said quietly. "If you wish to be alone..."

I turned and looked at him. Truly *looked*, as I had not done in days. So wrapped up in my own grief that I had selfishly spared no mind for his own. So determined was I to take the weight of guilt upon myself for Gawain's death that I would not give him more than a glance, for fear he would, what...?

Turn on me? Reject me? Accuse me?

Now, as I looked into his face, my heart splintered into a thousand pieces.

Because there was no blame or condemnation in those familiar green eyes. Only pure, heart-rending grief.

He had lost. Oh, how he had lost.

Love was more than sharing pleasure. It was taking on another's pain.

I had not done that with Draven. I had not even tried.

Seeing him now, standing there, alone, so alone, all of my doubt vanished, and the only grief I could think of was *his*.

"Did you know that I will love you forever? That I would die for you?" I took a small step towards him. "I will love you for a hundred thousand years. And then a hundred thousand more after that."

Nothing would take away what I had found. Nothing would take away the man who stood before me.

Every hour of my life. Every breath, every whisper, every step I took had brought me towards him.

And now that our hearts had found each other—now that our very blood was *one*—I would never let him go again.

Carefully, I placed the sickle on the ground beside me and took another step towards him.

Love, real love, was standing by his side even when I didn't think I deserved to be there. Real love meant sticking around even when all of the sorrows and horrors made me want to run the other way.

I brought my hands up to Draven's cheeks, cupping his face and tugging his head down to me.

His emerald eyes glistened with unshed tears. He was strong, ever strong and unyielding. But now he *would* yield. To me. At least for a little while.

"Let me kiss your wounds," I whispered. "Give me your tears, my love. Bury yourself in me and give me all of your grief."

A choked sound came from his throat. Still, the tears stayed put.

I pressed my lips to his and kissed him. Kissed him as if there were nothing else I should be doing. Emptying my mind and filling it only with this moment, as if this kiss were everlasting and immortal.

We had lost people we loved.

But there was still this. A kiss worth all of the pain and all of the heartache.

Then Draven's tongue swept into my mouth, harsh and demanding, and my lips parted in surrender. I could taste the wine he'd been drinking and wondered just how much he'd had.

And then the kiss changed. There was no slow build, no gentle request, no sweetness. He pushed my hands away and grasped my face, kissing me with hard tantalizing strokes of his tongue.

I gave myself up to the demand of his kiss. His fingers slid down the back of my neck, and my body rippled and shivered.

My eyes closed as he pressed against me, feeling the shape of him, firm like forged iron. My breasts yielded against his chest, soft and pliant. This. The feeling of my mate. His scent, his warmth, the feeling of his strength. Even with only a few days apart, I had missed him more than I'd realized. I needed him more than I knew.

He clearly felt the same, for he was drinking me in, taking my mouth greedily, his hands moving down to stroke the small of my back and caress my hips.

I pulled away, and he looked down at me blankly.

"Come," I whispered, and took his hand.

I led him over the crumbling rocks and beneath the lintel of the temple.

Inside, the air was chill and musty.

"Is this what you want?" Draven growled from behind me. With a slight movement of his hand, he whirled me around. I collided with his chest, the breath going out of my lungs. In an instant, his hands were around my throat. "To fuck in the house of a god? To fuck in the darkness?"

I could sense the torrent of emotions behind his words. The agony, the rage. I sensed how close he was to unleashing all of the pain he felt upon me, to letting me see the jagged wounds he could barely keep closed.

I made no movement, simply held still beneath his hands, feeling his breath hot upon my face in the dark as we stood there in the abandoned house of an ancient and terrible god.

"It doesn't have to be dark. Unless you like it that way. But perhaps you'd like to burn even better?" I lifted my hands, and torches along the walls blazed to life.

Draven hardly spared the flaring torches a glance. He simply looked down at me with a gaze that would have turned any other person to ash.

"If you start this," he said, his voice a hard, dark thing, "you should know I won't be able to stop and I can't be gentle." He dropped his hands from my neck. "We should go back."

"No," I said firmly. "I think we should stay right where we are." I took his hand in mine again and tugged him backwards.

I already knew what I would find as my body moved through the cool shadows.

My hips hit a slab of hard, cold stone.

Draven's jaw clenched so tight, I thought it would break. "If we stay here, your world is here. This. Me. I'll take you. Between your legs, inside your mouth. Everywhere I can. I'll hurt you, Morgan. I'm broken. You don't know..." His voice cracked. "You don't know what I'm capable of right now."

"And you do? You think you know what *I* need right now, Draven?"

I ran my hands down my body, cupping my breasts briefly, feeling how tight and heavy they already were. "What I need is *you*. What I need is for you to take me any way you need me."

Draven's eyes watched my every move.

"What are you waiting for?" I goaded him. "Unleash your pain. Heal me with it. Heal me, gods damn it, and fuck me like you know you want to, Draven."

That was all he needed to hear.

With a roaring, crashing sound, he rushed towards me, claws extending and tearing my tunic from my body like a feral animal.

His hot, hungry mouth fumbled to my breasts. Mouth biting and fingers tugging at my nipples, cupping and kneading my breasts until I was gasping and moaning.

My trousers were slashed off, falling to the ground in ribbons. I was shaken, scratched, but he had not harmed me otherwise.

Then he was lifting me up onto the stone slab and pushing me backwards, my breasts tilting upwards towards the high cavern overhead as if in a twisted distortion of worship.

But there was only one god I worshiped. And he had my body at his command now, to do with as he willed.

He sucked at one nipple, then the other, as my body arched. I pushed my hands to the stone, gasping, trying futilely to maintain some control. But as he dragged his tongue over one breast, almost painfully, I let out a ragged breath. He rubbed his wide palms back and forth, catching my nipples between his fingers and squeezing as pleasure laced through me.

I raised my hands, weaving them through his hair. The thick strands were damp from sweat and the misty air around us. I wrapped my hands through the thick, black tendrils and shamelessly urged him downwards.

He let out a low, hoarse growl, and to my surprise, stood back.

In the torchlight he stood there for a moment, his gaze raking over me, taking me in, stripped and naked on the cold stone, breasts upturned, thighs bare, and the place between them... wet and entirely exposed.

I shifted slightly, biting my lip under the force of that unsettling dark gaze. All too aware of how I must look, vulnerable and nude on the altar slab. A sacrifice to lust. To grief.

"What is it?" I whispered. "What do you want?"

He let out a raspy breath. "What do I want? I want to fuck you with my face until you come so hard screaming my name that the stones crumble around us. And then..."

There was more? I shivered, palms down on the cold stone.

He was unlacing his trousers, pulling out the head of his long, swollen cock and wrapping his fist around it. "Then I want to fuck you with my cock, fill you up as you clench around it, so good and so tight..." A look of near-torment crossed his face, as if waiting even another moment was causing him pain. "As I take you the way you were meant to be taken. Like you were made for me. And then, when we're through, I want you to wrap your lips around my cock and take me in your mouth while I lie atop you and take you in mine again and again until we're spent."

There was silence in the temple. In the distance, a pebble clattered.

I shivered though I did not feel cold.

"Do you have any objections to any of that?" Draven growled, breaking the silence. His voice echoed off the walls.

In the dim light, I quickly shook my head.

"None?"

"None." I wanted it all. Wanted him to do everything to me he had ever imagined. "I'm yours. Do with me what you will."

He moved towards me, grabbing my wrists and slamming them down on the stone, then pushing them over my head. I flinched, feeling the tender skin on my arms erupt in pain as it slid over the rough rock.

His mouth moved between my legs, snarling as he lowered his head like a ravenous beast, as if intent on devouring me whole.

His tongue slid over my folds, then went straight to my clit. A strangled gasp went through me as I reflexively moved my wrists, pulling against the confines of his hands.

Draven didn't loosen his hold. He simply switched my manacles, grasping both my wrists with one of his hands, squeezing them even more tightly in place as he moved his free hand between my legs and mercilessly slid all four fingers inside me.

I screamed. I screamed, and as I did, I wondered if the stones truly would fall around us.

As his mouth worked against my clit and his hand thrust between my legs, filling me again and again, I had no words for the feeling of pleasure coursing through me. He filled me completely. The touch of his mouth on my throbbing clit, the feel of myself soaking wet against his mouth. It was too much. Too much. I felt choked. Sweat fell in beads to the stone below me. I writhed against him, not caring who might hear, who might see.

He thrust his hand in and out of me, hard, and for a panicked moment, I wondered if he would care if I tore right now, and then I *was* tearing, exploding, breaking. A bright flash of light ripped across the temple as I burst, destroyed and devastated.

Above us, an ancient stalactite fell, landing with a crash far across the vast room.

I moved as if to seek his mouth, a plaintive moan escaping my lips.

But Draven was already atop me, pinning me down with his entire muscled body.

I couldn't move. Couldn't breathe.

And then his cock was inside me. My back scraped against the rough stone as he drove hard and deep between my thighs, impaling me against my father's altar.

He thrust into me again and again, picking up speed, then slowing, pulling out almost completely, letting the head of his cock sit there, notched against my pussy until I moaned and lifted myself, trying to spread my legs wider and force him back in.

Hazily, I looked up at him.

He was looking down at me like some almighty god, the hard lines of his jaw tight, his eyes like gleaming gems.

"Please, Draven, please..."

"Stop," he commanded. I fell silent. "Let me look at you." His hands tightened their grip on my wrists. It was painful. I felt my skin scraping against the stones and hoped I'd be rubbed raw.

A harsh and brutal kind of gratification. That was what we both needed.

No one could hurt me like he could. He wouldn't allow it. *I* wouldn't allow it. And the same was true of him.

Our love had blossomed into a dark flower, covered in thorns.

Only we could give each other what we needed right now. Enough torment and pleasure to somehow take away the other kind of pain.

And in this hurt, we would help each other heal.

"For fuck's sake, silver," my mate whispered above me. "Fuck, but you feel good. I don't want it to end. I don't want this to ever end."

I looked up at his face, saw the expression in his eyes, and finally understood.

He was mourning more than Gawain, more than Rychel. He was mourning for this. For us.

Because my love believed we didn't have much of us left. He thought we were going to die in the Black Mountain.

Or at least that he was.

"It won't end." I lifted my hips and forced a guttural groan from him as his cock re-entered my wetness. I tightened myself around him. "It won't ever end. Eternal, Draven. That's what you said. You and I are eternal. There's no going back on that."

And I knew it was true, in my heart of hearts, in my blood, in my very bones, in my soul. I was his for all eternity. No one could take us from each other. Not even in death.

"We found each other," I whispered. "Not for the first time."

His gaze narrowed on me as if I had said something strange but familiar.

"You've always known it," I said quietly. "I suppose I have, too."

He drew his hips back then slammed into me, and gods, I felt every inch of him.

"Every twisted part of me is yours. And every twisted part of you is mine. The good and the bad. All of it. Forever. You're fucking *mine*, Draven Venator. Don't you ever forget it."

He pulled out of me, teasing me, and I lifted my hips, my body clinging to him like a lifeline. I felt restless, frantic, desperate to have him inside me again.

And then he started to fuck me. Really, truly fuck me.

Releasing my wrists, he gripped my hips hard, slamming into me, hitting my core so deep, I threw my head back and screamed. His hands reached up to squeeze my breasts, so taut and so heavy. Every part of me was desperate and starving for his touch.

He moved his mouth down to one of my nipples, and I moaned, overwhelmed and nearly delirious at the feel of him, the fullness of him. His cock stroked in and out.

I closed my eyes, lost in the heady tide.

And then I felt his hand slip between us, finding the spot that would drive me to the edge and push me over. His fingers stroked my clit, and my head slammed back hard against the altar slab.

I cried out, clenching around him as his name left my lips and echoed over and over off the empty walls around us. Stones rumbled. The walls shook. The flames flickered in their torches.

And then I felt him coming, too, sinking into me so deep, I never wanted us to part. The cry that left his lips was wordless. A sound of ecstasy as he shook and quivered, throbbing above me like a molten surge.

Much later, we walked in the dark side by side.

Draven's cloak was around my shoulders. He carried the bundle of my tattered clothes under one arm.

We skirted the edges of the camp, watching the glow of the refugees' fires as they burned bright against the shadow of the mountain.

I shivered, and Draven turned to me in concern.

"Are you cold? We can go back."

"You mean because I'm completely naked underneath this cloak?" I moved the folds of the garment to give him a peek of my body.

With a groan, he stepped forward, slipping his hands under the cloak and wrapping them around my bare waist.

"Is it wrong?" he whispered, burying his face in my hair. "Wanting you this much? Doing what we just did when..."

I stroked his back, knowing what he meant. When they were dead and gone. When they could never love in such a way again.

"I don't think it could ever be wrong. I want you. I love you. That doesn't mean I'm not still thinking about Gawain and..." My voice hitched in my throat. "And Rychel."

Silence. The incredible silence was a void that would never be filled.

My mate's little sister was gone. I mourned her, yes, but it was also a heartbreak I could not come close to understanding.

Not unless I lost Kaye.

"I really thought we'd find her," I said, bitter grief slipping back into my voice, unable to help myself. "And not like this. I mean, whole. Alive. The way she was."

So vibrant. Rychel had been a bright spark amongst the Siabra court.

"I thought maybe she'd be imprisoned. I didn't think she'd have an easy time of it, but I really thought..." I trailed off.

Draven was silent.

"Did you?" I asked him. "Think we'd find her?"

"I truly don't know what I expected," he said quietly. "But it wasn't this."

No. Not seeing his younger sister transformed into an aged crone. Without the wisdom or experience or well-lived life an old woman like that should have had.

Rychel had been hardly more than a child. A child who had *saved* a child.

"She died to save a life," I reminded him. "She was extraordinary. Truly noble."

He nodded. "That's some comfort. I mean, I've always known she was stubborn. I should have known she'd never give up. Even if it meant giving everything she had." He stumbled over the words a little, and I pressed up against him as if I could soothe his hurt with more of my touch.

He kissed my forehead. "You're going to need a new sheath for that blade."

He meant the sickle. I carried it in one hand. I didn't want to think about how or why I had done what I'd done.

"There's a leatherworker in the camp who Madoc introduced me to. She's extremely talented. I'll go and see her. She should be able to make something for you," he said, glancing down at the curved blade pressed against the cloak.

"Before morning?" I asked in surprise. "She'd have to work through the night."

"I'll pay her well. She has children," he explained. "The more she has when they reach Camelot, the better she'll do with so many mouths to feed."

I nodded. "Give her enough to set up a shop."

He raised an eyebrow.

"Why not?" I challenged. "Our coffers are limitless in Myntra, aren't they? I decree this. As your empress."

He quirked his mouth. "We'll pay her more than fairly. If I give her too much, others will be envious." He touched my chin. "They'll all do well in Pendrath, Morgan. Have no fear of that. Sir Ector will see to it. You're doing much more than most rulers ever would with unwanted refugees."

"They're not unwanted," I said softly. "They're our neighbors. And with any luck and the goddesses' grace, they'll soon return to their own land."

"Grace, huh?" Draven ran a hand over his jaw. "I didn't think you thought much of that stuff."

"I don't," I said. "It's mostly bullshit, of course."

He coughed discreetly. "Was that why you picked such a sacrilegious place for our dalliance this evening?"

I tossed my head. "Absolutely no idea what you're talking about."

"An altar," he mused. "A fucking altar."

"Fucking on the fucking altar." I stepped towards him and ran a hand over his pelvis. "Do you like hearing the words?"

He took a hasty step back. "None of that now," he warned. "Save it for the tent."

I wiggled my eyebrows teasingly but did as he'd asked.

"I've been wanting to ask you something," I said casually.

"Are you wondering if we're going to be punished for violating a temple? Can't say I know the answer to that."

I snorted. "No. Nothing like that. I'm not concerned in the slightest. This is something else."

A question that had been a long time coming.

"How did you meet my uncle?" That was the easy one.

Draven seemed to think so too, for he raised his brows. "I met him at a tavern in Rheged, of all places. In a village close to Dornum."

"Before or after you murdered the royal family?" I asked sweetly.

He grinned. "You know that story already. I was still for hire though, if that's what you're really asking."

"And he hired you? Just stumbled across you there?"

Draven laughed. "Oh, there was no stumbling. He knew exactly who I was, Morgan. The man had an uncanny knack for knowing things."

"How did he convince you to do what he wanted? I suppose when you heard about Excalibur, it was easy to agree?"

Draven looked at me in a way that sent my heart fluttering. "Something like that."

"What do you mean?"

"I mean he told me he would help me find my heart's desire."

"And your heart desired a magic sword?"

"My heart had no idea what it really wanted. It was broken into pieces and full of rage at that point."

I knew he had been devastated after losing Nimue and his wife. A woman who had been his dear childhood friend but who he had never been able to love as one should love a wife.

"But he knew what to say. He told me about you."

My skin prickled. "What did he say?"

Draven shrugged, and I knew I wasn't going to get a straight answer to that one. "He told me you liked to read. That you were lonely. Lonelier than you even realized." He looked down into my eyes. "He told me you were in danger."

"But how did he know all of that?" I pressed. "And why did he arrange for all of this in the first place? If you hadn't come to Camelot, if we hadn't left to find the sword..."

Draven nodded. "I've thought about it, too."

We'd never have found each other. If it weren't for my uncle.

Or was there someone else to thank?

"Your mother."

My heart sped up. "What?"

Draven hesitated. "Your uncle... I think he must have loved your mother very much. When she died, he began to plan this. Set things in motion."

"Did she know? Do you think she told him things?"

Draven nodded. "How else could he have known all that he did?"

Had my mother wanted me to find my true father? To take him down as Draven and I were now trying to do?

Or was I simply executing my uncle's revenge scheme? One put in motion long ago.

Or was there another piece to this puzzle I was missing?

"Now it's your turn. Answer something for me," Draven said suddenly. "Who is your father?"

I looked at him as if it were a stupid question. "Gorlois le Fay. High King of the Valtain. You know this already."

"I know that part, yes." Draven was silent for a moment. "I also know he has the powers of a god. And your sister claimed to be the daughter of one."

I knew what he was asking. And I knew what he was waiting for me to say.

But I wasn't ready to say it. Not yet.

"I'm so tired," I said desperately. "Can we go to sleep? Can we go back to the tent? We can skip the sheath. I'll just carry it like this."

Draven smiled slightly. "I don't think your horse would like that very much. I'll walk you to the tent, then I'll go and find the leatherworker. You rest."

Rest. After what Amara had told me that night, I wasn't sure I could ever rest again.

But I simply nodded and let him lead me home.

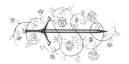

The air was crisp and cool as we broke camp the next morning. Around us, the refugees were slowly packing up their things, loading wagons, folding tents, and cooking breakfasts over the fire.

Madoc and Amara walked about, checking on the camp's progress and making sure everyone had something to eat. If a family did not, the healer or her husband would approach another group and see if they had anything to spare. Failing that, Madoc would rifle in a large satchel he wore and fish out some hard rounds of bread.

We had contributed all we could the night before. With one less mouth to feed, I had asked Hawl to bring our extra supplies to Madoc and Amara.

Now we were heading out. We would separate from the group and be on our own again. As I looked around at the tired faces of Rheged's people, I prayed that they would suffer no further losses along the way to Camelot.

My horse snorted, breath visible in the early morning chill as we set forth on a narrow trail that wound its way past the abandoned village we had camped on.

As the day went on, our route curved northwards. The trees began to thin, giving way to sturdier shrubs and rockier terrain.

By noon, the mountains had emerged on the horizon like ancient sentinels, their craggy peaks shrouded in clouds and mist.

We passed by rocky outcrops, dappled with lichen and moss. Tenacious wildflowers clung to stony crevices.

By nightfall, the temperature had dropped sharply, enveloping us in a chill. The air grew thinner, carrying a subtle tang of minerals and rock as we passed deeper into the mountainous expanse.

The landscape was beautiful but forbidding. As we set up camp that night, the wind whispered through the valley we sheltered in, carrying with it the murmur of a cascading nearby waterfall.

Soon the valleys would become deep ravines. The terrain would grow more steep and treacherous.

And we would draw ever closer to my father and the Black Mountain.

A summit one could see over the clouds, the man we had met on the road had said. A mountain that had appeared as if from nowhere.

I shivered. No fae could do such a thing.

But then, as I had refused to acknowledge to Draven, my father was no true fae, was he?

He had been worshiped as a god.

And me? I wanted to think about that part of things even less.

CHAPTER 28 - MEDRA

M y Aunt Sarrasine had lied.

She had brought more than two guards.

As I wound my way slowly down the tower steps, I passed more dead fae guards in their distinct, menacing, dark armor.

All had broken necks. I felt a flicker of pride. Odessa hadn't even bothered to draw her swords.

At the bottom of the tower, I walked down a long corridor that seemed too quiet, even for this time of night.

Every now and then, I would pass a body. Servants who had been running and mowed down by merciless blades.

A few were black-armored fae. In one case, a knight of Camelot lay beside a dead fae from Sarrasine's court. They had run each other through with their weapons and collapsed upon each other as they died.

I passed the stable boy who had flirted with me weeks ago. His eyes were still open. There was blood pooled around his head.

After that, I stopped looking at the bodies.

I moved by instinct, slowly, towards the center of the castle. I felt a strong compulsion to tell someone that Odessa was dead. To have someone other than me know what had happened. And besides, someone had to see to her body.

When I reached the Great Hall, it was still quiet.

Somehow, I had expected to come across more people. Sir Ector with a contingent of knights. But perhaps the fighting had moved outside. Or perhaps Sarrasine's invaders had delivered their blood and chaos and then left as quickly as they'd come.

I stepped into the Great Hall, letting my eyes become accustomed to the shadows.

There were bodies here, too. More of them. A few servants. A number of knights.

I walked slowly between the columns.

Then I saw him. Kneeling on the other side of the hall with a bow on the floor beside him. A few dead fae guards lay on either side, arrows protruding from their chests.

It was Crescent. He was cradling a small figure in his lap.

A child.

My heart sped up.

I walked slowly towards him.

When I reached his side, I looked down at the girl in his arms. Taina's eyes were closed.

"Is she..." I stopped, not wanting it to be true.

He looked up at me, his face impassive. "She'll live. She needs a healer."

I wondered why he hadn't already sent for one or begun carrying Taina to the temple. Everyone knew Kasie, the High Priestess, was the best healer in Camelot.

Then I took in the exhaustion on Crescent's face. The blood. The way he held Taina towards his chest so carefully that I had almost missed the way his own arm was twisted at an unnatural angle.

I opened my mouth to offer to help. Then remembered.

"They came for me."

He nodded. "I figured as much."

"Odessa..." I stumbled over the name. I couldn't finish. Couldn't say it.

I looked down at Crescent's face. He was looking at me as if he didn't want me to continue.

"Don't," he said quietly. "Please."

But I had to tell him. Someone had to know. I couldn't hide this from him. Not when she had died to save me.

"She's dead. Odessa is dead."

The words hung in the air for what felt like an eternity.

I could feel the weight of condemnation without him saying a single word.

Finally I could take it no more.

"She died because of me. She died saving me. Sarrasine—one of my aunts—came here for me. I was going to go with her. Odessa tried to stop me. Sarrasine killed her."

Still Crescent said nothing. In his arms, I could see Taina's small chest rising and falling and was strangely grateful to the girl for simply staying alive.

I wanted to tell him it was all right. That I had killed Sarrasine. That it was over.

But somehow, I knew it wouldn't be much comfort.

"You need to go," I said, trying to restore his sense of urgency. I couldn't understand what was taking him so long. "Odessa is dead. But Taina isn't. You need to take her to the temple."

I waited for him to tell me I had to join him. That it wasn't safe for me here.

Instead, he simply looked down at his daughter. "Yes."

"Go now, Crescent," I said as gently as I could. "I haven't seen any more of the..." What was I to call them? My grandfather's soldiers? "The invaders. I think they're gone now."

To my relief, he pushed himself slowly to his feet. Still cradling Taina, he turned towards the door.

"I'm sorry. I'm so sorry, Crescent. I didn't mean for her to die."

He froze. "I should never have brought her here."

They were the last words he said as he moved away from me.

Did he mean Taina? Or Odessa?

Perhaps both.

Either way, as he left the Great Hall, as he left me standing there alone, it was clear he blamed me for it all.

None of this would have happened if it wasn't for me.

I was a mistake.

I should never have existed.

If I had gone with Sarrasine tonight as soon as she had asked, perhaps this all might have been avoided. At least she had claimed to want me.

Or if I had said no and run when I'd had the chance, I might have been able to stop things, too. Odessa would never have mounted those tower steps.

But instead, I had done neither. I had wavered back and forth, trusting my aunt like a foolish girl. Until choices were taken and Odessa was dead.

Now I was trapped. In a place no one wanted me. With death all around me.

I was responsible. For whatever had happened to Taina. For Odessa's death.

I had brought all of this upon them. Simply by being born.

Why had my mother done this to me? Why had she given birth to me simply to leave me? Had she known I would grow up in this way, an unnatural, unwanted child?

I stumbled out of the Great Hall and down a new corridor.

I could have gone outside, sought out Sir Ector or Dame Halyna. But what would have been the point? I doubted they wanted to see me either.

Were they thinking about me? Soon, Crescent would find them and tell them what I had done. They would hate me then, too.

But not as much as I hated myself.

I went slowly up a narrow staircase and out into a corridor on the second level of the castle, above the Great Hall.

It was quiet here, too, but at least there were no bodies. The hallway was empty.

I passed chamber after chamber with the doors left open. The beds inside were empty, covers turned back as if people had fled quickly.

If everyone else was gone, shouldn't I leave, too? But where would I go? And why bother? There was nothing left to hurt me here.

I passed another room and glanced into the open doorway.

This bed wasn't empty. Someone was sleeping in it.

I paused, curious despite myself.

I took a step closer, standing in the doorway. Should I rouse them from their slumber? Or let them continue to sleep now that the trouble seemed to be over?

I stepped into the room. It was a lavish chamber, one of the most luxurious I had seen in the castle. Finer than my own. All of the trim was gold, and the bed was made of carved mahogany.

It was a room fit for royalty. I realized where I was and who this must be.

Intrigued now, I moved towards the bed.

A boy was sleeping in it.

He had long, light-brown hair that spilled over the pillow. It looked as if it had been a long time since it had last been trimmed.

His skin was pale. Almost translucent. As if he was never in the sun.

This was my uncle. Kaye.

I had never met him. I had never known him awake. He had been like this since I was born. Afflicted with this cursed sleep since that very first night I came into this world.

I stared down at him, curious for the first time about who he was and what had happened to him.

Why, he looked younger than I was now. Somehow, I had expected him to be older. He *was* older, of course, in human years.

What a strange life—to simply lie in this bed all day. Stranger than mine. How long would he rest here? Was he dreaming? It must be very boring to sleep and sleep.

Who cared for him? I glanced around the room but no one else was there. He must have had a caregiver. They must have panicked and fled, leaving him there unattended.

I scowled, feeling oddly angry with this unnamed person who had abandoned my uncle.

What did I do now? Leave him as I had found him? Try to carry him to the temple and find Crescent? I was strong enough to lift Kaye from the bed, yes, but I wasn't sure I could carry him all that way. I supposed I could make some sort of a litter and drag him along.

But then, he wasn't my responsibility. He seemed fine enough where he was.

I half-turned to go.

He was family. My family. He had been abandoned, just like I had been.

With a sigh, I moved back to the bedside.

Kaye looked so childlike, so frail. And there was no one to care for him. He was all alone.

My Aunt Morgan had left him, too. Did he even know that? I doubted it.

Feeling unexpectedly moved with sympathy for the boy in the bed, I reached out a hand and touched his cheek.

The world around me quivered and disappeared.

BOOK 3

CHAPTER 29 - MORGAN

I t was becoming abundantly clear to us all that things could not continue like this.

Guinevere was reaching her limits.

Oh, she hadn't shown any signs of advanced aging like Rychel. At least, not yet.

But she was growing weaker by the day. This morning she'd hardly been able to mount her horse, though she'd hid it well.

She had only fallen once and had blamed the wind. Convenient. She had twisted her ankle, and Lancelet had been furious. With Guinevere or with me, it was hard to say. But she didn't bother to hide the fact that she thought we were both mad.

The horrible thing was that I couldn't stop Guinevere. Because I needed her.

I needed sleep. I needed to stay alive. I needed to block my father until we reached the Black Mountain so that we could destroy the three objects. And try as I might to do it all myself, I couldn't. I needed Guinevere.

And she knew it.

So she kept on, urging sleep upon me like a doting mother.

Some days, I could get by with just three or four hours of rest. But that seemed to be my limit, fae-blooded or not. It was terrible to admit, but I *had* limits. Sleep, just as for mortals, was one.

Before we'd entered the mountains, three or four hours might have been nothing for Guinevere to shield me as I slept.

But now, I could see things had changed. Even those three or four hours were too long for her now. The closer our proximity grew to my father, the stronger his pull.

I didn't know what was involved in Guinevere blocking him from accessing my mind as I slept. If it was anything like what I'd gone through, I could easily imagine it and didn't need the details.

All I could do was pray we'd reach the Black Mountain soon.

Pray. Now that was laughable. And yet there seemed to be no other word for what I kept doing. Childlike, I chanted silently in my own head. Hoping beyond hope that I wasn't going to fuck everything up. For the sake of my friends. For the sake of Eskira.

In the meantime, Guinevere was stoic. Lancelet was furious. And Hawl... Well, Hawl kept cooking.

Good old Hawl did everything they could to make sure that we were properly fed.

And the further into the Mountains of Mist we got, the easier said than done that was.

They'd put no more moths in the food, but there were some scraggly looking rabbits Draven caught. After days on the road with no fresh meat, Hawl managed to turn those into a feast.

Sunstrike and Nightclaw guarded our flanks as we traveled, prowling by day, hunting at night. Throughout our journey, they had contributed to our meals from time to time. A haunch of deer, a leg from a boar.

But now that we'd entered the mountains, the terrain was rocky with sparse vegetation and even sparser prey. The most they seemed able to catch were rabbits, squirrels, and mice. I couldn't even imagine how many mice it would take to satisfy the appetite of a massive creature like Nightclaw.

So we'd told the exmoors in no uncertain terms to stop providing for us. It was a fair command, I'd thought, until I'd seen the hurt in Nightclaw's eyes. A hurt I'd forced myself to look away from.

I'd already refused to fly him. To use him in any way that might involve him or Sunstrike becoming injured again. I wasn't going to use the exmoor to fight my battles for me. Not like my father had done.

But instead of being grateful, he'd been hurt. As I should have known would be the case.

Nightclaw had chosen me. Chosen me to fight for. I should have understood what he was determined to give me wouldn't be that easy to reject.

We'd stopped for the evening. I sat on a large, not particularly comfortable rock, letting my mind wander as I watched Hawl butcher two skinny rabbits and toss them into a pot filled with small potatoes and herbs.

When Lancelet's hand grabbed my upper arm hard, I squeaked.

"Come with me," she ordered, dragging me off my rock and into the scraggly bushes nearby.

"Why is it you always grab?" I complained. "Why can't you greet me with a gentle pat on the back? Or, I don't know, a clasp of hands?"

Lancelet snorted as I'd known she would. "A pat on the back?"

I rolled my eyes. "So this isn't a friendly chat then?"

"Guinevere is not well," she said with her customary bluntness.

"Yes, so I've noticed. I suppose I should be grateful you didn't hit me on the head with a rock and pull me into these bushes."

"Don't think it wasn't tempting."

"It would solve your Guinevere problem, too," I pointed out. "I'm surprised you haven't done it already."

Lancelet grimaced through surprisingly feral-looking teeth. "Then I'd be left with a Draven problem."

"There is that," I acknowledged. "Not to mention Nightclaw."

"Not to mention you're my friend," she said, grudgingly.

"Oh, so you're still willing to admit that?" I made a show of rubbing my arm where she'd grabbed me.

"You're my friend, yes," she said. "But Guinevere... She's my... Well..."

"Oh, ho, so this is how we're finally going to get you to acknowledge what she is." I rubbed my hands together gleefully. "Yes, do continue, I beg. She's your...?"

Lancelet glared. "It's none of your concern. At least we're quiet and subtle, unlike you and your mate."

I hooted loudly. "Quiet and subtle? Is that what you think? I mean, I *know* Guinevere doesn't think that. Because by the Three, that woman is shockingly loud. But you? Yes, I suppose you just might be that naive about the soundproof-ness of your tent. But believe me, it is not soundproof. At all. Not by a longshot."

Lancelet had gone red to the roots of her short blonde hair. "Shut up."

"Why? What's the problem?" I grinned. "I'm just glad you're finally getting some well-deserved... Ouch! Stop pinching me!"

"Don't speak about her like that," Lancelet snapped.

I shook my head. "You're so far gone. Well, I suppose it's a good thing."

"A good thing?"

"At least there's one person you'll smile for. One person you'll have to take care of you when..." I trailed off as I realized what I'd been about to say.

Lancelet was staring at me. I quickly looked away.

"When what? When you're gone?"

I shrugged. "I don't know. It's possible, right? We don't know what's ahead."

"I certainly don't. You and Guinevere on the other hand? Who knows."

I took a deep breath. "I'm not going to let her die for me. I can promise you that much."

Lancelet didn't look all that reassured. "But you? You'll let yourself die?"

"I won't let myself. But I won't deny there might not be much escaping it."

There. I'd admitted it.

Draven thought he might die saving me. Well, that wasn't going to happen.

If it took a death, it was going to be mine. I knew that to my core.

"But... Guinevere."

"I need her for now." I looked away. "But she's not going all the way with me. I won't allow it."

"Good luck stopping her," Lancelet said, sinking down onto the ground and plucking a blade of grass. "She's more stubborn than I am."

"And that's saying something. I know. But she's not. Coming with me, I mean." I hesitated. "Neither are you."

Lancelet was back on her feet in an instant. "Like hell I'm not."

"You're not." My voice was sharp as steel. "As your friend, I won't allow it."

Lancelet glowered. "And as your *friend*, I don't think you can tell me what to do. You're the empress of Myntra, lest you forget. Not the empress of Pendrath. You might have been my queen, sure. But you refused that honor. Your choice, Morgan. Your choice."

I sighed. "Look, I'm not fighting about this. But you *will* stay behind. If you want to protect Guinevere, you'll have to."

Lancelet looked at me for a long moment then sank back down onto the rock. "Fuck. Well, fuck."

"Yes," I agreed. "I'm sure what you'd really like to say is 'Fuck you, Morgan.'"

She grinned. "Many times."

"Feel free. I feel like saying it to myself sometimes."

"We won't be left behind so easily, you know," she said. "Next you'll tell me you plan on leaving Hawl, too."

I looked away guiltily.

"By the Three, Morgan," Lancelet exploded. "Why bring any of us in that case?"

"Why bring you? I couldn't have stopped you. And back then..." I stopped. "It didn't seem real. Not until..."

"Not until Gawain."

I nodded. "But now..."

It seemed the time had come. I told her what Amara had told me about Guinevere. About what the shielding was doing to her.

When I was through, Lancelet looked shaken.

"Now you understand," I said softly. "I won't let there be another Rychel. Not if I can help it. Not when Guinevere is so special to you, Lancelet. You both deserve some happiness. Not to die on some miserable mountain."

"Not to die by my best friend's side, saving our world, you mean?" The look Lancelet gave me made me flinch.

"I already know you're self-sacrificing. You don't need to prove that to me or to anyone. We already know only one person can destroy these things." I gestured to Excalibur curved in its sheath at my side. "And it's me. Me. Not you. Not Guinevere. Not Hawl. So while I appreciate the loyalty and the spirit, I won't let you all be collateral damage just because you're all too stubborn to see my point of view."

Lancelet was still shaking her head, so I went for the kill.

"Besides, do you think Guinevere would really survive out here on her own?" I said brutally. "Alone? You think she's capable of that?"

"She'd have Hawl," Lancelet said. But she looked uncertain.

"Sure. A Bearkin. And they're incredible. But two protectors will always be better than one. You know that."

"Why not let Hawl join you at least? You know they'll be devastated if you try to leave them," Lancelet insisted.

"No. Draven and I will go alone. Just us. That's it." I bit my lip. "And I swear to you, Lancelet, I'd leave him, too, if I could manage it."

She stared at me. "I really think you would."

A bird called above us, and I lifted my eyes to see Tuva circling off in the distance.

"That damned bird. Half the time I forget she's with us," I complained, trying to change the subject.

Lancelet sniffed. "Try having her in your tent with you during... you know."

I burst out laughing. "No! Really?"

Lancelet looked grumpy. "Really. Just once, but that was enough. It was raining outside. I guess she didn't want to get wet."

I laughed again. "You had a tryst with an owl."

She punched me in the shoulder. "That is *not* how I would describe it, and if you ever say that again, I'll…"

"You'll what?" I was still snickering. "Make me eat moths?"

"Oh, I'll do worse than that," she threatened, stepping towards me.

I shrieked. "You'd have to catch me first."

And then I was flying through the camp, pebbles under my feet.

I raced by Hawl who looked up in confusion from their cooking.

Then past Guinevere who calmly glanced between me then Lancelet, who was hot on my heels, and then resumed her unpacking.

Screeching and laughing, I ran past our tethered horses and down towards the nearby stream. Draven was crouched by the water's edge, shaving with a dagger. He looked up in surprise as I approached, then grinned and shook his head.

I ran past him, plunging into the stream, just as Lancelet caught up with me. Unable to stop herself, she was up to her knees with momentum just as I swept a wave of icy water towards her with a huge sweep of my arm, drenching her from head to toe.

"You're soaked," I crowed, jumping up and down in glee.

She sputtered. "You are, too, you idiot!"

"Yes, but I got you first. Look at you!" I cackled like a mad woman.

"Look at me! Look at you! For all you know, there are leeches in these waters!"

"There are. Plenty of them," Draven said from the rocky bank. "I pulled three off my face just now."

Lancelet and I looked at each other. Then, shrieking and laughing and screaming, we ran for the bank.

CHAPTER 30 - MORGAN

W e reached the Black Mountain nearly a week later.

Except for the brief moment of levity Lancelet and I had shared days back, a subdued mood had fallen over our group and remained like a heavy cloud. One might have even called it a gloom.

I felt filled with a deep and troublesome melancholy the closer we came to the mountain that held my father's court. Nothing I said to myself and nothing Draven tried to say or do could dissipate it.

I knew the mountain was where I had to go. I knew what I had to do.

But the *doing* of it was hard. Harder than anything I had ever done before.

I was no hero. I was just a person swept up in events greater than myself. Wave after wave, the pull of fate had swept me along until I had finally arrived here at this place.

And I could not help but see it as a place of ending.

I knew I would give everything I had to succeed. But there were different measurements of success.

For days, we had followed a narrow, winding path through sheer cliffs and along treacherous slopes. Jagged rocks protruded from the ground, slowing our progress and wounding one of our pack horses so badly that we'd had to leave it behind. Occasional gusts of icy wind sweeping around corners and veils of mist that would block our view for hours carried with them reminders that darker days awaited us the closer we drew to the Black Mountain.

By the second day, the mist was beginning to feel omnipresent. At times, I felt as if we were walking through a dreamscape, so heavy and dense was the fog. Strange, ghostly shapes seemed to materialize and then vanish again, leaving an eerie sensation in their wake and goosebumps crawling over my flesh.

On the third day, the mist momentarily lifted, and as it did, there, towering over us, lying straight ahead, was the Black Mountain.

The sight of it was formidable. It cast a shadow over the entire landscape. Rock dark as the abyss seemed to absorb all of the light around it. My heart thudded as I stared at the ominous peak, dark and imposing, its jagged edges cutting into the sky and disappearing among the dense clouds that cloaked its upper reaches.

The air felt heavy with ancient magic.

The gloom that had begun to hang over our party seemed to tighten and intensify. We moved towards the mountain steadily but with an unmistakable sense of dread.

Just before twilight, we emerged from a winding pass and reached the base. Or to be more accurate, a portion of the base, for the Black Mountain was so vast that we might easily have traveled around it for days before encircling it completely.

We had come out into a rocky valley at the foot of the mountain. A small lake lay at the bottom of the dark cliffs. Narrow, winding stairs carved into the rock of the cliff led up to a stone platform that hung over the water. At the top, the face of the cliff seemed unusually flat, but from our position, we could see nothing else.

The air was filled with the chill murmur of the mountain breeze and the gentle lapping of the lake against the rocky shore.

All seemed very calm, very peaceful.

"This is it then," Lancelet said, breaking the silence. "We go up those stairs."

"And then?" Hawl questioned.

"I suppose we have to wait to find out," Draven said, his voice low.

I could feel Guinevere's eyes upon me. The dark brown orbs seemed larger than ever in her pale, drawn face.

"We could make camp and wait until morning," Lancelet suggested. "Or..."

"Or we could tether the horses and go up those stairs right now," Hawl finished.

"I say we go now," Guinevere said softly.

Draven nodded. "Agreed. Let's see what's at the top. Then we can make camp."

Lancelet's horse moved skittishly. "And if the entrance is at the top? Then what? We leave the horses down here alone?"

"It's not as if we're about to be sucked in," Hawl boomed. I felt the Bearkin glance at me in a way that was almost nervous, as if they worried there might be some truth to what they'd said. "We can return and make camp after we investigate. We'll decide what to do then."

I said nothing. I simply looked at the winding stone stairs carved into the cliffside. At the silver reflective surface of the lake.

We ascended the stairs one by one. They were narrow and there was no rail.

When had they last been used? Had my father ever made his way up these stairs? I doubted it. That seemed far too mundane for Gorlois le Fay.

I skimmed my fingers along the rock face as we climbed, feeling the stone, cold and solid beneath.

Under my feet, moss and lichen clung to the steps. As we ascended, the damp patches gleamed slightly in the fading light. The squelching of boots against the wet stones mixed with the rhythmic thud of our steps and the clatter of an occasional dislodged pebble tumbling down the slope and into the lake far below.

Draven had taken the lead. Behind me came Lancelet, then Guinevere, then Hawl.

We had nearly reached the top when a panicked gasp came from behind me, and I paused, turning swiftly to see Lancelet had slipped. She had sunk down onto her knees, her hands grasping at the stairs.

"A loose stone," was all she said as she pushed herself back up onto her feet grimly. "Fucking fae and their lack of handrails. It's not as if they all have wings, now is it?"

I couldn't even form a reply. My heart was pounding. We were so high up now that the lake below seemed no more than a puddle. If she had fallen...

"Here," Draven called from ahead. I looked to see him standing at the top of the platform. "It's narrow, but we all should fit." He glanced down at us. "Well, except Hawl."

He took my hand, pulling me up beside him, then waited for Lancelet and Guinevere to finish their ascent.

The four of us stood on the platform, looking at the cliff-face as Hawl, breathing heavily, reached the top steps.

"I'll stay where I am," the Bearkin growled. "Doesn't look as if the fae built that platform to hold more than a few of you scrawny creatures."

"Where's the door? Is there supposed to be one?" Lancelet demanded. She and Draven were already sliding their hands over the cliffside, searching for crevices. "How do we get inside?"

Guinevere and I stood side by side in silence.

"I don't see anything," Lancelet finally said in frustration. She glanced at me. "Do you?"

I shook my head. "Nothing."

"And yet there are stairs. And this platform," Guinevere said quietly.

"Exactly," Draven agreed. "Clearly there is something here or we wouldn't be standing here now. Why build a staircase to nothing?"

"Perhaps we'll be able to see more in the morning," I suggested. "The sun is nearly down. It will be hard to navigate those stairs in the dark."

"There has to be something here. Unless..." Lancelet scowled.

"What?" I asked.

"Unless this was half-built. Perhaps the stairs were supposed to continue higher." She looked above us as if expecting to see a sign. "Or perhaps a door was planned but never built."

"Or we need more daylight to see properly as Morgan suggested," Draven said gently.

"A good meal and some rest is what everyone needs," Hawl boomed. "I can provide one of those things."

I felt Guinevere's eyes on me and purposely kept mine down.

Guinevere could provide the other—if I let her.

But last night, I'd woken from three bare hours of sleep to hear her crying and moaning. From within my tent, I could hear Lancelet speaking to her softly, trying to calm her. I could picture her holding the former high priestess in her arms, her face full of worry.

I was putting them both through agony every time I indulged in "rest."

What was rest for one of us was torture for the other.

This cruel symbiosis that Guinevere and I had been forced into had to end. And soon.

As night fell, we made our way back down the narrow stairs and set up camp at the edge of the lake. After watering and tending to the horses, I leaned back against a stuffed pack and watched Draven build a fire as Hawl prepared our evening meal.

Guinevere had gone to lie down in her tent.

When she awoke after supper and offered to let me rest, I jumped eagerly at the chance. I caught a look of surprise on Draven's face but ignored it. Slipping into our tent, I wrapped myself in a bedroll and closed my eyes.

When he came in a few moments later and lay down next to me, I pretended to already be asleep. He slipped his arm around my waist, kissed the back of my neck, and soon fell asleep.

I listened to the sound of his breathing, trying not to let the comforting sound and the rise and fall of his chest lull me into slumber.

For a while, I could hear my friends talking in low voices around the fire. Soon, Hawl left the group to lie on their bedroll near the lake. The Ursidaur usually preferred the open air to what they described as the "stuffy confines of a smelly tent."

About an hour later, quiet had descended. Lancelet must have fallen asleep.

I pictured Guinevere sitting alone by the fire, struggling to keep her eyes open.

I wondered how much longer I would have to wait.

Sitting up, I crawled carefully towards the tent flap and peeked out.

Guinevere sat, resting with her back against a rock. Her head lolled against her chest. Her eyes were closed. Her breathing was heavy. She was asleep.

I drew a breath of relief. This was it. It was now or never.

A strong hand gripped my wrist and yanked me backwards into the tent.

"What the hell do you think you're up to?" Draven sounded furious.

There was no point in denying anything.

"I'm leaving."

"Like hell you are. You're not going anywhere. Certainly not alone."

"You can come with me. I didn't say I was going alone. But if you try to stop me..." I looked at him. Even in the dark, I could imagine those green eyes blazing back at me.

"Then what?"

"Then I'll do whatever I have to," I said quietly. "But I'm leaving here tonight."

"And the others? You're just going to, what? Leave them here?"

"Yes. They're sleeping. We can sneak out now."

Draven narrowed his eyes. "What did you do?"

"I... drugged them," I admitted.

The sleeping draught I had pilfered from Amara's tent had come in handy.

"The food?" Draven hissed. "I ate that, too."

"I didn't put it into your bowl. Only Guinevere's and Hawl's."

"Not Lancelet's?"

"No. She's sleeping, but..." I hesitated. "I'm about to wake her."

"She knew about this?"

"Only part of it." I looked at him and felt riddled with guilt. "I'm sorry, Draven. I should have told you but... I couldn't. I needed you to react... Well, you'll see."

The hurt in his eyes hadn't faded but he nodded. "I don't like it. But I'm coming with you. A thousand harpies wouldn't be able to stop me."

I forced a smile. "That's the spirit. Hopefully there won't be any harpies."

I slipped out of the tent quietly and into Lancelet's.

"This is it," I whispered as she woke up. "You need to look after Guinevere and Hawl. They're both asleep."

"Tonight? Guinevere was supposed to let you sleep."

"Yes, well, I didn't give her the chance." I explained what I had done and watched her expression turn troubled. "You need to stand watch until the sleeping draught wears off. Just in case."

She nodded. "I understand. How long will that be?"

I hesitated. "I have no idea. They each had half a draught. A few hours, I should think? By morning at the latest. I suppose they'll be groggy, but…"

"Morgan!" Draven was calling from outside the tent.

We scrambled out.

His back was to us, his sword drawn. "I heard something."

"What?" I murmured, moving to stand beside him.

Lancelet quickly took up a defensive position by Guinevere.

I glanced at where Hawl lay over by the lake. Maybe this had been a terrible idea, I thought with a sinking heart.

"I'm not sure." Draven was glancing all about, scanning the area.

I followed his gaze, listening intently. But the night air hung heavy with stillness. I could hear only the distant rustle of leaves and the soft murmur of the lake against the shore. Above us, the moon, obscured by fleeting clouds, cast intermittent beams that danced across the campsite.

Down by the water's edge, Hawl groaned in their sleep, and I turned towards the sound.

There was a ripple on the lake, seemingly innocuous. I struggled to see anything out of the ordinary.

Hawl groaned again, and I took a slight step forward, keening my senses.

Then the moon emerged from its veiled sanctuary, and I saw it. A serpentine form materializing within the cascade of light.

A creature, previously concealed within the darkness, now shimmered with other-worldly luminescence.

Undulating with sinuous grace, it slid towards the sleeping Bearkin. Moonlight danced upon its silvery scales.

A snake. Larger than anything I had ever seen.

Urgency surged through me. "Draven!"

My mate's head instantly swung towards the water's edge. Immediately, he extended his hands, weaving blades of shadows towards the serpentine form.

But the shadows bounced off the creature harmlessly, dissipating without effect. Born of shadows and darkness, the snake seemed impervious to Draven's particular brand of magic.

As the serpent shimmering in the moonlight began to coil itself slowly around Hawl's foot and slide up the Bearkin's leg, Draven darted into action. His silhouette cut through the night as he grabbed the Bearkin under the arms and began dragging them away from the water's edge.

I stared as if in a trance, frozen and indecisive.

"Morgan," Draven shouted. "A little fire would be nice!"

Grimacing, I nodded. Raising my hands, I pointed a torrent of fire towards where the serpent's body still lay coiled on the beach, and targeted its lower half.

The beast writhed and hissed as the scorching flames licked at its scales. Letting out a haunting, horrific sound, it pulled itself off Hawl and tried to slither back towards the water, but it was too late. Unable to withstand the searing heat, the serpent's spectral scales melted and unraveled. The air filled with the sounds of melting flesh and a sickly hissing.

A yelp from Lancelet drew my attention, and I whirled to see her being yanked to the ground by an invisible foe.

The moon had retreated once more behind a cloud.

The serpent that had Lancelet in its grip blended seamlessly with the inky night. I couldn't make out anything. Lancelet had pulled her sword and was swinging all around herself, striking out at the ground again and again, but it was futile. The snake attacking her pulled her across the camp, raking her over the rocks and down towards the edge of the lake.

I let out a cry of fury and raced towards her, just as the fickle moon emerged from behind its concealing clouds, casting silvery radiance over the scene. In the newfound light, I could see two serpents had coiled around Lancelet's legs and were dragging her down to the water.

Lifting my hands, I directed fiery tendrils at the serpents. Flames erupted, illuminating the camp and consuming the creatures at the far end of their long bodies. As the snakes hissed in agony and were incinerated, I tugged Lancelet to her feet as the coils binding her were released. She stumbled backwards with me, sword still gripped in her hand.

On the other side of the camp, Draven had dropped Hawl down beside Guinevere and was shouting something at us, pointing back to the lake.

More ripples were forming on the surface of the water. I counted to five, then ten, then began to lose track.

"No, no," Lancelet moaned. "This is not good. This is not good timing, Morgan. We could really use Hawl right about now."

I gritted my teeth but said nothing, already feeling as if I were suffocating with self-blame. How could I have been so stupid?

Then—a glimmer of moonlight shot across the camp. I followed it as the beam of light meandered upwards over the cliffside of the Black Mountain, up the stone stairs and to the top of the platform we had been standing on together only hours before.

Lancelet followed my gaze. "Holy shit."

There, at the top of the platform, illuminated with moonlight, a doorway glowed, etched with blue and silver lines.

We looked at one another.

"You have to go," she said slowly.

A scream cut across the air. We whirled towards the cluster of horses tethered further down the beach near the water's edge.

Serpents had emerged and wrapped themselves around two of the horses legs. They had already brought one down and were dragging the poor creature into the water.

"Fuck," Lancelet exclaimed and began racing towards the horses, her sword gripped tightly in her hand.

I looked up at the doorway outlined on the cliffside, filled with panic. This was my chance, and I was missing it. Could we afford to wait another night?

I looked at Lancelet running down the beach, then back at Draven who stood protecting Hawl and Guinevere with a dagger in each hand.

We couldn't leave. Not now. I had made a horrible mess of things. We couldn't leave, and we couldn't stay.

The beating of wings filled the air overhead. I looked up, relief flooding my veins as Nightclaw and Sunstrike came into view. Moonlight gleamed on the cats' sleek fur and glinted along their sharp claws as they descended, eyes gleaming as they prepared to join our struggle.

The sound of my quickened breath mingled with the rhythmic thuds of the exmoors' wings, air vibrating with the impending clash.

And then the battlecats touched down.

Instantly, their powerful roars exploded, reverberating off the mountains and shaking the stones around us.

The clash of claws against scales mixed with the beating of heavy wings and the whistling of wind. Sand churned and rocks heaved as the exmoors attacked the serpents with ferocity, claws finding purchase on the snakes' invisible forms wherever they could catch one.

Heavy paws stamped upon serpent heads with sickening accuracy. Sharp exmoor teeth tore into invisible flesh, ripping through their adversaries with primal determination.

Then it was over. The once-invisible serpents lay dead or writhed in agonizing defeat.

The exmoors stood in the moonlight, their claws stained with spectral ichor, breath billowing hot in the aftermath of the struggle.

I lowered my hands and stepped forward, my eyes linking with Nightclaw's. The cat sat on his haunches, looking at me with inhuman intelligence. I gazed back at him with pride and sadness, remembering a time when his sleek and lustrous gold-and-black striped fur had been unkempt and matted, when his true worth had been ignored, undiscovered.

Now, his amber eyes were filled with reproach, as if he were asking why I had not called for him as soon as we had been attacked.

I cast my eyes away, tears unexpectedly pricking at the corners.

"I will not use you," I said aloud. "I will not be like him."

The cat stared back at me in silence, then lifted a paw and heavily slammed it down onto the ground. He gave a low growl and prowled towards me.

I held my ground, waiting, until finally the exmoor lowered his majestic head and pressed his furred forehead against mine.

"I chose you," he told me. "There is a difference."

The tears pricked more painfully. I squeezed my eyes closed. "You have your own life to live. I won't have either of you risk yourselves." I opened my eyes and looked at Sunstrike who was watching us in silence. "Besides, you have your mate to think of. I know what she's been hiding."

Draven had come up behind me. Now I sensed him freeze.

"She's carrying your cubs," I said aloud, not caring who heard anymore. "You can't tell me that doesn't matter. I won't put either of you in any more danger."

Nightclaw let out another low growl and turned his head towards his mate.

Had he known? Surely he must have. Animals could sense these things. They could even smell them. And Nightclaw and Sunstrike were no ordinary animals.

"If you truly want me to ask for your help," I said, trying to keep my voice steady. "Then please keep watch over my friends tonight. I... I did something stupid. They need me, but I can't be here." I turned and pointed upwards at the door that was, thankfully, still glowing in blue and silver. "I'm going inside there. Only Draven can come with me."

Nightclaw's growl was loud enough to shake the ground this time.

I flinched but continued, "I need you to stay with Lancelet and take care of Guinevere and Hawl. Where I'm going, you can't come. Please accept that."

I reached out a hand and lifted it, gently running it over his head. "You have no idea how much I wish you could be with me, Nightclaw. Don't you know how much strength you give me just from knowing you exist? That you care?" My voice broke. "But Sunstrike needs you, too. You have to take care of her now. Only her."

Now Draven stepped up. "I'll watch over her for you. You have my word. She'll return to you."

I brushed a hand over my eyes. "We have to go now." I looked over at Lancelet. Her face was grim. "Things didn't go according to plan. I'm so sorry."

"We're all alive," she said. "I suppose that's all that matters."

I nodded. Crossing the camp, I grabbed my pack from beside my tent. Draven's was already across his back. He was wiping his daggers on the rocky ground, trying to clean off the filth from the serpents.

"Time to go." I tried to make my voice cheerful. "Say good-bye to them for us in the morning, will you?"

"By the Three, they'll be pissed," Lancelet said gloomily. "I'm not looking forward to it. I don't know who will be worse to deal with, Guinevere or Hawl."

I stepped towards her and, gripping her shoulders, pulled her into a tight embrace before she could resist. "I love you. You fucking know that, right?"

I felt her nod against me. "I know."

"Be happy. That's all I..." I stopped, my throat closing up. "Be happy. You deserve it."

And then I turned and walked towards the stone steps and the Black Mountain for the second time that night.

CHAPTER 31 - MORGAN

"You knew it was here," Draven said from behind me as I stood before the door, looking at the intricate tracework. "You knew when we were all trying to figure it out. Yet you said nothing."

I didn't reply, simply lifted both my hands and pressed them flat against the stone.

"What's happening to you, Morgan? Talk to me."

I closed my eyes, feeling a needlelike pressure in my palms. I held them steady, knowing pulling back now would mean my death.

Then my hands were pulled even tighter against the stone. I was locked in a vise. I couldn't have yanked myself away even if I'd wanted to.

"What's happening?" Draven's voice had turned sharp. "What's it doing to you?"

"Just... wait." I could hear the strain in my voice. "Please."

It hurt. I didn't want him to know how much.

He was quiet. I saw him put a hand on his hilt. But he made no move to touch me or draw his sword.

I took a deep breath, then another, waiting, waiting.

And then the pressure was gone. I pulled my hands away.

"Fucking hell, Morgan," Draven swore, grabbing my wrists and turning my palms up.

They were raw and stained with blood.

"What did it do to you?"

But the answer was evident. My blood had opened the mountain.

Behind me, the stone panels were sliding apart, revealing the mountain's dark interior.

I heard a shout. Far down below us, some kind of commotion was occurring.

I looked down at our campsite by the lake and could just make out two struggling forms. Guinevere was awake.

"We have to go now," I said tightly. "Ask me later."

"Morgan," I heard Guinevere call. "Stop! Please!"

I pulled my hands away and slid between the panels. There was just enough room for Draven and I.

"Morgan, stop! I need to speak with you first! I need to tell you..."

I forced myself to shut out the sound of Guinevere's pleading. I told myself there was nothing I could do now. She was safe with Lancelet. They couldn't pass through the doorway, even if they tried.

The mountain wouldn't let them.

Draven was following me in, squeezing through just as the panels began to slide closed.

Inside, we stood together.

It was very dark.

"Well, fuck." His voice echoed off the stones around us. "We're here. Now what?"

I took a deep breath. "Now this."

I felt for him in the dark and wrapped my hands carefully around his waist, then pressed my ear to his chest, listening until I found the steady beating of his heart.

We stood like that for I don't know how long.

Together, in the dark.

Eventually, his arms came around me. He held me tight against him. His chin came down to rest atop my head.

"Oh, Morgan. Why do you do these things?"

"Do what?" My voice was muffled. I felt on the verge of panic. I made myself keep listening to the sound of his heart, willing myself into a calm I didn't truly feel.

"Act as if you're alone in this when you're not. I'm here, my silver one. I'm always, always here."

"I know," I said, my voice small. "Sometimes I know that too well, I think. I know you'll always be there. And so I... I did what I had to."

He was quiet for a moment. "I think I understand. It would have been harder to tell me first."

I nodded. "You would have had so many questions."

I could almost feel him smile. "That's true. I would have. Damn curious mind. Can you blame me?"

"I love you for it," I said truthfully. I lifted my mouth to his.

"Even in the pitch black of this mountain, I want you here, now," he said against my lips. "Is there a wall, do you think?" He shifted. "There's a floor at the very least."

"Decidedly *not* a good idea," I said, suppressing a grin, my voice strained. "We need to move on."

"On to where exactly? It's not as if we have a map. Or a light."

I bit my lip, then wincing a little, slid my hand into my pack and pulled out an item wrapped in velvet cloth. I gasped as the cloth brushed against my raw palm.

"The mountain knew you." Even in the dark, I could sense him looking towards my hand. "It took your blood, then let you in."

I nodded. "I've been here before. Somehow. I don't know when."

Carefully, I unwrapped the grail, tucked the cloth back into my pack.

Holding the chalice, I stood. Waiting for what? I wasn't sure.

And then it happened. The cup began to glow. I held it aloft in both hands and the light intensified.

I could see Draven now, standing beside me. I could see the way we had just entered.

"Care to let me in on how that works exactly?" Draven's tone was lighthearted, but I could sense his worry.

"I'm not sure I know the answer to that myself."

I was... remembering things. If it could be called that. Things I had once known. Small things.

I'd known there was a door. Beyond a doubt, I had known it.

I had known it would appear at night. And I had known it would let me in.

But more than that?

I held the grail higher using both hands, and a beam appeared.

I turned slowly in a full circle, letting the long ray of light illuminate our surroundings.

We were in a colossal hall. Towering pillars rose around us like silent guardians. Their surfaces were covered with runes and carvings. The ceiling above us was so high, it was lost in the shadows.

The hall seemed to stretch endlessly before us, disappearing into the darkness, creating an illusion of infinite space within the mountain's depths.

The atmosphere was grand, the architecture imposing. But the place was empty.

"Where is everyone?" Draven said, his voice low. "Is this your father's court?"

I finished turning the grail's beam.

"Stop." Draven's voice was sharp. "Look. There. The light."

The grail's light had grown brighter and the beam longer as I pointed it towards a particular area of the hall in front of us.

I moved the grail from side to side and the beam dimmed. When I moved it back again, it grew stronger.

"Well, that answers that," Draven said. "We have a guide."

I nodded. "We follow the grail."

He winced. "Not something I'm keen on doing. But I suppose we have no other choice in this place."

There were no torches. No lamps to light our way. No sunlight streaming in from skylights above. The grail was our only light. And for it to shine, one of us had to hold it aloft at all times.

Hours passed as we moved from one hall into another, following the beam of light.

The pillars around us seemed to absorb and amplify the echoes of our boots on the polished stone floor. At times, a low hum resonated from unseen depths beneath us, pulsating through the cavernous halls.

At some point, the night must have ended. We walked on through the day.

Once, the intermittent whisper of a breeze suggested that somewhere in this vast place there might be a way back out to fresh air and sunlight. Other than that, the air was cool and dry, without the hint of an earthy aroma one might expect to find within a mountain such as this.

We began to lose track of time. Walking on and on, through one hall to the next, down one long corridor into another vast, pillared room and into a corridor again.

We might have been going in circles, so similar were the rooms, so uniform were the designs of the pillars.

Only the carvings on the columns and walls seemed to have any variation. But after pausing once to examine them closely, I made myself stop looking. They seemed to share the same brutal themes of violence and degradation. Evidently the carvings were meant to show my father's strength, his triumph over his enemies. But I couldn't look at them without disgust coiling in my belly. They seemed only a horrific reminder of a past long forgotten but one which might easily come again.

Eventually, we stopped for the night, laying our bedrolls on the cool, polished stones.

We could not even make a fire. There was nothing to burn. No abandoned furniture. No wooden decorations of any kind. Only drab, hard stone.

Draven sank down onto his bedroll, pulling an apple out of his pack, and looked over at me as I positioned the grail a little ways away.

"I hate the thing," he said casually, taking a large bite out of his apple. I watched him chew, enjoying the normalcy of such a simple thing. "And yet now it's our beacon of hope."

I shuddered. "Well, I wouldn't go that far."

"Here's a question for you. Why don't we try to melt the thing right now?" Draven's eyes were angry as he looked at the grail. "What's stopping us?"

I undid the piece of leather holding my hair back in its long braid and shook out the strands. "By us, you mean me."

"Of course. I get you to do all the hard work." Draven grinned.

I forced a smile. "I've already tried."

"You've what?"

I bit my lip. "I tried to destroy it. The grail."

"How? When?"

"One night, after... after Gawain." I hesitated. "You were sleeping. I snuck out. Went far away from the camp. I threw everything I had at it." I looked at the grail, wanting to kick the cursed thing across the endless, empty room. "I was furious at myself for not trying before. But it was no use anyway. The thing wouldn't burn."

"Yet here we are on a quest to destroy it. What a delightful challenge that will be."

"Yes, well," I said tightly, "we'll find a way."

"At the very least," Draven said, finishing his apple and tossing the core over his shoulder, "we'll destroy your father."

"Yes, we will," I promised him. "But there's a way to destroy the objects, too, and it's here. Somewhere. I know it is. We'll find it. We're getting closer."

"Do you believe that? Or do you feel it?"

I shifted uncomfortably. "What's the difference?"

"There is a difference, Morgan. A difference in you. You're..." He shook his head. "You're hiding things."

"I'm not. What things? I told you about the door. The grail... that was just a guess. I didn't know for sure."

"Didn't you?" He was watching me closely. Finally he shook his head again. "Fine. It's not that I'm upset. I'm not angry with you. If you want to keep things from me, that's your right."

"I don't," I protested. Was I lying even to myself now? "It's a belief. A feeling. Can't it be both?"

I looked at him over the light of the grail. A poor replacement for the warmth of a campfire.

But while our surroundings might have changed for the worse, Draven—he was the same as he'd always been. In the very best of ways.

I watched as he leaned back on his elbows, clad in traveling leathers that contoured to the clean, strong lines of his warrior's physique and grinned.

"What?"

"You look more like a vagabond wanderer now than a prince," I observed.

"These leathers were exceedingly costly, I'll have you know," he complained. "Are you saying they look badly tailored?"

I laughed. "I'm saying you look more like a man I'd meet on a dusty road than a prince of a royal court."

He tugged at the opening of his tunic, and my heart hammered a little at the glimpse of bronzed skin it revealed.

"Dusty, no. Sweaty from walking all day and night, yes."

The mention of sweat didn't dispel my desire. If anything, it heightened it. I found myself suddenly imagining licking the sweat from Draven's chest as he lay back on his elbows, looking down at me from those wicked, emerald green eyes.

As if reading my thoughts, he suddenly sat up and leaned forward, resting his body on his hands like a prowling cat.

"You were licking your lips," he observed.

His glossy, raven hair was tousled and hung around his face. I looked at the slant of his jaw, the sleek, onyx horns and felt the familiar, raw pull of longing.

"I wasn't," I said automatically.

"Were, too." He reached up to grab the back of his tunic and yanked it over his head with one smooth tug.

Now I *was* licking my lips.

With the shirt gone, the space between us seemed to pulse with heat.

I couldn't take my eyes off the hard, taut planes of his body. The play of muscles beneath the surface of his sun-kissed skin.

He glistened with a sheen of sweat. I could smell him, not unpleasantly. The scent carried the essence of pure masculine vitality.

"Always with the sandalwood," I complained.

He smirked. "This is pure, unbridled me you're smelling. Perhaps you're imagining things when you add in the spices."

"Ha! That's what you'd like me to believe, isn't it? You're carrying a bar of fragrance in your pack, aren't you? Whatever you rub all over yourself to smell like this." I leaned forward suddenly as if I was about to rise and dart towards his pack and, in an instant, found myself pinned to the floor.

Draven's powerful frame hovered over me. "This what you really wanted?"

"Perhaps." I gasped as he nudged my thighs apart with one knee. "Although the time and place is... a little unusual."

"From what I recall, we've had more *unusual* than this."

He leaned down and licked the line of my jaw. "Mmm."

I was afraid to ask. "Sweaty? Disgusting?"

"Sweaty, yes. We both are." He grinned. "Disgusting? Never. You taste good to me. Always."

"You have terrible taste. I suppose I should be grateful," I teased.

He slid my tunic up over my stomach and kissed my belly button, then started licking a line down to the top of my waistband.

I shivered.

"Do you think he's watching us?"

"Who?" I frowned. "My father?"

I felt him nod. "Him. Them. Anyone."

I looked upwards, trying to glimpse the highest point of the ceiling that arched overhead and failed.

"I don't know. I don't care. I want you."

"The feeling is mutual, I assure you."

And then my trousers were being yanked down over my hips, and I had no time to think of who may or may not have been watching us. As Draven mounted me, we were alone in our own private universe.

There was no one else who mattered.

CHAPTER 32 - MORGAN

I slept uneasily, dreaming of a long-forgotten civilization where my father ruled as king. I dreamed of my brothers fighting over a mortal woman until they had torn her asunder. I dreamed of my sister, Tempest, sitting beside a fountain filled with blood, drinking from a red-rimmed goblet.

When I woke, Draven was already packing his things. I watched as he lifted one of his water flasks and shook it, then grimaced.

"You let me sleep in," I accused.

He shrugged. "Did I? We don't even know what time it is here. For all I know, you're up early."

I made a face. "How much water do you have left?"

"Enough to get me through today. You didn't expect this to be the greatest threat we faced in the Black Mountain, did you?"

"I hadn't expected to die of dehydration before I finally found my father, no," I said ironically. "We'll just have to find water."

"Find water. Find a way to destroy the most powerful objects in existence. I adore your optimism, silver one." He rose to his feet. "Well, if my mate says we must, then we must—and we will. Shall we?"

I gathered my things, and we resumed our march.

This time, Draven held the grail aloft as we walked through the hall.

For the next few hours, we followed much of the same dreary pattern as the day before. Walk through endless hall after endless hall into an endless corridor into a new endless hall. Repeat.

By afternoon—or what felt like it, we emerged into a space larger than any we had seen before. Before us stretched a winding staircase leading down into the depths of the mountain.

This staircase had guardrails, which was the best that could be said for it. The worst was that on either side, as far as we could tell, lay nothing. Nothing more than a black abyss.

Draven leaned over the edge of the rail and tossed a pebble down.

We stood, waiting for the sound of it hitting the floor below.

And waited.

Finally, a tiny thud.

I held the grail higher. There was no end to the staircase that we could see.

I swung the light around. There was no other way to go. Not unless we went backwards.

But to do so would mean finding our way on our own, as the grail's beam of guiding light went only down the stairs in front of us, forcing us forward.

"Wonderful." I stared down the steps. "Lovely."

"Really? Bleak and barren, I would have said." I stuck my tongue out at Draven's back as he stepped around me and set his foot down carefully on the first step. "Do you think it's leading us to your father, or leading us to our deaths? Guess we can't do anything except follow and find out."

Clenching my jaw in frustration, I went after him.

Soon it seemed as if we had been walking downwards for a day and a night.

Step after step, step after step. The staircase seemed to never end. It simply spiraled down and down.

At first, we talked to pass the time. But after a while, with our water reserves diminishing, we began to try to save our breath.

Draven stayed in the lead, carrying the grail in front of him like a torch. After what felt like at least three hours, I forced him to switch places with me and held the grail as I led the way.

About an hour after that, I stopped.

Draven hit my back, and I nearly stumbled.

"Sorry," he said, sounding tired. "What is it?"

"I thought I heard something. Did you? Listen."

We stood there in silence. I swung the grail around slowly, but no matter where it swung, the beam of light continued to point to the steps right in front of me. Downwards. And down again.

"There." Draven sounded excited. "I heard it."

We listened again.

There it was. A drip. Like the fall of water.

Eagerly, I held the grail out over the side of the stairs and we peered downwards.

Far below, there was a gleam.

"Water," Draven said, squeezing my arm.

We picked up our pace, continuing our descent, anticipation building with each step.

When we finally reached a floor of solid stone, the grail's glow revealed a scene so welcome, it took my breath away.

A wide, shallow, rectangular pool. Marble statues of fish and other sea creatures decorated each corner, frozen in lifelike poses. In the center of the pool lay a huge fountain. Somehow, even in this empty, abandoned place, the fountain's streams continued to cascade downwards, filling the pool with fresh water.

We approached the water's edge silently. I lowered my hand, dipping it into the pool. The water was cool. It smelled fresh.

"It knew," I said, looking at Draven.

He nodded, then pulled out his flask and lowered it into the water. "Well, if it wanted us dead, there are simpler ways than this." He took a swig from the flask before I could stop him.

"Really?" I narrowed my eyes. "Such as?"

"Such as leading us straight off a cliff," he said cheerfully.

He tugged his tunic up over his head, then tossed it into the pool.

I glanced around nervously. "If you're planning on taking a bath…"

"Oh, I am," he assured me. "I certainly am."

I eyed him as he began to shuck out of the rest of his clothes. "I'll stand watch."

He waggled his eyebrows at me. "If that's what you want to call it. Go right ahead."

I grinned. "I didn't say I wouldn't enjoy it."

My hand was, in fact, on the hilt of my blade. Just in case.

The scene was tranquil as Draven dunked himself under the waters a few times, then scrubbed his shirt and wrung it out.

I switched with him quickly, refreshing myself in the pool and rinsing out the tunic I had been wearing before donning a clean one from my satchel and slinging the wet one over the leather bag to dry.

It was hard to say for sure, but it felt as if it were evening or thereabouts.

"Should we camp here?" I asked.

"It seems as good a place as any. Less exposed, for one."

He had a point. The pool was a smaller, more enclosed room than most of the ones we had come through.

"Where does the grail want us to go next?" Draven asked as he drained a flask of water and leaned down to refill it again.

I lifted the light. The beam pointed towards an arched doorway.

I stepped closer towards it, peered through the arch, and groaned. "You'll never guess."

Draven came up behind me. "For fuck's sake."

The beam of light shone ahead of us, pointing to a flight of stairs across the room that ascended up and up, the top reaching higher than we could see.

"We're going to live in this mountain forever, aren't we?" Draven complained.

I turned around and kissed him. "I could think of worse people to be stuck with."

He grimaced. "Small comfort when we run out of food."

"Perhaps the grail can lead us to that, too." Then I shuddered, remembering what else the grail had done. And what it might find acceptable as a food source.

"It won't come to that," Draven said, looking down at me. He turned back to look at the pool. "I'm going to trust its serenity while accepting that, like everything else in this place, it could be a lie. Let's camp here and move on tomorrow."

We ate and then lay down beside one another.

It was only when I had started to close my eyes that the gleam of the grail caught my gaze one last time and I realized something.

I had slept the night before, wrapped in Draven's arms. But I had not dreamed.

My father had not invaded my mind, though I had been unshielded.

My heart thudded. What did it mean?

Perhaps he had given up. Stopped trying to batter his way into my true dreamings. Or perhaps it had been a rare reprieve. He had been distracted by something else or had forgotten.

Or was it the place? The mountain had recognized me, opened for me. The grail led me. Could one of those things somehow be shielding me now as we traveled to what I hoped would be the heart of my father's court?

Draven was already dozing. I listened to his breathing until I was sure he was fully asleep, then carefully sat up and, pulling away from him, crawled over to the edge of the pool and leaned against it.

I sat awake there the rest of the night.

CHAPTER 33 - MORGAN

We had gone down. Now we traveled up.

In the morning, we climbed flight after flight of winding stairs, leading up and away from the tranquil pool until, by about noon, we seemed to have reached a new area inside of the mountain.

Torches glowed along the walls in every room and every corridor, burning without flame and without end.

The mysterious new illuminations were welcomed. We had become so used to the grail as our only light source.

The rooms here were constructed in a smaller style with lower ceilings—still higher than any mortals made but low enough that we could finally glimpse their vaulted tops.

After a few hours of this, the grail's beam of light led us out onto a parapet that bordered a vast chasm. We followed along the edge of the low wall until we came to a place where a long, wide bridge jutted out over the chasm. Immense stone arches spanned it in sections, above and below, supporting the weight of the monumental construction.

Far on the other side, we could see a fortress carved from stone. A new region of the mountain. My heart hammered. Was my father's court on the other side?

Great iron doors marked the way in.

The beam shone straight along the stone bridge.

There were no guardrails this time.

"At least there's no breeze," Draven observed, catching my gaze. "No air, no wind, no breeze."

I looked down at the chasm sourly. "Truly, we are blessed. That's the last thing I'll be thinking as I fall to my death. Thank the Three there was no wind."

He laughed. "Ready?"

But there was a worried look in his eyes as he grasped my hand. Turning it over, he raised it to his lips and kissed my palm lightly. "We can always hold hands as we walk across."

The bridge was easily wide enough to traverse side-by-side. Four people might have stood upon it, shoulder to shoulder.

That still did not mean I didn't wish for guardrails. A low wall. Anything.

"Linking your fate to mine once again?" I teased.

Mischief flashed across his face. "I suppose I could tie you to me with a rope. Would you like that?"

"Which part of me would you tie?" I asked before I could stop myself. "No. Don't answer that. Not right now." I willed myself to stop imagining the possibilities. "Hands would be nice."

Clasping hands, we began to walk. I tried not to think about the vast chasm below. The gaping maws of space to either side.

Or the faint breeze, not quite a wind, that caught strands of my hair. Nowhere near strong enough to push us off the bridge but distracting nonetheless.

We kept walking. A quarter of the way.

Then a third.

I glanced downwards. Blackness. A bottomless valley of stone.

Why did the sight of it terrify me so much?

I shifted the grail in my sweating hand.

Draven glanced at me. "Do you want me to take it?"

I shook my head but let go of his hand, switching the grail to it and wiping the sweat from my other.

We walked on.

We were drawing near to halfway when a rumbling began far below us.

I looked at Draven uneasily.

We quickened our pace a little.

The rumbling increased. The bridge beneath our feet began to quiver ever so slightly.

We moved more quickly, passing the midpoint.

The rumbling noise was growing louder, becoming a thunderous roar.

Stones shifted uneasily. The arches overhead groaned in protest.

Dust rained upon us from ancient crevices overhead.

The bridge's trembling intensified.

Draven's hand found mine and squeezed. "Run?"

"I like your plan," I gasped.

We ran forward. I held the grail at my side. We didn't need the beam to direct us, we already knew where to go.

But it was too late.

The bridge trembled violently beneath our feet.

Something was coming.

A brilliant glow rose from the abyss below. Vivid and fiery like a burning star ascending from the darkness.

"Stop," Draven ordered. "Back to back. Weapons out."

We halted in unison, standing pressed against one another. I held the grail in one hand, my scythe in the other.

The luminous fireball was drawing closer. I raised the back of my wrist to my forehead and wiped the sweat away.

What entity born from the abyss was drawing near? What foe would we now face?

I imagined my father riding on the back of an exmoor and braced myself.

The fireball exploded upwards on my side.

At first, I was blinded.

All I could make out were pure flames.

And then, something began to take shape.

A creature of fire. A creature made entirely of flame.

The contours became discernible within the bright brilliance.

An outline. A silhouette.

A woman.

Every inch of her form was flickering flames. She was the embodiment of fire itself.

She loomed over us, a towering, titan-like being. Flames trickled down past her waist, going far below the bridge into the darkness where they wound together. A flaming whip crackled and danced in her hand, casting sparks in all directions.

Draven moved to my side, his weapon already free. Defensively, he started to raise it.

I grabbed his arm. "No. Wait. Look."

An anguished expression twisted the flaming creature's features, as if she were under the weight of unbearable torment.

She looked down at us, and her beautiful, burning mouth opened in an agonized scream.

Abruptly, she lifted her whip streaming with flames, and I flinched, expecting the weight of the heavy, punishing lash to be flung down upon us at any moment.

But instead, the woman extended a single burning finger.

Its tip blazed like a beacon in the darkness towards where Draven and I stood on the rattling bridge.

She was pointing at me.

A guttural wail emanated from the flaming woman's open mouth. The tortured sound echoed off the mountain stone.

My heart raced. No, not me. She was not pointing at me.

The grail.

I lifted my arm, holding the chalice high.

The flames surrounding the burning lady seemed to flicker with intensity. Another unearthly wail burst forth. A communication beyond words but the meaning of which was clear.

A plea. A yearning.

I looked at the flaming being, something deep inside of me resonating with memory.

She was glorious. She was tragic. Suspended between the realms of life and death, of fire and earth. A spectral wraith of flames trapped in a purgatory of darkness.

Her beauty burned so bright, it was divine. A corruption of what she should have been.

"Zorya?" I whispered. "Is it you?"

Beside me, Draven inhaled sharply.

The woman gave a keening wail that sent stones falling from high above.

The answer was clear enough to me.

I lifted the grail higher. "The grail? Is this yours?"

Long ago, the stories went, the three objects had been created by the gods. The sword, Draven had once told me, had been made by Perun. His sisters created the other two objects. Marzanna made the grail. Zorya, the spear.

But what if the stories had gotten it wrong?

Very, very wrong.

The flaming woman who had been goddess of the dawn looked down at me with her blazing eyes, terrible in the pain they held.

"Do you know me?" I demanded. "Do you know who I am?"

"Morgan," Draven whispered from beside me. "What are you doing?"

I ignored him.

I already knew one part of the story that had been badly misshapen.

Perun was not Marzanna's brother. He was her father.

But the name which he went by in this world of fae and mortals was not Perun, but Gorlois le Fay.

I shook the grail. "Did you create this? Did you create any of the objects? The sword by my side, this sickle? The spear?"

My questions lingered in the charged air. I stood waiting, shaking with anticipation, gazing up at the burning deity.

Zorya shook her head mournfully.

"Was it made *from* you?" I pressed her. "Against your will? Is that why you're here? Like this?"

The flaming woman pulsed with energy as another scream ripped out, filling the space around us with a deafening sound. Draven gripped my arm, and we braced ourselves as the bridge beneath us danced and trembled with the power of it.

When the shaking had stopped, I looked back at the corrupted goddess, undeterred.

"Something was stolen from you. Taken to make this... this horrible thing. You were trapped here. You've been here, like this, ever since."

Another blaze of flames as the woman lowered her head, nodding her assent.

"Can we destroy it?" I cried. "Here? Now? Together? Help me! Let me set you free."

I felt Draven stiffen, but I didn't have time to worry about what he must be thinking.

"I will never let my father have it. The grail or the sword. Never again," I swore to the woman. "Tell me what I need to do."

She moved and sparks flew around her. Slowly, she lowered her head to my level and peered into my eyes.

I met her burning gaze unblinkingly, looking back into orbs of scorching red that burned as brightly as the sun.

A jolt went through me. She was inside of me. Not like my father had been in my dreams—invading my mind against my will. This was different. Gentler. She was not taking. She was placing. Placing her thoughts very carefully as if afraid even touching me in this small way might break me.

No one has ever asked.

No one has ever cared.

No one ever came.

"Well, I'm here now," I said aloud and clearly. "I've come."

You are. So different. Yet the same as before.

The voice was fond, wistful. Sadness welled inside me.

The object you hold is a violation.

A pause.

This hurt was old. So old. And yet I could feel her horror even now at what had been done to her.

There may be a way to destroy it.

The thought was careful, controlled. As if hope was something she had long since forgotten. Still, I sensed a seed of it there. Growing in the light inside of her.

"Let's do it. Here. Now. I'm ready," I said quickly. "I've tried on my own. I wasn't able to destroy it. But with the two of us..."

Not so fast. You say you tried to destroy it alone.

She was thinking. There was a pause.

Together, it is possible. Yes, I believe it is. But you do not understand.

"Tell me."

It will take something. From you and me both. As for me, I am willing to give up anything to do this. Anything. To cease existence would be better than this state I am now trapped in. But for you, it will be something you can never get back.

"What? What will it take?" I asked.

A wordless motion. The equivalent of a helpless shrug.

"I don't care," I said stoutly. "I'm ready. I'll do anything."

"Morgan." Draven's voice was sharp. "Morgan, what are you promising her? What's happening?"

He could only hear one side of our conversation, I remembered.

"We're going to destroy the grail," I explained. "Right here. Right now."

"You and that... thing?"

I stared at him. "She's no *thing*. You don't understand who she is to me."

"Tell me then," he said quickly. "You called her Zorya. But how do you know this? How is such a thing even possible?"

I tried to quell my rising impatience. "Look, I'm not a believer. I never have been. You know that. But parts of the stories are true." His eyes widened slightly.

"I don't know what she is exactly now," I went on. What *I* was. What *we* were. "But before she was turned into this... thing, she was Zorya. I know it beyond a shadow of a doubt. And I also know that"—I took a deep breath—"she's my aunt."

There was shock in his eyes as the words passed my lips, yes. But no denial. No disbelief. Only rapid acceptance.

Draven believed me. He would always believe me.

"And what does she say will happen to you if you do this?" he asked, looking at me carefully.

I forced myself to meet his gaze steadily. "She's not sure. But the process will take something from both of us."

Draven exhaled.

"But that's nothing I didn't already know, Draven." I clenched my jaw. "I already expected to die in this place. Don't deny you've had the same thought. And if that's what it takes, we're here willingly, aren't we?"

He shook his head, but said nothing.

"Anyhow," I said, suddenly weary, "I'm going to do it. I'm going to help her. Especially if it rids Aercanum of this cursed thing once and for all." The grail pulsed with light in my hand, and I stared at it. "Besides, I think it wants us to."

"To destroy it?"

"Yes. It never asked for any of this. It's been used for terrible things, but ultimately, it's part of *her*, Draven. Part of her that was wrenched from her without her consent. Some aspect of her being. Call it a soul. Call it her heart. The taking of it left her like this. We can't even begin to imagine what she must have been before or what she's been through since."

"You know she's your aunt, but you can't remember that? What she was... before?" Draven's voice was very soft.

I shook my head. "No. Only small parts of... my history."

He nodded. "Very well. I'm here. I'll help however I can."

"I don't think there's much you can do for this part. But thank you."

I shot him a grateful look, then lowered the grail to the bridge, setting it in the center of the path.

Then I slowly unsheathed Excalibur.

The curved blade gleamed bright as if recognizing the other object of power. Did the sword know what I had to do?

With a quick intake of breath, I raised the blade to my palm and slashed before Draven could stop me.

Drops of blood welled up from the cut.

I slid my hand along the sickle, coating the blade in red.

Then I looked up at Zorya. She stood, waiting, trembling in flames.

"Ready?"

I lifted Excalibur in both hands, ignoring the sting of pain from the cut.

The air hissed with energy. Heat radiated from Zorya's form, turning my skin hot and burning.

I stood firm, holding the sword upwards as the corrupted goddess of the dawn moved towards me across the abyss like a restless spirit.

Lifting her blazing hands, she held them over my head.

A glow of light erupted, and I cried out, closing my eyes tightly from the intensity of the heat.

Now. Do it now.

Her voice in my head was urgent.

I forced open my eyes and swept Excalibur downwards, hardly taking in the flames dancing all along the blade as the sword suffused with elemental power, steel bursting with more magic than I had ever seen.

There was a sound like nothing I had ever heard before. Like waves breaking on a beach. Like the shattering of glass.

Then it was over.

The grail lay cut asunder. Its light had gone out.

A cry pierced the air. Not of suffering or pain, but elation.

I turned towards Zorya and saw her form beginning to flicker.

She was dissolving.

The sound of the grail breaking had faded away, but now a new one came in its stead.

The chamber was vibrating and rumbling. The stones beneath our feet were shaking once more.

A low roar built from the depths of the chasm. A primal sound that filled the air with fury.

Something was coming. Something angry.

I realized Draven was still watching me. Meeting his gaze, I saw him quickly wipe the expression from his face. Awe. Shock.

Then there was only concern. He reached out to grip my arm as the bridge shook harder.

My sword still out, we braced ourselves for the arrival of whatever was coming up out of the deep.

The rumbling grew louder.

A creature of nightmares loomed into view. Its massive form was shrouded in an inky veil, tendrils of darkness swirling and coalescing around its monstrous frame. Eyes gleaming with a baleful light pierced through the blackness, fixing upon us with a hatred that sent shivers down my spine.

With a guttural growl that sent heavy stones from the ceiling crumbling downwards, it moved towards us.

I stared at the creature. It was a being of pure darkness, a twisted counterpart to the fiery goddess.

Clearly it was seeking retribution for the destruction of the grail. My father must have sensed what we had done and sent this minion to punish us.

Only one thing could cast out the dark.

I lifted my hands to call upon flames.

My palms out, I shot fire forwards.

Only, nothing happened.

My brow furrowing in concentration, I tried again, waiting for the blaze to extend from my fingertips and dance towards the demonic creature of darkness.

Nothing.

Beside me, Draven was watching.

He raised his own hands, thrusting them forwards. I knew what he was doing. Would it work?

Nothing came forth. No flames. No fire. No spark of heat.

He tried again, opening his palms and creating a sword of shadows, larger than any I had seen him make before.

Lifting into the air, he swung it just in time as the creature lowered a dark, swirling arm towards us in a sweeping motion.

Draven's shadow sword hit the arm. I watched him clench his jaw and brace his feet, struggling to stay upright as the strength of the creature pushed against him.

The sword was holding the creature at bay but doing nothing else.

With a cry of pain, Draven dropped the sword and stepped back, grabbing me and pulling me downwards as the creature's arm swept over and above us, narrowly missing knocking us backwards off the bridge and into the chasm below.

The shadowy sword was now stuck in the creature's arm like a pine needle in a bear's massive paw.

As we watched, the sword of shadows was absorbed into the creature's own blackness.

We had no flames. And Draven's shadows were useless.

What else was there?

I looked down at Excalibur. Compared to the massive creature that threatened us, the sword that had destroyed the grail looked pitifully puny.

But if the creature just got close enough... If I could get higher somehow. If I could...

Meanwhile, Zorya was fading. Her form flickering and dissolving as she grew closer to embracing the ether.

I knew she longed for this release. I would not wish to keep her.

And yet...

There was no need to ask. No time to say anything.

She swung her flaming head towards me once, just once, and I felt her presence.

I am sorry for what you have lost. I go now, but I will do what I can to aid you. One last time.

With a fierce cry, the goddess of the dawn hurled herself at the shadowy creature.

Flames clashed with shadows, each blow resonating in an epic struggle for dominance.

Zorya's flames were fading, but still she flung them at the darkness with an unyielding determination.

For a fleeting moment, it seemed as if she might prevail.

But as her fiery form flickered and waned, the monster of shadows' dark tendrils enveloped her in a suffocating embrace.

With a final, defiant cry, Zorya erupted in a blaze of incandescent light.

As the flames subsided, the chamber was briefly silent, and in the darkness, I saw that my aunt was gone.

The creature of darkness still stood before us. Zorya's sacrifice had not been enough to vanquish it. But at least she had tried.

Around us, stones began to fall. Heavy ones from the ceiling. Then, looking back, I saw that the bridge itself was crumbling behind us.

Only one way out remained now, and it lay before us. I followed Draven's gaze to the heavy stone doors that lay on the other side. Could we make it?

A new cry pierced the air. The call of a hunter.

A shadow fell over my face, and I looked upwards.

A golden owl was swooping down from the cavernous chamber.

Following close behind it came a dark battlecat, its wings beating in a forceful rhythm. Tuva. And Nightclaw.

In our hour of greatest need, my exmoor had come. Even when I had told him not to. Pride filled my heart, but I opened my mouth to cry out, to tell the exmoor to go back.

It was too late. With claws bared and teeth gnashing, Nightclaw flew straight towards the creature of shadows.

My breath caught in my throat. It was futile. It had to be. A small owl and a single exmoor against such a massive creature of darkness.

There was no way we could win this battle.

"Morgan." Draven's voice sounded strained in my ear. His hand gripped my wrist. "Morgan, we have to go."

"No." I shook my head frantically. "Go? We can't go now. You don't understand..."

"No," he said, his jaw tightening. "It's you who doesn't understand."

As he began to pull me down the bridge, I looked behind us.

The way we had come was falling away. Entire swathes of stones collapsed noiselessly into the chasm below. The sounds of the ancient bridge disintegrating were joined by the sounds of Nightclaw's roars and Tuva's sharp cries and the creature of darkness's own guttural exclamations of fury and hate.

As the two creatures of light battled the creature of darkness, Draven continued to pull me down the bridge.

But I had no plans to leave. This was Nightclaw. My Nightclaw. He should not have been there. I would not leave him now that he had come.

How had he even found us?

I forced Draven to a halt as I paused to watch the battlecat, wings spread wide as it glided through the air then descended upon the shadowy demon, unleashing claws and teeth, landing blows anywhere it could on that terrible sinuous form.

Meanwhile, Tuva—looking miniscule as she flew high above—swooped close to the creature, darting and weaving, distracting the demon and sending it into a swatting fury as Nightclaw sought to wound it.

Too late it dawned on me what the bird and the cat were doing.

A sickening crack filled the chamber as the shadow demon struck Nightclaw with a devastating blow. The massive feline, caught off guard, let out a pained roar as it was thrown back by the force of the impact.

A deep gash marred Nightclaw's flank. The exmoor's fur rapidly matted with blood as he struggled to maintain his flight.

Despite the wound, I saw Nightclaw's eyes burn with that familiar unyielding golden fire.

He soared back towards the creature of shadows. I let out a cry of protest, hands trembling and clammy, blood draining from my face.

"Here, Morgan!" Draven was shouting. "Inside! We need to get inside."

The doors. Somehow we had reached the massive iron doors that led the way off the bridge.

Draven had managed to get one of them open. Now the towering door parted in a space wide enough for us to squeeze through.

"I'm not going anywhere," I screamed.

As he tried to pull me through, I thrust my hands out, wedging myself in the space.

Vesper. It was Vesper all over again. The hands pulling me away from Lancelet. The hands pulling me from Nightclaw.

"Stop!" My voice was shrill and desperate.

I looked back towards the battle.

Nightclaw had simply been buying us time.

Now, with each beat of his wings, blood fell from the wound on his flank. But the battlecat was unrelenting, flying straight back towards the creature of shadows.

With a roar, the demon struck out at the exmoor as it flew, this time with a force so great, it sent the cat tumbling backwards through the air.

Nightclaw let out an anguished roar as he spiraled downwards into the abyss, his wings drooping by his sides.

I screamed, hands reaching out towards my exmoor. But before I could step past the doorway, Draven's arms were tight around my waist, pulling me across the threshold and kicking the heavy metal door shut behind us with a deafening bang.

As we stumbled forward into the dim chamber, I wrenched myself away.

My head was spinning. Nightclaw's cry rang through my mind unendingly. I would never forget the sound.

"Open the door," I demanded.

Draven said nothing, simply leaned back against the wall and slid down to the floor. His face was numb.

I yanked against the iron door. It wouldn't budge. Of course it wouldn't.

"Open the fucking door, Draven," I screamed at him.

I was a gaping wound. Bereft. Emptied. I had no flames.

And now... I had no Nightclaw.

Over and over, the image of the exmoor tumbling through the air replayed in my mind.

I reached out for the battlecat with my senses, searching and scanning with my mind harder than I ever had. Nothing.

I looked at Draven again. He was sitting with his head in his hands.

"Draven."

He wouldn't look at me.

"Draven," I said again, softer this time.

I forced myself to take a step towards him.

Draven wasn't Vesper. He was my mate. He was the furthest thing from hurt or treachery or betrayal that I could possibly imagine.

He had known why Nightclaw had come from the very start, and he had refused to let the exmoor's sacrifice be in vain.

He had saved me. Even though he'd known I would hate him for it.

"Draven, I'm..." I started to say just as he lifted his head.

"What was that?" he said quickly, looking around. He sniffed. "Do you smell that?"

"I don't smell anything," I began, just as a sweet, honeyed scent filled my nostrils and my vision dimmed.

CHAPTER 34 - MORGAN

I woke to the sound of an owl hooting.

Slowly, I sat up. I was lying on a bed in a large but otherwise empty room. The chamber was colorless. Everything from the bed furnishings to the walls was a stark, soulless white.

Despite the hooting I had heard, Tuva was nowhere to be seen. I was alone.

I walked across the white marble floor towards a tall, arched window and stopped.

I was no longer within the mountain. The window I looked out of commanded a view of the clouds.

As I leaned against the windowsill, I could feel a gentle sway beneath my feet and realized the building, the palace, was itself in motion.

I watched as a mountain peak appeared in the clouds below, then vanished again, and my heart sped up.

My father's court was not inside of the Black Mountain. It was above it.

I turned slowly around the room. I could have sworn Tuva's hooting had woken me. But the owl was nowhere to be seen.

There was a slight sound from across the room, and a door pushed open.

A maidservant stood there, clad in a long, white robe. She was very pale, with white, almost translucent hair. She would not meet my eyes, simply stood with her eyes downcast. Her arms hung by her sides. Her limbs were slender and elongated in a way I found both fascinating and disturbing. I had never seen such features in a fae.

When she spoke, her voice was cold. "My God summons you. You must come now."

I took a curious step towards her. "God? You mean my father?"

"The God." The maidservant sounded displeased. "The Divine One beckons you to his glorious presence."

I laughed at her. "He is no god. And there is nothing glorious about his presence, I assure you."

She lifted her head to look at me, and I saw the cold dislike there.

So much for having anything in common with these strange people.

"He's a monster," I said quietly. "And if you belong to his court then you must already know this."

"Follow me," was all she said.

I went with her. Not because I enjoyed following commands. But because my most pressing goal was to find Draven. He must be in this floating palace somewhere. Or worse, already with my father.

I followed the young woman down empty white corridors until we reached a set of silver doors.

Four guards flanked the entrance, decked in pristine white uniforms. Each held a spear made of silver, ornately decorated with gemstones. The spears looked more ceremonial than practical. I supposed my father didn't particularly require protection.

The maidservant who had led me now pushed open the doors to the throne room. They swung open with a soft creak and she stepped back to let me pass, then pulled them closed behind me.

Passing over the threshold, I took in the scene before me.

A towering throne of obsidian rose atop a raised dais of gleaming white marble.

Upon the throne, rising to his feet as I entered, was a figure who immediately commanded my full attention.

My father.

He looked nothing like how I had imagined.

This man, this being, bore only a vague resemblance to the man in my dreams and his portraits.

He was alien. Inhuman. Un-fae.

Pale with a hairless head, his skin stretched taut over a rigid and angular face. Like the maidservant, his limbs were unnaturally elongated and his fingers long and sinewy with muscle, like the hands one might imagine in a nightmare clambering out of a grave.

Once, perhaps he had possessed a semblance of beauty with the same sharp features and high cheekbones I had seen mirrored in my brothers and sisters. But now, the sight of these protruding bones only served to accentuate the terror he inspired. My instincts screamed at me to flee as he rose before me, towering over us all like a specter of death.

The god of thunder he might have been, but everything about him reeked of rot and decay.

And he was not alone.

Sitting on the dais was a woman. She was smaller but similarly formed. In contrast to my father, she still possessed vestiges of her former youth and beauty. Pale gold scales wound down her left cheek and stretched down her slender neck, disappearing below the low-cut neckline of the silver clinging gown she wore.

She looked at me with viper's eyes of a radiant turquoise and smiled as she caressed Draven's cheek as he leaned against her, seated between her legs with his head nearly in her lap.

I looked at my mate, taking in his dazed expression, the bite marks trailing down his neck, caked with spots of dried blood.

She had touched him. Tasted him.

I had to fight the urge to vomit all over the throne room floor.

"Hello, Vela. It's been a long time," I said.

She smiled and traced a line down Draven's golden brown throat, making sure to hover her fingertips over the marks. "So good to have you finally home again."

"Do you mean me?" I said calmly. "Or my mate who sits beside you?"

Vela laughed, but I could see the fury in her eyes. "Your mate?" She turned to look up at my father. "Your daughter has no respect."

"Perhaps that's why the bold little thing has always been my favorite," he said, looking past Vela at me. "She entertains me the way no one else ever could."

"I survived when no one else could, you mean," I retorted. "After all you sent against me."

My father simply smiled.

Vela's eyes narrowed. "Do you even know who you are?" She gestured to Draven. "Who *he* is? Have the scales finally fallen from your ignorant little eyes?"

"I figured it out long ago," I answered.

She hissed at me with pleasure. "Then you know who he truly belongs to. Who he gave himself to long ago."

"I know the truth. What you say is only your version of it." I looked at Draven's glazed emerald eyes. "You cannot keep one who wishes to be free. No matter how much you may wish to." I forced myself to smile very calmly at Vela. "He *is* my mate. He doesn't want you. He hasn't wanted you in a very, very long time."

She hissed again and raised her hand as if to strike me, but my father made a warning gesture and she lowered it again, shooting daggers from her beautiful viper's eyes instead.

"He's mine," she snarled. "He is Khor."

Vela rose to her feet. My skin crawled as she leaned down to run her fingers through Draven's black hair—as if he were no more than a pet. She kept her eyes on me all the while, making sure I was watching every touch, every caress.

My hands had tightened into fists. I forced them open, trying to exude a calm I didn't feel.

"Your Draven, my Khor," Vela crooned, "has fought by my side and your father's countless times against the Three. You and your aunts, Perun's rebellious sisters and his headstrong daughter, all with their weak spots for mortals."

"You see weakness. I see strength. I've gotten this far," I said.

Vela laughed and turned to look at my father again. "Even now, she tells her own twisted version of the story."

"There are many stories," I said. "Most are twisted. Most are untrue."

"Where may one find the truth? It is a question as old as time itself," my father mused. He did not seem particularly invested in what was happening between Vela and me. He watched, half-bored, as if simply waiting for what would come next.

Had he even really expected me to get this far? How much of what had occurred in the Black Mountain had he been able to see?

"Have you forgotten, stupid girl?" Vela snarled. "Have you forgotten that we *killed* you?"

I looked at her steadily. "I remember."

I remembered it all.

Mortal stories said that Vela and Perun had been rivals. That they had battled against one another.

These stories were all lies.

"You killed us both," I said softly, meeting Vela's eyes, then my father's.

"Oh, my child." My father sighed. "Oh, Marzanna. No father should have to do what I did. I have waited for you to return. Waited countless mortal lifetimes. And now that you have, I have been so disappointed."

"Pardon me for not caring," I replied.

"As I have waited for my mate," Vela agreed. "And finally, he has returned to me. My precious Khor. How desperately I have missed him." She smoothed Draven's hair, and I forced down the bile that threatened to rise in my throat.

"He may have loved you once," I said. "That part of your story is true. But he grew to despise you."

"He fought by my side," she countered. "Our love knew no bounds. We were as one."

"Don't forget the details, Vela. They're rather important, I'd say. He grew to loathe your cruelty. You were vicious and cold. He fought beside you, struggled to be loyal, until he could stand it no longer." I paused, grappling with a tide of rising ancient memories.

Khor, the most powerful fae in existence aside from my father, had spent centuries by Vela's side as her loyal companion. Like all of us, he had been worshiped like a god, by faes and mortals.

Then he came to me. He had asked for my help. He had wanted to switch sides.

It was a dangerous desire. Joining my aunts, Zorya and Devina, and I would have made our alliance much more powerful.

My father and Vela could not stand for that.

But perhaps even worse than wishing to change sides, Khor and I had become lovers.

He had abandoned Vela. Rejected their bond utterly.

"Our love was forbidden. He was bound to you, though he had no wish to be any longer," I said clearly.

"Our bond was eternal," Vela said, smiling. "You really thought he had a choice?"

I looked at Draven with his passive expression, his docile pose, and thought of the thousands of years we had lived before this.

If one couldn't make a choice on who to love in such a long life, what was the point of it all?

"He loved me, Vela. You couldn't stand that. You wouldn't change. You had no wish to. And so his heart abandoned yours. Instead of accepting that, you killed him for it. You killed your own mate rather than letting him go free. And in killing him, you finally broke the bond between you as he could never have done on his own."

I looked up at my father. "And you. You killed your own sisters and your own daughter. Not because you had to. But because you wished for even greater powers than you already possessed."

I looked beyond my father's throne.

The room was not walled behind the dais. Instead, it opened up onto a grove of oak trees surrounded by white marble arches. In the center of the grove lay a familiar-looking table.

"But you were a fool."

From the corner of my eye, I caught my father's frown.

"You lost a part of your own power as you stole ours." I met his eyes. "I took the most, didn't I? As I died? It's the real reason you wanted me back here. Not because of some pretend love you supposedly bear for me. You are no real father." I shook my head. "I don't think you've ever had any comprehension of love. Not a single moment in your existence have you ever truly known or understood what it is. If you had..."

"If I had?" My father's eyes were glacial.

"You would have known it was more powerful than anything you could ever have dreamed. You waited for me countless lifetimes, you say? Now I'm here. Not because you waited. But because of love."

Vela gave a low chuckle. "She's as naive as any mortal girl, Perun. Have you really missed her stupidity?"

I ignored her and looked at my mate, sitting there by Vela's side.

He had mixed his blood with mine in a Siabra ritual so powerful, it had merged our abilities and our lives.

I thought of my mother, who had passed all of her magic to me before she died, even though it had left her exposed and weak to Uther's killing blow. She had done that. For me. To safeguard me.

I thought of the fae that Fenyx had killed. How I had set them free.

Their spirits had passed through me and out of me. Each one recognized me, thanked me. A gift, they had said. I had given them the gift of eternal peace. I had brought them the deaths they had longed for and ended their liminal torment.

But they had given me gifts as well. Gifts for the lady of night, for the daughter of darkness.

For the one they called the goddess of death.

Marzanna. My other name.

"You both killed the ones you claimed to love. You stole souls to feed your lust for power. The souls of innocent children," I said to my father and Vela. "If only you had learned at one point in your miserable, overly long lives where true power lies. Not in taking. But in letting go."

CHAPTER 35 - DRAVEN

I watched Morgan with a reverence that never waned. My mate, my empress, my heart. She was utterly magnificent.

A perfect mingling of grace and strength. She radiated with a luminescence that could rival the stars themselves.

As she stood there before the throne of this corrupted court, I saw her past, her present, and her future. I saw who she was and who she had become.

Both her fierceness and her fragility left me in awe.

There was a fire behind her eyes, a hard-won wisdom, a silent testament to the trials she'd faced and conquered. Yet beneath the veneer of flame and steel, I saw a vulnerability that spoke to the depth of her compassion, her empathy—a reminder of the passionate heart that beat firmly in her chest.

Her gaze met mine, and I was lost in the depths of her soul, reminded of all we had shared. The triumphs and tribulations that had forged us. The paths we had walked hand in hand to bring us here, to this place. To this ending.

However it ended, amidst all of the chaos of our world, she remained my anchor, my solace, my hope.

Yet here I sat. Ensnared.

Or was I?

Beside me, another woman wrapped around me like a sensual vine. Her thighs pressed against my body. Her fingers slid possessively over my skin. She was a vision of temptation in silken finery. Her touch was a tantalizing caress.

A sickeningly familiar one.

Morgan's eyes flickered. I caught the glint of uncertainty, the shadow of doubt that threatened to cloud her thoughts.

While her expression remained a perfect mask of composure, I felt the weight of her scrutiny, the silent questions that lingered unspoken.

Did she doubt my loyalty? My devotion? Did she question the bond that tied us together in this lifetime and for all the ones to come?

Her thoughts remained a mystery, but I knew her heart, her soul. I knew the depth of her love, the unwavering faith she placed in me.

I rose to my feet, casting aside the chains of deception that bound me.

My destiny lay not with the woman who sought to claim me as her own, but with the one who had always held my heart in her hands.

CHAPTER 36 - MORGAN

I could almost feel the ripple of shock coursing through the room as Draven came towards me. Vela's expression was a mask of incredulity as she watched my mate rise and walk away from her, her hold over him shattered like a fragile mirror.

But I paid her no mind. My focus lay elsewhere. Drawn towards the man who was my heartline.

At last, he stood before me. The embodiment of all that was good and true in this world.

There was a lump in my throat. I had hoped. Hoped that being here in this place would trigger for him all that I had already remembered.

But that didn't mean I had not still feared I might be wrong.

As our lips met, the throne room faded away into obscurity. There was only us, entwined, unbreakable, enduring.

When we parted, Vela was laughing. It was a high-pitched, strangled sound.

"It's not possible," she gasped with a hand to her mouth. Her eyes narrowed. "Get back here," she commanded Draven. "Now."

In answer, my mate languidly lifted one hand. Instantly, Vela flew into the air, dark ties pinioning her wrists, her ankles.

With a flick of his wrist, Draven sent her plunging across the room and into the nearest wall.

She screamed as she slid to the floor.

"Enough," my father's voice rang out. "What is the meaning of this?"

"I'm sorry," Draven said, not sounding sorry at all. "Isn't this what we're all here for? I thought I was simply moving things along. Or did you want to keep reminiscing about the past for another few hours?" My mate put his arm around me. "We came here to destroy you. And you're here because you think you can stop us. Is that an accurate summary?"

My father's face darkened. "Where is the grail?"

"You know damned well where it is," I said. "Gone."

Something flickered over his face. So he had not known. Not for certain.

"That's not possible." Vela had pulled herself off the floor and now stood closer to my father, a few feet from the throne. "There's no way to destroy any of the objects. Not without destroying the world."

"The world? Is that what he told you?" I looked at my father. "As if he's ever cared about this world."

"It would destroy us," Vela insisted. "We'd lose everything. Aercanum could collapse."

"Lies," I said calmly. "The grail is gone. The world is still standing. And it'll remain that way, if I have any say in it."

"You don't know what you've done," Vela said angrily. "Without the three objects..." She glanced at my father.

"What?" I prompted. "What will you lose? Are we not gods, after all? What do we have to be afraid of?"

A look of dismay passed over Vela's face, and I smiled slightly.

"Ah. Not gods then."

My father snarled. "She didn't say that."

"But we're not," I said quietly. "You may be Perun. The real Perun. She may be Vela. Somewhere inside of me, I may even have the seed of your daughter Marzanna. But we're *not* gods. I don't even know if such things as gods exist. But either way, you didn't make this world, did you, Father? You simply arrived in it."

He said nothing.

"That's what I thought." I shook my head. "Creators? We didn't create anything. You probably don't even know who did."

"You dare to speak to your father in such a way?" Vela exclaimed. "He is the oldest, the most powerful, the most ancient..."

"The most powerful *what*? The most ancient *what*? He's not a man. But he's not a god either. He's a being." I shook my head. "No, not a being. A *thing*. A monster. An abomination."

My father's eyes were cold as ice as he stared at me in silence. What had he expected? My worship?

"We can never die," Vela whispered. "What creature can say such a thing? Of course we are gods."

"Deathlessness is not a blessing but a curse," I said stingingly. "All creatures who live should also die. It is the way of things. The right way. You've both had far too much time on this plane of existence as it is."

"You say that," Vela retorted. "Yet you stand here in a new body. A new woman with Marzanna's memories. Each time you fall, you'll rise again. Reborn to a new life."

"Perhaps," I said softly. "Or perhaps it will end with this one. If I choose."

She paled, as if understanding how far I was prepared to go, here, today, with them.

"The grail is gone," I said to my father. I touched Excalibur. "The sword hangs by my side."

"And you would destroy it? After all it has done for you?"

I nodded. "It is a part of me. You made sure of that when you killed me to create it. But as long as it exists, you can use it. I will not allow that to happen again."

I looked between them. "Two down. One to go. Where is the spear?"

Vela exchanged a look with my father, shooting him a small triumphant smile.

"If it's here, we'll find it," Draven declared.

Vela laughed. It was a real laugh this time. "Stupid man. You already found it."

"What does that mean?" I demanded, my heart sinking.

Vela gave me a knowing, secret smile. "You met it. It died."

Suddenly, I understood.

"When I found Excalibur," I said slowly, "the sword wasn't alone."

Draven looked at me. "Orcades."

"She had been trapped in an underwater prison for who knows how long. She never told me why." I looked at my father. "She was your greatest warrior. Why would you have imprisoned her there?"

My father said nothing.

I thought for a moment. "Unless she was more than a warrior. More than your general. Unless you wielded her like a weapon. Like a spear. Until one day, she refused to be used by you any longer."

"Was she Devina?" my mate asked, his lips curling in disgust as he looked at Vela and my father. "Did she *know* she was?"

"She never had Devina's—what would you call it?" Vela tapped her lips. "Her charm. Or her memories." She smiled at my father. "You saw to that quite successfully, didn't you, Perun?"

"She was much more pliant without them," my father agreed. "Devina had always been so stubborn. Even as Orcades, she was frustratingly unreliable to wield."

I felt sick inside. So my other aunt was truly gone. Devina. The goddess of the hunt. Not even a vestige of her remained somewhere in Aercanum as it had with Zorya.

"Then your spear is gone, too," I pointed out. "Orcades died in Camelot."

My father exchanged a knowing look with Vela.

Instantly, Orcades's last words poured into my mind.

"Who meets their death devoid of love shall surely face their end. But one who gives their soul away, eternity extends."

Fuck.

Medra.

CHAPTER 37 - MEDRA

I was flying. Soaring over mountains. I was a bird with golden wings.

A flash of motion far below caught my eyes, and in an instant, I was diving.

The taste of fur and blood. I had caught prey. A mouse.

My vantage changed.

I was a child.

Around me stared a thousand pairs of similarly empty eyes. Devoid of life. Devoid of expression.

There were no colors here. All was a sickly gray. I stumbled through the dark, my senses dulled, cold and alone.

I had been something else once. More than this. There had been warmth. A bed. A life. There had been love.

Now I dwelled underground, huddling for hours in an insensate trance. At times, I swarmed with the others. Tasting sour blood and rank flesh when a poor traveler fell into our cursed lair.

I had to get away. I pushed upwards and out.

I saw my aunt. I saw Draven. They were fleeing across a bridge inside a vast black mountain. A creature of darkness was flinging its wrath upon them.

Behind them, on the bridge, two pieces of charred metal lay forgotten. A broken cup, caked with dried blood.

I swooped downwards, my sharp beak tearing into the creature's face, ripping apart pieces of dark tendrils that fell like rotting flesh into the chasm below.

I watched my aunt and uncle pass through a heavy iron door and felt a rush of relief. They were safe.

But my eyes looked beyond the doors, as a true bird's never could. I watched them as they fell. Saw them carried away to a place of great danger.

I pushed my mind further, looked higher. Above the mountain, to where a palace floated in the clouds.

Inside the palace, a dead man sat upon a throne.

Careful now, a voice inside me warned. Go back. Turn back.

But I ignored it. I pushed on.

The man on the throne was bored. His head rested on one hand.

I flew closer, curious, heedless and bold.

The man's head turned towards me, and his gaze sharpened. He smiled, then reached out a hand.

I screamed.

My eyes opened.

My uncle was sitting up in bed.

"Kaye?"

Light brown hair tumbled around a pale young face.

He was older than me, I reminded myself. Or was I older than him?

It didn't matter now.

I picked myself off the floor where somehow I'd fallen and went over to the bed.

"I know you," he said, looking up at me with wide, brown eyes. "You were in my dreams."

My mouth felt dry. "I'm Medra."

"Medra?" he said. "But you're the spear."

"The spear? I don't understand. I'm Medra. I'm your..." I tried again. "I'm your niece." I looked around the room. It was still night and all remained quiet. "The castle was under attack. I came in here to see if you were all right."

"I know," he said. "I saw it. Odessa... The fae woman. I saw it all."

I stared at him. "How is that possible?"

His lips twitched. At another time, I thought, I might easily have liked this young uncle of mine. "How is anything possible? How do we know? I was asleep. But I dreamed... I dreamed many things. I saw from many eyes."

"Eyes that weren't yours," I said. "So did I. Just now. When I touched you."

He nodded. "We were connected to the grail."

"Is that what that was? The object on the bridge?" I thought back. "But it's broken now."

"Yes." He hesitated. "I should have died."

"But you didn't." I stared at him. "You're still here. Why should you have died?"

He shook his head. "The grail was my lifeline. By rights, when my sister destroyed it, I should have died, too. I could feel it. Couldn't you? Did you sense its power going?"

"I didn't feel anything. Nothing from that broken cup."

He looked at me oddly. "Yet you're the spear."

"You keep saying that," I said, starting to feel annoyed. "What does it mean?"

He licked his lips.

There was water on his bed table in a pitcher. I poured him a glass and passed it over.

He drank it quickly. "It means..." He stopped as if frustrated with his own inability to explain. "Don't you understand? You saw the woman. The attack tonight. He's coming for you. The one who made them all."

My heart sped up. "What do you mean? Who is?"

Kaye shot me a look that said I wasn't fooling anyone. "Your grandfather."

I looked around the room. "He's not here now. He can't reach me here. We're all alone."

"Medra." Kaye's voice was gentle and patient. "Stop pretending you don't understand."

"But I don't." My voice was shrill. "What are you talking about?"

"You saw the children," he said. "I know you did."

"What do they have to do with this? What were they?" I thought of the eyes I had seen through. Children? I wasn't sure they were that.

"Your grandfather made them. Turned them. He's done that and oh, so much worse. If he succeeds in getting to you, he'll do much more. My sister and her husband went to stop him."

"And what? You don't think they'll succeed?"

"They destroyed the grail. They're close. But with you here..." He trailed off. "Don't you understand? You're not just the spear."

"What am I then? Tell me that," I demanded. "My mother made me to fulfill a prophecy. Is that all I am to everyone?"

"You're whatever you choose to be. You could be his, if that's what you wish. Or you could be..." He hesitated.

"What? Tell me," I said, furious.

Everyone was keeping things from me. No one had told me the truth. Perhaps no one knew what the truth even was.

Only my mother. Perhaps she had known.

"The grail showed me. You're the king-killer. Not just kings. You're the destroyer of worlds."

I stared at him. "But I don't want to be any of those things."

"I know." Kaye's voice was gentle. "I know you don't. You just want to be you."

I nodded.

"But the problem is, Medra... he won't let you. He'll use you like he used your mother."

"I won't let him," I whispered.

"Then you'll have to stop him," Kaye said.

"How?"

A look of sadness passed over his face. "I can't tell you that."

I felt my cheeks redden with anger. "Can't? Or won't? Aren't we family? Doesn't family stick together? Tell me, Kaye."

He shook his head. "It's not like that. You have to see for yourself."

"Where? Where do I go to see?"

"Where they all are now. You glimpsed the place. I know you did."

"The man on the throne," I said automatically. "He looked at me."

Kaye looked startled. "He saw you? Here?"

I felt a twinge of fear. "Yes."

"Then, Medra, there's not much time. You must either go to him or he'll take you there himself. If he does, you won't like it."

Panic welled inside me. "What does that mean? How do you know all of this?" Stubbornly, I stomped my foot. "Who are you, anyway? Look at you! You're just a boy in a bed. You're no older than I am."

"I'm older, and I've seen more," Kaye said with a wistful smile. "I was tied to the grail. Believe me, I saw far more than I would ever have wished to."

"What is this? What's going on here?"

I turned towards the doorway.

Crescent stood there. He was alone. "Medra, what have you done?"

"Done?" I blinked at him in confusion. "I haven't done anything."

"Kaye." He seemed to take in the boy in the bed for the first time, to realize my uncle was awake and sitting up. "Kaye, are you all right?"

"I didn't hurt him, if that's what you're implying," I said, feeling angry. "He was all alone when I found him. Forgotten."

Just like me, the word implied.

But Crescent ignored me as he strode into the room. "We need to get you out of here." He was talking to Kaye.

"You could ask him, Medra," Kaye said urgently. "Ask Crescent to take you there now."

"Take her where?" Crescent frowned. "Has she told you?"

"Told me what?"

"Told you that her family attacked the Rose Court. That my sister..." His voice hitched, and for a brief moment, I glimpsed the pain he was in. "My sister is dead."

"They weren't my family," I started to counter. "They're as much my family as they are Morgan's. It wasn't my fault."

I heard the words as they left my mouth. Hollow and empty.

The truth was, it had been my fault. Deep inside, I knew it was. All of it. Odessa's death. The attack.

If I was the spear, if I was the king-killer... then I was the problem. I had always been the problem.

My mother had created me that way.

"Can Crescent take me to Morgan? Is she with my grandfather now?" I asked Kaye.

He nodded.

"I'm not taking you anywhere." Crescent frowned. "We have to get Kaye to safety." He looked at my uncle. "Taina is at the temple. We'll take you there, too." He glanced at me. "Both of you," he conceded. "You'll both be safe there."

"Take me to my aunt," I demanded. "Kaye says you can stitch me there."

"I can show you the way," Kaye said quickly. "If Crescent will just take my hand..."

"This is ridiculous. You're both children. There's no time to waste. I don't know what you think is going on, but the castle was just attacked. We can't stay here. Come, Kaye. I'll help you up." He reached the bed and began to help Kaye up. "I'm not stitching Medra anywhere. Certainly not to Morgan. We agreed stitching would never be used while she was away. And I'm not about to send Medra when I'm supposed to be protecting her."

"Protecting me?" I exploded. "Is that what you've been doing?"

But it didn't matter. Even if Crescent somehow agreed, it was too late.

A pain was inside my head. There was a knife stabbing me from the inside out.

I cried out in pain, sinking to my knees, covering my head with my hands.

"Medra." From a distance, I saw Kaye sliding out of the bed. I caught a glimpse of Crescent's shocked face.

Kaye fell to the floor and started to crawl towards me. "It's happening. Medra, you can stop him. Try!"

"I can't," I screamed.

I was being torn asunder. Was this stitching? If so, I feared I would be torn to pieces. There would be nothing left of me.

"What's happening to her?" Crescent's voice came from a long way away. "What do we do?"

The room was spinning.

Blurrily, I thought I saw Crescent crouching next to me. He reached out his hands to grab me, but they passed right through.

"Kaye, she's slipping." His voice was frantic now. "Who's doing this? Kaye..."

But it was too late.

I was gone.

CHAPTER 38 - MORGAN

"Shall I reach for her now?" My father smiled at me. "Shall I show you the spear? The new one?"

Medra. Little Medra. Baby Medra. My innocent niece.

I shook my head frantically. "No. Please."

"What does he mean? Morgan, what does he mean?" Draven demanded.

I clutched his arm, feeling sick inside. "Medra... She's the spear. Orcades... This is what she meant."

Draven's eyes widened in horror. "No." He turned to my father. "Not the child. Leave her in peace. I beg you."

"Beg?" Ancient lips thinned in a grimace. He was foreboding and alien. A being that had no right to strip more life from Aercanum than he already had. "You *will* beg. Assuredly. Once I have brought the spear here to wield."

He gave me a look I thought was meant to be paternal. Even reassuring. "It will be better this way, Marzanna. You'll see. The child was never meant to exist. But now that she does, well... It's not too late for you at least." He turned slowly to the grove of oaks that lay behind his throne.

For the first time, I let myself fully take in what lay in the center of the circle of ancient trees.

An altar.

Once, I had been tied to a tree there. My blood was taken and used to forge Excalibur. As Marzanna, I had died in agonized betrayal.

What was my father planning to forge in blood and agony today?

"She will die so you may live. The power I should never have given up will be repurposed. Funneled into something newer, greater."

"You would let this one live?" Vela hissed. "Even after all she has done? Even after the grail?"

My father frowned. "A loss, to be sure."

I thought of the three children of Gorlois le Fay, or Perun as I now thought of my father, who Draven and I had killed.

Lorion. Tempest. Daegen.

Did he consider their deaths a lesser loss than the grail? It certainly seemed so.

"She is here now. She is finally here. This is your chance! Kill her now! End this and take back the power she stole," Vela pleaded.

"Silence!" My father's voice boomed like thunder.

He glanced at me, and suddenly, I realized I had heard something I should not have.

A revelation. A confirmation.

"You lost something when you killed me," I said slowly. "I was right. Power went into me. And now you want it back."

My father was already powerful. Perhaps he was the most powerful being in Aercanum. If he got back what lay dormant inside me and combined it with the might of the sword and the spear, he would be unstoppable.

"A new world awaits us, Marzanna," he promised me now. "Aercanum—the way it was always meant to be. The people are weak. Ripe for the plucking. They will serve us as their gods as they have always been meant to. There will be no one higher than you or I. We will be adored, worshiped. No desire will go unmet."

"I have my heart's desire," I said, repulsed. "I have no need for anyone's worship."

His lips thinned. "And yet worshiped you still are, Daughter. The platitudes and devotions of thousands go up to you in temples across these lands each day."

"Not to me," I contradicted. "To who I used to be." My heart ached briefly as I thought of the people of Eskira praying to the Three, never knowing the truth. "The temples are a lie. All of this is a lie. We were never meant to be worshiped. We don't deserve to be."

My father's face flushed a color I hadn't known it could change—turning from icy white to angry red. "We are the most powerful beings Aercanum. We were meant to rule these lower creatures as kings and queens! Gods and goddesses! And you speak of *deserving*? Does an insect deserve to be stepped upon? There is no deserving. No right, no wrong. There is only power and weakness."

"Mortals are not insects," I said furiously. "There is no such thing as a lesser creature. There *is* such a thing as right in this world. And what you have done with your time here has been beyond evil, Father."

I saw the disdain in his eyes. "Then there is no escaping it. You are not my child. No trace of the old Marzanna remains in you."

"If she possessed anything of your cruelness, then I am glad for it," I retorted. "But I doubt she did. She fought you. *I* fought you—with my aunts and with Khor by my side. You and Vela stood alone. Then and now."

"You and your stolen mate will fall today," my father warned. "My patience has been tried, and I have no more left to bestow. You might have stood at my side again, the most blessed and most powerful of all my children."

"I'd rather die," I said honestly.

He smiled. "Then so you shall."

"Finally we are getting somewhere," Vela snarled. "Finish her and take back what is yours, Perun."

My father turned to her. "Take him. You know what to do."

The fae woman nodded, smiling eagerly. "At last."

She turned to Draven as my father lifted a hand.

I had no time to move, no time to scream. The floor was yanked out from under me.

I was pulled. I flew across the throne room like a child's toy as my father marched out into the grove.

My father flicked his wrist and my back hit an oak tree. I hung suspended there with no need for bindings.

Then Draven was in the grove. Flying towards my father with long blades of slivered shadows in each hand.

With a cry of rage, he threw himself over the altar, his dark knives slashing towards my father's chest.

The knives never reached their target. My father lifted his hand, and a gust of wind so strong it sent my head slapping back against the tree erupted around him.

Draven went reeling backwards into the throne room, sprawling onto the floor.

"Vela," my father snapped. "Take your revenge. Finish him quickly or I will."

The fae woman was already rubbing her hands together. She laughed gleefully as Draven picked himself up off the floor, and she carefully aligned herself between him and where I hung in the grove.

"It's too late," she crooned to Draven. "Perhaps if you are very, very good, my handsome Khor, I will let you watch her die."

And then she sprung upon him. Long claws extended from her slender fingers, narrow and dagger-sharp.

She opened her mouth to snarl, and long, pointed fangs descended, dripping with a thick and viscous liquid.

Vela was a shapeshifter. With a whispered incantation, the silk-clad woman became a monstrous hybrid of human and beast, her form twisting and contorting into a fusion of scales, claws, and fur as she propelled herself towards Draven.

I twisted on the tree, helpless and trapped, able only to watch as Draven charged to meet her head-on.

With a swift motion, he raised his blades and lashed out.

But Vela was quick and agile, dodging and weaving, evading his strikes, her shifting form making her a difficult target to pin down.

Meanwhile, my father approached me, a silver knife in his hand. Without meeting my eyes, he slashed open one of my wrists.

Blood dripped down my hand. My father caught it in a small wooden bowl.

"Making a new grail?" I asked.

He ignored me. Walking back to the altar, he poured the blood he had taken from me upon it, then raised his hands towards the sky.

Lightning crackled overhead. White energy channeled down.

Across from the grove, the throne room had darkened, becoming a swirling vortex of shadows illuminated only by the flickering light of Draven's and Vela's clashing powers.

I watched Draven leap up from the floor where his former mate had thrown him down, and I caught my breath at the sight of his wounds.

His leather jerkin had been slashed to pieces. Blood flowed in ribbons from countless cuts over his chest and shoulders. When he turned, I inhaled. His back was a mess of blood and tangled flesh.

Vela had been wounded as well. She was moving less quickly. One of her legs had been broken, and she was dragging it behind her.

Draven showed no signs of noticing his injuries or of slowing down. With a roar, he ran back towards her, delivering a flurry of blows.

The fae woman shrieked, but instead of recoiling as I had expected, she pushed herself towards Draven. As her head came near to his, she opened her mouth. A long, sinuous tongue darted out, and she licked the entire right side of his face.

My mate let out a cry of pain, and I heard the shapeshifter laugh.

When Draven next turned towards me, I saw his face was a mess of blood and melted flesh.

Every particle inside me writhed to come to my mate's aid.

"Draven," I screamed. "Take it. Take everything."

I prayed to Aercanum itself that he would hear me and understand.

Finally, he heard. He turned to me, his handsome face a wreck, his poor body broken and bleeding.

I met his gaze and held it. Take everything, I pleaded with my eyes.

Our bond was strong. Our connection was deeper than anything Lancelet and I had ever shared.

I saw him understand.

Lifting a hand, he held it upwards.

Excalibur flew out of its curved sheath, away from its place at my side and towards Draven, as if it were a bird with wings coming home to roost.

The weapon's hilt slammed into the palm of his hand just in time as Vela sprung towards him, her claws already extended and lifted to slash across his chest.

But Excalibur was raised and gleaming.

Draven raised the blade just as Vela's mouth opened again. I saw her long, wet tongue emerging, coated in its thick, menacing acid.

A whistling sound from above.

Something flew in from the open sky above the grove. Buzzing through the air like an angry wasp.

Suddenly Vela was screaming—a horrific, wordless sound.

A long, sickly strip of pink flesh flew through the air and landed with a splat at Draven's feet.

Tuva hooted in triumph as Vela sank to her knees, her hands covering her mouth.

For a moment, my mate hesitated. Then his face hardened.

Lifting Excalibur, he landed the killing blow. The sickle cut through the shapeshifter's chest, separating her into two.

Vela fell to the ground, her screams silenced forever.

Tuva lifted into the air again. As the golden owl flew towards me, the world around us blurred and then stopped.

I looked at where my father stood by the altar. He was frozen in place, his hands still raised, lightning still channeling downwards. The scene had become like a tableau from a painting. Lifeless and still.

I turned back to the owl.

But Tuva was a bird no longer.

A woman stood before me, ancient but unaged. Her hair was gray and tangled, but I could see glimpses of its former gold. Lantern-like eyes stared into mine, full of sorrow and wisdom.

"Tuva?" I whispered.

"I have been called by many names. And that is one," the woman said. "There is no time to list them all." She lifted a hand and touched my cheek.

I looked into her eyes. "I know you," I breathed. "Nedola."

My aunt, the third sister, nodded, then turned her head, looking around the grove. "Once, this place was sacred. It was the beginning of it all." She looked to where my father stood frozen by the altar. "Then it was corrupted."

"You weren't there that night," I remembered. "The night it happened. Why?"

She turned back to me, her visage tinged with bitterness. "I was spared. If one can call it that. My brother decided I was not powerful enough to kill. He replaced me. With you."

She had lost her sisters that night. And ever since...

"No punishment would have been great enough for living while my sisters died. And so I cursed myself. I had been spared while you three were not. My sisters were gone. And you, my niece. Alone, I could restore none of you. Devina was the most lost of all. She had left the fabric of this world so completely..." Nedola paused, and I heard the grief in her voice. "I could find no trace of her at all."

"You've been following me," I guessed. "All this time."

She nodded. "I've waited for you. Traces of you have always lingered in the world. I watched and waited for your rebirth. Many times, I thought I had found you only for it to be some other girl who bore merely a passing shadow of resemblance to my Marzanna."

She glanced around. "Now look at us. Finally we are here again. At the end of this dark road."

"Can you stop my father?" I asked. "Is that why you're here?"

"I cannot destroy him for you, no. I'm here for my end. Like my sister Zorya, I have been waiting for it for a very long time. But along the way, I'll help you as best I can. Just as I have always done."

I felt a lump in my throat. "Thank you, Aunt."

She nodded. "After this, it will be over. For me at least. I shall not choose to be reborn. I will pass on." She looked upwards to the cloudy heavens. "Somewhere, my sisters are waiting for me. I will go to find them."

She turned her head back to the throne room where Draven stood, frozen like a statue, his arm still poised over Vela's fallen body, Excalibur clasped tightly in his hand.

"But before I do..." She gently touched her hand to my cheek one more time, then touched my arm, tracing the markings that gleamed on my skin like silver paint. "I will return all of you to yourself."

And then she was the bird again. The beautiful golden owl I had first seen with Merlin.

Her wings spread wide as she soared across the room, straight towards my mate.

I gasped, for a moment not understanding.

And then she blazed, flaming with the power I used to have as her feathers flared with fire and she became a golden arrow heading straight towards my sword held aloft in Draven's hand.

Bird met sword.

There was a sparking, crackling sound of power upon power. Impossible to fully describe.

A blast of light filled the room, and I shut my eyes.

I felt a tingling over my body. My skin began to glow with heat.

I opened my eyes. My markings were gleaming, not silver but gold. They writhed like living, breathing things along my arms.

I felt suffused with life. Rejuvenated.

And as I looked across the grove into the throne room, I realized why.

Excalibur was gone.

My mate's hand was empty.

The sword had vanished, and so had Nedola.

I had only enough time to take this in before the world around me resumed its pace.

Draven's arm fell to his side, empty of the sword it had held just a moment before.

My father's lightning sizzled on the altar.

And I pushed myself off the oak tree and stepped across the grass towards him.

Perun looked at me in disbelief, then confusion.

"Vela is dead," I told him. "Excalibur is no more."

His eyes honed in on the empty place at my waist, then he scanned across the room to where Vela lay dead, slain by a blade that would never again exist.

"Its power is back where it belongs," I said. "Within me. As is my mother's." I flexed my hands ever so slightly. "And yours."

Perun's lips thinned. "So this is it."

Draven took up a position at my side. Blades of shadow formed in each of his hands.

"The grail is gone. The sword is gone," I said evenly. "Soon, you, too, will be gone, Father."

"It's over," Draven added. "You're alone. Soon all will be as it should be. You'll be forgotten once again."

My father shook his head. "Do you truly think you can subdue me so easily? Before we were worshiped, I lived alone in this world. The sword was a stubborn, stupid thing. The grail always fickle. But the spear... Ah, the spear. The most faithful of the three. The most powerful of them all. And that is all I need now."

He slammed his hands down on the bloody altar, and with a chill, I realized what he had been doing all this time.

Charging the stone. Preparing to summon the spear.

"I call upon you," he cried, raising his voice skywards. "Daughter of my daughter, the so-called spear of kings. Deliver vengeance to me now!"

He was calling her. Calling Medra.

I looked at Draven. His face had drained of blood.

We had to stop him. We had to do something.

I felt my newfound strength, felt the quiver of power in the markings that covered my body. I could fight. But just how did one stop a mad man summoning an infant to be his spear?

I cast out blindly with everything I had, not knowing what would emerge from me. Would it be fire? Ice? Darkness? Or something else?

A gust of wind as powerful as any storm of my father's shot out from my hands, pushing my father away from the altar.

For a moment, he looked surprised. Then he laughed. "Too late." He pointed upwards. "Look. She comes like the dawn. The child of my blood. My granddaughter."

Draven and I looked up as the lightning that had been forming overhead parted like a veil.

A form began to take shape upon the altar, wrapped in a swirl of mist.

With bated breath, we stood, waiting for Medra to appear.

Little Medra. So small and helpless. I waited for her piercing infant cries to fill the air.

But when the mists cleared, another figure lay on the altar.

Not a baby. A young woman.

Her eyes were closed.

"Medra?" Draven breathed.

My father laughed, and the room shook as if with thunder. "Not what you were expecting?"

"What have you done to her?" I demanded.

He ignored me, looking down at Medra hungrily. "She's so pure. So beautiful. Something has changed. She's fuller. Brimming over. I can almost taste it. She's more powerful than her mother ever was."

He reached down as if to touch Medra. "What a pair we will make together. The true child of the god."

Draven erupted. Leaping over Medra's prone form on the altar, he positioned himself between the sleeping girl and my father.

"Keep your hands off her," he growled. Over his shoulder, he called to me, "Stop him, Morgan. We can't let him do this to her."

Nodding grimly, I pushed my might outwards as I had done before, channeling the wind, the sky, the very light.

The room around us trembled. My father shook where he stood. For a brief moment, I thought he might fall.

Then he smiled. Leaning forward, he touched a single finger to Draven's chest. My mate flew backwards over the altar, crashing into one of the great ancient oaks, his blood coating the bark.

Draven rose and charged again towards Perun, that powerful being of lightning and thunder, that false god we were sworn to bring down.

"You shall not touch her," my mate roared. "You shall not have her. I swear it to you."

My father lifted a hand, and Draven skidded to a stop, his face rigid with strain as he pushed against an invisible wall.

"I will rip you into pieces, here and now," my father said lazily. "I will hang your limbs one by one from the trees for the birds to peck."

"Never," I screamed, and I lifted my hands.

Instantly, a fissure appeared, growing beneath the altar.

The oak trees around us began to split and crack. Branches and leaves fell around us.

My father turned slowly towards me. "I'll finish you both. Then I will descend out into the world and do what I should have done in the beginning. I will force my will upon creation. I will bend it to my liking. All who will not bend will be destroyed. All who will not kneel will choke and die." He looked down at Medra. "And she will be with me every step of the way. The daughter I should have had."

I looked at my mate's face. It was a portrait of agony. I knew that as he looked at the girl lying on the altar, all he really saw was the small baby he had held in his arms.

The baby we had sworn to Orcades we would always protect.

"Never," I said again, quietly this time.

My eyes met Draven's, and he nodded.

This was it. Our time had come. We would destroy my father together.

When Medra awoke, I prayed she would remember us. I prayed she would somehow find all the happiness she deserved.

CHAPTER 39 - MEDRA

There was pain. Blinding pain. Darkness.

Then cold. Icy cold.

My body was pressed to something flat and hard.

I pushed my eyes open. At first, there was only a brilliant, flashing light.

I focused my gaze. Above me, lightning sparkled, illuminating the sky overhead.

My other senses were returning slowly. I could hear someone shouting.

Through a sliver of sight, I saw them.

My uncle, splattered with blood, breathing hard as he stood over me, tendrils of darkness spiraling into a shield that formed an impenetrable barrier from the storm that raged around us.

My aunt, dancing with death itself, her every movement a symphony of destruction as she unleashed torrent upon torrent of magic upon...

A man. The dead man on the throne I had seen in the vision Kaye had shared.

My grandfather. The man who had not stitched me here but *torn* me, *wrenched* me, *forced* me to this place to do his bidding. I was a child. A mere child. And he had violated my body and my will.

He was battling my aunt. I knew if he emerged victorious, what he had done to me would be only a taste of things to come.

I touched my hands to the thing I lay upon. Flat, cold stone.

An altar.

So, it came to this. I was to be his ultimate sacrifice.

Transfixed, I lay there, still half-dazed with pain, and I watched. And I saw. I saw this fight was taking everything my aunt and uncle had. And they were giving all of themselves, unquestionably, to save me. To save my world.

Lightning crackled through the air. Flames licked at my grandfather's heels. Cracks ran across the grove, meeting in a giant fissure that grew with every moment.

The trees around us were fractured and splitting. The marble chamber that held it all together was crumbling.

Destruction and death. I had arrived just in time to witness all of it.

I snuck a look up at my uncle. His eyes were closed with the strain of shielding me.

His face was different from how I remembered. One half was a mess of torn flesh. His upper body was slick with blood, the skin ripped and shredded away.

He opened his eyes, not to look down at me, but over to where my aunt spun and wove her body around the grove. She was engaged in a deadly duel. Blades of darkness swirled around her as she met my grandfather's thunderous blows. A fire of defiance burned bright in her eyes.

And in my uncle's? I saw the fear and the pain.

He loved her. And he thought she was going to die.

He looked down at me then, and our eyes met. His expression was shocked. Then the shock vanished, and in the next instant, I saw something so familiar and so long-forgotten on my uncle's face that tears pricked my cheeks before I could stop them.

Love.

I knew it with a certainty I had no need to question.

I thought of Odessa, and in my mind's eye, I knew exactly what would happen next.

Their deaths. Their sacrifices.

I might go on, but it would be alone.

My grandfather was laughing as he fought his defiant daughter, his pale skin stretched across ancient bones that I suddenly longed to break.

He moved closer to the altar, deftly avoiding my aunt's blows, and I saw my chance.

My body trembled as I reached deep within myself, grasping hold of the dark, roiling currents of magic I had always known were there.

My grandfather's gaze fell upon me. I saw the malevolence in his eyes. He would take and take and take until there was nothing left.

But it didn't have to be that way. Not when I could stop this. Now.

With a primal, mutinous scream, I launched myself, sitting up on the altar and throwing myself towards him. My arms wrapped tightly around his steely, corded neck.

His furious cry echoed through the grove like the stampeding of thunder through the clouds.

I knew he saw me as a momentary impediment. Nothing more.

From across the grove, I heard my aunt cry out my name.

From the corner of my eye, I glimpsed my uncle running towards us, and I smiled. Fitting that his would be the last face I ever saw.

And then, with a blinding flash of light, I imploded.

Like a prisoner breaking free of the chains that had bound them for so long, I surrendered myself to the darkness, wrapping my manacles around myself and my grandfather and strangling us with them.

We were both one with the darkness now.

As my vision faded to black, I reached out my mind and felt the heartbeat of the stars.

CHAPTER 40 - DRAVEN

I coughed, feeling dust leave my lungs. There was a ringing in my ears. I felt the roughness of the ground beneath me, the jagged edges of broken stone digging into my skin.

I pushed myself up onto my elbows. Across from me, Morgan lay sprawled stomach-down on the ground.

Crawling towards her, I gently flipped her onto her back, brushing pieces of broken stone and grit off her pale cheeks.

Pale. So pale. Her eyes were closed. Her body was still.

I touched a finger to her throat. She wasn't breathing. There was no rise or fall to her chest.

Heart hammering with adrenaline, I lowered my lips to hers, breathing in life as my hands moved against her chest, compressing again and again.

A cough. A sputter. She stirred beneath my touch.

A gasp escaped her lips as her chest began to rise and fall.

She turned her head, looking up first at me, then scanning our surroundings, taking in the devastation that surrounded us.

We had fallen from heaven and somehow survived.

Around us lay the twisted wreckage of Perun's palace, the remnants of our battle scattered like fallen leaves on the wind. Chunks of white marble littered the ground like fallen stars, their surfaces marred by cracks. Shattered pieces of gold glinted dully amidst charred wood and smoldering ruins.

Morgan was pushing herself up. I helped her to her feet.

The Black Mountain lay not far off in the distance. We were back where we had started.

A shouting broke through the ringing in my ears.

"Here! I've found them! Come quickly!"

Morgan looked at me in silence, tears trickling down her face.

There was no need for words. No point in them.

Nothing would bring Medra back. Nothing. We both knew that.

Morgan wiped quickly at her face as Lancelet burst breathlessly through a cluster of nearby trees.

"Morgan! Draven!"

A roar followed as Hawl emerged. The Bearkin was wounded on the shoulder.

"An arrow?" I asked.

The Ursidaur nodded. "We were attacked while we slept."

They might have said something then, a jibe at Morgan for what she had done when we'd left. But instead, the Bearkin seemed to take in our state and said nothing.

"We've fought nonstop," Lancelet said. "We wouldn't leave this place without you. We knew you'd return."

"Guinevere?" Morgan asked. "Is she...?"

"She's safe," Lancelet replied. "Here. She's coming now."

Guinevere broke through the trees, panting, carrying a satchel. "I have herbs. Healing salves. Dressings and bandages. Do they need anything?"

She looked back and forth between us, and her jaw dropped.

For the first time, I looked down at myself. My jerkin had all but crumbled away. My chest was raw and ribboned. When I let myself dwell on it, I could feel my back was much the same.

"Your face," Morgan said quietly, gesturing.

I touched a hand to my cheek, and Guinevere cringed. "Please. Don't."

I lowered my hand.

"This is beyond me." Guinevere took a deep breath. "But I'll try, when we get back to camp."

I nodded curtly. "I don't need to look pretty."

"What happened?" Lancelet asked eagerly. "Did the peak of the mountain collapse? Was it an eruption? How did you get down?"

We looked at one another. "Not the peak of the mountain," I said slowly. "A palace above. Floating in the clouds."

Lancelet stared. "That sounds... beautiful. But since Morgan's father was involved, I assume it wasn't." She bit her lip. "Is he...?"

"He's gone," Morgan said simply.

"You did it then," Lancelet said, sounding awed. "You truly did it."

"We did nothing," Morgan said, her voice unexpectedly sharp.

Lancelet seemed to take in the tracks of tears. "But then... who?"

"Medra." My voice was hard and brittle.

Guinevere gasped. "Medra? But how?"

"Where is she? Where is the little thing?" Hawl boomed. "Tell me at once and I'll go to her. Did she fall far from here? Were you separated?"

My throat constricted at Hawl's kindness. "Separated. Yes."

Morgan reached out a hand and touched my arm. It steadied me.

"She's gone," my mate told them all. "Medra is gone. We should go, too. We can talk about it more later."

It was clear this wasn't the joyous reunion our friends had been hoping for.

We were alive. But I was finding it hard to be grateful.

My grief was swelling inside me like a tempest, tearing at me with merciless claws.

I had sworn to protect the child at any cost, to shield her from harm with every fiber of my being. I had tried, and I had failed.

Now a ghostly whisper lingered in my heart. I could still see her face, so innocent and brave as she embraced her fate.

She had been a pawn in a game she had never asked to play. A victim of forces beyond her control.

I closed my eyes. I remembered the scent of the baby I had held in my arms. The sweet fragrance of her hair. The pink bloom in her tiny cheeks. The way she had smiled up at me as I sang to her while she lay in her cradle.

She had been such a precocious baby. Always so bold, so curious.

I had looked forward to teaching her so many things. How to fish, how to fight. Would she have made giant bubbles in a fountain like Rychel? Or adored baby animals like Morgan's brother Kaye?

How could she really be gone?

Morgan's hand slipped into mine. I realized she was leading me forward.

I followed numbly as our party moved through the trees.

My mind drifted back to the final moments in the palace of clouds.

There had been darkness. All had gone black.

Yes, but before that, there had been an explosion of light. Something had wrapped around me, enveloping me.

A shield.

The child had shielded us. Wrapped Morgan and me in a veil of protection as I had been doing for her—just before she had destroyed herself.

I remembered the look on her face as her eyes had met mine.

I stopped in my tracks.

Peace.

The expression had been one of peace.

"What is it?" Morgan murmured. She gestured to the others to go a little ways ahead without us. "Draven, what is it?"

"She saved us. Medra saved us."

"She sacrificed herself. I know. I'll never understand it." She shook her head. "The power it must have taken."

"Not just that. Not just her sacrifice. She shielded us, protected us as we fell. She's the only reason we survived."

Morgan looked startled. "I thought it was you. I thought you'd done that somehow. I didn't even have time to react. It all happened so fast."

I shook my head. "It wasn't me."

"I still don't understand. She was only a baby when we left. How is it possible? It's like a terrible dream. Will she still be there when we get back? I can't accept it. I can't believe that she's gone." Tears were trickling down Morgan's face again. "I know you loved her more than I did, Draven. I know you cared for her more. But I cared, too. I swear I did. I just… I didn't know how to show it like you did."

I was shocked. I pulled her to me, heedless of my wounds. "I know. Morgan, believe me, I know."

"She was so small," my mate sobbed. "How can she not be so small still? How can she have saved us? She should be home. I thought she'd be there. I thought I'd have more time. I thought…"

"I know, silver one," I murmured against her hair. "I know. I know."

It was all I could say as we stood there beneath the trees.

Around us, the air was heavy with the scents of earth and pine. The forest rang with the chorus of birdsong and rustling leaves. Shafts of golden sunlight trickled down from above, dappling the forest floor with patches of golden light.

The world was alive, and we were still in it.

We stood like that, together in silence, for a long time, listening to the sounds of the world Medra had saved.

CHAPTER 41 - MORGAN

It was coronation day.

There was a saying from Tintagel that I had read in a history book once: "A valiant sword does not craft a wise scepter."

Courage in battle or in adversity did not necessarily translate to the wisdom to rule.

We returned home to Camelot in mourning—for Medra, for Nightclaw, for Gawain, for Rychel. And then, once we had exchanged news of our losses, for Odessa.

But amidst the weeks of bleak mourning, there was always a seed of joy to carry me through. Because my brother Kaye had woken up.

To learn Kaye had met Medra and spoken with her in her last moments in Camelot... Well, it was a bittersweet blessing for Draven and me.

But with Kaye's awakening, a new challenge arose. For, as it turned out, Kaye did not wish to be the new king of Pendrath.

Oh, my brother was not some irresponsible youth. It was not simply the call of freedom that made him refuse kingship. He was convinced—wrongly, I still felt—that I deserved to sit on that throne first.

Nothing I said or did could convince him otherwise. And in the end? What won me over was a simple plea.

A plea to let him have a childhood.

The childhood I had not had.

He did not say so in as many words, but the implication was there when I gazed into my little brother's eyes and saw the weariness that should not have been in the eyes of a boy so young.

After that, I could not refuse him.

Instead, I looked. I looked forward into the future and saw Kaye having years to grow and explore without the threat of Arthur or some terrible war hanging over him. I imagined him surrounded by friends and family who truly loved him and would teach and protect him. I saw him becoming king not as a child, as Arthur had been, but as a man—ready and mature, confident in his abilities, and surrounded by a court of friends and advisors who would be there to support him every step of the way.

There was another tempting incentive to do as my brother had asked.

Given a few years, I knew I could rout out any lingering vestiges of corruption from Arthur's court. Get rid of all of the Lord Agravaines and Fenyxs. Make the Rose Court into something truly worthy for Kaye and a new generation to take over.

And so I agreed—but with conditions.

My term would be limited. A maximum of fifteen years. If Kaye changed his mind, I would agree to step down before that.

Should I have any children while I was queen, they would not supplant Kaye in the line of succession.

I was tempted to ask for wording to be written in, declaring any future children of mine would be removed from the line of succession altogether. But then, I strongly doubted Draven and I would ever have any of our own. Not only were our hearts still too raw for that, but with the lingering curse upon the Siabra, Draven's Nimue had already been an exception.

Meanwhile, the group of supporters who had called upon me to reign Pendrath had grown and grown until they'd become an influential flood. Upon my return to Camelot, I'd had to contend with the existence of a powerful faction capable of swaying not only Pendrath but Tintagel, Lyonesse, and Rheged.

Perhaps someone else might have been flattered. I was not. Instead, I saw only another source of trouble for Kaye.

The faction called upon me to expand my dominion as empress not only over Myntra but over all of Eskira.

I refused—but offered a compromise. As Empress of Myntra and temporary Queen of Pendrath, I would form a council of kingdoms made up of representatives from all over both of our continents. The council would be equal parts fae and human and would include, of course, a Bearkin delegate. Should other intelligent races be discovered, they would be invited to join us as well.

In the meantime, over my fifteen years of temporary rule, I saw an opportunity. An opportunity to quietly and carefully suffocate the faction of these ardent supporters so that when it came time for Kaye's ascent, he would face no issues from that quarter.

Aercanum did not need the greater coalescence of power in one woman's hands.

I was not the world's savior, despite what many had convinced themselves based on the stories being told of my friends and my deeds. The people of Aercanum would have to learn how to save themselves. Without my father's baleful presence, they had every chance of doing so. Now was the time for a long and lasting peace.

Of course, a cross-continental council—which King Mark quickly labeled the Empress's Parliament—would have been an impossibility in Arthur's time, considering the complications of travel alone. But with the new arches that Crescent and Draven had been overseeing construction of, the issue of travel between kingdoms and even continents melted away. In a heartbeat, Lady Marjolijn of Lyonesse or King Mark of Tintagel could step over and be in the Rose Court for a meeting or even a festival. Or a funeral.

State funerals for Gawain, Odessa, and Rychel took place as soon as we returned, all in Myntra. We had brought back Gawain's ashes for Crescent.

But in Medra's case, there was no body to bury or to burn. She had no resting place, even in Rheged. And there were few who had known her.

Even fewer who had truly loved her.

So, Draven and I grieved in private, torn with indecision on how best to honor her memory.

Until one day, Crescent had come to our suite.

He'd been withdrawn since we'd returned. We'd put it down to the loss of his husband and sister. But in private, Sir Ector had told us there was more to it than that. He'd tried to explain the dynamic between Crescent and Medra. And suddenly, so many small things seemed clear. The way Crescent looked at us—not with resentment but with guilt. Because he believed he'd failed her.

Now he stood before us, his hands behind his back, his eyes downcast.

"I'd like to show you something," he said quietly. "If you have a moment?"

We were staying in the Rose Court then, preparing for a meeting to discuss the refugees from Rheged.

Draven and I left our notes and maps behind and followed Crescent through the castle until we reached the western wing and stopped on the outskirts of a small room.

Before Crescent pushed the door open, he paused. "We haven't spoken of Medra a great deal since you returned," he said, his voice tight. "But I wanted you to know that she has never left my thoughts. Not once. We may not have gotten along as I once dreamed we would. I failed her..."

With a quick glance at me, Draven started to protest weakly but Crescent held up a hand. "No, it's true. I failed her, Draven. And in failing her, I failed you both. I failed your trust." He shook his head miserably. "She was like no other child I'd ever known. She was difficult. Willful. Rebellious."

I could feel Draven tense up. "A typical teenager then?" he said, his tone light but full of implication.

Crescent forced a smile. "In part. She certainly was more like you or Gawain. Perhaps one of you would have been better suited to deal with her. I was a quiet child. Too gentle, my father always said. I wasn't who she needed."

"But you brought her Odessa," I reminded him. "And from the sounds of it, Odessa was exactly who Medra needed."

But in doing so, he had lost her. His only sister. The words didn't need to be said. They hung in the air all around us.

"You and Medra may not have gotten along," Draven said carefully. "But I'm sure she knew you cared about her. Why would you have brought Odessa to her otherwise?"

"You're right about one thing. Odessa loved her. That much I know for certain." Crescent looked at us almost pleadingly. "I loved her, too. I don't think I ever succeeded in convincing Medra of it, but I did." He licked his lips. "That doesn't mean I didn't also misjudge her. Wrong her."

I got the sense there was more to the story. Perhaps some day, he would tell it.

Crescent turned to the double doors behind him and began to push them open. "I had this room set up for you. I thought perhaps... Well, a place you could go. To remember her."

We stepped inside the little room, and I gasped.

Whatever I had been expecting, it wasn't this.

The little room had been turned into a gallery.

A gallery of Medra.

Along the walls hung large oil paintings in silver frames. And in each frame was an artfully rendered portrait of Medra.

Medra as an infant, gurgling and smiling in Draven's arms.

Medra sleeping in her cradle, looking cherubic and peaceful, her soft cheeks tinged with rose.

The rest of the pictures were Medra as Draven and I had never had an opportunity to see her.

Medra toddling across the Great Hall. Her hair was a mess of black curls around her face.

Medra holding a wooden sword and looking determined as she stood in the practice yard across from Sir Ector. She looked about seven or eight years old, but I knew it must only have been a few weeks after we'd left.

I glanced at Draven and knew he was feeling the same shock I was.

It was one thing to be told how Medra had grown at such an incredible pace. We knew it was true from having seen her at the very end. But still, I knew neither of us had really been able to imagine it. Not until now.

We moved to the next painting. It depicted Medra hunched over a book in the castle library. She looked lost in thought. A half-eaten apple sat on the table next to her.

I covered my mouth with my hand. The girl in the picture was so familiar—for so many reasons.

"She didn't know it, but I was always checking up on her," Crescent said softly. "She loved the library. From what Sir Ector says, she was a great deal like you in that way, Morgan."

I nodded, my heart too full to speak.

If she had lived, I could have shown her all my favorite books. I pictured us sitting in the library for hours, reading quietly, and the lump in my throat grew, knowing the dream would never be.

The next picture showed Medra astride a chestnut stallion, her head lifted high. She looked beautiful and regal. She also looked at least fourteen years old.

"Medra had a complicated relationship with animals," Crescent said. "We were working through it." He hesitated. "She had a lot of rage in her."

Draven and I looked at one another. This was the first time anyone had told us.

"But I know Odessa was teaching her to be... Well, to be more gentle," Crescent continued. "And Medra loved her horse. She never harmed it."

I nodded slowly, thinking about all of the reasons Medra had had to be angry.

"She knew we'd left her then," Draven said, looking at Crescent.

The dark-skinned man nodded. "That was one of the reasons for her anger, I think. She was not a typical child. Her mental capacity increased as rapidly as she grew. She was well on her way to being a brilliant scholar, even without tutors. But even so, I don't think she ever truly understood why you left her."

Draven's eyes met mine, and I saw the haunted expression there.

"She did," I reassured him, my voice low. "In the end, yes, I think she did."

He nodded. Fumbling, his hand found mine, and we moved on to the last painting.

Medra was holding a sword in this one. A real blade this time. She was not alone in the painting. The artist had captured the moment her blade clashed up against Odessa's. The two women were pushing up against one another, neither one ready to surrender.

Medra had a huge grin on her face. Odessa's expression was more serious, but I could see the hint of a smile beginning to form.

"Who painted these?" I asked, turning to Crescent.

"I sketched them out, then took them to a local artist. One you might be familiar with." He gestured to the doorway.

Galahad stood there, his dark eyes solemn. "I wasn't sure I should come in."

"Yes, come in. Please do." Wiping my eyes quickly, I walked over and embraced him, then held him by the shoulders. "You painted these? All of them? Truly? I had no idea you could paint."

"It's been something of a hobby, the last few years. Someone kept up and leaving me so I had the time to spare." He grinned.

I punched him lightly on the arm. "Leaving you! You were joining the temple, remember?"

His face sobered. "Well, that's where I learned, in fact. You remember Christen?"

I nodded. The young spy who had died. "Of course I remember him. Your dear friend."

Galahad nodded. "He was also a wonderful artist. He had been a painter's apprentice before joining the temple and then the rebels. He helped me to hone my skills."

"Well, they're incredible. Really, Galahad. Incredible." I turned around and looked from one painting to the next. "But when I think of how much we missed..."

I bit my lip and glanced at Draven. His back was to me. His arms were crossed over his chest. He hadn't budged.

"Perhaps we'll leave you two alone for a while," Crescent said, following my gaze.

"Thank you. These paintings are... a wonderful way to remember her." I stumbled over the words, hearing how cliched they were, but knowing they were true. "We'll treasure them always."

When the two men had left, I approached Draven.

"My heart is so sore, Morgan," he said simply as I touched his arm.

"I know." My heart ached for him.

"I have no tears to shed. It just... hurts too much."

I wrapped my arms around him, burying my face against his chest. "I know, my love, I know."

His hands came up to touch my hair.

"It's cruel and unfair," I murmured. "But oh, Draven. She was so *good*."

"She shouldn't have had to be," he said, his voice cracking. "She should never have been there."

"But she was," I said tiredly. "She didn't ask for any of it. Neither did we. We just... did the best we could. And we'll remember her for what she gave. And always, always love her."

There was a bench in the middle of the gallery. I drew Draven over to it, and we sat there for a long time, looking at the pictures.

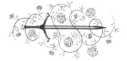

Now I stood in a different room, alone and surrounded, not by paintings of Medra but by lavish gifts from every known land in Aercanum. Around me, ornate chests overflowed with treasure, each one more splendid than the next. Golden ornaments adorned with precious gems. Richly woven tapestries. Colorful jars of exotic spices. In one corner of the room, a gleaming suit of armor stood on display. King Mark had sent it from Tintagel. There was even a beautifully crafted sword next to it. A matching set.

I was in need of a new sword, it was true. I ran my hand over the hilt. Tintagel steel was said to be the finest in Eskira. Perhaps I would test the blade out when I had the chance.

There was a rap at the door, and I whirled about, suddenly conscious of the fact that I still had not put on my coronation dress as I had promised my ladies-in-waiting half an hour ago. The dress still lay on the bed, a monstrosity of crimson and gold silk and chiffon with a heavy brocade cape to accompany it.

"Morgan?"

I put a hand to my throat. "Oh, it's just you."

"You're still not dressed?" Kaye stood in the doorway. "I thought the coronation began in an hour."

I looked at my brother fondly. He looked very dashing in a tailored doublet of deep red velvet. A ruby-studded brooch in the shape of a rose was on his collar. "You look very handsome."

"You look... very nice, too," he said tactfully.

I looked down at myself and laughed. Draven and I had gone for a walk in the woods that morning. I was still wearing trousers covered in burs and thistles. "I'll get dressed soon. But I swear, that dress is so heavy, the less time I'm forced to wear it, the better."

Kaye nodded as if he understood. "I came to say thank you, again. For doing this for me. I know it's going to be a lot of work."

My face softened. "Of course, little brother. It's no trouble. Not for you."

"I will be a good king someday, Morgan," he said. "I promise."

I stepped towards him and touched his cheek. "I know you will. There's plenty of time for you to grow up first though."

A strange sound came from behind his back, and he took a step backwards quickly.

"What was that?" I asked, frowning. "Kaye?"

"I brought you a coronation present," he said hastily. "I've been waiting for the right time to give it to you."

I had a sinking feeling I knew what he had brought. "You don't need to give me anything. It's not as if I need anything else, Kaye. But thank you for the thought." I reached for the door as if to pull it shut. "Anyhow, I think you're right. It's growing late. I should get dressed..."

"Morgan, wait." Kaye stepped back into the room.

I sighed. "Kaye, please."

"You don't want to at least see it?"

"Not if it's what I think it is."

Kaye frowned. "Well, I think you should see it. Then decide."

There was another sound from behind his back. This one was distinctly mewing.

My brother moved his hands.

"Kaye, please."

But it was too late.

He held out a kitten.

Not just any kitten. I was staring at a tiny version of Nightclaw himself.

The cub was diminutive compared to its father, larger than a regular kitten but still barely filling both of Kaye's hands.

Despite its vastly different size, the kitten possessed the same velvety obsidian coat Nightclaw had had, albeit with softer, more delicate fur. Golden stripes covered its small body, but less pronounced, like faint whispers of the powerful markings Nightclaw had borne.

The cub stared up at me, its eyes a mesmerizing amber just like its father's. Full of curiosity and innocence, the cub's eyes were completely devoid of the bitterness and anger that had been there when I'd first met Nightclaw in the menagerie.

The kitten swatted a paw towards my face enthusiastically and gave a playful growl, revealing tiny yet sharp-looking fangs and reminding me of the wild instincts waiting to awaken within this adorable bundle of fur.

"They're very sweet," I said. "But no." I started to turn away. "You should take it back to its mother."

"Don't you want to know if it's a boy or a girl?" Kaye inquired. Closing the door behind him, he set the kitten down on the floor.

"What are you doing? Kaye, I have to get ready."

"No one will care if you're late. Besides, you're the queen. Isn't it fashionable to be late?"

"That's just something people like to say," I said distractedly, watching as the kitten raced across my room straight over to the bed hangings, where it began to attack the tassels hanging from the coverlet. "They don't really mean it when they're the ones having to wait."

"Sunstrike took the other kittens hunting," Kaye said. "But she left him behind."

So it was a boy then. A little Nightclaw.

"Why didn't she take this one, too?" I asked, already secretly worried. Was there something wrong with this one? Was he smaller than the others? Was Sunstrike rejecting him? I hadn't even been to see the female exmoor since we'd returned. It had been... too painful to contemplate. Now I wondered if I should have asked Draven more questions about the cubs.

"She told Draven this one is too wild to take along. The two girls listen to her better." Kaye grinned. "So I offered to watch him."

"You're catsitting," I said. "Catsitting on coronation day. My chamberlain will be thrilled." My eyes widened. "Oh no. No, Nightclaw, down!"

But it was too late. While I had been distracted, the cub had pulled himself up onto the bed, digging his claws into the coverlet, and proceeded to pounce upon my coronation dress. Now he was worrying at the lace on the bodice with his teeth.

Rushing over, I grabbed the little cub and gently tried to extricate him from the gown. But it was too late. Part of the lace trim had already pulled away.

"They're going to murder me," I said in horror, holding the cub under one arm and trying to smooth down the dress with the other.

"Who?"

"My ladies-in-waiting!" Lady Eve headed up the troupe of women. "The dress took a month to sew." As Lady Eve reminded me every time we had a fitting session. "Oh, the pins. The pins, Kaye!"

"The pins?"

"They'll stick more pins in me," I moaned, sinking onto the bed and leaning back.

A rumbling sensation against my chest drew my eyes downwards.

I was still holding the cub. It had nestled against me, paws down, and was now looking at me with interest.

"You called him Nightclaw," Kaye said softly. "Just now."

Almost against my will, I stroked the cub's sleek head. "I never got to see Nightclaw this small. Was this what he looked like?"

The kitten's purring was soothing. Comforting. It made me forget about the gown. The coronation. The hours I would have to spend standing in front of a large audience while the master-of-ceremonies and visiting nobles gave speech after speech lauding my future reign.

"You see?" Kaye sat down on the bed beside me and smiled. "He's sweet, isn't he?"

"If I had ever dared to call Nightclaw sweet, he would probably have ripped my head off," I murmured, still stroking the cub. "But yes." I sighed. "He is rather sweet. Now take him away."

Kaye's eyes widened. "But…"

I pushed the kitten off my chest gently and sat up. "Take him away, Kaye."

"Morgan…"

The door to my room pushed open, and Draven stood there.

"You brought the cub?"

Kaye nodded at my mate. "She wants me to take him away."

"What did you expect me to do? Bring him to the coronation?" I said a little testily.

"Why not?" Draven grinned. "You're the queen. You can do anything."

"I can't have a cat running around during a coronation ceremony." I frowned. "Can I?"

"He could be the official exmoor-of-ceremonies," Kaye said eagerly. "A symbol of peace and friendship amongst kingdoms."

I raised my eyebrows. "I highly doubt little—" I stopped myself. I had almost called the kitten Nightclaw again. "I highly doubt the cub would enjoy that."

"He's very sociable, actually. More than his sisters or Sunstrike. He'd probably love to attend the coronation. Wouldn't you, little fellow?" Kaye said encouragingly, pushing the kitten over and tickling its stomach.

"Fine," I said suddenly, watching them. "Fine."

"Fine?" Kaye stopped and looked at me. "Really?"

"Really. Call him the royal mascot." The thought of a tiny Nightclaw running wild around the temple, racing underneath noble ladies skirts and between the legs of visiting dignitaries was too good to pass up. "But he'd better not get stepped on." There was another tapping at the door. Probably Lady Eve. Oh, I was in for it. "He can't fly yet, remember."

"I'll watch him," Kaye promised. He grinned at Draven and me. "I think you're making the right decision. This will really spice things up."

"It will ensure it's a coronation to remember for the ages," Draven said. "That's for certain."

He came up behind me and lifted my hair to kiss the back of my neck. "What made you change your mind?"

"He is rather cute, I suppose," I said lamely.

But the truth was... now that I had seen the cub, I could hardly stand the idea of letting him out of my sight.

"When his mother's back from her hunt, we'll have to return him, you know," Draven whispered in my ear.

"I know," I snapped. "It's not as if I were going to catnap him. This is just for Kaye. I'm doing it for Kaye."

"Of course you are, silver one. Of course you are." He nipped at the back of my neck and I let out a tiny shriek.

Across the room, Kaye grimaced. "Ugh. If you're going to start that, I'd better go." He came over to where the cub was rolling around on the carpet, then stopped. "Do you want me to take him, or should I leave him?"

The tapping at my door was growing louder. I suddenly imagined carrying the Rose Court scepter in one hand and a mewling exmoor kitten in the other as Lady Eve looked on aghast.

"Leave him," I said decidedly. "What's the cub's name?"

Kaye and Draven looked at one another.

"What is it?" I asked.

"Sunstrike wanted to leave his name up to you," Draven said quietly.

It was an honor. A great one.

A lump had immediately formed in my throat.

"Oh." My voice was small. "I see."

"Well, I'd better go," Kaye said, stepping over to the door. He smiled encouragingly at me. "Maybe we can think of a list of names at dinner after the ceremony."

I nodded. "I'd like that." Especially as it would be a four-hour-long event with sixteen courses.

"You just have to get through the next few hours. Now get that thing on." Draven nodded towards the dress on the bed. "I have my own instruments of torture to don." He kissed my forehead. "I'll see you at the temple soon."

I looked at the retreating backs of the two men I loved more than anything else in the world and then at the little cat attacking its own shadow on the carpet.

In a moment, a group of well-meaning women would burst in to dress me to become their queen.

But in this instant—in this split-second of freedom—there was only love.

Love, the one force in the universe that no one could ever fully explain. Love, the candle in the dark that led us through the night and softened all our sorrows. Without love, life was a starved and empty thing, for there was no hope, no joy without it. My father had never, ever learned that lesson.

But with love, there was strength. Love held us up and kept us from falling. When we found it, we clung to it and we never let go.

Love made us strive to be better than we were. Love lifted us. Love carried us. Love made our flaws forgettable.

Love was our saving grace. Love was the greatest adventure.

"I love you both," I called just as Draven yanked the door open. My brother and my husband turned back to me. Their faces shone. They were so beautiful, it made my heart ache. "So much. Don't ever forget it."

And then the room was full of women and noise and their replies were drowned out in the din, and they were gone.

EPILOGUE - MORGAN

I breathed in the crisp autumn air as I stood alone on the stone terrace at the edge of the lake. Autumn had fallen, and the city of Noctasia had been transformed into a tapestry of fiery hues, falling leaves, and the soft glow of harvest lanterns.

In the heart of the city, the town square had become centerstage for the autumn harvest festival. Tonight, the square was already alive with the sounds of music and laughter. A boisterous band played spirited tunes upon a stage covered with wreaths of leaves and ribbons while pairs of dancers in vibrant costumes swished and twirled on the wooden dance floor in front.

Slender towers swathed in trailing bright-red ivy and vibrant orange blooms stood along the shores of the lake, its surface shimmering with the reflections of the brilliant foliage. Along cobbled streets, market stalls overflowed with seasonal produce and spiced beverages. Carved, white stone bridges spanned the waterways that flowed through the city, adorned with garlands of colorful leaves, leading revelers from one district to the next.

Alongside the terrace, brightly-painted gondolas floated past me, draped with cozy blankets and hanging lanterns as they carried chattering, laughing passengers over the lake.

I leaned against the railing and looked back towards the town square, watching as a tall slender woman in a red jerkin whirled her companion, a petite curvy woman in blue, until both were breathless and laughing. Across from them, two dark-haired women danced to a slower beat, their arms wrapped around each other tightly.

"I fear the stars themselves will envy your radiance tonight, my silver one," a husky voice said from behind me.

I turned, already feeling my cheeks heating up.

Kairos Draven Venator stood at the edge of the terrace, his hands clasped idly in front of him. He looked very handsome and very charming and very, very dangerous.

He wore a high-necked black jacket with a crisp, white shirt beneath, its fabric pristine and immaculate against his bronzed skin. The sleeves were gathered at the wrists with black velvet cuffs, embroidered with subtle silver accents that caught the light. The shirt was unbuttoned, giving a glimpse of part of the tattoo he'd recently had emblazoned on his chest.

A bursting star surrounded by a pair of wings. For Medra and for Nightclaw. Unseen beneath the shirt and jacket, on his back, I knew a broken chalice atop a pair of criss-crossed swords marked a spot of remembrance for Gawain, Rychel, and Odessa.

"A man could lose himself in eyes like yours, Morgan." Then he whistled, his eyes moving over my body until my skin felt as hot as an oven. "And that gown..."

I glanced down at myself. The gold gown was molded to my figure and cut so low, my breasts seemed to threaten to spill from the bodice. The skirt of brilliant oranges, reds, and golds billowed slightly in the breeze off the lake, pooling around my feet in a cascade of silk, like liquid flames.

He gestured over his shoulder. "You didn't want to join the rest of the group? Taina is begging to go bobbing for apples."

I looked to see where he was indicating. At a large round wooden table bordering the dance floor sat Crescent, Taina, Hawl, Sir Ector, and Dame Halyna. Galahad stood nearby, idly clapping his hands to the music as he watched the dancers. I watched as the song finished and Lancelet dragged a laughing Guinevere towards the table with Lyrastra and Laverna following a little ways behind.

"I thought we were supposed to be opening the masquerade ball. That's the reason I'm dressed... like this."

Draven grinned. "We are. Don't worry." He opened his jacket and fished out two objects. "But I thought we could mingle first. With a little anonymity?"

He held one of the objects out to me, and I took it.

A mask of gold and silver filigree. Delicate swirls and flourishes mimicked an owl's plumage, every feather meticulously crafted.

Draven lifted his own mask to his face, and an exmoor's sleek silver whiskers extended outwards. "Would you care to attend incognito, my lady?"

He lowered the mask, examined my face more closely, then frowned at whatever he saw there. "Or perhaps skip the ball entirely?"

"Can we?" I asked dubiously. "I thought it was tradition."

"Screw tradition. We can go or we can not go. Or we can go late. It's all up to you, empress of my heart." He stepped towards me and placed his hands on my hips. "You look tired."

I tried to smile. "Just a little."

"We could use some time alone. Just the two of us. Away from everything."

"That would be nice." I closed my eyes, listening to the strains of the music. The tempo had slowed. I could hear the lapping of the lake against the terrace. "Somewhere with water just like this. Far away from it all."

I nestled in against him. How strange, the sense of safety I now felt, nestled in the arms of this dangerous man.

Draven touched his hand gently to the small of my back and wordlessly began guiding me in the steps of the song.

In an instant, the world around us faded away.

"I've never said sorry," he said suddenly as we moved to the music.

"For what?" I asked.

"Back in your father's court. With... Vela."

Weeks had passed. And yet we had somehow never spoken of it.

I tried not to let my body tense up at the memory of him crouched at that woman's feet, but it was no use.

"There's nothing to say sorry for."

Yet a sour taste had filled my mouth.

"I was playing a part. I know you knew that. But still... It was a despicable part to have to play," he said. "In that moment, you have no idea how much I hated myself."

"I know you had no choice," I said quietly. "Believe me, I do."

He was silent for a few moments as we danced.

"You need to know, I'll never love anyone else, Morgan," he said finally. "What we have is eternal—and those aren't merely words."

"What do you mean?" My heart had started to hammer. Somehow, he was touching my deepest fear, the one I hadn't had the guts to speak aloud since the mountain—not to him, not even to myself.

"What I did to you, when I saved your life in Meridium—it took blood and it took the grail. But more than that, it took..." He hesitated.

"What is it?"

"Nedola. She was there."

I caught my breath. "Nedola? You never told me that before."

He nodded. "Odelna. Nedola. They were one and the same. The real child had died some time before. Nedola was... inhabiting the body. Like she did with that dead soldier on the battlements that night in Myntra."

I finally understood. Even the names were a play on words. I wrinkled my nose.

"I suppose we should be glad she chose an owl in Camelot," I remarked with a shudder. "And not a corpse."

Draven winced. "Though if you knew some of the things I said to that owl when I was frustrated..." He shook his head. "Anyhow. That's not what I needed to say. What I needed to tell you was..."

"Yes?" I prompted.

"That I took a risk. Doing what I did. The bonding ritual saved your life, yes. But... I might have lost mine."

My heart sped up. "I never knew that. You never told me."

"It didn't really matter." He quirked his mouth. "If I'd failed, we'd both have been dead."

"But it didn't fail," I said. "It very much succeeded."

He nodded. "But bound us, against your will."

"Not against my will anymore. I would do it all again in a heartbeat, if I had the choice."

"Even if you knew..." Again that hesitation.

I raised my eyebrows. "Tell me, Draven. That's an order. From your empress."

He smirked. "Well, in that case."

The dance was over. Draven let go of me and, stepping back, ran his fingers through his dark hair. "We're bound until death. To death and... beyond death."

I stared at him. "What does that even mean?"

"It means..." He paused. "It means what you and I have goes beyond anything Vela and I did." He flinched. "Gods, but I hate even saying her name."

I thought of Vesper. "She was your childhood. Your past. What we have together is another lifetime. Quite literally. Don't be ashamed of your mistakes. We've both made some." I smiled. "But to hear you say 'gods' sounds quite strange now."

"Doesn't it? Standing in a temple is even stranger. During all of those prayers to the Three during your coronation, I kept wanting to laugh hysterically."

"That's probably because Nightpaw was climbing that courtier's trousers," I reminded him. I thought for a moment. "But what does that even mean? Beyond death?"

"You remember Zorya and Nedola? How they didn't want to be reborn in Aercanum? They didn't want to stay. They wanted to... go on."

"I remember."

"Well, for you and me... What I think this means is... we can't do that. We can't go on. Not without the other."

I stared at him. "So you couldn't really have died for me?"

"I might have died. You might have, too."

"I don't understand."

"Death isn't necessarily the end, Morgan." He shrugged helplessly. "I don't know how it all works. Gods—" He caught himself and grimaced. "Even the gods, or the ones we grew up thinking might be gods, didn't know. Isn't that what we both learned up there that day?" He took a breath. "Nedola said there would be a price. It might have been my death and yours. But since we both lived..."

"We're bound, through this life and the next. If there is one. Not just words," I said slowly.

"Not just words," he repeated.

My pulse thudded in my ears. "Perhaps we've been missing something else."

"Something else?" Draven tilted his head.

"If Nedola and Zorya wanted to leave Aercanum. If they wanted to go on, then maybe they knew something we don't."

"Or they simply wanted a chance at peace. At nothingness." Draven shrugged. "We'll never know."

"Oh. Right." For a moment, I'd been excited. Thinking of the idea of Medra somewhere else, out there. Anywhere.

But if Medra had somehow gone on, if there really was *something* out there for her, then that meant it might be out there for my father, too. And that didn't bear thinking about.

"The fae didn't originate in this world," I said slowly. "At least, the ones everyone believed to be gods didn't."

My father. His sisters. The original pantheon.

Draven nodded. "I think your father confirmed that essentially, yes."

"So then where did we come from? If not here, where?"

Draven shook his head at me in amusement. "I hope you don't think I have the answers to that."

"No," I admitted with a sigh. "Not really. I mean, that's not to say you're not a brilliant man..."

"Thank you." Draven smirked.

"But... no. I don't either." I frowned in disappointment.

"Maybe we can find the answers together," Draven suggested. He pulled me against him and kissed the top of my head. "If there's anyone who could find answers that even the gods didn't have, it would be the beautiful, stubborn, unstoppable woman I'm holding in my arms right now."

"I'm flattered you think I'm unstoppable and even more relieved to hear you understand that's all I am now—just a woman," I said, laughing. Albeit, an unusual one.

To my surprise, he held me by the shoulders and looked down into my face intently. "That's the sound that makes my life complete."

"What?" I laughed again, a little awkwardly this time.

"That. Your laugh. The sound of your voice. Anything, really." He leaned his head against mine gently. "Before we go about trying to answer questions of life and death, I have a request."

"Yes?"

"Perhaps we could just live a little. You and me. We've come through all of this darkness, this devastation. We've earned our due, Morgan. I want what we deserve."

"No one deserves happiness. Or else everyone does," I quickly pointed out.

"Very true. But I still want it. With you. Irrationally or not, I don't care." He kissed me. First one cheek, then the other. Then my forehead. "I want you." He kissed my lips briefly, and my heart began to speed up. "You have no idea how much. Or in how many different ways. But I just want you. Tell me I can have that, Morgan."

I looked up into my mate's face. "You can have that," I whispered. "For eternity."

THE END

Keep reading for a sneak peek from the first book in my new series...

ON WINGS OF BLOOD (TEASER)

I stirred to life atop a mountain of corpses, my body battered, my skin stained with the blood of the fallen.

The air around me reeked with death.

With a groan, I shifted my weight, the movement sending ripples of pain down my back. Something was pinning my legs down.

I stirred again and, this time, glanced downwards. A chill ran through me. Not something. *Someone.* Someone dead.

My ears pricked at a sound, straining to decipher the muffled murmurs.

Footsteps marched against hard ground. People were coming.

I sat up and pushed at the heavy body that had fallen over my legs, struggling to free myself.

The voices were growing closer now.

Like a specter, a figure appeared on the edge of my vision, bouncing up the mounds of bodies like a weasel.

A man. Small and wiry. A smirk played upon his lips, revealing a row of ratlike yellowed teeth.

I lay very still, hoping he would think me just another body. But it was too late.

With another leap, he was on top of me, pinning me down.

I could smell the stink of something rancid on his breath as he lowered his face to mine and sniffed.

"Barnabas!"

The voice was young but strong. Commanding.

The man sitting astride me froze.

"Yes, Master?" His voice was like the crawling of serpents. Odious and simpering.

"What have you found?"

An intake of breath. The man's face was very close to my ear. He inhaled again, drawing in my scent as if it held the fragrance of a rare wine.

And then, to my horror, his tongue snaked out. Red and foul-smelling, it approached my neck.

"Barnabas." The voice was sharper. Annoyed now. "I asked you a question."

The tongue slid back into the man's mouth. I saw the look of disappointment in his eyes.

"This one's alive."

A pause. "Impossible."

There was a glint in the man named Barnabas's eyes I didn't like. I held my breath as we looked back at one another. Then he smiled.

"Even so, she's alive. And she smells"—he sniffed the air again like a hungry mongrel, and I flinched—"exquisite."

He lowered his mouth to my neck again, and I shouted, raising my hands to push him away as I saw the glint of sharp teeth.

"Get off her," the other man's voice snapped. "Don't taste her. That's an order. Bring her here."

"Just a small taste. Just a little taste, pretty one," Barnabas whined so quietly only I could hear. "You smell so good. Better than anything I've ever had."

I flailed, reaching up to hit him, but his arms easily pinned me down. He was stronger than I'd expected. Or I was weaker. One of the two.

I closed my eyes as I waited for the inevitable bite.

Instead, there came a soft crunching sound.

I felt a wetness on my face and opened my eyes.

Barnabas still knelt on top of me. But his head was gone.

Shuddering, I sat up and shoved his corpse off me, glancing to the side to see his decapitated head rolling down the mound of bodies.

I wiped my arm across my face, trying to clean off the blood.

That was when I realized I was very inconveniently naked.

"Get up. Come down here," the other voice ordered.

I rose slowly to my feet and heard gasps from below.

Focusing my eyes, I saw a line of soldiers, some standing, others on horseback. All work red and black armor.

A man sat at the front on a black steed. He held a bow in his hands. The one that had killed Barnabas.

As I stumbled slowly down the mountain of rotting corpses, he slid down from his horse.

He had saved my life. Killed one of his own men to protect me.

But as I saw the arrogant expression painting his features, the cruel twist of his thin lips, I felt no gratitude.

Hair as pale as moonlight fell around the man's shoulders. Piercing gray eyes glinted as they looked at me, assessing me from head to toe as I approached, lingering slowly on every inch of my flesh, stripping away all of my modesty.

"Take a good, long look," I snapped, finally unable to bear that gaze any longer. I tossed my hair and was disconcerted to feel it fall on bare skin. "Because I assure you, it's the last one you'll ever get."

There were some hoots of laughter from some of the soldiers down the line. A glare from their young commander silenced them in an instant.

"Get her some clothes," the man said coldly to a soldier standing nearby, ignoring what I'd said. "No, on second thought, give her your cloak. Take it off. Now."

I saw the soldier's eyes widen. "But, Master," the man whispered, glancing at me surreptitiously. "You saw what she is. She's a…"

"I know what she is," the one they all called Master responded. "Give her your fucking cloak. We're taking her back with us."

Hurriedly, the soldier unfastened his cloak and tossed it over to me. I caught it gratefully, trying to ignore the look in his eyes. Fear or hostility—I wasn't sure which.

"You're quite mistaken if you think I'm going anywhere with you," I said to the commander as I wrapped the cloak around me.

A moment later, I wished I hadn't spoken.

The commander had mounted his horse. Now he turned to look down at me disdainfully. His nose was crooked and hawk-like, as if it had been broken before.

Still, despite his strange features, there was something about him. A magnetism I could feel holding me fast. His eyes locked with mine in a silent challenge.

"No one asked you what you wanted. You don't have a choice. But if you plan to resist…" He shrugged, then snapped his fingers to the soldier. "Find her proper clothes. Then bind her."

And they did.

Preorder your copy on Amazon today.

TRIGGER WARNINGS

A bduction
   Abuse
Alcohol Consumption
Amputation
Animal Abuse
Animal Death
Bullying / Harassment
Cannibalism
Child Abuse
Child Death
Childhood Trauma
Decapitation
Deceased Family Member
Domestic Violence
Drug Use
Explicit Sexual Content
Infant Death
Murder
Physical Abuse / Torture
Poisoning
Suicide
Violence / Gore
War

ALSO BY BRIAR BOLEYN

Blood of a Fae Series

Queen of Roses

Court of Claws

Empress of Fae

Knight of the Goddess

Historical romances written as USA Today Bestselling author Fenna Edgewood...

The Gardner Girls Series

Masks of Desire (The Gardner Girls' Parents' Story)

Mistakes Not to Make When Avoiding a Rake (Claire's Story)

To All the Earls I've Loved Before (Gwen's Story)

The Seafaring Lady's Guide to Love (Rosalind's Story)

Once Upon a Midwinter's Kiss (Gracie's Story)

The Gardner Girls' Extended Christmas Epilogue (Caroline & John's Story – Available
to Newsletter Subscribers)

Must Love Scandal Series

How to Get Away with Marriage (Hugh's Story)

The Duke Report (Cherry's Story)

A Duke for All Seasons (Lance's Story)

The Bluestocking Beds Her Bride (Fleur & Julia's Story)

Blakeley Manor Series

The Countess's Christmas Groom

Lady Briar Weds the Scot

Kiss Me, My Duke

My So-Called Scoundrel

About the Author

Briar Boleyn is the fantasy romance pen name of USA TODAY bestselling author Fenna Edgewood. Briar rules over a kingdom of feral wildling children with a dark fae prince as her consort. When she isn't busy bringing new worlds to life, she can be found playing RPG video games, watching the birds at her bird feeder and pretending she's Snow White, or being sucked into a captivating book. Her favorite stories are the ones full of danger, magic, and true love.

Find Briar around the web at:

https://www.instagram.com/briarboleynauthor/

https://www.bookbub.com/profile/briar-boleyn

https://www.amazon.com/stores/Briar-Boleyn/author/B0BLWFKHWC

https://www.tiktok.com/@authorbriarboleyn

Made in the USA
Las Vegas, NV
26 April 2024